THE PURLOINED SKULL

A TWIST OF POE MYSTERY

Also By

VELDA
BROTHERTON

TWIST OF POE MYSTERIES
The Purloined Skull
The Tell-Tale Stone
The Pit and the Penance
Masque of the Rising Moon

THE VICTORIANS
Wilda's Outlaw
Rowena's Hellion
Tyra's Gambler

THE MONTANA SERIES
Montana Promises
Montana Treasures
Montana Dreams
Montana Fire
Montana Destiny
Montana Legacy

OTHER TITLES
Beyond The Moon
A Savage Grace
Once There Were Sad Songs
Stoneheart's Woman
Wolf Song
Remembrance

THE PURLOINED SKULL

A TWIST OF POE MYSTERY

VELDA BROTHERTON

LAGAN

OGHMA CREATIVE MEDIA

www.oghmacreative.com

Library of Congress Control Number: 2018944182

ISBN: 978-1-63373-372-5

Interior Design by Casey W. Cowan
Editing by Gil Miller

Lagan Press
Oghma Creative Media
Bentonville, Arkansas
www.oghmacreative.com

This book is dedicated to everyone who worked with me on
The Observer *staff for so many years.*
This series would not have been possible without you.

Thank you, Parker.

ACKNOWLEDGEMENTS

A special thanks to my publisher, Casey Cowan—who also happens to design my kick-ass covers and layouts—and my editor, Gil Miller. I also want to remember the rest of the Oghma Creative Media gang. Here's to Venessa, Gordon, Amy, Mike, George, Cyndy, Vivian, and Andrew. Thank you all for your continued and unwavering faith in me.

1

CHAPTER

Jessie was alone in the newspaper office when the call came in about the bones. She was writing an article about the monthly Golden Agers' meeting. Agnes Mhoon had celebrated her 98th birthday with a chocolate cake and their guest speaker, a ranger from the state park, spoke to them about bats. Bones would be a lot more fun than bats any day.

Being alone meant she had to go out to Kyle Foster's place and check out the call herself. She stuffed her camera, pad, and pens into the carry-everywhere backpack that contained everything she might need on a two-day safari, except the guts to follow through on this.

What if they were human bones, like Kyle thought? Damn and double damn. This was not why she returned to Arkansas or why she agreed to work for a weekly newspaper.

The deal was, no big stories, just boring dreck.

Hefting the pack over her shoulder, she headed for the Jeep. Maybe someone had buried their old dog or a prankster had found some cow bones and thought it a good joke to pull on poor old Kyle Foster. Most people couldn't tell the difference between animal and human bones, so hopefully it was a false alarm.

What would she do if they were human? Christ, she didn't need this. But someone had to go, and her boss, Seth Parker, was taking chemo. Which left her, more or less, in charge. The title of city editor was a joke, but not so funny anymore.

Damn again.

Half an hour later, she stood in the woods near a bluff overhang and stared at the camera's screen and a cluster of human rib bones scattered in the dark soil. The glowing green light mesmerized her, kept her from pressing the button.

An image of Steve's face, twisted with rage, intruded. A breeze kicked up, dried the sweat beading on her forehead, and blew away the memory with a scattering of last fall's leaves.

Back to the bones. Concentrate.

She'd come home to lick her wounds and figure out how to atone for what she'd done. Getting involved in a story that could call attention to her was no way to do that. What was she doing here anyway?

Hide. Run and hide. All she wanted was to be safe and let the guilt fade away. Why hadn't she found a job flipping burgers or working at Walmart and let it go at that?

Bones, for crying out loud. Things like this simply did not happen in small-town Arkansas. At least they weren't supposed to. This would be a big story, no doubt of that. No way would she write it. She didn't dare.

Take pictures, talk to Seth, take notes, leave them on her boss's desk, and get back to her bat story.

She leaned back on her heels and blew a strand of hair out of her eyes. Gazed at the deep-woods grave. Not a scrap of flesh clung to the bare bones. And they were human. Someone had died out here a long time ago. And they hadn't buried themselves.

Now what? Parker would never let her walk away from this story. He'd make her write it, no matter what. And Heaven help her, she ached to do just that.

As if he stood over her now, Steve's voice raged. "You bitch, have you ever thought of anyone but yourself?"

"It was my job. I wrote a story," she whispered into the quiet morning, and knew it for the lie it was. She'd ruined his life and her own.

Way more than that. She didn't blame him for hating her. She hated herself. Had then, still did. The comfort of this place didn't extend to gaining forgiveness because she dared not own up to what she'd done. As long as no one knew, she was safe.

"Are they a archology find?" Kyle Foster whined, jerking her out of the mental interrogation.

Sucking in a tremulous breath she rose to her feet without replying and framed and snapped the first of several shots, shuffled around, framed, shot, over and over until she'd covered every angle. No danger she'd compromise the crime scene. Kyle's nosy dogs had already done that.

Bare tree limbs rattled in a gust of wind that carried the scent of rotted leaves and a vague whiff of marijuana emanating from Foster. The bones waited in eerie silence, sad remnants of someone's life. They made no sound, put off no stench, nor were they impatient to be identified. Just a pile of bones, that's all. No heart to ache, no spirit or mind to remember and regret.

With a shiver that chattered her teeth, Jessie glanced at Foster hovering nearby, whiskered face screwed into a message of desperate misery.

Without disturbing the dig further, she rose and took some long shots, carefully leaving him out of the frame. She understood his need for anonymity all too well. She could use some of the same. So take the pictures, call the sheriff, and let Parker handle it from there. Refuse to get involved. Go back to writing her feel-good pieces for page five. No more big stories for this gal. No more the award winning JJ Stone and dreams of a Pulitzer. These days she was just plain old Jessie West. Hiding out where Steve could never find her. If he did, he'd kill her. That he'd promised, and she believed him, didn't really blame him because she deserved the worst he could do to her.

She licked her lips, returned to the present, and replied to the farmer's question. "Sorry, but these aren't artifacts."

"Shoot. So, maybe we just cover em back up, say we never saw em."

"You know I have to call the sheriff."

"Huh-uh, nope." He shuffled backward, cast a nervous glance upward, as if he expected the drug task force helicopter to sweep down from the sky and carry him off.

"Should have re-buried them, then, Kyle. You called a reporter, for Christ's sake. I can't ignore this."

The claim echoed mockingly. She'd like nothing better. The taste to do so on her tongue like bitter ashes. Discovery of the bones would bring her more hurt than they would the mournful marijuana grower. Cedarton, Arkansas was a small town firmly steeped in the old ways, fenced off from criminal activities, from gangs and drug dealers. The only crime out here these days was growing marijuana, which had replaced whiskey stills of earlier days. Somehow that was acceptable to most everyone but the law.

So what was a dead body doing buried all the way out here in the middle of nowhere?

"Aw, dang and blast, girl. I called you so—I mean, all I wanted was to gather them bones all up in a tow sack and take em to the University, maybe get me a reward. Like them fellers what dug under Jacob's Bluff and found them artifacts before they started blasting for the new highway. Paper said they was worth a heap of money."

"I know, but I'm afraid this is not a prehistoric find, this is a body someone buried." No use trying to explain to him about the intrinsic value of artifacts. He expected cash in hand. "Someone was probably murdered, since most folks don't go around burying their loved ones under bluffs."

She dragged her gaze away from the grave. An honest-to-goodness story lurked here, and the urge to write it grew inside her, scared her half to death. Did she dare take a chance she would mess up again? Worse, reveal her whereabouts to Steve?

She swallowed. Hard. Turned to Kyle. "When did your dogs bring in the bones?"

Squinting into the sky, he scratched his butt through filthy britches that hung on him like he was a broomstick. "First one, a week ago yesterday. I didn't think too much about it at the time, thought it was some dead cow ole Snoop'd come across. But then this morning in he comes with what looks like a dang finger bone, and Howler, he's got him one too."

He dug around in his pocket, came up with the appendages, and offered them in his dirty palm. "Anyways, I knew right away it wasn't no cow. Could have me a archology find was what I thought." Glaring at her like it was her fault, he dropped them into her outstretched hand.

They were cool and smooth, like a series of bony dice meant for a macabre game. Shivers raced through her. The inevitable reporter's questions jittered to be free. Who had this been? And what terrible thing had happened that the body ended up here?

Someone committed murder, Jessie, and the story is yours. Take it and run. You know you want to.

Shaking off the temptation, she peered at the pitiful man. Why didn't he get a job? "I'm sorry, Kyle, but these bones aren't thirty thousand years old. In the first place, they're buried too shallow. This is all silt, and it's been washed in for thousands of years. We'd have to go down several feet to reach artifacts from the archaic period."

"But Snoop and Howler dug all around in there." His nasal voice raised an octave, the whine grating on her nerves. "Couldn't they have dragged em up from way down deep? Maybe even found em somewhere else and buried em here? Look how the ground is all tore up."

His furtive glance skittered away when she glared at him. Both knew he'd been at the grave looking for something he could sell, but she waited for him to go on.

He didn't.

He just stared at her with eyes as hang-dog as those hounds of his.

At a loss for anything further to say, she shrugged in his direction. Soon she had to call the sheriff, and there was nothing either of them could do about the consequences.

"Oh, heck." Kyle shrugged bony shoulders. "The way things go for me, I shoulda known it'd only mean trouble. Shoulda just covered the dang things up and kept my mouth shut." He shifted from one foot to the other, sending an aroma of smoked dope and body odor her way.

Fingers itching to snap a picture before he could protest, she glanced at the anxious man. Parker expected pictures of people. Readers want to look at people, not things, he'd repeated a dozen times or more. But this nervous marijuana farmer would never agree to pose beside his unearthed treasure. The long dead bones would have to do.

How would he react when he saw the photos of an open grave containing a partial skeleton and nothing else?

He'd give her one of those looks that said she should know better. Mutter something like, "Needed the fellow who found them, at best the dogs."

But she didn't do that anymore. Take pictures of people who objected. Dig up dirt about folks, like some cheap tabloid reporter. With a grimace at the dreadful pun, she stowed the camera in her backpack and pulled out pad and pen and a bottle of water. Taking a sip, she contemplated the site. Aching. Hurting deep down to follow this through.

The need to write this story tied a painful knot in her chest. She took another long gulp of water and concentrated on the site. Might as well take a few notes. Get a feel for the scene.

Earth sifted from the edge of the hole, revealed another bone that pointed at her like an accusation.

Tears filled her eyes and she scrubbed them away. Damn the demons anyway. She dragged in several deep breaths, closed her eyes. Forget the past. Envision what happened here. A grave should emanate a lingering vestige of its inhabitant, shouldn't it?

But she got no vibes. If ghosts existed they never talked to her. Maybe she just wasn't good company. All she sensed on this lovely day was the fragrance of earth warming to spring, a mossy dampness in the air, the cheerful song of birds celebrating new life, the moist caress of soil through the fabric of her jeans when she knelt for another look.

A few quick words scribbled in the pad would help with recall later. Face it. Parker would insist she write the story. He was the boss. She would decline, and he would gaze at her, exhaustion from the chemo painting bruises under those dark eyes. And she'd give in. But only for the initial story. Staff Writer signature. No follow-up, no research or digging about for clues. No ruining lives. No calling attention to herself. Crawl back in her hidey-hole. Let the big boys down at the Harrison daily take over from there. And in the end, Parker would back off. Not because he agreed with her reasons, but because he didn't have the strength to try to convince her she was being foolish.

Kyle glowered at her reflective silence. "Miss Jessie, you know I can't put up with the sheriff and his deputies tramping all over my place. That's why I called you. I thought... I hoped maybe you could get me something from them archology folks you wrote up in the paper." One dirty hand gestured toward the dark grave and his morose, chocolate brown eyes gazed at her in desperation.

To keep from meeting that soulful stare, she studied the disturbed grave. "Come on, Kyle. Even here in the boonies we have to put up with law enforcement."

"So I reckon there won't be no danged reward, either." He twisted his hat, scratched at lank, dishwater blond hair. "Reckon I ought to learn to keep my mouth shut, hadn't I? I'll walk you back to your rig. When you think they'll show up?"

"I've got a phone in my pack here." She traded the water bottle for her cell phone and flipped it open. Probably wouldn't be a signal, but she tried anyway.

No Signal flashed on the glowing blue face, and she turned a half circle, held it at arm's length.

Something moved on the ridge above. She froze, stared up into the deep shade. What was that? Nothing visible. A deer maybe.

"I don't suppose I could talk you into waiting till tomorrow?"

"What?" Startled by the sound of his voice, she swung around. "We could both get in a great deal of trouble here, Kyle."

Foster picked at a dirty nail. "I 'spect I already am in a heap of trouble, ma'am. Last time I'll be this foolish."

One could only hope, but she doubted that. She walked a ways up the slope, squinted in the direction of the moving shadow. Nothing. Glanced at her phone. Still no signal.

"I'm sorry, Kyle. I don't have a choice."

"Ruby's gonna kill me for this."

"It'll be okay. You know that." She moved along the rise, peered at the blue window again. "Darn it. The court will fine you and turn you loose so it can fine you again next time. You're money in the bank."

His feeble grin turned lopsided. "All I know is my kids got to eat, and there ain't much cash money in row cropping these days. Wouldn't be so bad if I'd a crop other'n rocks on that hard scrabble farm, and I ain't about to get me no public job." A common vow of most of the older hill folks accustomed to making a living off the land and surprised when it was no longer possible.

A feeble grin revealed yellow teeth. "Aw, hell and damnation, this early I can plant again, I expect. Next time I'll mind my mouth, you'll see."

He wouldn't though. Men like him were bent on searching out trouble, as if they weren't born knee deep in it.

"I'm truly sorry. I don't know what else to do."

He lifted his thin shoulders and the hems of his overalls rose to reveal dirty bare ankles. "I reckon there ain't naught you can do." He gestured at the phone. "Might have to go plumb back to town to make that call. Useless little gadgets."

When she continued to swing the instrument around in an effort to get a signal, and to maybe spot the intruder, he glanced once or twice toward his farm.

"Well, reckon I'll get moving. Might have time to do something afore they get here, seeing as how you can't make that thing work. Besides, they'll be concentrating on these bones, at least for a while."

"Does anyone else live up there?" She gestured toward the ridge.

"Nope, why?"

She raised her shoulders. Nerves pecking at her was all it was.

Kyle took off, grumbling words she couldn't understand.

Below the grave, perched on a rock beside the creek where she'd parked the Jeep, Jessie checked her phone again, found three bars and punched in the number for Sheriff Mac Richards's office. She spoke to him briefly, then followed his instructions to notify Dave and Kathy Spacey, the resident forensics experts who also taught at the Junior College in Cedarton. A breeze lifted her hair and she leaned back on her arms, stared through the white, scaly limbs of a huge sycamore at an incredibly blue spring sky.

Might as well face it. She wanted this story. Bad. Ached for the excitement that came while composing that lead paragraph. The anticipation of researching and following leads. But did she dare? It wasn't as if the *Observer* was the *Los Angeles Times*. And she was certainly no longer the infamous but fictitious JJ Stone whose star had flared so brightly and briefly out in LA. That was all in the past. This was her life now and she'd make the best of it. If she could.

Lost in thought, she jumped when Kyle fired up his ancient tractor. Watched him drive off, the chug of the beat-up old Ford engine echoing back from the peaks that skirted the valley. Beside her Cedar Creek chattered merrily, forming crystalline pools for crawfish and minnows.

The air smelled of new birthing. The dogwoods were in bloom, lacing the rugged hills in creamy white. Warm sunlight dappled her face and she leaned back to bask in its rays. She'd been a kid when the family pulled up stakes and moved to California, but it was true what they said about these mountains. They called you home, no matter how long you stayed away.

Along the road that curled out of Cedarton, a speeding white car left a trail of dust in its wake, its roof reflecting bright shards of light. Sheriff Mac headed for the crime scene, and as usual he was flying low, lights flashing, siren silent so as not to stir up the cattle grazing on both sides of the road. The curious animals raised their heads, jaws moving, and stared at the interloper.

She rose and waved both arms over her head.

The patrol car went into a skid that put its front wheels on the narrow lane to Kyle's place. Out of the ford of the creek, another wild slide and the SUV rocked to a stop near her Jeep, bumper dripping water. You'd have thought she'd reported a shoot-out in progress.

For a moment a dust cloud obscured the cruiser. Out of that settling debris two men appeared like aliens off a mist-shrouded spaceship. Just like in the movies. Ought to be men in black with dark glasses, outrageous weapons in their hands, perhaps even a little green monster or two. Instead, there appeared the lanky sheriff in his gray Stetson, a roll of crime scene tape dangling from one hand, and beside him a stranger. Tall, well built, with skin like tarnished copper. A black t-shirt showed off wide shoulders and a flat belly, tight jeans hugged some fine equipment, and long, muscular legs carried him toward her with the mere vestige of a limp.

Sometimes God was good.

This had to be that new guy the department had hired. According to her friend Tinker, who worked at the sheriff's department, he was an exnarc off the streets of Dallas. And hot. Tinker always did know her men. He was mostly Cherokee and rumored to be a psychic or something. Tinker wasn't exactly sure what.

"Some Indian thing," she'd said. "He communes with the dead or demons or spirits. I'm not sure."

A strange thing to contemplate. But he definitely looked like all of the above, tough and mean and on the warpath. Whatever the dead told him, he wasn't too happy about it. His black, wide-brimmed hat sported a rattlesnake skin band that matched his boots. Probably caught the reptile barehanded and bit its head off. As for that psychic crap, it was a pile of just that. Crap. But that was her opinion. Some put plenty of stock in it. Maybe he would talk to the bones, solve the case right off the bat.

The sheriff halted in front of her, thumbed his natty gray Stetson back an inch, and squinted sparkly blue eyes. "Jessie. Came as quick as we could."

She couldn't help but smile. "Saw you did. Didn't want to give those bones a chance to get up and run away, I guess."

The man with him cast a dark look at the sheriff, grunted in what she guessed might pass for speech where he came from.

Maybe he didn't speak English. Or maybe he only talked to the dead.

With eyes dark and secretive he settled rapt attention on her. A shiver skittered down her spine like a blue-tailed lizard. Something fingered around in her brain till she wanted to run and hide. But she held his gaze, because, by God, she wasn't about to let him know what he was doing to her libido. But he'd do just fine.

The sheriff interrupted the stare-down. "You two through looking each other over, I'll introduce you. Jessie, this is our new deputy, over from Dallas. Told you about him. Starting our new crime scene investigation unit. Name's Dal Starr. This here's Jessie West." Mac smiled like a father taking credit for his offspring.

The deputy shifted and sunlight slashed across the sharp angles of his face, reflected in eyes that weren't black at all, instead were green as oak leaves in full summer. There was no humor in his stoic gaze. Must come from all those dead folks telling him all about hell and such.

Determined to overlook that, she stuck out her hand. "Pleased to meet you. Dal, is that short for Dallas?"

His big hand turned hers palm down, and for a moment she thought he was going to kiss it. He didn't. But he didn't let it go, either. "As a matter of fact it is. My momma's fault. She always wanted to go there. But as it turned out, I'm the only Dallas she ever laid eyes on." He paused, but before she could reply asked, "What's Jessie short for, Jessica?"

The lazily drawled inquiry, when she'd expected at best a grunt, caught her unawares, and she felt captured, swallowed up. Trapped. Under his warm touch her skin tingled and she wanted loose.

He held on tight.

She angled a quick glance upward into his features, shaded by the hat he hadn't removed, and remembered to reply to his question about her name.

"Here I was having my doubts about your psychic abilities, and then you go and guess Jessie is short for Jessica. I'm impressed."

To reward her for the sarcasm he allowed a corner of his mouth to twitch like he wouldn't laugh, no matter what, but he sort of wanted to. "Nothing psychic about it. Purely a lucky guess, ma'am. Lovely name."

The same emotionless tone colored everything he said. Probably soothed the ghosts.

Stop it, Jessie, before you get plumb silly.

A rousing snake uncurled in her belly. This man's feral watchfulness made her nervous. Like he might be reading her mind or whatever it was he did. God forbid he asked for anything, because she'd give it to him, even though he scared her. Never could tell what a man like this one would do if pushed. He still held her hand, and she wanted it back. Who was she kidding? What she wanted was for him to drag her off somewhere and rip off all her clothes. And that would just be the start.

When he finally let go, the fantasy skittered away, disappointment replaced it, and she stood there like an idiot. Struck dumb. At last she found her own voice, but it sounded like someone else's. "Well, I'm pleased to meet you, Deputy."

"And I you, Jessica."

Mac broke in. "Just what is this about a body? It's a little out of your field, isn't it? Not like you to be poking around a grave that ain't yet a hundred years old."

"Wasn't me found it. Poor old Kyle's dogs Snoop and Howler did that little job." The sheriff's teasing relaxed her, and she spared another glance for the tall deputy, who continued to study her like she was prey. Made her nervous, and she wished Mac would let her be on her way, or tell his new guy to behave.

"And so, Kyle being like he is, called you instead of us."

She shrugged. "Can't help that. Maybe he likes me better than you."

Mac joined her in laughing.

"Why don't you take us to the scene, then?" he said.

Like he couldn't find it on his own. Giving orders and showing off for the psychic. She sighed. "Come on. It's up here a ways, under that overhang."

Relieved to be on the move and out of reach of the deputy's intent scrutiny, she led them across a field carpeted with tiny pink spring beauties, and up the incline.

To the north a gargantuan concrete bridge sprawled across the valley on enormous legs, its elongated dark shadow slashing the fields and forests below. The span of the new highway under construction would one day open a four-lane route from Tulsa on the west to Branson on the east, bypassing Cedarton by a few miles. Lord only knew what its coming would do to the small town. Plenty of time to worry about that though. Construction was already eighteen months behind schedule and trudging right along.

She continued talking to Mac as if the deputy weren't there. "When his dog came in carrying the bones, Kyle thought it was a prehistoric find, being so near Jacob's Bluff. By the way, I called Dave and Kathy Spacey, like you asked. They didn't have classes today. I saw them arrive up there a while ago. Took the logging road in. The site's pretty badly messed up, I'm sorry to say. Those dogs have had a field day. Kyle penned them up, but it didn't do much good. I'm afraid he's been digging around himself. Looking for treasure. I took some photos. It was way too late to preserve the scene, but I didn't touch anything."

"Are you in law enforcement?"

Starr's husky query ran roughshod over her senses.

Before she could reply, the sheriff did it for her. "Jessie here is a reporter for the *Grace County Observer.*"

"Why'd he call a reporter?" He actually growled the question.

First time she'd heard a man growl, though you read it in books a lot. It appeared that some things did rile him after all. Plenty of law enforcement officers disliked members of the press, but since coming back here she'd had no problems. Maybe because of her relationship with Mac. It didn't hurt that her folks had been well-liked before they'd left for California. And she was what you might call connected, having kin all over the county.

Maybe this man was psychic, after all. At one time he would've been right on the money with his quick assessment of her integrity. But she didn't get the chance to object to his misconceptions of her life now. They had arrived at the grave.

The Spaceys' red SUV gleamed through the trees, parked on the old logging road once used to haul hardwood timber from these woods. The couple busily unloaded equipment. A blue tarp lay at the upper side of the burial site where a few bones had been placed. Several wooden boxes and screens were stacked nearby.

Kathy noticed their arrival first and rose, wiping gloved hands on the seat of her pants. Dave remained on his knees, absorbed in taking pictures of the exposed bones.

The couple were exact reflections of one another. Each had sandy hair, blue eyes, and a sturdy body. They were dressed in their official uniforms—jeans, baseball caps, and flannel shirts they could shed down to t-shirts as the day warmed. Kathy did most of the talking, while Dave tended to ruminate quietly. Anytime, anywhere you saw one of them, you saw them both, as if they were attached by invisible bonds. To look at them one would never guess they were forensic anthropologists.

Mac approached them. "Dave, Kathy, this here's our new crime scene investigator, Dallas Starr. Deputy Starr, this is Dave and Kathy Spacey. They're with the anthropology department at BJC. They give us a hand on cases like this." He chuckled, watched the three take each other's measure. "Murder and mayhem around Cedarton's rare. Don't too many skeletons turn up, not even them that's ten thousand years old. But it happens. And with that new highway giving access to our fair backwoods, it'll happen more and more." Mac laughed again, and everyone joined him except the psychic Cherokee, who appeared to be visiting with the departed. Someone needed to tug on his chain, bring him back to this world.

He didn't shake hands, but nodded at both the Spaceys, an underlying tension obvious in his manner. She wanted to scream, "Speak," at him.

"I'll just hang this out." Mac took off to stretch the yellow and black tape along the perimeter of the crime scene.

Eyeing the churned soil, Starr stepped gingerly to the edge of the hole and squatted beside the bones. "We can't do much more harm here than's already been done."

After a glance toward Kathy, with an expression that revealed nothing, he checked out the burial spot. He gazed into the hole for a long while, then raised his face to stare into the sky with his eyes closed. After a minute or so, while Jessie expected him to break into a chant, he spread a hand flat against the earth and took a deep breath. Features unreadable, he remained in that position for at least a full minute before rising.

Damn, he was good. It was hard not to stare, so everyone did. Maybe he was having a séance, or communing with the spirits. It looked like he was serious about this stuff, unless he was just putting on a show.

"When do you think these bones were put here?" He shoved his hat back with a thumb and glanced at Kathy.

"I thought you'd know that," Jessie said before the other woman could answer. "Being psychic and all." She bit her tongue when he shot her a look that could've singed her hair.

Kathy squinted in his direction, mouth tight. "I'm not sure we can tell you that. I can tell you that it's probably been here at least ten years. Not a sign of flesh so far. We'll do some tests, get you more information. Too bad the dogs tore this place up so bad. We could've gotten some idea of how long ago he was planted by the growth of plants over his grave."

She grinned.

Dal didn't.

The man was sexy to look at, with absolutely no sense of humor or social skills. He probably burped and farted at the dinner table.

Clearing her throat, Kathy went on. "As soon as we take measurements for height, pinpoint age and gender—we haven't found the pelvic bone or skull yet—this body will be tagged and sent down to the medical examiner in Little Rock for cause of death if it's possible to determine." She grimaced. "From the looks of this place, I doubt we'll find all the bones."

Dal nodded. "Then it's true you-all don't have an ME here."

"No, just a coroner. Roy Bean. And yes, it really is his name. Anyway, he's not an MD. Old Roy runs the mortuary, so he has a working acquaintance with dead bodies. Any death that's suspicious, we send the body down to Little Rock for autopsy."

"This one's definitely suspicious," Starr said like she might disagree.

Jessie swallowed a smart retort. She'd gone about as far as she dared with him.

Wisely, Kathy remained the professional she was, though her expression told another story. "So far all we have is some of the appendicular skeleton, though there's some of the axial there." She pointed and everyone acted like they might know what she was talking about.

Jessie chuckled and suppressed a remark no one would appreciate.

Kathy got it, though, grinned, and went on. "Again, we'll know more in a few days."

Starr glanced quickly at Dave, who hadn't said a word, but continued to busy himself snapping preliminary photos. "So what we've got here is a headless, naked, partial skeleton. Any clothing remaining?"

Dave let his wife reply.

"We'll have to excavate deeper first. There'll be some remnants of clothes if there were any buried. Threads, buttons, zippers, shoes, something. Haven't found a sign so far."

Starr nodded. "I'll just hang around a while, do some of my own looking. I like to handle the evidence on a case myself."

Kathy gave him a sharp glance that Jessie read as resentment, and she didn't much blame her, considering his tone of superiority. She braced herself for Kathy's reaction. This might be fun to watch. During Jessie's extensive coverage of the Jacob's Bluff dig the previous fall, she and Kathy had become friends, and she knew enough about the forensic anthropologist to know she'd not let Dallas Starr tread on her expertise.

True to Jessie's surmise, Kathy came right back at him. "As Mac told you, we've worked with the police before. We do understand chain of evidence. You're the investigator here, but don't come around with that big city attitude says you're gonna teach us how to do our job. Maybe they have more sophisticated ways in Dallas, but we do know what we're doing."

The stony-faced deputy took it right on his square chin like he might have deserved the retort, but a glint in his eyes warned Kathy not to go too far. "I'm sure you do, and I didn't intend to suggest you didn't. But I know my job too, and we'll work better together if you keep that in mind."

There he went, making friends already, and he hadn't even taken off his hat.

Kathy continued in a tight voice. "We, Dave and I, have a good reputation in archeology and anthropology as well as forensics, and we're the best you've got, detective, so don't presume to shove us around."

"I wouldn't think of it, ma'am. Where is this lab?"

To Jessie's surprise, he grinned. Dimples gentled the harsh line of his jaw and sparks lit his eyes. His voice softened around the edges. From the look of it he totally disarmed Kathy. Her own animosity slipped away.

"At the Junior College in Cedarton," Kathy managed to reply to his question. "You'll find it adequate for your needs. If not, the State Crime Lab can back us up. As you can imagine, we're not kept too busy with dead bodies in this remote county. A different story down in Little Rock though."

The tension had eased a bit, so Jessie decided to educate him. "There's not a town in the entire county with a traffic light. Cedarton is the county seat and it's the largest city, with a population of two thousand four hundred two, unless Marie Orrendorf has had her kid. There's a couple of four-way stops and we do have a Walmart. The newspaper I write for, the *Grace County Observer*, is a weekly. The nearest daily is in Harrison, about seventy miles southeast, in Boone County. Not much excitement goes on around here, but it is about time the county rated a CSI, even if it is a lone Texan." She dared a smile, but he'd gone back to stoic, almost as if she weren't there.

That was fine with her. Now that Deputy Dallas Starr had been thrown into the mix, she was determined to write this story. Eager to get her teeth into investigating all the leads, staying out ahead of this psychic Cherokee. This time she'd do everything right. And she might even solve the crime before he did. Wouldn't that rip him a new one?

2
CHAPTER

Dal watched the sheriff circle one small tree after another until he'd enclosed the scene with crime tape. This was about as far from the streets of Dallas as he could get. But it was already okay. Except for the reporter, and he'd handle that real quick. He spared her a quick glance and was startled to see her staring at him. Her fear zinged through his brain. Good. Better if she was afraid of him, would keep her at arm's length.

Sheriff Richards joined them, took off his hat, and combed blunt fingers through thinning silver hair. "Well, I can see y'all are gonna get this sorted out. My phone won't get a signal up here, so I'll get on back to my rig and call in. Wish they'd get those danged towers up. One day one of us is gonna need help real bad and won't be able to get it cause some farmer was scared microwaves would make his cows give sour milk. Reckon that's what we pay for living in God's Country." He doffed his hat at one and all, started away but found more to say before taking his leave.

"Probably go on back to town to keep an eye on things and leave Dal here to his business. Jessie, I expect you're not about to light out for a while. Likely you'll be wanting some pictures as they work. You'll see we get copies, and you, too, Dave? Dallas here hasn't had time to assemble all his equipment. Reckon I sort of grabbed him right off the plane. You wouldn't mind giving our new deputy a ride, Jessie?"

Dal sent her a glare. Just what he needed. Cooped up in a confined space with a nosy reporter. He made to object to the sheriff's arrangements, but the man's steely glint stopped him. It hadn't been a question. The girl glowered at Richards, too. She didn't like it any better than he did. Something about her drew him. Something stronger warned him off.

She was grinning now, nodding at the sheriff. Did she do everything he said, like it or not? An odd relationship he'd like to know more about. Cops didn't crawl in bed with reporters where he came from. Surely the old man and her weren't sharing the sheets? Stranger things happened.

Richards glanced at Dallas. "I'll have a county car ready when you come back to the station. You'll take it home with you since you'll be on duty twenty-four hours a day. Where you staying?"

"I don't have a place yet. I'll have to get a motel room until I find something. But I don't want to be a nuisance for Jessica here. I'll just ride on back with you, pick up the car, and drive myself back out here."

She appeared relieved and looked away.

"Nonsense, boy. You might as well get used to the way we do things around here, and it's easy does it. You act like you're still walking the streets of Dallas protecting your back from a knife or bullet. Loosen up. Jessie won't mind a bit taking you into town when you're done here, will you, hon?" Mac shot her one of his looks that barred any disagreement.

She wanted to stick her tongue out at him. Dal experienced her desire as if it were his own and couldn't help but chuckle.

Her brow furrowed and her gaze darted from him to the sheriff. "Of course not. Tinker and I are going out to eat at Ortega's later anyway. I can swing through the square easy as can be. Be glad to drop Deputy Starr off at the jailhouse." She mimicked Dal's earlier stiff tone.

Dammit, now he was beginning to like her. That would never do. Clearing his throat, he turned to the strange burial scene. Dave continued to place small numbered tags beside newly uncovered bones and take pictures.

An odd prickling sensation lifted the hairs on the back of Dal's neck. Whatever else this was, it wasn't a crime scene. The body had been carried in. Dead. By someone scared out of their wits. A woman, possibly two. Their terror lingered like the stench of a long-ago forest fire.

He'd best keep that to himself for now. A reporter hanging around the scene of a crime was a definite no-no in his book. And playing house with the law, even worse. No telling what kind of story she would concoct if she knew too much about his methods. This being his first case on a new job, he wanted to do everything right. Reporters told lies when the truth would do. He had good reason not to trust any of them, and held a deep resentment for the stories they concocted with so little remorse.

It was not so easy to ignore this one. She was country pretty in her jeans and crisp white shirt, streaky blonde hair tied back with a blue scarf, and eyes splashed with gold so in certain light they looked like cat eyes. Smooth skin free of makeup except for a bit of pink on her lips. Though she was afraid of him, she had the guts to sneer at that fear. Once again he damned the visions handed down to him by his Cherokee grandfather. He did not welcome communing with the spirits of the dead. Most especially those who had suffered and longed for peace. They could not go to their rest without wreaking vengeance. His head was filled with their pleas. Yet, it was worse to catch a thread of thought from the living, as he often did.

Tamping down the voices like his grandfather had taught him, he managed to concentrate on working with Dave and Kathy Spacey. He hadn't gotten off on the right foot with them, and vowed to make amends.

A sensation of being watched from above hung with him, but he couldn't see anyone. Probably that old fellow whose dog found the bones. He made himself scarce quick enough. Time later to hunt him up. Squaring his shoulders, Dal watched the Spaceys at work. He had little to do other than keep an eye out for what surfaced as they screened the loose dirt.

Around midday, Dave brought out a basket filled with sandwiches and a large thermos of lemonade, which they all shared while perched on large boulders nearby. The Spaceys had finished removing and recording the bones uncovered by the dogs, and after lunch began the task of digging and screening within the grid they'd laid out. Dave supplied Dal with a pair of surgical gloves like he and Kathy wore so he could join in.

"We'll photograph, measure, and tag each one, and Dave'll note them on his chart," Kathy explained. "We'll use a body bag for transport. It is a body and needs to be treated like one."

The loose humus was carefully dug and sifted through screens, smaller bones picked out and anything of a suspicious nature bagged and tagged. Dal welcomed the work, but kept glancing at Jessie, who remained busy writing in a pad and taking pictures.

Why in the hell he couldn't keep his eyes off her, he didn't know. Women, even ones pretty as her, were definitely off limits after what happened with Leeann. Yet, he caught himself staring at Jessie as they worked and thinking it was too bad she had chosen such a dishonest profession.

With a great deal of effort he dragged his attention from her and back to the screen where Kathy piled soil. While sifting for smaller bones, he paused and spread a palm in the loose black earth. Feminine fear and raw panic slammed through him, kicked his heart into high gear. Lightning and thunder, cold rain, a terror so gut-wrenching he jerked his hand back. His Cherokee grandfather proclaimed his a natural gift and one he should celebrate, this ability to sense both ghosts and evil spirits, known as *asgi`na* and *anasgi`na*, in Cherokee, as well as their lingering emotions. Most of the time, Dal wasn't sure he agreed.

The feeling of being watched grew stronger, and he twisted to stare toward the top of the bluff. Brief movement quickly vanished into the shadowy trees. A twist of rage and hatred.

"What's wrong?" Kathy asked.

"I thought I heard someone up there."

"Probably a deer. They're thick around here."

Only an animal? No. Deer didn't have such a scramble of thoughts. But he nodded, continued to study the terrain.

Up on that bluff, hidden by underbrush and rocks, lurked someone with human intelligence. Whether it was ghost or evil spirit, or just that Kyle fellow keeping watch, he wasn't sure. He sensed fear and a babbling hysteria in the mind of the watcher. Closing his eyes, he reached for that mind, touched hate and confused fury. Once more he glimpsed a body and a rainy night lit by flashes of lightning. The scene darkened, to be replaced by a savage rage that shook him to the very depths. Whether it came from the past or from whoever hid above them, he couldn't tell, but he would find out soon enough. Of that he was sure.

The interloper's thoughts disappeared like mist rising in early morning air. Dal relaxed and watched Kathy Spacey place yet another tiny bone beside the others, alongside rows of Polaroid photos lying to dry on the blue tarp. Then he went back to sieving dark soil through the sifting screen. Scoop after scoop revealed pieces of the intricate jigsaw puzzle.

First time he'd ever been involved at this level of an investigation, and he found himself enjoying it.

And this place was peaceful, even in the midst of a murder scene. The surrounding woods were anything but quiet. Birds squabbled and sang, squirrels scolded and darted from one limb to another, limbs rattled and brush whispered in a light breeze. The conglomeration of odors was far removed from what he'd grown accustomed to in Dallas. Fresh earth, the fragrance of flowers, a vague wafting of animal scents from cattle grazing in the valley below.

A skull hadn't turned up yet. They might never find it. Those dogs had done a damned fine job, and there was no telling what they'd carried off. A small, shiny black object, definitely not a bone, peeked from the soil jumping about on his screen. Excited, he gently brushed away the dirt like the Spaceys had demonstrated.

"Dave, got something here."

"Coming." Dave approached, placed a numbered tab beside the object, and snapped a shot.

An ebony arrowhead caught the flash of the camera, and Dal picked it up in gloved fingers.

Terror vibrated through him, set his nerves on edge. Okay, he had to remain calm, so no one would think him totally nuts. Everyone was so entranced by the object he held that he needn't have worried. The reporter hovered nearby, camera aimed, flash going off in quick repetitions.

"Look at that, would you?" Dave whispered in awe. "But something's wrong with it."

"Looks perfect to me," Dal said.

Kathy studied the arrowhead. "That's what's wrong with it."

Jessica's camera flashed again.

Anger rising, Dal turned on her. "I'm afraid I can't allow you to keep those. We can't release information to the press on what we find here during the investigation."

Holding the camera tightly against her midsection, she pinned him with a stare, sorrel eyes sparking gold in the sunlight. "Oh, get over yourself. I know better than to publish unauthorized photos or write anything until Mac releases it. I'm not a tabloid reporter."

"Oh, sure, and there really is such a thing as off the record, too. I'll believe that when elephants fly."

"Pigs," she said. "It's when pigs fly."

Though said jokingly, the scathing look told Dal he'd hit a nerve. Hadn't she ever heard of Dumbo the Elephant? He wanted to push the argument, but didn't pursue the matter. By God, he would get the last word, though.

"This is my department and I will not work hand in glove with a member of the press. As far as I'm concerned, you shouldn't even be here. And I intend to take it up with Sheriff Richards." He had plenty more to say, but he made the mistake of taking a breath, and she filled the space with a sudden blast of her own.

"You go right ahead and do that, Mister Dallas Starr from Dallas. You don't like reporters, that's pretty clear. I suppose you feel justified in taking it out on me, but we're both professionals, and I would appreciate it if you treated me with respect. Mac happens to be the boss, your boss, and he trusts me. Sometimes I can get information he can't... you can't. Some folks hereabouts don't like to talk to the law. I'm kin to a lot of them, and they'll talk to kin. They trust me. You come up needing to know stuff I can supply, then you'll be glad to have me around, so why don't you curb that temper of yours? This is not Dallas, and I am not the enemy."

God, she was gorgeous when perturbed. Sparks flew from those magnificent eyes and every time she clenched her lips, dimples winked in her cheeks. But beauty or not, no reporter would ever get the best of him again, and he shook away the fascination. Be damned if he'd trust her, ever.

"So maybe we should consider you a CI?" he shot back.

Oh, man, how badly she wanted to throw something at him. Had she not valued her camera it would have come sailing at his head. He went on before she could explode.

"I was hired to investigate crimes, and it's my considered professional opinion that we have an ongoing criminal investigation here. I would appreciate it if you'd let me do my work in the way I see fit and not interfere." His emphasis on certain words were intended to mock her.

She snapped him a brittle look. "And you can do the same. You'll get copies of these pictures, as Mac requested, and none will be published without his authorization. But until he or my boss takes me off the story, I'm on it whether you like it or not."

Rage rode through him and he clenched his fists. Jessica rose on her toes and stuck out her chin, daring him. What a handful she'd be. "You might think about getting that corncob out of your butt."

Both Kathy and Dave paused to study the two of them, and he reined in his anger. Smothered a laugh. Corncob? In his butt? Damn, that image was hilarious. All he could do not to laugh. He simmered down. No sense in this sort of trouble, even before he got started on the job. What he wanted was to completely dismiss Jessica from his mind, but on the defensive, she was dangerously attractive to his dark side. Maybe he'd poke around in her head again sometime. He always had liked women who stood up for themselves despite being threatened. But dammit, a reporter?

Intense emotion lent a flush to her sun-kissed complexion. A few strands of ash blonde hair had escaped the blue scarf and framed that determined chin still tilted at a dangerous angle. Those remarkable, wide-set eyes continued to shoot sparks in his direction. It was like being faced-off by an alley cat that knew its enemy was bigger but fought back anyway.

Her heated gaze awoke the slumbering beast within him, and he had the distinct feeling he might get burned badly if he wasn't very careful. She had plenty of bad stuff to hide and it'd made her defensive as all get out. The idea that the two of them shared something dark annoyed him and he decided to let the matter drop. She had his urges stirring like a rattler uncoiling in the warmth of the sun. It'd do to block her churning thoughts.

Sighing, he turned away. He was tired and had probably misread the circumstances. She was right, this was not a big city and all the rules were different. But be damned if he'd apologize.

Shaking off the remnants of her stubborn defenses, he studied the black arrowhead, handed it to Dave. "What is it? Looks like an artifact."

Kathy touched it with the tip of a gloved finger. "I'm not sure, but I don't think so. I think it's obsidian, but so perfect it may have been polished. Though we occasionally find obsidian here, it's not indigenous to this part of the country. At one time Indians probably traded for it."

"Could I see it again?"

Dave dropped the arrow head into Dal's gloved palm. "Fingerprints?"

"I doubt it." The artistically crafted flint belonged to the victim or the one who buried the body, he couldn't yet be sure. No early American native had ever handled it though.

An essence of renewed terror tingled up his arms and he tamped it down. He got the message, loud and clear. Violence hovered here as if reluctant to leave until justice was done. And the lovely shaped stone had something to do with whatever terrible deeds had occurred. He carefully slipped the arrowhead into a bag and sealed it.

Miss Jessica West continued to watch him, and he shifted under her gaze, infuriated that she could get to him so quickly.

Dave had gone back to sifting dirt. "Hey, look here." He held up a smashed hunk of lead, and Dal pushed away the distraction of the reporter. "Well, that isn't an artifact, unless those fellas were more advanced than we thought."

Dal touched the misshapen bullet with the tip of a finger and jerked away. Anguish, pain—*betrayal.*

"My God."

"What? What is it?" Kathy asked, and Dave gaped.

"I think you'll find our victim was shot," he said.

"I take it back, deputy. You're good," Jessica said in a mocking tone.

He chose to ignore her. "Looks like a thirty-caliber. Hunting rifle, perhaps?"

"Another good guess." Jessica sidled closer, daring him to say something.

"Well, we've got something else here," Kathy said. "I'm not sure what. Looks like a shoestring or leather thong." She reached for an evidence bag. "We'll have it analyzed, see what it is."

Sensing Jessica's stare, Dal turned on her. "Aren't you going to take a picture?"

He almost staggered with her silent retort. You wouldn't think a pretty little thing like her would know such language.

3
CHAPTER

Sitting on the sidelines didn't appeal to Jessie and she sucked on her water bottle like an angry child. The new deputy was really getting to her, and her initial fascination wasn't helping matters one bit. If she hadn't promised the sheriff she'd take him to town, she'd have already run for her life.

No use telling him what she thought about his smart mouth, so she did her best to become invisible while framing her shots, then retreating to the sidelines. What Mac saw in this guy, she had no idea. Darned Texas cretin needed an attitude adjustment, and she just might be the one to give it to him.

Parker would not forgive her coming back without a story and plenty of pictures. That she would do, but nothing more. It wasn't much of a story yet anyway, and she'd be glad to turn it over to him. A body that would probably never be identified, a case never solved, too much attention falling on the small-town reporter who broke the story. And worst of all, Dallas Starr involved. All she wanted was to get back to her ancient burials and let this guy play his games with someone else. Parker could give him a dose of his own medicine. Darn that Mac anyway, saddling her with this horse's ass.

Dave raised a hand. "I found the pelvic bone."

Kathy took a look. "We have us a male. I measured the humerus earlier and figured as much. So, we're definitely dealing with a man around six feet, give or take half an inch or so."

Jessie snapped a few quick shots of them studying the bone. People. That would make Parker happy, though Starr would probably have a cow when he saw it.

Starr slipped off his hat and ran fingers through thick, black hair. "That's probably all we'll ever get on this poor devil, unless the head turns up, and that's doubtful." He fitted the hat back on and tilted it just so. "Let's hope we can find someone missing and this can be tied up quickly. At least we'll have a place to start."

While Dave tagged and photographed the pelvic bone, Jessie ignored Starr as if he weren't there and addressed Kathy. "What about DNA?"

"We'll try," she said with a sigh, "but if our vic isn't in the system or we can't find relatives to compare with, it doesn't do much good. Won't do to be in any hurry getting the profile back either. This isn't CSI. There's at least an eighteen-month wait on DNA results from the state lab unless it's an emergency, which this sure isn't. They're working on that, but the back-up is horrific. And then there's a question of who we compare the results to."

Jessie nodded. Starr glared at her till her brain itched. If she stayed around him much longer, she wouldn't be able to think at all. The idea of hauling him to town in her car gave her the heebie-jeebies.

To her relief, everyone went back to their jobs, the only sound the rattle of dirt sifting through the fine metal screens and the serenade of birds. The sun slipped behind the mountains and long shadows crept over the remote spot in which they worked. Damp air settled around her like a cloak, and Jessie shivered.

Why didn't they call it a day?

As if she'd joined Dal Starr in reading minds, Kathy wiped her brow with a shirt sleeve and addressed the deputy. "We can keep digging if you want, but we're already deep enough we're picking up some tool chips and pottery fragments. It looks like we've got all the bones that haven't already been carted off by animals. I'd hoped we could find the skull, but if it ever was here, it's been carried off. It's your call."

Grunting, he rose from his knees, grimaced, and dusted his jeans. "Dogs probably used it for a toy. If we had the manpower we'd set up a search grid outward from here. I'll talk to Mac about that."

"Sometimes we use classes from the college to walk search patterns," she said. "But—"

"Yeah, I doubt anything would turn up. A body buried that long… hell, there's not going to be anything left lying around by the perp either. You'll let me know what you find before you send the bones to Little Rock?"

"Certainly, Deputy. You'll have our report as soon as we've done some more testing."

"No sign of clothing?"

Kathy shook her head. "Not one single thread, so I reckon you were right. You have yourself the skeleton of a headless, naked murder victim. We will try for a sample from the bones for DNA testing, for all the good it may do." She shrugged in resignation, then smiled up at him.

Oh, Christ. Jessie groaned. He'd charmed Kathy to hell and back. Well, his charm, such as it was, wouldn't work on her. She didn't want to like him. So she wouldn't. No trouble there.

Kathy went right on talking to Starr like they were old friends.

"Good to have you, Deputy. It's about time the Grace County Sheriff's Department moved up in the world, with its very own criminal investigator. I'm not sure just what you'll find to investigate. That highway will change things, though, one of these days. If crimes pick up, maybe you can talk the powers that be into a lab as well." She grinned wryly. "Heck of a thing to have to depend on lawbreakers to keep our jobs, huh? Glad Dave and I have our day jobs." She pointed a fond smile toward her partner.

"I don't reckon we'll have to worry about our jobs," Dal said. "Every time you get progress, you get more people, you get more troublemakers. We'll just have to work with what we've got on this case. I appreciate anything you can do for me." The white teeth flashed.

For maybe half a second there, he seemed sincere, but Jessie didn't believe it for one minute. Like most men, he just knew how to get what he wanted out of women. Most women. She'd pass, though.

Kathy touched her husband's arm and suggested it was time to pack up and leave.

The taciturn Dave nodded and everyone helped gather the equipment and the body bag and load it in the SUV.

"You ready, Deputy?" Jessie asked.

He came away from staring off over the mountains.

In the distance sunlight played a golden farewell across the tops of the peaks. Shadows crept into the clearing on silent feet. It would soon be dark, and Jessie didn't wait for him to come to his senses. This act of his gave her the willies. She certainly didn't believe in psychics or any of that drivel about communicating with the dead. It was just plain creepy. Communing with the living was bad enough on some levels.

She told the Spaceys goodbye, stowed her camera and pad, shrugged into her pack, and started off down the trail, fleeing whatever made the hairs quiver on the back of her neck. Behind her, Dal's boots kicked up rocks on the rough path. Once she heard him mutter something, and turned to see his hat had been knocked off by a low-hanging tree limb.

"Flat lander," she muttered. His lack of agility on the rough ground surprised her, but she didn't slow down.

"I heard that," he called.

"Doesn't matter to me. I thought you people were supposed to be more fleet of foot."

He caught up. *"We* people? You mean Texans, Cherokee, lawmen?"

"Well, I guess I meant Cherokee?"

"Well, I'm Cherokee, or I once was, a long time ago. However, we Texans do better in the saddle or on flat land, that's true. Lawmen, now, we're a mixed bag."

She kept stomping along, grumbling under her breath. "Smart aleck." No need to try to get on her good side. It wouldn't work.

"Now, as for you people, do you always have such smart mouths?"

"Okay. Okay. I apologize." Don't know why, though.

"No need."

She hurried across the field toward her Jeep, persimmon saplings flipping at her britches legs. He soon matched his pace to hers and, wrapped in an uncomfortable silence, they moved side by side across the meadow. It was good they didn't agree on anything. She wanted no common ground between them.

After a while, he spoke in that low-pitched, sing-song drawl. "Look, I guess we got off on the wrong foot. I don't want to make an enemy of anyone in the press. I don't want to make any enemies, period. Do you think we could start over?"

"Oh, shit," she muttered under her breath. He had to go and get friendly. The last thing she wanted was friendship with him.

"What?" he said.

"You seem good at reading minds. Why don't you figure mine out? Come on, will you?" His nearness and the timber of his voice sent a warm sensation through her. She was sure she blushed.

"I heard, just not sure what you meant."

"I meant, oh, shit. You don't fool me with your insincere apology."

That she would experience a typically feminine reaction to a sexy man, especially this one, annoyed her. No sense in going there. She brought out the worst in men, and that wasn't the half of what they did to her. Mostly this one scared her, for a variety of reasons.

To cover her confusion, she lit in on him. "I don't care whether you dislike me or my profession or it's a bit of both. That's your problem. Seems to me like you're afraid I'll catch you doing something you're not supposed to do. You don't like reporters, that's too bad. Someone has to do the watchdogging. Usually those who shout the loudest about the sins of the media are the ones with the most to hide." She almost bit the end of her tongue on that one. Talk about misplaced self-righteousness.

His gaze darkened. "Well, so much for a truce. I want it on the record that I tried."

"Wait till I get out my pad, I'll make a note of it."

"You do that. I suppose you believe the public has the right to know everything, no matter the consequences to the innocent. Doesn't it bother you in the least that what you write might do extreme harm? And if you're the entire free world's watchdog, tell me this. Who's watching the watchdog?"

Stomach churning, she whirled to face him, blocking the way so he couldn't get past without wading through a growth of thick brambles. He halted, gazed down at her, eyes smoldering with challenge.

Answering him took all her strength. She could barely reply and pressed her lips tightly to still their quivering, then plowed on. "You don't know anything about me or what I'm like, so keep your ill-mannered remarks to yourself." Way to go, Jessie. That was real bright.

Without a word in rebuttal, he turned away.

"So much for starting over," she muttered.

Despair burned her throat, her eyes filled. She swallowed hard and faced into the wind to dry her tears. How close he had come to her secret, but damned if she'd let him see her cry. She would do well to stay far away from this man who had the uncanny knack of seeing through her carefully constructed façade. She was relieved that he hadn't pursued his question, which she had so pointedly not answered. At one time she had made a terrible mistake, and could indeed have used a watchdog.

She guided the Jeep along the crooked road toward Cedarton in silence. Leaned against the headrest beside her, he appeared to be sleeping. Good. She was tired of arguing with him, defending herself against his accusations.

Infuriated with both him and herself, she glanced back at the road. Sometimes it was hard to be a woman. What was this need to nurture, anyway? Just because a man looked like an angel when he slept was no reason to trust him when he was awake.

A quick stop at the newspaper office revealed Parker had left for the day. She tossed her notes and the digital card from her camera on his desk and locked up. Tomorrow would be time enough to discuss the story with him so he could hammer it out before they went to press. She wanted as far away from this one as possible.

She delivered the brooding deputy to his vehicle at the sheriff's office, which was housed along with the county jail in a rock structure built along the eastern side of the square in the early 1900s. The office was closed, but a blue Chevy Tahoe waited out front, with *Grace County Deputy Sheriff* emblazoned on its doors and a rack of blue and white lights across its roof.

After she let him out she gunned the engine and zoomed off before he could thank her for the ride. In the rearview mirror she watched him, standing beside his unit, staring after her as if frozen in place.

No way to keep from running into him. She didn't want this, needed only peace and privacy and her safe little job. And then along comes this story and with it Dallas Starr, a man so intriguing and complex she couldn't help but want to peel off his layers to discover the person beneath. Best if she never had that chance and she'd do her damndest to see it didn't happen.

So, she'd go meet her friend and enjoy the evening with her. Forget all about the handsome lawman. But a voice inside said that wouldn't happen.

She had met Tinker Mattewan soon after she returned to Cedarton and went to work for the paper. The only female on a force of six full-time and occasional part-time field deputies when needed, Tinker worked as a jailer/dispatcher with dreams of someday working in the field.

The day they met she had been assigned to accompany Jessie during an interview of prisoners for an article about the drug treatment program the sheriff had implemented at the county jail. Tinker soon slipped away as the men crowded around Jessie to be first to tell their story, some so young they didn't yet shave, others calloused and defeated, each with heart-wrenching tales. Clearly a few were fabricated, but their experiences tore at her heart. Many of those caught in the trap of drug addiction were not criminals, but rather ordinary people who made unfortunate choices.

She and Tinker had enough in common to balance out their differences. That could make for an exciting friendship. Tinker called it "like" at first sight. Both lived alone, were fiercely independent, and shared a deadly attraction toward men who lived on the edge. Where Tinker liked to taste of her fascination, Jessie denied hers. That gave them plenty to discuss, sometimes heatedly. Their efforts to deal with their bad habits formed a bond between them. Despite that, she hadn't confessed her darkest guilt even to this new friend.

Tinker had no immediate family, and since Jessie's parents had been killed in a car wreck out in California a few years earlier, she had none either—only a large scattering of cousins, aunts, and uncles in the county. As a result she and Tinker gravitated to each other. They became an occasional foursome with Dave and Kathy Spacey, keeping Jessie in a comfort zone that excluded a man partner. Whatever relationships Tinker had with men were kept outside the bounds of hers and Jessie's friendship.

The fake adobe structure known as Ortega's was located several blocks down the gentle roll of the hill off the square, and once inside Jessie instantly spotted Tinker's unruly mop of flaming hair. Feeling gritty and slightly frustrated, she threaded around a few occupied tables to the cubbyhole near the back, dropped her pack on the floor, and sank into the padded booth.

"Hard day?" Tinker asked. "Well, never fear, your drink is on its way."

A darkly handsome diminutive waiter with flashing black eyes immediately brought her a large-stemmed, frosted goblet filled with pale green slush. A lime hung on the rim glistening with salt. The margarita in front of Tinker was almost gone.

Catching the waiter's eye Tinker pointed out that fact, then watched the young man's tight butt wiggle away. "My, oh, my. How sweet."

"Nope. Too young, too innocent."

"Says you." With a shake of her head, she dragged her attention back to Jessie. "I took the liberty of ordering for you. Thought you might need sustenance after your run in with our new deputy. Did you ever see anything so formidably gorgeous in your life?"

"Probably not, the key word being formidable. His beauty runs no deeper than that snakeskin on his hat."

"You mean he's just another pretty face?" Tinker giggled, covered her mouth. "Beauty only skin deep? Shit, Jess. You're bad to the bone." Emptying her own glass, she peered over the rim. "What did you say to him, anyway? He was set on burn when he popped into the jail a while ago." She sucked the lime slice and made a face.

Jessie shrugged. "It wasn't exactly what I said. Besides, he started it."

"And you couldn't hold your tongue, could you? The least you could've done was wait till after you'd had your way with him before mouthing off."

"He's a shit-kicking weirdo. He talks to dead people, for God's sake."

Tinker laughed heartily and licked the remaining salt off the rim of the glass. "So tell me, did this—umm—altercation begin over the pile of bones?"

Jessie drank deeply of the tangy margarita. "Oh, that's so good."

It didn't surprise her that Tinker knew about the eerie discovery. Everyone in town had heard the news by now.

"Ah, yes. The bones. I don't think I've ever had such a day. What with Kyle glaring at me like it was somehow my fault he would lose his marijuana crop, crying to me like I could do something about it when he knows the task force will catch him when they do their flyover this fall before he can harvest those plants anyway."

Tinker peered at her. "I do wish you wouldn't drop those tasty little tidbits about your marijuana-growing acquaintances. I am a cop, after all."

"Oh, get real, Tink." Not to be deterred from her main target, she plowed on. "Then, that psychic wonder has the nerve to shoot off his mouth about the responsibilities of the media and how we do more harm than good." She dragged in a breath and took another long drink.

"I can't believe he could dare criticize the fourth estate," Tinker said. "My goodness, what's the world coming to?

"You should've seen him, slinking around acting like he has some deep-seated psychic ability. And Mac…."

The teasing glint in her friend's eyes got the better of her and she let it drop, surrendered her mood, and chuckled. Tinker didn't know about her past. She'd never been able to confess to such a degrading action. So she kept up the teasing mood.

"Okay, okay. I'll admit I'm touchy. But I'll swear, I expected any minute for him to rip off his clothes and start chanting."

"Now that I would've paid to see. And you would've too, you know it."

Jessie laughed with her.

Sobering, Tinker played with her silverware a moment. "You know, honey, you can't remain celibate all your life."

"With men like him around, I can sure give it a try."

"Why are you so afraid to have a little sex and a laugh or two? It's good for what ails you."

Jessie sighed. "I'm not afraid. Well, maybe I am. A little."

"If I were you I'd charm the socks off that hunk of an Indian and drag him off to some den and screw his brains out."

"Tinker, I swear."

"Well, I would—if I were you."

"And since you're not, what would you do?"

"Drag him off somewhere and screw his brains out. That is, if you're not going to. And if he ever notices I'm alive."

Tinker's laughter tinkled like bells and Jessie joined her. Her friend always could cheer her up.

"He keeps looking past me like I don't even exist, I'm gonna stick my foot out and trip him, get his attention." Tinker scowled and played with her drink.

"I should be so lucky."

Tinker pointed a finger, azure eyes twinkling. "Aha. Next time he looks at you, go to it. I'm serious, friend. You won't regret it."

Jessie shook her head. "Honey, you're impossible."

Along with Tinker's fresh drink, the waiter brought a basket of steaming chips and hot salsa. Both dug in with relish, washing down mouthfuls of the fiery appetizer with long sips of the tart drinks.

By the time their meals came, they had caught up on each other's week and lit into the food with relish.

Between bites Tinker spoke. "You know, seriously, I wish you wouldn't talk so openly to me about marijuana crops."

"Why? Everyone knows who grows it. It's common knowledge."

What would Tinker have to say when she saw the coming week's issue of the newspaper? Parker, who loved to prod the bureaucrats and their complacent constituents, was working on his editorial on this very issue. She'd seen the final paragraph, which said that readers were naïve if they thought that such publicity stunts as cops pulling up marijuana plants was a serious effort to wage a war on drugs. He also had some stuff to say about why the purveyors of other far more dangerous drugs were ignored in favor of arresting those who grew marijuana.

As usual, he'd stir up the town into taking sides and debating the issue, which is what he wanted. And he really didn't care if they hated him for it. Everyone would buy a copy of the paper just to see what he had to say.

He once wrote that occasionally he almost fell into the trap of wanting respect until he remembered that his job as editor was to make his readers think, not to make them love him. He'd added, *Got to respect me for that.*

And indeed, Jessie did respect him. She also loved him, though not in a sexual way. More as if he were a close brother. She dragged her thoughts back to the conversation and Tinker's despair over her career.

Her friend's porcelain skin flushed a bright pink. "I'm as much of a cop as the guys who go out on call. Just because Sheriff Mac sticks me in the office or jail all the time doesn't make me less of one."

"Of course you're a good deputy." Jessie understood her friend's frustrations. "Mac's just old-fashioned. He's not about to let a woman go out on calls where she might get hurt. Southern chivalry."

"Ha, no such thing. It's the Bubba principle, and it's firmly in place in Grace County."

Laughing, Jessie dipped a chip in salsa and transferred it to her mouth, chewed, swallowed, and changed the subject. "Want to rent a movie? It's Friday and we can stay up late." She scooped up another dollop and downed it, blinking away tears and pouring margarita on the fire in her mouth.

"Richard Gere," Tinker said.

"Whatever."

"What, no argument? Is Mel Gibson out of favor? My place?"

Jessie caught the slightly abashed tone. "Tinker, when are you going to seek help?"

"Help? I don't need help."

"You never come to my cabin. It's not normal for a grown woman who carries a gun, for goodness sake, to be afraid of the dark to the point where she can't drive around in the country at night."

"Carrying a gun doesn't help. I can't shoot the dark and make it go away. I can't help it. I just can't stand to have all that black stuff hanging around me hiding God knows what. Going to your place, it's like driving into a black hole. Why do you live out there in the boonies anyway? That's what isn't normal, my friend. Woman was meant to be surrounded by sidewalks and traffic and lights and noise, Walmart and clubs."

Laughing, Jessie held up a hand. "And where around here do you find traffic or noise and clubs? Unless you consider Junior's Beer Joint a nightclub." Though she wondered how Tinker expected to drive a patrol car around the county and take her turn at night duty, Jessie didn't bring it up.

"We do have a Walmart," Tinker insisted. "My place?"

"Okay, fine. We'll watch the movie at your place if I can grab a shower there. But I don't understand how anyone can live in these beautiful mountains and choose to do so in town, even one as small as Cedarton. It simply doesn't make sense, with all that lovely, wide open space out there filled with trees and wild flowers and creeks and—"

"Bears and snakes, and don't forget the dark." Tinker shuddered.

Both laughed and chatted amiably about the bones and who they might belong to. An hour or so later they left Ortega's. The video rental store was on the way to Tinker's apartment, two rooms above the Jantzen's carriage house at the back of their hundred-year-old Victorian house down the hill from the west side of the square.

It was nearly two in the morning when Jessie parked the Jeep in the clearing near her cabin. A late moon bathed the land in a silver glow that dampened the yellow shimmer of the yard light. She swung down from the high seat and the strap of her backpack hung on the floor shift. As she bent forward to free it, a stealthy movement in the edge of the woods caught her eye. Squinting, she stared at the spot for a full minute, but nothing more stirred. Hair rose on the back of her neck, shivers raced down her spine.

Stop being so dumb. There's surely a logical explanation. Some of Tinker's nervous jitters had rubbed off on her, that was all. Even so, she moved quickly to the porch, crossed it, opened the door, scurried inside, and shot the bolt. Even if something was out there, it was probably a deer or one of the small, shy black bears common in these parts, or her neighbor's dog. At least, that's what she kept telling herself.

The last time Steve had found her he kicked in the door and barreled into her apartment shouting obscenities.

They argued and he hit her. She didn't blame him. She deserved it for what she'd done to him. That was it, though, and she'd never seen him again. A week or so later she packed a few things and scurried straight home to Arkansas.

Oh, God. What if he was here? What if he'd found her?

Wrapping both arms around herself, she hunched against the kitchen cabinets, shaking so hard she couldn't move.

She had to stop this. Get hold of herself. Steve wasn't here. He'd moved on, even if she couldn't. No one was here but her exploding imagination. Giving herself a shake, she stumbled to the sink and filled a glass with icy well water, drank it while gazing out the window. The cabin had become her hideaway, bordered along the back by thousands of acres of Ozark National Forest. She had rented the place when she first arrived, but was now buying it, including the five acres of land cut in two by Cedar Creek out back. Thick stands of cedar, oak, hickory, maple, and sycamore offered homes to multitudes of wildlife.

The arch of the new highway spanned the valley a few miles to the north. Far enough away so that the noise of future traffic wouldn't disrupt the serenity of the location. But she could see the damned thing, and wished it would magically disappear in a poof of dust.

She finished the water, set the glass on the counter, and went into the only bedroom. Switching on the light, she closed the blinds, checked out all the corners, then the closet. At last, she stopped shaking and shucked out of her dusty work clothes. She was safe here.

Kicking the jeans and shirt in the direction of the clothes hamper she wrapped herself snugly in a terry robe and padded into the adjoining bathroom to take another shower. Uncovering the bones had made her feel dirty and a bit antsy, that was all. She would not allow what had happened in LA to follow her here. The hot water helped wash away the earlier fear that someone was out there. Watching her.

Yet, a vague uneasiness settled within her that she couldn't shake. Kicked off, no doubt, by her run-in with Deputy Dallas Starr and his particular brand of hatred for her kind. Not to mention his weird ability. No wonder she had this terrible feeling she couldn't shake.

"Face it." She spoke aloud while she adjusted the hot water with hands that shook. "You don't find a pile of bones buried in the woods every day. It's made you jumpy, that's all."

And you don't meet a man like Dallas Starr every day either. Don't start with him.

In spite of the rationalization, terror stirred deep within her soul. What would she do if her demons had returned?

4
CHAPTER

Monday morning Jessie sat at her desk in an empty office. Parker hadn't shown up, and her notes on the bones lay on his desk beckoning her. She ignored them to finish a story about a shooting that had taken place Saturday night. Not unusual or deadly.

Slightly inebriated, Thurman Slakey and his cousin Lennie Rawls, who both worked at a chicken processing plant over in Springdale, came out of Junior's Bar engaged in an argument over who would be the designated driver of the 1963 Chevy pickup belonging to Lennie. Unable to settle the dispute, they both went for their guns, Lennie's in the rack in the cab window, Thurman's crammed under the seat. Both too drunk to drive, they weren't much in the shooting department either.

No one was hurt in the shootout, though the blast from Thurman's shotgun shattered the windshield of Lennie's truck and a .30-06 bullet from Lennie's deer rifle ricocheted off the pavement, killing a hapless squirrel in a nearby oak tree. The dead animal fell into the wading pool in nearby Happy Trails apartment complex and was discovered a while later by a stray dog who carried it all over town, depositing it on the front stoop of the Red Bird diner for Wanda Jean Cross to find on her way to open up for the after-church dinner crowd. The episode was par for a Saturday night.

Wendy breezed through the door and Jessie glanced up to wiggle her fingers at the girl.

"Morning, Jess. You okay?"

"Sure. You?"

"Fine, but Mikey went to work and forgot to reset the alarm. Sorry I'm late, but I'm here now." She sat at her desk, gestured toward Parker's office. "He in yet?"

"Nope, you lucked out yet again."

Mikey, huh? The girl definitely got around.

Wendy giggled and started opening the mail. Jessie went back to her story.

Though both Lennie and Thurman were out on bail and had been spotted having coffee together at the Red Bird Sunday after church, the story had to appear in the paper. It would be expected, or word would get around that Parker was ignoring the real news.

His wry sense of humor could add a twist to the tale. By the time he cooked up a catchy headline everyone would be talking about the incident. The byline would read *Observer* Staff, but everyone in town would know who wrote it, and who twisted it. Besides volunteers who sent in community news from around the county, she and Parker were the only writing staff.

And he, in his peculiar cynical way, kept one faction or another in town incensed at him continuously. His latest, an issue concerning the legalization of marijuana, would soon be hot and heavy and letters to the editor would arrive by the bundle.

Despite the friendly animosity between Mac and Parker, she'd get a quote from the sheriff about the shootout involving the death of one unfortunate squirrel. Mac could usually come up with some humorous aside to every occurrence short of rape and murder, which was so rare as to be nonexistent.

She dialed his office. Tinker answered and transferred her call in a businesslike manner, with no allusions toward the new deputy.

When Mac picked up, he cut her off before she could ask her question.

"Glad you called. Want you to do me a favor."

Uh-oh. "What?"

"Our criminal investigator will be there in a minute. I want you to set up a time you can ride with him and show him around a bit."

"Mac, dammit. What'd you send him over here for?"

"Girl, watch your mouth around this old man. In my day ladies didn't use such language."

"In your day, Mac, I wouldn't be considered a lady. Consarn it."

"There, isn't that better?"

"Sure. Okay to think it, just don't say it, huh? Reminds me of my grandmother. She used to cuss, but covered it up with innocent sounding expletives like 'my stars and garters,' as if no one would know what she was really thinking."

"I knew Effie well, and everyone knew exactly what that grand old lady thought. But back to Deputy Starr. I'm not asking you to walk out with him, just show him around. Besides, there might be a story there. You interviewed our other new deputy and took his picture for the paper. Why be different with him?"

"Because he is different. It'd be like interviewing a snarling wolf in his den."

Mac cleared his throat, and she stared across the office and out the front window while he continued. "I had a talk with him. He agreed he came on too strong out at the crime scene, and he's gonna back off, give you a chance to prove yourself."

"Prove myself? Prove myself? To him? My stars and garters, Mac." She was forced to continue over his outburst of laughter. "Since when do I have to prove myself to the local law enforcement? Get one of the part-timers to show him around. All they do is sit on their butts at the Red Bird telling tall tales anyway."

"Nope, all busy keeping down crime in the county. Take it easy there, girl. You sound just like Josiah."

"Yeah, well Grandpa was a bit more outspoken than Grandma." It wasn't half what she wanted to say, but she let it go at that and seethed in silence, waiting for Mac to pick up the thread of the conversation.

He waited a second or two, then asked, "Well, you taking him or not?"

"All right. I'll do it. But for you, not him. He'd better behave himself, and if anybody has any proving to do, it's him, not me. Got anything new about the murder investigation?"

"You'll have to ask our new investigator about that." Mac laughed. The old fart. He'd done it to her again, led her about until she tamed right down and did precisely what he wanted.

"I love you, Mac, but watch out. One day you'll go too far. It's Parker's story. He'll deal with your mind-reading deputy."

"Oh, so that's the way it is. Glad you told me. Have to admit, I was sure surprised to see you out there." He chuckled. "I'd appreciate your showing Starr around, though. Good deeds come back to us."

"That's what I'm afraid of."

He laughed.

"What about the squirrel killing?"

"Oh, yeah. A quote. How about 'Though the deceased was found to have double-ought buckshot in his chest, at this time, we don't have enough evidence to hang the culprits'?"

"Not up to your usual standards, but it'll have to do."

He was still chuckling when he rang off.

She went back to the keyboard and was immersed in editing the story when Parker came in, and right on his heels, Dallas Starr. Both chattering like they were old friends. Great. Now she'd have to deal with their friendship.

Parker greeted her, waved at Starr, and disappeared in his office, leaving the deputy's hulk to crowd the small waiting room. He leaned on the counter and peered through the opening at her.

"Met your boss. Nice fella."

"Noticed." Peeking from behind the computer screen, she beheld his granite-like features and black hat, framed like a picture. "He's a real peach."

"I see *you're* in a good mood this morning. And here I came to make amends."

"I know what you're here for. I talked to Mac."

Starr's wide grin shook her to her roots, and made a new man out of him. If she wasn't careful he'd have her shoved up against some wall with her clothes off. All things considered, she agreed with Tinker. That wouldn't be half bad.

Steady girl, you don't need this.

Without returning the grin, she went back to work, unable to stop her fingers from trembling on the keyboard.

"And…?" he said, after a decent interval.

There he went, carrying on like an ordinary human being instead of the gruff animal he'd been at their last meeting. She ignored him and continued to work on her story. Or pretend to.

Wendy, whose duties included taking care of walk-ins, answering the phone, typesetting the handwritten scraps of community news that came in from all over the county, and helping label papers, all of which she managed to do around a wad of bubble gum, decided to get in on the action. She rose, rubbed her palms down the sides of her ample, denim-covered thighs, leaned both elbows on the counter, and stared up at the handsome deputy.

"Could I help you?"

Like she hadn't listened in on their earlier conversation. The man obviously had a strange effect on women, but Jessie did her best to concentrate on the computer screen and ignore him. Truth be told, she was afraid of her own feelings. The man was too damned attractive for his own good, and had the nerve to act as if he hadn't a clue the effect he had on her. On all women, it appeared, the way Wendy vamped him.

"I'd like to talk to Jessie, if she's not too busy," he told Wendy, gathering her firmly into his fan club. Some women loved dark, brooding men who held their secrets close.

From the corner of one eye she saw Wendy flip her bleached yellow hair at the tall deputy, who had the audacity to wink at her.

Way to go, girl.

"Jessie? This gentleman—"

"I heard. Tell him I'll just be a moment. I have to finish this." Gentleman, indeed.

Deliberately, she typed some more nonsense that she would only have to delete when she returned to the keyboard. The poor, deceased squirrel had jumped over a quick, brown fox on his way to animal heaven.

Dal cleared his throat and backed away from the opening so that all she could see was his midsection, cut by a silver belt buckle. Wendy, bless her soul, just stood there staring, first at Starr then at Jessie.

Probably picturing what he had bundled in those jeans. Not that she blamed the girl. He did know how to package his merchandise. Where was his uniform? Why didn't he leave her alone if he disliked her so much? She worked up a definite resentment toward him for coming here, and at Mac for sending him, while the squirrel did some more leaps, bounding about as if very much alive.

Wendy stared at her, blue eyes wide. "Jessica?"

"Yes, I'm coming." Rising, she hit save and struggled to compose herself for the confrontation.

She crossed the small room, opened the door into the smaller waiting area, and held on to the knob in case she got a chance to slam it in his face.

"What is it?"

Her heart beat so hard he could surely hear it.

Brow furrowed, he looked her directly in the eye with no shame at all. "The sheriff insisted I come by and talk to you about some of the folks around here. Something about your keen insight. Said I need to learn my way around. He thought maybe you'd show me the county so I wouldn't get lost wandering the back roads. You seem pretty busy right now. If there's a better time, perhaps I could come back?"

Taking part in a ride-along with a law officer was coveted by most reporters and, in her other life, she'd attained a few herself. When she refused to jump at the chance with this guy, he snatched off his hat and began again.

"Dammit, I'm sorry we got off on the wrong foot. I shouldn't have shot off my big mouth. I've come to realize that this is a really small town, and I sure don't need to be in trouble up to my earlobes with the press."

Lord, how the man hated to apologize. He almost, but not quite, sounded as if he meant it. She couldn't help but enjoy his discomfort.

"Don't tell me apologizing was your idea. I expect Mac has chewed said ears."

His grin totally undid her. "I wouldn't say it was my ears he chewed, not exactly. He aimed a little lower, as a matter of fact."

There went the attempt to charm. Anger tinged her reply. "You know, I'm not any crazier about this than you are. I'll accept your apology, for Mac's sake. But you can keep your distance."

Though his lips curled, the grin remained stuck on his lips without reaching the smoldering green eyes. "Not to worry. I have no intention of coming near you. I'm not wearing my fireproof britches. This is strictly business."

She glared at him to let him know she meant every word.

"That man sure does respect you." He twisted the hat in both hands. On he plowed, getting in deeper. "Everyone's hinting pretty strongly that I was a perfect jackass. It seems you have quite a following in the department."

She expelled a breath, surprised that she had been holding it, and allowed a small smile. "Well, nobody's perfect."

"That's a relief." He laughed as if he had been taking lessons in the art of enjoying a good laugh, but didn't yet have it down.

It was her turn, and she made a good job of glaring at him some more. "Look, I agreed with Mac to set up a time we could go for a drive, but it can't be today. We go to press tomorrow and I've got some deadlines to meet. I won't be finished here until quite late."

Dal fitted the hat back on his head and spent more time than was necessary adjusting it. "I knew coming here was a bad idea. Why don't

I let you off the hook? I understand your reluctance, and believe me I'm with you. Putting the two of us together would be a little like throwing gunpowder in a fire."

Unable to hide her curiosity, she shoved an errant strand of hair away from one cheek. "And just which one of us would be the fire?"

He halted, turned. "You, no question about it."

"And don't you forget it." Considering his expression, like he wanted to drag her off and screw her brains out, she might ought to slap him upside of the head. Tinker's words had come back to haunt her, but she met his stare, pursed her lips, and refused to look away.

Made him a little nervous too, the way he shifted his feet and looked for something to do with his hands. He finally forced some words out. "Well, you know how it is on a new job. Best to try and please the boss. But it's all right. I'll just tell Mac you were too busy."

"I really am today, but I promised him, and I keep my promises. How about Wednesday morning?"

Dal studied her closely. Something crawled around way down inside her. The last thing she wanted to do was be shut up alone in a car with him. He was speaking again and she had to concentrate to hear over the roaring in her ears.

"I really do get lost every time I wander off the main highway onto one of your meandering gravel roads. Half of them are marked with a number that doesn't match what folks call them. Earlier I was on what a fellow told me was Flat Rock Road but it was marked number three thirty-eight. Maps dot com doesn't bother to mention that."

Despite an alarm tolling somewhere in the back of her brain, warning her to back off from him and run like hell, she was going to do this. Clearly he did need help. And she had told Mac she would. So by golly she would.

"Okay, you've convinced me," she blurted.

Oh, crap. All along, she'd known this would be the outcome. They'd have sex a few times, then every time they met it would be shifting around looking in all directions for both of them. Why had she bothered to fight it?

"Pick me up here Wednesday about ten. I'll be free for the day."

On came the charm she'd seen him use on both Kathy and Wendy. "I really do appreciate it. The department is so shorthanded no one has had time to ride along and show me around. It would be embarrassing to get lost on my way to answer a call. Someone could die. If that happened, Mac might lock me up." His eyes glittered.

Damn him, he did read minds. "Next time, Dal Starr, I'll just think 'You can get bent' and save the effort of saying it."

"That'd do just fine, ma'am," he drawled, not bothering to deny her allusion. "Anything else?" Once again, the green eyes sparked. Without waiting for a reply he touched the brim of his rattlesnake-banded hat and eased out the door as if afraid to turn his back on her.

Just as she settled down enough to get back to the shooting piece, Parker stuck his head out of his office.

"Got a minute?"

She glanced up at the mild-mannered, gentle man who appeared to hold nothing sacred in heaven or on earth. He had stepped quickly into the role of a mentor and friend when she'd had no one to turn to. She never knew a man and woman could love each other without the idea of sex entering the picture. Even knowing all about her past, he'd given her a job and hope for some sort of future. She couldn't have let him do that without telling him the truth, but he was the only one in Cedarton who knew.

Capturing the squirrel article from the printer, she tossed it on her desk and went into his office. He must want to talk to her about the notes on the bones. Inside, she saw he'd downloaded the photos into the computer and had one up on the screen.

After she was seated, he leaned back in his chair and played with a pack of matches. What he did nowadays to replace chain smoking. "Have a nice visit with our new deputy?"

The chocolate brown eyes revealed his enjoyment. He'd rather tease than eat.

"Not near as nice a one as you obviously had. You two acted like old buds."

Parker shrugged. "Nice enough fella. Be careful, though."

"Hmmm. Don't I know it."

"Okay, long as you do." He paused, stripped a match, and lay it carefully in the clean ashtray. "I scanned your notes. Good job. When can you write it?"

"I'm not doing the story, Parker. And you well know why." She gestured toward his computer. "You better get busy because I'm not writing it."

He peered at her over his half-glasses and pursed his lips.

"That hangdog look won't work. It's your story. You have something for me?"

"Well, at least you're interested in doing your job on some level. Do you know Mary Smith?"

Jessie nodded. "Yes, we're friendly. She's in her fourth term on the city council. Seems to have found her niche. Keeps her out of Harold's way while he runs around all over town like the big shot he isn't. What about her?"

"She and her first husband owned eighty acres out near the new highway. He passed on, you know, drowned in the flood of 'eighty-nine, the night of the double twisters…."

"I vaguely remember hearing something about that."

61

"…yes, well, anyway, word is that she's been offered a huge sum of money for that land. Check it out. See if we're looking at some kind of subdivision out there, or worse yet, a shopping mall. I knew that highway would bring no good."

"For this week's edition?"

"No, it's too late for that. I want you to poke around a lot. Next week will be fine. What are you working on?"

"The shootout that resulted in the death of that poor squirrel is ready for your deft manipulation." She ticked off the rest on her fingers. "The rural water board meeting and the verbal disagreement about the right-of-way for the new lines to the southeast end of the county. Aunt Sally Jenson's hundredth birthday party. The school board meeting and—and I think that's it. That story about the woman running the new free health clinic for the county over in Rossville won't be ready till next week."

He turned and spread the files she left on his desk. "Jessie, I wish you'd reconsider doing this story." Before she could object he held up a hand and went on. "Now, listen. I understand your fear, but the worst thing we can do is run away from what scares us. You'll never ever be whole again until you face up to those fears."

"I need to forget."

He shrugged and caught her gaze with a somber one of his own.

What if he told her it was write the story or lose her job? Would it matter that much? She could always go to work at Walmart. The expression on his face told her he would never make her chose between her job and this one story. They were too close for that, even if he did think he knew what was good for her.

"Okay, tell you what. I'll put this together and let you take a look at it, since you were there. But I want you to edit it for me. No arguments."

She didn't want to, but agreed rather than back him into a corner. He was pretty put out at her.

"You'll find some quotes in there from that close-mouthed deputy. He all but forbade me to write anything until he said I could."

Parker chuckled and slipped off his glasses. "That'll be the day. You were on site. I'll write the story from your notes. As for the investigation itself, we'll abide by the rules and use Mac's release."

"Mac said he'd get one over to us before sending one to the Harrison News. I have a feeling this is going to be a big story."

His grin grew wider. "I certainly hope so. And I'll want your feature to tie in to this story. Folks around here appreciate your ties to the past. We'll need to keep all our sources clean by making friends with our large Cherokee friend. We don't want the department shutting us out."

She angled a look and saw he was joking. "If anyone gets us shut out, it'll be you. Don't forget I saw your editorial for this week."

"I only spoke in general terms, didn't get personal at all."

She laughed. "Well, you know me. I'm always fair. People figure if they want to read all the dirt, there's always the Democrat-Gazette in Fayetteville or the Harrison News. I'll give our readers what they want. A local angle."

"Precisely why I hired you. What else?"

"You want me to do your library piece so you can concentrate on this?"

He nodded. "Thanks. It's pretty simple, and I'll edit it for you. I'm also doing something on the battle they had at the council meeting Friday over stray dogs, and we've got some canned pieces and plenty from the school, plus my usual knock-em-dead editorial, which you've had a look at. There'll be plenty of letters to the editor on legalizing marijuana that'll take up a lot of space." He laughed and poked a finger at a letter lying on his desk. "This one is from a fellow who's started a church. The parishioners smoke marijuana in its religious ceremony. He claims the law is harassing all eleven of them."

"You gonna run it?"

"Damn right I am."

"One of these days, Parker…."

"Yeah, but ain't it fun? As soon as we have this one in the can, you take some time on that land deal with Mary Smith. It's always a hassle running down something like that. We'll do it next week or maybe even the following." He fiddled with a pencil and peered at her over his glasses. "I just had a thought. Remember that story you did a few months back about how the highway department handles the discovery of historical sites along the proposed route? Why don't you dig it up—no pun intended—and we'll run a capsule rewrite next week as a follow-up to the bones story. Mention the prehistoric site and the bones those archeologists from New York dug from under Brown's Bluff back in the twenties. That would be a great slant. Another body after thirty thousand years. I think I've even got a picture in the files."

"Good idea. I found it interesting that the Spaceys treated this crime scene in exactly the same way as they did their historical digs and I can tie that in. Anything else?"

"Not unless you've got something."

"Nothing else. Oh, I almost forgot to tell you why Deputy Starr dropped by. He wants me to do a ride-along Wednesday, sort of show him around the county. Seems our Native American gets lost easily."

He laughed with her. "Great idea. Show him around. Being on his good side will give us a better story on this than the dailies will have. And once this breaks, there'll be boar hair in the butter with reporters wandering all over the place, even though they don't know bee from bulls foot about this area. They consider it a waste of time to poke around much out here in the boondocks unless there's something really sensational going on, so they'll be using press releases and stealing from our articles for the time being. These people always open up to you, though goodness knows why."

"I'm a native, and you're that damn Yankee who came down here from Boston, and you know that's the truth of it. But you keep practicing on your quaint remarks and maybe one day you'll be accepted as one of us."

"I know. I've only been here twenty years. You'd think that'd be long enough." He made a rude noise. "Just cause you were born here almost thirty years ago. I've been here longer than you. Till you came back last summer you hadn't set foot in these hills since you were in high school, and you know it."

"I'll be twenty-nine this summer. Don't make me older than I am. Actually, my folks and grandfolks were born here from good country stock and I'm kissing kin to half the people around here. That counts for a lot. If that's all, I'd better get back to work."

He waved her away, then called her back before she could escape. "One more thing. While you have the new deputy captive, do an interview with him, get a picture. We'll do something on him in next week's paper. You know what folks like."

She nodded without telling him that Mac had suggested that as an excuse for sending her with Dallas. It would only complicate matters to get into this further with Parker. He'd guess at the real truth, that she was scared to death of her reaction to the deputy and would rather keep her distance. Instead she returned to her desk, but it was a long while before she went back to work. She couldn't stop thinking of Dal Starr, and how he wasn't going to like her doing a story about him. Not one bit.

5
CHAPTER

One minute the woman's actions amused the hell out of Dal, the next they made him madder than hell. To shake off an urge that had lain dormant so long he thought it'd rusted, he drove to the Red Bird, the local gathering spot in Cedarton. Time to get acquainted with and learn something about the small community.

Once he introduced himself, the coffee drinkers filled him in on the lay of the land. Relaxed in their company, he sat back and listened. A steaming cup of black coffee appeared in front of him, along with cream and sugar in old-fashioned blue dispensers. He thanked the plump, pretty waitress and she dimpled.

The rattle of dishes from the kitchen accompanied the conversations, while the men spoke of places like Dogtown and Flat Rock, Cedar Hill, Cedar Run, and of course the county seat, Cedarton. Two Black Oaks, one over by Esther Town, the other out past the old abandoned SEFOR plant.

What the hell was a SEFOR plant?

He wanted to ask, but settled for listening. These men were proud of where they lived. Bragged about stuff he wouldn't have ever thought about.

"Not a single traffic light in the whole county, not even in Cedarton, and it's the biggest town," a man in overalls declared.

"That's amazing," Dal said. "What's with the road numbers and names? Hard to keep straight."

Theron hitched up his dragging britches. "Well, that's cause of that crazy nine-one-one mapping. Cause they hired in folks from Iowa or Illinois or some such place, it took em a few years to get it right. Never knew why they didn't hire someone who lived in these parts. Time they finally got it done, they'd changed danged near ever one of our road names. Put up numbers ever'where. Two numbers on a road means one thing, three another, four yet another." The old farmer shook his head. "Just caused a tangle of confusion, if you ask me. All our fire departments knew where to go from a feller's name. And we sure as thunder all know where we live."

This brought on a round of belly laughs that Dal joined.

Relaxed, he enjoyed another cup of strong, black coffee. Damn, being here sure beat a day in Dallas.

Talk soon turned back to the bones uncovered out at Kyle's.

The fella who'd introduced himself as Fudge started it. "Yeah, them bones were found under Jacob's Bluff, off Cedar Creek Road. We allus called it Jacob's Road, now it's got a number and a new name. Tell me what sense that makes."

"None, none at all," a short, chubby man named Billy Dale said. "I heard that there grave belonged to an outlaw wanted by the FBI for untold years." He cast a questioning glance at Dal.

Fishing for information. Dal grinned, and said nothing.

Fudge snorted. "Naw, I figure it was only the first of many that'll be found. We most likely have a serial killer on the loose."

Others had theories about the identity of the body, ranging from that of Caveman Jake, who hadn't been seen all winter, to a man who deserted his wife a few years back, running off with that cute little redhead who waitressed at Bea's Restaurant, to the fellow that drowned the night of the twin twisters and his body'd never been found.

So, two men unaccounted for. Dal made a mental note to check that information further.

"Coulda been some transient off the train, though," offered Theron.

The man in crisply-ironed overalls—whose name Dal could not understand, though it sounded like *Woofer*—chimed in, "Don't spect the paper in Federal'll cover it, though. Heard Jessie Ann was there first. She's a true Arkansawyer and she'll write what's really up. Tells the truth, that gal does. The papers in Federal and Hareson has got so uppity they only report politics and stuff going on at the University, and put the Hog's doins on the front page, like we cared a whit about that or what country's fighting what war over the waters."

Theron leaned back and twinkle-eyed Dal so he knew he was about to get some true Arkie leg-pulling. "Most of them reporters aren't from round here anyways, and don't know the first thing about us. Think they're natives just cause their folks moved here to born em. Hell, if your cat had kittens in the oven you wouldn't call em biscuits."

That broke everyone up, including the waitress, who had to sit down and wipe her eyes. Dal nearly choked on a mouthful of coffee.

"Theron, you'll be the death of all of us yet," the woman cried when she could speak.

Dal had given up getting their names straight, or half of what they said. The charming, thick hill accent left him wondering if he'd come to an alien land. He'd have to work on that, for they'd surely expect him to know and understand them the next time they met. He did figure out from the context of what was said that the town they called Federal was Fayetteville to the west. And Hareson was Harrison, a good-sized town in another county to the southeast. He sure had a lot to learn, but the prospect gave him a good feeling inside.

After listening to a few of those wilder tales Dal figured he was being put on. After all, he wasn't from "round here" either. The way they talked about Jessie West, an informative article from her should put a stop to some of the outlandish gossip about the bones. And damned if he didn't hate to admit that.

Odd why someone like her worked for a rinky-dink weekly newspaper out here in the back end of nowhere. Running from something, that was clear. Learning she was a native surprised him. She acted too city polished for that.

"Has Jessica always lived here?" he asked.

All heads turned to give him a good going over, like he'd committed a grave error.

The man with the theory about the serial killer looked up from blowing at a steaming cup of coffee. "Nope. She went away for some years, out to California with her folks, but she come back. Wests is kin to the Reeds and the Spencers. You interested, you'll be the first gits anywhere with her. Been here a while now, but keeps to herself. Heck of a nice girl, though. Fair and knows her history. Always digging around in someone's past for stories, but don't abide anyone digging into hers."

Everyone nodded and no one else offered more information. Obviously they figured it wasn't any of his business.

Without being asked, the pretty waitress brought him his third cup of coffee. The breakfast crowd departed, and Dal was going to leave as well, till he got a whiff of hamburgers and french fries. Time for lunch, and his belly was growling. Four men dressed like construction workers entered and sat at the table next to him.

The topic of the mysterious discovery under Jacob's Bluff soon came up.

One man ventured a suggestion aimed at Dal. "If I was you, I'd talk to Caveman Jake. If anything happens in these woods, he's bound to know about it. Less'n he's the one buried up yonder. Ain't seen him in a spell. Course, don't reckon, were it him that he'd be a skeleton already. Saw him over to the store last fall buying baloney."

Everyone laughed heartily.

"Well, I don't know," another drawled. "He was mostly a skeleton last time I seen him. Near seven foot tall, if he's an inch, and soaking wet won't weigh a hundred twenty-five pounds. Rough, scary looking fella. More likely he done the killing."

Dal set down his cup. "Where might I find this Caveman person?"

"Caveman Jake," a red-faced man supplied. "Lives up the creek a ways from Kyle's place." The man paused, studied Dal, then said, "In a cave. Kinda close to the bluff where y'all found the bones but you gotta take the old logging road out past Levon's place and then walk on in. Reckon old Caveman's been living out there thirty years or more. One of them burned-out hippies, they say. Early on some of the women stewed about him, like women will, but he never bothers anyone. Can't say he's the cleanest man around, but he keeps to hisself and never has caused a breath of trouble. Them that's talked to him say he's fair educated, just not real smart, if you get my drift." He blew on his coffee and muttered, "Seen him at the post office yesterday."

"So don't reckon he could be your skeleton," a handsome young man said. Laughter filled the café.

Dal waited until the appreciative chuckles died down. "Where's he from? How does he make a living?"

"Shoot, no one knows where he's from. He just drifted in here one day back in the early seventies along with all them other hippies. Most of them what stayed took up somewhat normal lives, and live like the rest of us, but not Caveman. He just clung to his strange ways."

A lank-jawed man wearing blue coveralls with the name Banjo embroidered above the breast pocket snorted. "I don't reckon he makes a living. I hear he picks up a Social Security check at the Post Office every month, but it must be disability, cause he ain't that old."

The waitress, whose name was Norma, came out of the kitchen with three plates layered up each arm. All were heaped with enormous hamburgers and piles of french fries.

"And you think this Caveman Jake might know something?" Dal asked, eyeing the food.

She returned to his table with the coffee pot. "He might know plenty, but good luck getting him to talk to you. He's pretty close-mouthed and teched as well." She filled his cup. "Aren't you hungry, honey?"

He couldn't help but grin at her motherly concern. "As a matter of fact, I am. Bring me what they're having." He gestured around the room, to a round of laughter.

While he waited for his burger and fries, Dal decided he had done the right thing coming here. This job, this place, and these honest, hard-working, friendly people were just the tonic he needed. Beginning with his meeting with Jessica this morning, he hadn't enjoyed a better day in a long while.

"Anybody here know of a place I could rent?" he asked of the room.

"That's a tall order, son," an older man said. He leaned toward Dal and stuck out a gnarly hand. "Name's Bud Granger. I run a cattle ranch out on Sugar Mountain."

Dal took his hand. "Good to meet you."

"Likewise. I don't know of any places to rent save a few old rundown shacks you wouldn't want your pigs living in, was you to have any." He paused, rubbed his chin. "Tell you what, though. If you're not real particular, there's some trailers over nearby the state park. They're small and old, but would do for a spell. Mostly rented out to fellas working on the highway now. There's RV and camping in the park, but that's a ways from Ina Mae's trailer park. You wouldn't be bothered much. That spring over at the park is said to have curative powers, and there's fishing and swimming. Seems city folk like to rough it in the country." He laughed at the idea. "They're not real fancy but the place is reputable and the widow woman who runs it'll do you right."

He lifted his hamburger in both hands, eyed it, picked something off the side of the bun. "I heard one of them was going to be empty soon. But you'd best hurry. It'll be gone once the word gets out. Them fellas coming in to work on the highway snatch stuff up quick as it comes available. RV park is full of em, just setting down there in them campers happy as hogs in a mud waller." He took a big bite, chewed a while. "Damn me, Norma, but that's fine."

"Where is this park?" Dal asked.

One of the construction workers answered for the man whose mouth was stuffed. "Few miles north, you want to veer off to the left at the sign for the state park and it'll be on your left a ways out the road. Can't miss it. Shingle says Hidden Holler Trailer Park. Right pretty place. Tourists used to come and go, but since the workers come in for the new road, it's been full up with them. Tourists have to trek on down to the KOA if the park's full. Reckon when they finish this highway, if they ever do, things might get back to normal and we'll all be broke again." He paused for everyone to chuckle, then went on. "Trailers aren't too bad. I reckon I've seen worse. For that matter, I reckon once or twice I've lived in worse."

More laughter that Dal joined. He didn't remember when he'd laughed so much. Had been a lot of years.

When he finished his meal he headed toward the RV park in the blue four-by-four Ford Explorer, the small model, but equipped with a powerful engine and a rack of blue and white lights. Inside, a radio, and locked beside the driver's seat a wicked baton for taking down perps, and a short-barreled pump shotgun for when nothing else worked.

At the park he explained who he was to Ina Mae Carter, the owner, then quickly added that his uniforms were on order in case she didn't believe him. He needn't have worried.

Tilting her head back to gaze up at him, she said, "Oh, I heard all about you. I'd be tickled to have the law around, if you can stand the place. It's not real fancy or anything."

It looked like this new job would be an asset, not a liability, and that gave him a fine feeling.

"Having you here might keep some of these yahoos from getting caterwauling drunk when they come off work of a Friday night. Want to see the place? I was fixing to get an ad in the paper this week, but I'd as soon let you have it without going to the trouble."

He followed her past a neat garden, rows laid out with seed envelopes stuffed down on stakes at the end of each. The gravel drive wound down along the banks of the wide, shallow stream that ran through town.

On its banks, five older model mobile homes were nosed into the trees. Dogwoods bloomed like drifts of snow against bare trees just beginning to show green. The trailers were far enough apart to insure a certain amount of privacy, and were separated by ten-foot-high solid slab wood fences.

She was right, they weren't fancy, but neither were they dilapidated.

Ina Mae chattered all the way, but he scarcely listened. The place was far enough from the highway the traffic sounds were muted. Water flowed swiftly over the creek's rocky bed, making its own music. Everything that was evil in the world was shut out except what he kept stored in the dark recesses of his mind.

"I haven't had a chance to clean it up yet, just been too busy," Ina Mae explained as she unlocked the door. "I'm going to have to ask two hundred dollars a month, what with the price of electric and water nowadays. You'll pay for your own heat and phone. Seems an awful amount, I know."

He almost staggered, but not from the odor of mustiness that met them. He had expected to pay much more. The place was a mess, but it was big enough to suit him for the time being, and he had always been good at scrubbing and fixing. A double window above the worn couch looked out back over the creek and secluded valley, cradled by mountains on all sides.

Eyeing the tiny rooms, a vision of a very young, beautiful Leeann twirling circles in their first small apartment, eyes glistening, yanked him into the past. His heart turned over, kicked him in the ribs. Not a good idea to call back those happy days. There was too much darkness in his soul to deal with the memories.

The eerie feeling he'd had yesterday at the grave site prickled at the back of his neck, stirring the hairs there. Even the most peaceful of places harbored evil.

Only a murmur of voices from the morgue on the other side of the wall broke the quiet of the newspaper office Wednesday morning. The blank computer screen stared back at Jessie, the blinking cursor like a skinny black roach she'd like to squash.

She yanked up the phone and punched in Mary Smith's number.

When the woman answered, she spent a few minutes exchanging trivialities, then asked about the offer on the old property where Mary and her first husband had lived.

After a long hesitation on the other end, Mary replied. "I suppose this is for the paper."

"Yes, it is." No, I wanted to put it in my diary. Geez, she was in a bad mood. Itched to go out and dig into someone's private life, as if it might be any of her business.

Another long pause. "I don't understand why you want to know."

"Do you have any idea what plans the buyer has for the land."

"How in the world would I know that? And what would it matter?"

Jessie's ears perked at the defensive tone. Something definitely going on here. She and Mary weren't exactly friends but, being a member of the city council, the woman was usually at least sociable. This morning her tone was downright rude for someone who might ought to consider keeping her options open with the press.

Best to make light of it until she could learn more. She wasn't in the mood to pry into someone's private life. At this moment, what she wanted was to spend hours visiting old folks eager to talk about the past, write their story, then go home and eat chicken noodle soup and take a walk in the woods.

Like that was going to happen. Onward and upward. She firmed up her voice. "We thought it might be significant to our readers if the buyer has plans to build oh, say, some sort of tourist attraction because of the highway? Would you mind telling me who the buyer is?"

Nothing, no reply at all. She was still there, she could hear her breathing. "Mary?"

"Perhaps I should speak to Harold."

The woman hung up abruptly.

"Sorry I bothered you," Jessie said to the dial tone. How odd. Why get so bent out of shape over a simple question about the sale of some land?

Fleeing the accusing blank computer screen, she rose and poured herself another cup of coffee, stood at the window to drink it. Rather be out in the sunshine chasing around for an interview or strolling through a peaceful old cemetery, like she usually did on a Wednesday, than playing guide to Dal Starr.

She'd read Parker's story yesterday, and thought how clever he was in his approach. Thought further how she might have written it. Yearned to do so, but stubbornly caught a few typos, made a suggestion or two, and handed it back to him.

If he thought making her do that would change her mind well, he was almost right. What the hell was wrong with her? Why couldn't she get past the guilt? The fear she'd do the same stupid thing again.

A burst of laughter came from the morgue, interrupting her reverie. Wendy, who helped Joe and Martha Dowling complete the inserts and label and bag the week's papers for delivery. A normal Wednesday morning, but she sensed that normalcy had come to an end for her. And just as she was getting the hang of hiding out. Damn that Dal Starr, who had strode onto the scene like a panther on the prowl, all sleek muscle, lithe limbs, and shiny coat. Challenging her. A dangerous predator if ever there was one, and her the prey. Mmmm. That was something to think about.

A stack of this week's papers lay on a table in the visitors' area, and she picked one up. On the front page, above the fold, was her photo of the open grave and Parker's story of the mysterious find near Jacob's Bluff. Page three continued the story and included another photo of the Spaceys and Starr with a bone, plus a sidebar of the importance of the Spaceys' work in relation to the gruesome discovery. On page nine she'd tied her feature to the news story. Beside a picture of the human skeleton discovered at Brown's Bluff were succinct comments from residents who'd been around then. The kind of historical fill her readers enjoyed. All laid out perfectly by Parker who knew how to draw the reader's eye from one important point to another.

The bell on the door tinkled. Squaring her shoulders, she drew a deep breath. Deputy Dal Starr filled the opening, in full uniform and wearing a sidearm.

She dropped the paper. Blood roared in her ears. Unarmed, he was dangerous enough without a gun on his hip. Though she opened her mouth, nothing came out.

A tentative, let's be friends smile tugged at his lips, and for a brief instant did something breathtaking to his moody features. "Sorry I'm late."

"Oh, I didn't notice." Her heart trembled. "Guess I forgot the time. I'll get my things."

What an idiot she could be. She crossed the room on wobbly legs, pawed around under her desk for the bulky backpack that held everything from camera to breath spray, then straightened with what she hoped was a neutral expression. "I'm ready."

But she really wasn't. How could she climb in his car, close the door, trap herself in there with him? A far too unnatural fear darkened her vision until he was only a shadow in the bright sunlight.

He stepped back to allow her to go first. There wasn't enough room for her to go through without touching him. He wasn't about to move. Her thigh brushed his. He touched her elbow, then pulled away as if burned. A fragrant warmth closed over her. Shivers chased a trickle of fear up her spine, and she hustled into the sunlight.

Damn it, she had to *stop* this. Either settle down or don't go with him. Simple as that. But it wasn't simple at all. The explanations she'd have to make to Parker and Mac overwhelmed her desire to back out. Maybe she could make him cancel.

"It's clear you don't like me. Why did you insist I do this?"

"It's not you, you're probably okay," he said. "It's your profession that puts me off."

"How kind of you," she muttered. Probably okay. "The same back at you, you self-righteous son of a bitch."

He didn't bat an eye. In fact, she had the feeling she amused him. That made her want to sock him one.

"Hey, let's do this and get it over with. I have an investigation, and everyone's too busy to show me around. Besides, I figure what Mac says goes, even with you. Just come on. It'll be over with before you know it." He moved quickly to open the door of the Tahoe, gazed at her. "I promise not to bite."

It wasn't his bite that worried her. "I don't understand why you couldn't just get yourself some maps off Yahoo, or something."

"Oh? And what do I type in? Caveman Jake, cave number three south of the river above Levon's place?"

No escape, no out. No matter which way she looked. He was right.

Do it and get it over with. "Okay, but I get to use the interview with Jake." When she moved toward him, he took her arm, his strong fingers rendering her breathless. He guided her into the high seat before she could scream out in panic and wrench away.

"Only if it doesn't contain information sensitive to our case."

"This isn't negotiable, unless you plan on killing me to keep me quiet." Stomping on his foot was out, so she settled into his vehicle and tried to appear calm. Not good to scream let me out and make a complete fool of herself.

"I don't kill women, just truss em up and toss em in the back seat. Haul em around till they capitulate." His hand lingered at her elbow.

"That's reassuring." She pulled away.

Eyes darkening, he let go of her. "No need to get prickly, but I'm sure you'll do your best to depress me, and on such a beautiful day, too." Shrugging, he went to the driver's side, swung into the seat, and glanced at her before sticking the key in the ignition.

She stared out the window and gave him directions.

"Turn right at the corner. I'll show you around the area of the scene of the crime, and Caveman's habitat."

"I appreciate it." He steered into the turn, wheels slipping on gravel.

He drove like he did everything else. Full speed ahead and damn anything that got in the way.

"This is Parker's story. I have to warn you, though, your tough guy act won't get you squat with him. He's been there before."

"Yeah, I'll bet." He cleared his throat, stared out the windshield. "You going to tell me what you know about Caveman Jake or not?"

She bristled at his manner, but decided to ignore it, at least for now. "Don't worry, I know who Caveman Jake is, but nobody really knows much about him. He's an enigma, might as well be a ghost. He's schizophrenic and takes some kind of medication to control it. Vietnam is the romantic conclusion. I think maybe he just fried his brain on drugs in the sixties, which I guess if you think about it, is romantic as well, in a warped kind of way. What sense do you hope to make out of him? I don't see what help he could possibly be."

"Well, then, it's a good thing you aren't running this investigation, isn't it? Schizophrenia is a disease, not the result of something we do to our bodies. God knows, we do enough on our own to destroy our good sense." His jaw clenched, and that funny noise must be his teeth grinding.

Mr. Smart Ass. At least he kept his eyes on the road while they argued. And a good thing, too, at the speed he drove.

Unable to let him have the last word, she went on. "It's my job to ask questions and get at the truth, and then print it."

He snorted. "The truth? I didn't know reporters knew the meaning of the word. Besides, I thought you said this is Parker's story."

The sarcastic tone did something nasty to his drawl so it was no longer pleasant. She was almost sorry to have caused it, but plunged full speed ahead.

"Well, that could change anytime, especially if you keep being such a sanctimonious son of a bitch. It's always the media's fault when anyone in law enforcement does something stupid."

Her heart hammered in her throat. The argument kept growing, they'd be out on the road duking it out. She'd never let him know how close he came to being right about her. But why defend herself when she wasn't even that person anymore? And why in the world let him think she might be doing the story?

He took a deep breath and drove on in silence. At least she'd shut him up.

Soon the two-lane paved road narrowed to gravel, the Ozark style houses spaced farther apart. They rode along between fenced green pastures dotted with grazing beef cattle. He keyed both windows down and it felt good just to breathe in the air smelling of fresh-plowed soil. Nothing was turning out like she'd planned. Penned up in here with him, golden sunshine lying across their laps, the warm breeze tickling through her hair. His so black it reflected blue like the wing of a crow. What a fool she was, for her mouth went right on as if her tongue were loose at both ends.

"I was rude the other day, and I'm sorry. If we're going to spend the day together it'll be much more enjoyable if we're not being perfect jackasses."

"This isn't exactly a picnic. Besides, nobody's perfect," he said.

"Wanna bet?"

A harsh laugh that sounded forced prompted her to join him. Relieved, she leaned back against the warmth of the seat and dragged in a deep breath. It was downright scary the way he studied her, like he wanted to scoop the insides out of her brain and contemplate them.

"What's wrong? Watch where you're going!"

He jerked the wheel in time to prevent the right front tire dropping off in the ditch. Her head thunked hard against the window frame, and he jammed on the brakes, throwing her forward.

"Take it easy. Trying to kill me?" She rubbed at her head.

He leaned across and took her arm. "Hey, you okay? Let me see."

His hand raked through her hair, fingers entwined with hers. When she twisted around, his lips hovered so close they blurred. Flinging her hands up, she batted at him. "Stop, get back. Stop it."

Eyes scrunched tightly, she fought a desire to let him kiss her, fought harder the fear that gathered in her gut.

She could not, *would not* get involved with this man.

6

CHAPTER

Amazed at what he'd almost done, Dal reluctantly jerked away.

What the hell was wrong with him?

Stupidity and lust, that's what it was. He hadn't had a woman since Leeann, but that was no excuse. This one wasn't for him. Just because she smelled like flowers and sunshine and looked like an earthy goddess in faded jeans and patchwork shirt. Just because she made him laugh for the first time in years.

What was wrong with *her*, anyway?

She hunkered back in the corner like he was about to rape her. Streaked hair blew around a face flushed with anxiety.

Must be a way to smooth this over. No telling what she might tell Mac. "Hey, I'm sorry. Didn't mean to hurt you, or scare you. You okay?" He wanted to be angry with her, was angry with himself instead.

"It was just a tiny bump," she said softly. "A very tiny bump."

He almost didn't hear the words. "I'll pay more attention. I'm really not a careless driver." He pulled back onto the road, changed the subject as if nothing had happened. "So you think we can get any sense out of this Caveman fellow?"

"You think he had something to do with the bones?"

"Can't tell. I'll know when we talk to him." But he wouldn't tell her. She was itching to get at this story, no matter what she said.

She stared at him, checked her seatbelt, and scooted as far away as possible, like he might run off the road or pounce on her.

"So, about Caveman Jake?" He cocked one arm in the open window, drove with exaggerated care.

"I… uh… doubt if he'll make any sense, but don't take my word for it. I'll show you where he lives if you want to give it a try. Right up ahead is the Norville place, the one Parker said is being sold for mucho dollars. The forty acres borders on Kyle Foster's land."

The old house hunkered within a gathering of trees, limbs furry with expectant spring growth. When summer leaves clothed the trees, the house wouldn't be visible from the road. He grabbed glimpses as they passed by, but mostly kept his eyes on the road. What a sorry looking place. It hid plenty of secrets that pecked at him. He shut them out, preferring to drag information out of the reporter for the time being.

"Kyle Foster's place is where the bones were found." A statement, not a question.

"Yep."

"Where's that at from here?"

"Yonder, just past the fence line, that road that angles off toward the creek. See?"

She pointed, and he recognized the lay of the land. Ahead, the new highway span cut across the narrow valley and disappeared into the distance.

"Where's the off-ramp around here?"

"To the north of town about four miles. Two state highways converge at the square. One comes over from Fayetteville and Springdale, goes east to Red Bird then north to Blue Springs up in Missouri. The other comes from Harrison and goes through town, past the state park and on to the access to the new highway. Why?"

"Well, that might explain why someone wants to buy this old place off out here. Interstate access is an attraction for some companies or a speculator buying it for residential lots."

"Or it might just be rumor. Mistaken gossip." She studied him then looked away. "I can't imagine people wanting to buy a house way out here."

"There's usually some bit of truth, even in gossip. You live here and so do I. Now."

"Yes, I suppose, but I don't write gossip."

Well, she had him there, unless he wanted to start another argument. "So, is it a story? This land sale thing?"

"I really don't know yet. Couldn't get Mary to answer my questions. There's always been talk about how valuable the land around the highway is bound to become. Even so, there hasn't been an unusual amount of buying and selling so far. Not openly, at any rate. They're going to build a Casey's General Store at the exit. Other than that...." She shrugged.

Pleased to engage in an ordinary conversation with her, he attempted to keep it that way. "Tell me more about these archeological finds. I'm surprised by that."

"I'm not an expert, but I've done a couple of stories, especially since they began to break ground for the interstate. In the twenties the body of a young woman was dug up under Jacob's Bluff, but she was several thousand years old, and even if she had been murdered, no one really cared." She spared him a grin, and he basked in its warmth.

"Actually," she went on, "it took some archeologists from New York to dig her up. Folks around here thought it better not to disturb a grave. Superstition or religion, or maybe a little of both."

Shifting in the seat, she warmed to her subject. "So no more digs. Anyway, while this new highway route was being laid out, Dave and Kathy were called in to see that the Jacob's Bluff dig and any other known historical sites were protected from the construction. Some Civil War soldiers are buried in an old deserted field out that way too. As it turned out none were in harm's way, and so highway construction moved along on schedule."

"Is that usual around here? Finding artifacts buried under bluffs?"

"Pretty much so. At one time archaic man lived all through these mountains, and sites of settlements and burial grounds that date back several thousand years have been uncovered. Of course Native Am—" She broke off and glanced at him. "Uh… American Indians, as we think of them, came later, but they were, for the most part, civilized. Osage, Cherokee, Arkansa tribes. Some people mistakenly refer to the archaic bluff dwellers as… as Indians—"

He held up a hand. "You don't have to dance around the word. I'm a Cherokee, an American Indian, simple as that. That other PC crap is just that—crap. We're all native Americans, aren't we?" His grin softened the sharp tone of voice.

After a moment, she went on. "…and I suppose they were Indians in the truest sense of the word, but not in the way we tend to think of the term. It stands to reason they buried their dead somewhere. And then there were the Civil War battles at Pea Ridge and Prairie Grove, plus all the skirmishes that left the dead buried where they were killed. Even though it's against the law for people to dig for or possess artifacts, where they're on private property, it happens frequently. But, like I said, folks around here don't cotton to digging up the dead."

"And that's why this, uh, Kyle fellow, called you? He thought he'd found some of these artifacts? Guess he didn't mind getting paid for bones of the dead."

"Well, of course there are those who value money over morals. Especially when their kids are hungry. But who knows what we might do in the same situation? I'm not sure why he thought he'd get paid for them. I guess when folks call something valuable, others think in terms of dollars and cents. The University wouldn't pay him anything, they'd just confiscate them and put em in a box in the basement."

She glanced at Dal, and he felt her scrutiny, but kept his gaze riveted to the road and let her talk.

"Folks around here don't take kindly to the government telling them what they can do on their own property. Otherwise unsavory politicians win office because of their stand on property rights in Arkansas. People mostly just dig for souvenirs, something to display on the coffee table or hang on the wall, and they defend their right to do so. There's not a landowner in these parts who doesn't have a cigar box full of arrowheads, stone tools, and pottery shards he's come across plowing his own land. In this part of the country no law will stop a man doing what he wants on his own land, and that includes digging and keeping what he finds." She paused, and he threw her a quick glance, but she was staring out the window.

After a moment, she went on. "Laws aren't going to stop the cultivating of our biggest cash crop either. Growing marijuana has taken the place of making whiskey in these hills. And the revenuers will have about as much luck stopping it as they did putting an end to stills in the woods. The government spends thousands of dollars busting marijuana growers just to make a big show, when the law would be better served working with hardcore drug dealers and education."

He squared his shoulders, both hands tightening on the wheel. "I agree big drug dealers ought to be busted, but that's not going to happen. Too much money changes hands and too many governments get rich off drugs. It's a hopeless challenge for narcotics officers. God knows why we keep on doing it. In many cases drug use begins with marijuana, though. I agree with you there. If we could educate young kids to stay away from it, one day the demand for the hard drugs would drop."

He ground his teeth, but the anger took over anyway. "How can people be so stupid as to assume marijuana is harmless? You sound like you think it's okay to start little kids eight and nine years old smoking that poison so that by the time they turn thirteen they're ready for crack or smack, or better yet, the killer heroin? Who do you think your friendly farmers sell to?"

"I didn't say I agree with drug use. I'm just saying — "

"That growing it is okay if you can't find a job doing something else?"

"Not that either, But I do know that Kyle couldn't feed his wife and six kids growing cucumbers or strawberries. I've heard most of the marijuana growers bundle it up and leave it in their mailbox for pick-up by people coming through. They can't make any money off it here. It goes to the big cities where it's worth more."

He gripped the wheel, sat straight and stiff. Glared over at her. "If you believe that you're pretty naïve for a reporter. And even if what you say is so, what makes that right? Only the city kids get their hands on it? Talk about not-in-my-backyard mentality."

"Dal, we're talking about marijuana, not heroin. Some believe it should be legalized."

Now he hammered at the wheel, long past controlling his rage. "In the long run, there's very little difference in marijuana and heroin. Do you know how many kids I've seen killed by drugs in the streets of Dallas? Kids who started out smoking weed."

Leeann's dead body, needle hanging from one arm. Dear God, his poor Leeann. Through his rage, he tried to make this woman understand, though he wasn't sure why.

"Drugs are the scourge of our society. Nothing is worse, not organized crime or street gangs or serial killers or handguns. None take the toll that drugs do. It's the most destructive thing to ever happen to the human race, worse even than AIDS. Four and a half million may be infected with AIDS, many as a result of using drugs, but how many do you suppose will die from using drugs in the next ten years? Not to mention the collateral damage. Double that. Hell, triple it. And people have to open their eyes before it's too late. Too late to save our society."

She was talking, but he couldn't make out what she said. In the center of the darkness lay his once beautiful wife, destroyed by drugs. And his own life exploded into ruins by the accusations that followed her death. And the hopeless days and nights spent on the street trying to stop up the dam with one finger while drugs flowed in a never-ending tide.

The road ahead became a black tunnel through which he hurtled.

Shouted words echoed around him. He vaguely sensed he was losing it as the Explorer fishtailed on the gravel road, floating as if it were about to become airborne. His diminished vision registered a switchback curve ahead. It raced toward them. He was helpless to lift his foot from the accelerator.

His passenger's scream penetrated the trance and snapped him back to reality. He touched the brake, let off, touched it again in the split second it took to maneuver into the tight curve. He just might make it if he was very, very lucky. He hoped to hell his passenger had her seatbelt fastened. Too late to check, too late for anything but to ride this out.

If he wrecked the unit, Sheriff Richards would have his hide. Sweet Jesus, what if he killed her?

The Tahoe slid sideways along the narrow road, front tires on one shoulder, back tires on the other. The skid went on and on, an interminably slow motion, sickening ride. At last the vehicle came to a halt, rocked up on two wheels, hung there for what seemed an eternity, then dropped back with a thud that slammed his head against the roof.

He couldn't let go of the wheel. Nor could he breathe normally. Dust and gravel rained around them, a cloud drifted in through the windows. She coughed, yelled at him, penetrating the dull roar in his head. From the sound of her healthy scolding, he had scared her, but she wasn't hurt.

Frantically, he clawed at the seatbelt until it popped loose. Stumbling from the car, he ignored her calling his name, sloshed through the watery ditch and up the other side where he ran smack into a barbed wire fence. He grappled with the top strand, tried to tear it out of the way. Wicked barbs ripped the flesh of his palms. Pain yanked him back to reality. Though he stopped struggling, he remained jammed against the wicked wire, gazing across the field while a deluge of memories engulfed him.

Would he forever relive that day he'd found her, pale and lifeless on the bathroom floor?

A fresh wind brought him back to the reality of a sunny day. Blood oozed through his fingers, but he continued to grip the barbed wire, using the pain to stop the visions.

In the car, Jessie struggled to regain her equilibrium. Dust clogged her throat, gritted between her teeth, scratched at her eyeballs. A mix of terror and anger boiled within her until she feared it would burst.

What in the hell was wrong with this man?

Grappling fingers fumbled at the seatbelt until it released. She clawed the door open and staggered into the middle of the road, stood there a moment, disoriented. Looking for him so she could wring his neck. Dust settled around her until she could barely breathe. And when it cleared she was alone. No sign of Dallas Starr.

Where had he gone? What in God's name had come over him? Was he a madman?

There he was on the far side of the ditch, doing battle with a barbed-wire fence. He wrestled with the thing as if he wanted to tear his way through, escape a fearful beast that pursued him.

Heedless of the possible consequences of her own actions, she raced toward him. By the time she reached his side blood dripped from his hands that continued to battle the barbed wire.

Rage drifted away like the dust. Trembling, she reached out, touched his shoulder. Repeated his name, as if he were an animal that might strike out at the one who meant to rescue him. The danger could well be the same. He turned and stared at her with eyes dark as a bottomless spring.

"Back off." His voice was a rumble deep in his throat.

"You're bleeding, let me help." Her heart kicked, catching at her breath.

"Just. Back. Off." Muscles bunched along his jaw, and his tone brooked no interference.

Despite his reaction she could not leave him standing there like that, bleeding. She should be afraid.

"I'm going to call nine-one-one. Just stay right there."

"No, I said no." One torn, bloody hand clamped her wrist so hard she cried out.

Frozen and helpless, his blood hot on her skin, she waited for him to let her go or strike her down.

Instead, he jerked her forward into the wash of his breath, and something else, something ugly. A thick, coppery stench that tainted the warm spring air.

"I said back off. You'll call no one." He leaned so close his eyes, brittle as chunks of emeralds, captured her vision.

Something warm trickled down her arm. His blood! Her breath came in jerky gasps and she was struck speechless by sheer terror. It was the closest she'd ever come to fainting, had always thought such an act was something women did to escape an unpleasant situation. Well, hell, it sounded like a good idea.

Steve had hit her once, so hard and fast she hadn't the time to contemplate what he would do next. She'd sworn no man would ever do that to her again.

Gritting her teeth, she fought the darkness drifting over her. Be damned if she'd wimp out. "You let me go. Now. You hear me?"

Jesus, was that her voice? Sounded like someone else. Someone much braver, much stronger than her.

Must not have been though, for he scarcely reacted. Just kept holding her, staring down into her face. What now? Fainting was out, but she knew better than to fight him. He was too strong, could break her in half easily. Whatever he would do to her, she couldn't stop him, and might only make things worse by struggling. But she would not bend or break though terror clawed through her like some wild thing.

Breathing harshly, she waited while his hard gaze changed to a pure jade washed by unshed tears. He didn't so much turn her arm loose as throw it from his grasp as if she were filth. And she *wanted* to run—God how she wanted to flee this madman. What held her there, she didn't know, unless it was the fear. She'd felt such fear once before, when Steve learned about her story breaking before the planned raid on the drug kingpin. She'd gotten what she deserved that day, but this… this was not the same at all.

In silence, Dallas gaped at the bloody print around her wrist. Extending shredded palms he stared at them as if they weren't his. "I'm sorry. I didn't mean…."

Breaking off, he turned and stumbled toward the road like a wounded animal. Should she follow him or simply wait there until he drove away, leaving her free to flag down a ride? There might be no one along for hours. Or a simpler solution. Let him go, then walk the four or five miles back to the office. On wobbly knees, she crossed the pasture and climbed from the ditch to the road, not eager to catch him. No danger of that. The Tahoe moved out of sight, trailing dust.

The experience left her drained and sick to her stomach. It wouldn't take much to barf in the bushes. But she swallowed down the hot bile and dragged in a great breath of relief. He was gone. When her knees stopped shaking, she headed in the opposite direction.

She must have walked more than a mile before tires crackled on gravel. Shoving strands of hair from her sweaty face, she turned to wait for the approaching car. Whoever it was would pick her up. How should she explain the blood smeared on her arms?

When it was too late to escape, the cruiser driven by Dallas Starr came into sight. He passed by, nosed the Tahoe toward the ditch to block her way.

Panicked, she whirled and started back the other direction. But she'd never been a good runner, even though her legs were long, and he caught her easily, jerking her around to face him.

Too numb to scream, she could do nothing but gaze up into his shattered expression.

"I won't hurt you," he said in a shaky voice, but he didn't let go. "We need to talk." Not an order. "Please."

Compassion replaced terror. Yet, it was time to be careful, not stupid. "Please, don't grab on to me like that. You're scaring me." She tugged against his strong grip.

Surprisingly, he released her and held up both hands in a gesture of surrender, the cuts on his palms seeping blood. "Okay. Have it your way. Run. Tell whoever will listen. Tell them all about the crazy cop the sheriff has hired. Go ahead. I won't stop you. I won't hurt you. I can't do more than say I'm sorry."

Like hell, she'd run. Instead, she slipped out of his reach and challenged him with a silent stare. "Yes, you can. You can explain why you acted like that."

"I don't think I can. I can only say I won't hurt you." His expression closed and locked a door to keep her out.

"That's not enough. You scared the life out of me. There's no excuse for that." It was bizarre, how she wanted to run, but at the same time couldn't leave him there hidden within his pain. Hard to forget his earlier need for understanding. She said his name once, a question.

His head jerked, his eyes batted. "Go on, leave."

Intrigued, she took a step forward, then another, heart hammering until she gasped for air. Damn, what was going on inside his head? The same curiosity that had driven her to become a reporter was about to get her in deep trouble. She knew what it was like to be misunderstood, to have your actions used as weapons against you. To have no one wait for explanations, as if the destruction brought about by your actions had been intended. How in God's name could she dare to judge him?

She slipped into his space, where she could smell and taste his desperation, took his hands gently, and turned them so she could inspect the cuts and abrasions.

He endured her touch without comment, towering over her, ominous and silent, breath going in and out in noisy waves. She should be terrified, but suddenly she wasn't. And that didn't make any sense. None at all.

"Let's get you cleaned up," she said, surprised she could utter a word. "Then we'll talk. I'll drive."

Without speaking he plodded to the passenger side of the Tahoe and climbed in. She didn't say anything either, but drove them to her place, the wheel under her hands sticky with his blood.

He followed her inside, stood beside her while she filled the bathroom sink with warm soapy water and washed his blood off herself. She drew clean water and, without her bidding, he plunged both hands in, screwing his eyes shut but making no sound.

That must have hurt like the very devil.

She dragged over the small stool from the dressing table. "Sit."

Amazingly, he obeyed, and she went to work doctoring his hands.

In silence, he watched while she uncapped a brown bottle of hydrogen peroxide, grunted when she poured the liquid over his wounds, then asked, "Why are you doing this?"

"To clean away the dirt. Now hold still. Eww, that's ugly. Hope you've had your tetanus shot."

"I meant, why do you care? You just like assholes, or what?"

"Only perfect ones."

"No, really. I'd like to know."

"Uh-hum." For a long moment she watched the peroxide foam in the palms of his hands. There were so many answers to his question that she didn't know where to start. Nesting his damaged hands in hers because she desperately needed the contact to ground her in the moment, she replied, "Big question, why. What if I say I don't know why?"

"That I understand," he murmured. Tousled hair partially shadowed his expressive eyes. Eyes that now refused to look at her.

She couldn't tell him about herself, not yet. Maybe not ever. It had been months before she'd opened up to Parker. Maybe one day she'd tell her best friend, Tinker, and Mac. Difficult, maybe impossible to admit to her dreadful failure. Hard to admit to doing something so bad. Besides, Dal's vulnerability left him open to destructive emotions, and he was a dangerous stranger.

So, they'd both keep their secrets. At least for now.

"You know what? I think you need to get out of those clothes and into the shower. When you finish I'll bandage your hands." She let go of him and started to pull the tee shirt up to remove it. A silver chain hung around his neck, and she glimpsed a small, delicate woman's ring against his hairless chest.

He shoved her hands away. "Don't. I can do that."

"You've got blood all over you, you may be cut somewhere else. I trust you don't have AIDS." She thought to ask it lightly, but deep inside fear crawled.

"I said don't." A return to the sharp and unyielding tone.

A refusal to answer her questions sent the fear raging. He worked with drug addicts, for God's sake. How stupid could she be?

Stiffly she pressed her lips together to keep from shouting into the face of his stubbornness. Managed to mutter, "You really ought to go to a doctor. You need a tetanus shot."

He didn't answer, instead fumbled at the belt buckle. His injured hands proved awkward, and he gazed at her with an expression so furiously perplexed she wanted to laugh or cry or take him in her arms. She did none of those. What she ought to do was pound him on the head. That she didn't do either.

"Want me to help?" she offered, instead.

"Just unfasten it and then get out."

"Fine." Stubborn jackass.

With her own fingers trembling, she worked the buckle undone. Too bad she couldn't keep from touching his warm skin. Beneath that hook on the waist band, more bare skin, sleek with a fine sheen of sweat. He even smelled dangerous. She fumbled, released the hook. Good, that's over. Now, for the zipper.

"I guess I'm not too good at this. I never had any brothers and I've never been married, but I wear Levi's a lot, so how difficult can this be? A zipper is a zipper."

The teeth snicked apart to reveal tiny curls of black hair that tickled her fingers, sent a desolate longing through her. What was she *doing?* Undressing this man in her bathroom when she couldn't go near him without coming undone.

Just unzip the damn thing and get the hell out of his reach. Yeah, or put him out of your reach. Who was in danger here, anyway? Taking a deep breath, she raised her eyes for a fast look.

He stared, not at her or what she was doing, but at the mirror across the room, and their ragged, dusty reflection. He didn't even know her fingers were touching him

And that pissed her off bad.

Anger chased her arousal and she opened the fly with dispassionate precision. Leaving the removal of his clothing to him like he'd ordered, she turned to the shower.

"I'll adjust the water, it's stubborn sometimes. Want it hot?" The voice didn't sound like hers.

His silence was beginning to frighten her as much as his earlier crazy actions and she turned to scrutinize him. The top of her head was on a level with his chin.

"Are you all right?"

He studied both hands, then gave her a poignant grin that transformed his features, revealing a glimpse of a younger, less battered man. Then that face disappeared, replaced by a mask of primitive indifference. Her throat closed up just like it did when she thought about her mom and dad.

"Why wouldn't I be all right?" He waited a minute. "And no, I don't have AIDS."

He had a hell of a way of dampening passion. "Nice of you to finally tell me. I'll see if I've got a shirt you can wear. About the pants I don't know. Hand those out when you get them off, and I'll see if I can clean them up enough you can wear them home."

While she dug around in the closet among a collection of oversized sleep shirts, the shower washed blood off the frightening, naked man on the other side of the thin wall.

Grandma always said good food cured all ailments so, after rinsing the blood from his pants in the kitchen sink, she tossed them into the dryer and prepared a large omelet, nuked bacon in the microwave, and dropped bread in the toaster. Though the pants were still damp around the pockets, she put them inside the bathroom door when she heard the shower cut off.

The coffee pot had finished gurgling by the time he came out. Even the largest t-shirt she had was too tight across his wide shoulders, but it covered him. Some. His belly was the same color bronze as his arms and face. Tinker's advice bounced through her head. It was a damn good thing he had on pants.

"Smells good," he said.

"Sit there. When you finish eating I'll bandage those for you."

Every time she glanced up he was staring at her but she couldn't read the expression. She sat across from him at the small, square table, while he lunged at the food like a starved wolf, holding the fork awkwardly. She picked at hers, stomach in such a turmoil she couldn't force herself to take a bite. Going on a wild rampage certainly did things for his appetite.

Like a wolf. Lord, what had she gotten herself into? Better get him out of here, quick as she could, and tell Mac he'd better get someone else to show his new deputy around. That would be the end of that.

If she were very, very lucky.

7
CHAPTER

Dal still doubted Jessica's sincerity, and he sure couldn't tell her why he was so defensive, why he didn't trust her. How could he ever trust a reporter after what had happened with Leeann? But that was none of her business.

So, while he regretted having frightened her, he chose the coward's way out and told a partial truth. It was his only defense against the past catching up with him.

"I burned out, too much undercover work. I guess I turned into the filth I was trying to put away. I just couldn't handle it anymore. They put me on suspension, and eventually let me go because I wouldn't take a desk job. Like I said, Mac already knows all the sordid details, so it'll do you no good to tell him." He bit at a piece of toast. If that explanation didn't satisfy her, it was too bad.

"I wasn't planning on telling Mac anything. Why would I?"

"Because you two are way too close for the law and a reporter. I figured you told him everything."

"We're friends, that's true. Beyond our jobs. It wouldn't hurt you to make a few friends yourself. I suppose some reporters were mean to you, back there in the big city of Dallas. Did you kill someone?"

"In my job, hell yes, I killed someone. In the line of duty. Besides, it's okay to kill someone. That's what we're paid to do, isn't it? Keep the streets safe so people like you can dig up all the garbage for the entertainment of your readers?" He could almost see her licking her lips in anticipation.

In reality she only regarded him with those incredible cat's eyes of hers. "You have a real hang-up, you know that? Hope no one gets around you with a chainsaw, they're liable to make a king-sized pile of sawdust out of that chip you carry around on your shoulder."

"Look, thanks for dragging me here and playing Florence Nightingale. I appreciate it. If I hurt your feelings, well, hell, I didn't mean to—and I sure didn't intend to scare you."

She hugged away a shiver. "You didn't. It's okay."

The way she sucked in several deep breaths before she could speak in a normal tone told him it wasn't okay at all. That he'd terrified her. But he didn't much care, and he wasn't about to open up to her hidden fears. He had enough of his own.

"And so you just go all nuts once in a while and try to hurt yourself?"

"No, it's not like that. Must be the stress of moving, the new job, falling right into a murder case." He held out his wounded hands in a wide shrug, tried to make amends. This reporter could do him a lot of damage if she wanted to, and he would be wise to stay far away from her, but be damned if he'd beg. "It won't happen again."

"Oh, you can control it?" The implication was loud and clear. Why had he let it happen in the first place if he had control over it?

What a strange and unusual woman. After the performance he put on, she takes him into her home where there are no neighbors around, no one to help her. Was she crazy? He chuckled at the thought.

"That's funny?"

He watched her anger building, and tried to ward it off. "I was thinking about something else."

Her lips tightened, but she appeared to relax a little. "Why don't you let me bandage up those cuts, since you refuse to see a doctor? Then you can take me back to the office. I think it might be best if you got someone else to show you around."

"Me, too." He held up the hands again. "I can handle this. Don't bother."

She didn't argue. "Well, let's go then. Hope you don't mind if I drive."

"Not at all."

She took a handful of wet paper towels to clean off the steering wheel. He watched in silence for a moment, then said, "You should be more careful. I could have had AIDS."

She jerked a frightened glance at him, like a rabbit caught in the headlights and unable to react. "You said you didn't."

Muttered through trembling lips. He was again sorry. Then she went back to scrubbing the sticky wheel, her anger like a live barrier between them.

"That's true, I don't. I was just saying—"

"Never mind, I get it."

He nodded. "All the same, you should be more careful."

"I said I get it. Now leave me be."

They rode in silence, were nearly at the newspaper office before he asked what he had to ask, no matter what.

"What are you going to do about what happened?"

"Do?" She kept her eyes on the road.

Damn her, she knew exactly what he meant. "Are you going to expose me, tell all your readers how the sheriff has hired this lunatic?"

"If I decide to expose you, as you so adroitly put it, it won't be in the newspaper for everyone to read. I may talk to Mac or Parker about what happened. So you'd better tell Mac first. Friends share things, you know. But you won't read about it on the pages of our newspaper, I can assure you of that. I don't write that kind of trash, and I won't, ever again. What's private is private." Her cheeks flushed and she shot him a quick glance.

He caught the admission that once she had written trash, but didn't pursue it. He wasn't at all surprised and certainly not interested.

He did wish he could trust her to keep her mouth shut, but he didn't. If she'd done it once, she'd do it again. Wouldn't be able to help herself. It was only a matter of time before she told all, unable to resist the temptation of such a juicy story. And she wouldn't much care what it did to him, at least not enough to stop her writing it. Dammit, why couldn't he have kept his rage bottled up inside?

Still, he couldn't worry about it. He had a murder to solve and an explanation to cook up to explain his injuries to the sheriff. If he put his mind to it, maybe he could forget the crazy attraction he felt toward this intriguing woman who posed such a threat to the life he was struggling to put back together, piece by tiny piece.

By Thursday afternoon Jessie convinced herself that what had happened wasn't nearly as bad as she remembered. It was her vivid imagination at work again. There was work to be done and thinking of Dallas Starr wasn't helping at all. She'd heard nothing from Mary Smith on the sale of the old Norville house. Time to go looking for the elusive councilwoman, get something out of her, one way or another.

A special city council meeting had been called for that evening, and she caught Mary at the Red Bird. Despite the Freedom of Information Act that forbade a gathering of more than two members without the press present, the aldermen gathered here regularly.

This afternoon, she could keep them from breaking that law.

The nine members sat around a table in the rear where a huge window offered a view of the river and the sunlit peaks beyond.

When Jessie walked in, Mayor Artie Jessup glanced her way, all innocence and light. "Ah, the press. Does this mean we can start our meeting early? Join us, Jessie."

She remained standing. "I need to speak to Mary, about something else."

All heads swiveled toward the councilwoman, most especially Harold Smith's, who glared at his wife as if to ask, *What you been up to now?* Carrying a tall coke, Mary rose to join Jessie at another table rather than make a scene. Butch, who owned—and sometimes waited at the Red Bird—set a cup of coffee in front of Jessie. The luscious fragrance mixed with that of hamburgers and fries left over from the lunch crowd.

Before Butch retired to the game room, he said, "Holler if y'all need anything. I'm gonna try to break my old record."

By this time Mary had nibbled her lower lip clean of its awkwardly applied lipstick. Something was definitely up with the Smiths, and it made Jessie's inquisitive mind itch.

Mary threw one last glance over her shoulder at her peers and sank into a chair across from Jessie. "What did you want to talk to me about?"

She appeared ruffled, her usually neat brown hair spiky and her makeup not quite perfect. A pair of delicate ebony arrowheads hung from silver wires looped through her ears.

Speechless, Jessica stared at them. Were her two stories melding into one? She reached for the pad and pen in her pack, watched Mary watch her.

"Well, what did you want?" Her words sounded irritated beyond what the situation called for.

"Like your earrings. Where'd you get them?"

Mary darted her fingers to one ear, made an effort to smile that didn't come off. "Forgot which ones I had on. Thank you, but surely that's not what you came to talk to me about." Anger strengthened her demeanor and her pointy chin lifted.

"They're black arrowheads. Are they real?"

"Real what?" Mary appeared dazed.

"Real arrowheads. I mean as in dug up somewhere?"

"Uh—oh, I don't think so. I've had them for ages. Don't even remember where I—" She broke off, slipped the wire from her ear, and held the bauble in her hand, staring at it as if she'd never seen it before. At last, she regained some of her composure, threaded the wire through the piercing, and raised her thin shoulders.

Jessie shrugged right back at her. "Doesn't matter. They're pretty, that's all. I tried to call you a couple of times to explain my questions of the other day. I think you misunderstood. Parker asked me to look into the sale if it was going to affect the community, and that's all I was doing. I had no intention of upsetting you."

A tear leaked from Mary's left eye and she swiped it away, gazed into her Coke. Maybe there was trouble at home, her husband being the jerk that he was.

"You okay?"

After spending an inordinate amount of time stirring a straw around in her drink, Mary replied, voice trembling. "I've tried to sell that place since Ken drowned. And then after I married Harold, it just sort of became unimportant. We leased the pastureland out and forgot about it." She peered up at Jessie with soulful brown eyes. "I read in the paper about the body. I thought that's what you wanted to talk to me about."

"Why, no. Why would you think that?" How odd. "I asked about the place earlier."

Mary jerked her shoulders in another shrug that made her look like a puppet whose strings were being pulled by a drunken marionette. "I know, but I thought you were just getting around to it." She sipped at the cold drink. "It was a long time ago. It can't be him."

Excitement kicked at Jessie's insides and she traced a dark square on her notepad, fingers shaking. "I'm sorry. They never did find his body? That must have been terrible for you. I never heard what happened." A tiny lie to get at the truth. Maybe.

"It was a long time ago. He drowned. I don't want to talk about it." Her eyelids batted and she pinned her gaze on Jessie. "Somebody that's been dead so long. How will they ever find out who it is?"

An eerie sensation crept up Jessie's spine. What were they talking about here? Her long lost husband or…. "Oh, you mean the bones? They have ways."

Mary's voice came as if from a well. "I don't like bringing up all this old stuff. Why is it so important?"

"Are we still talking about the body? I asked about the land. The Norville land, Mary. Let the sheriff's department handle the investigation of the bones. Parker's concerned that we're going to end up with a mall or a bunch of condos right on our doorstep. It would ruin our peaceful valley. And you know him. He'll be apt to start petitions, write letters to congressmen, anything he can to stir the pot against something like that. Anyway, no matter what it is, he thinks there might be a story there. And so, I will get one."

Mary's cheeks flamed, but she didn't reply right away. Jessie drew smiley faces on her pad, then slashed daggers straight through their smug little grins, and said softly, "It must have been awful for you, Ken dying that way."

Mary's eyes took on the look of a doe caught in headlights.

That trick usually worked. Ask a question too tough to answer, turn the subject back to the real question. The easier one.

"It was a long time ago in another life. I'm so sorry. I've been so upset and confused. Of course they found Ken. We buried him. Anyway, I never talk about it. It's too painful. What does Ken have to do with any of this anyway?"

"Nothing, of course. So what about the buyer? Who is it?" Switch back, zero in with an easier question in safer territory, even though Mary's spooked reaction to the discovery of the body had dragged Jessie's attention away from the land deal. Something bigger and more mysterious was going on here.

My God—what if the two were connected?

Relief washed over the woman's drawn features. "Parker's almost right. It's the Allen Beekman Associates that want to buy the land."

Jessie whistled. "The retirement people? The ones that built Buena Falls Estates up in Blue Springs?"

Mary nodded. "Harold's been dickering with them for months, wanted it kept quiet. How'd Parker find out?"

"Well, you know this town. Nothing's a secret for long. Especially not from him."

Mary nodded, drew lines on her napkin with a thumbnail. "We can't sell it without my sister-in-law's signature, and she hasn't answered any of our letters. It's a lot of money. Harold's fit to be tied. About Jolene, I mean. We've called and left messages which she doesn't return. I don't understand it. There was a time when all she wanted was to be shut of that old place. It belonged to their folks, Ken's and hers. And then…." Mary gnawed at her lip some more, began to finger the obsidian earring hanging from one ear.

Boy did that ploy work. The woman had said much more about the Norville place than Jessie expected. She jotted notes on the land deal, then wrote *BONES?* and underlined it twice. Odd how upset Mary became when she talked about Ken's death. It had been a very long time ago, and she'd built herself a new life. Yet, she'd brought up the body, even though any fool could tell she didn't want to talk about it. Her first marriage must've been a doozy, and she hadn't been much luckier with the second. Though on the surface she and Harold appeared to get along, he was a loud-mouthed control freak. You sure never could explain why someone loved someone.

Sitting there in the bright sunlight Jessie gazed thoughtfully at Mary, and decided to check back issues of the paper concerning Ken's death. There might be one heck of a story here besides this deal on the land. Especially if the two were connected in some bizarre way. An intriguing thought. What a story that would be. The old desire to be the first to sniff out a story caught fire deep in her gut. She knew the feeling well, and everyone better get out of her way. If she decided to do it, that is. Parker did want her to, thought it would be good for her.

She clenched the pen till her knuckles whitened.

Don't do this, Jessie. A whispered warning.

But what if she did? While investigating the two stories, she could do a historical piece for the regular feature. Interview some of the old timers who would remember the floods and the night of the twin tornadoes, the night Ken drowned. Maybe she'd get a different slant than what had been written in the paper at the time. Capture some of those priceless statements that often came from the mouths of those who do so love to reminisce, and let the readers draw their own conclusions.

Excitement kicked in like an old, old friend, and in her mind she began to write the lead to the second story. The follow-up to Parker's. Her story. The idea both frightened and intrigued her.

Mary rose abruptly. "I don't think there's a story here, not unless Jolene gets in touch. We can't sell until that time, and Harold is furious and... well, I've said enough. See you at the meeting later?"

"No, I've got something else to cover. Parker'll be there, though. Too curious about y'all calling a special meeting to miss it. He may pick at you some more about this. You know how he is. Worse than an old hound dog on scent."

Mary laughed nervously and waved goodbye as she went out the door, leaving her fellow aldermen to stare after her in silence.

Since Jessie usually didn't read Parker's stories prior to publication unless he asked her to do so, it wasn't until the next day she found out that Mary failed to attend the city council meeting. And she still hadn't talked to him about taking over the Bones story. Wasn't sure how to go about it.

"When you saw her, did she seem okay?" he asked, prodding her with typical gentleness. "I mean about the property thing? Harold was in a terrible mood. You know how he gets when things don't go his way. Worse than his usual bellowing self. And he could've waited for the regular meeting to request replacements of neck braces and backboards for the first responders. You know him, though. Always in control. Even though the council voted with him he ranted and raved over every point that came up, and for no apparent reason. He made some lame excuse about Mary not feeling well. Looked madder than a scalded cat about it, not sympathetic at all."

There was a story hidden here all right, and Mary was right smack in the middle of it. Okay, now. Tell him.

"She must have fallen ill awfully fast. She did seem really upset, but more because of the bones out at Foster's. Do you know if Ken's body was found when he drowned? She says it was, but I'm not sure I believe her."

He pinned eyes the color of sloe berries on her. "Come to think of it, I have no idea. What are you suggesting?"

Might know he'd see past her casual discussion. "I don't know. We know the body Kyle found is that of a tall man, but it was definitely buried. It didn't just float up there and bury itself. Still, I'm always curious when someone disappears and their body is never found, then one turns up."

"Well, I wouldn't jump to that conclusion." He scratched his chin. "You know, that was before I bought the paper. I'm not sure about a body. Are you saying you want to follow up on this?" One dark brow arched in incredulous wonder.

"Oh, I don't know." Coward. Chicken. Tell him yes.

Of course she wanted to look into it in the worst way. Climb back on the horse that had thrown her so many months ago. Yes, she'd missed wading into a story like a tiger on the prowl. But somewhere in the back of her mind was the fear that she'd do anything for a story. Just like the last time. And if she did, what then? Who would she hurt?

There'd been no immediate reaction to the front page story about the bones, but if she dug around in this, it would surely stir up some daily reporters, maybe even television news. And she'd been blackballed in California for inventing sources, not to mention all the trouble she'd caused.

God, she needed to stay out of this.

"If you want it, you know it's your story. Go ahead. Follow it up. No telling what you might find." He watched her closely.

She squirmed. Grinned like an idiot. "I think—I think I'd like to do the story."

"Well, Hail Mary and whoopee. About time you came to your senses. This is yours, darlin. Go to it." The normally withdrawn demeanor had shelled away and he hugged her. Whispered in her ear. "Good for you. I knew you'd come around."

Nothing he'd like better than some fresh controversy. He might never admit it, but that was probably why he hired her. Not in spite of her background but because of it. Not that he wanted her to lie or cheat, but just push the envelope. Walk the edge. Could she do that without falling off? More importantly, could she do it without getting burned?

"First," he went on, "contact Beekman and get some quotes on what they plan to do out here, see if Harold will talk to you. And keep in touch with Mac and the Spaceys on the bones, but let's keep our priorities straight. Don't jump to any conclusions where Ken Norville's death is concerned."

With that, he headed into his office. She could almost hear his palms swishing together in victory. Trying to tamp down her excitement, Jessie went back to work. What had she said that rattled Mary so badly that she missed the city council? Had to be the unearthed body.

A secretary at Beekman Associates, who probably was supposed to keep her mouth shut, verified that the company planned a retirement village in Cedarton. Jessie could get no more than that out of the young woman. Harold didn't answer his cell, so she left a message with his voice mail, but doubted he would return the call. Without his input, she only had enough for a short story filled with speculation that would set the town to talking. She entered contact information in her planner, and penned in black ink *BONES MARY?*

After leaving messages on voice mails of both Mac and Kathy Spacey, she drove to the Red Bird. There she might run into Mac or Harold. Or even Dallas Starr, who had remained elusive since his run-in with the barbed wire fence.

Once inside the café, it was impossible not to order a hamburger and french fries. There was no sign of Mac, Harold, or the deputy, but she did learn that the latter had rented a trailer near the RV park. Not much of a place to live.

The remainder of the day passed in a blur as she followed up leads on both stories and jotted notes into her computer ferociously. It felt good to be working on a big story, and despite some doubts, she worked away the afternoon in a delightful frenzy.

That night she sat on the deck and watched stars emerge in a lavender sky. Something moved in the woods near the cabin. A furtive figure that shifted about in the shadows like some kind of predator. The old terrors overpowered her as if they'd never left and she hurried inside, closed the sliding glass door, and pulled the drapes, heart pounding in her temples.

Infuriated by her immediate reaction to the mysterious shadows in the trees, she dug around in a drawer in the kitchen, came up with a flashlight, and stomped out across the yard, ready to do battle. The night air was sweet with honeysuckle, abuzz with frogs and crickets and the melodious song of Cedar Creek. Clusters of stars filled the moonless sky. Bears came out at night, as did bobcats and cougars and snakes. None of them as dangerous as an imagined two-legged monster out for revenge.

But no one was there. She tromped around beneath the sycamore and hickory and oak trees, the earth underfoot soft beneath a carpet of last year's leaves. Tiny creatures scurried about and she felt like a fool.

"Okay, okay," she muttered. Stop acting so goofy and go back to the house. And so she did.

Saturday afternoon, completing the mindless tasks of housekeeping, she turned her thoughts to Dal's investigation, and the strange behavior of Mary Smith. Monday she would call the deputy for an update and finish the follow-up piece on the case of the bones, provided he would give her some new details. Dave and Kathy were still running tests, but had promised to have something soon. It would be a long while before DNA results came back from Little Rock. Time to rattle some cages and chase this story until something turned up.

After shaking rugs, she tossed them over the rail of the deck, went inside, and poured a glass of lemonade. Fetching her cell phone, she went back outside into the soft warmth that promised summer, punched in the sheriff's beeper number, and leaned against the rail. At that moment, sipping at the tangy drink and basking in warm sunshine, a sensation of being stared at crept along her spine, stirred the hairs on the nape of her neck.

She squared her shoulders and dragged in a deep breath. This would not happen again. She had paid enough. But suppose someone was here for quite another reason? Something to do with the bones… or that irrational new deputy.

When the phone rang, she jumped out of her skin, and took her time connecting. It was Mac.

"How's the investigation going on the bones?" she asked without preliminaries.

"I take it that you're on the story now. Congratulations. Dallas is in charge. Why not call him? What went on between you two the other day? And how in hell did he get tangled up with a barbed-wire fence? He had some cock-and-bull story about driving off the road and getting his rig tangled. What are you doing to my deputy, girl?"

She hesitated.

"Jessie, what's going on?"

"He told you what happened?"

"Not to my satisfaction, he didn't. I thought you and Dallas had hit it off after a kind of rocky start. Did you send him packing like all the rest? How do you ever expect to get yourself a man that way?"

"No, I didn't send him packing. I… I haven't seen him lately, that's all. I guess I've been busy. And who says I'm looking for myself a man? Even if I was, he doesn't fit the bill."

"Oh, ho. Too busy to follow up on a story this big? If you're not careful the daily will leave you behind, and this is right in your own backyard."

"Are they on the story?"

"A reporter called the office this morning. Said they'd be sending someone out to take pictures. Better get moving."

"Mac, I—oh, hell."

His friendly voice took on a tone of concern. "Girl, you okay? Not sick or anything."

"No, nothing like that. I just, well, I didn't—I *don't*. I'm not sure I can deal with Dallas Starr right now."

"I know things have been rough for you, honey. But he's had a rough go of it, too. Since he was a kid he's climbed over obstacles bigger than you or I can even imagine. And he's a good man. Wouldn't hurt you to give him a break." He paused, the unsaid words clear.

Everyone here had given her a badly needed break, hadn't they?

Mac and Parker. Tinker and the Spaceys. She stared blindly across the mountains, mind skittering in fits and starts.

Mac took up again, jerking her back into the present. "This isn't like you at all. Aren't you the one who always gives everyone the benefit of the doubt, who understands motives the rest of us don't even think about? You're such a softy you don't like me getting after Kyle and his marijuana crop because he can't read and write and has a family to support. What happened, gal, our big city narc with his rough edges get under your skin?"

"Don't be ridiculous." On the verge of telling him about Dal and his frightening behavior, she bit back the words. She would not be the cause of someone else's bad luck, not ever again.

The phone rang the moment Jessie disconnected from the disturbing conversation with Mac. Startled, she pressed the button.

Kathy Spacey's well-modulated voice meant business. "I thought you might want to know, the arrowhead we found with the bones? Well, it was a piece of modern jewelry, hand crafted from obsidian, I'll admit, but modern, just the same. A bit of a print on it, but unfortunately not enough to identify. And I think that item we found that appeared to be a shoestring was some type of leather thong that was probably clipped around it somehow to make a pendant or necklace. The wire or clip must've broken or come loose. Someone was wearing it for jewelry."

"The corpse?"

"Could be, I don't know."

"I thought you gave that to Deputy Starr."

Kathy laughed. "He's a smart man. It was his evidence, but he brought it out here for us to take a look. Said we could tell him if he was wrong, but he didn't think it was an arrowhead crafted by early man."

"Have you told him?"

"Yep, he came by and picked it up just a few minutes ago. Said something about stopping by your place. That's why I really called, to tell you he's coming by and ask if you might cut him some slack."

The sound of a car door slamming echoed from the mountain out back, and she caught her breath.

"You still there, Jessie?"

"Yes, I'm here." After chewing her lip a moment, she asked, "Kathy, you must trust him or you wouldn't ask me to be nice to him."

"Deputy Starr? Well, yes, Dave and I both like him, now that we're past his big city ways." She chuckled. "He's too serious for his own good, but he's smart, thinks real deep, if you know what I mean. Dave calls him a muller." A pause while she chuckled some more.

In the background Dave's laughter joined hers. Did they ever get more than two feet apart? Kathy went on. "And Dave ought to know one when he sees one. He really is a very nice man. Calls me Doc."

"Oh, how cute. And I'd like to know how you figured out he was nice. What's a muller? Some kind of fish?"

"Go ahead, change the subject. That's a mullet, and you know it. A muller thinks things over and over, and then over some more." In the background Jessie heard Dave's deeply resonant voice, but she couldn't tell what he said. Kathy laughed, then continued. "As for nice, well, he just is, that's all. Maybe you aren't giving him a chance. Dave wants you to lighten up and have some fun."

"You tell Dave I always have fun. And it's not true I haven't given him a chance."

What a lie, on both counts. All she did was work, which she enjoyed, but she certainly hadn't given Dal a chance to explain himself. Having a man in her life was definitely not on her agenda. It was too distracting, too painful, and besides, she always….

Knuckles rattled on the door, disturbing her thoughts, and she almost dropped the phone. "Kathy, I think he's here. Talk to you later."

"Uh, huh. Was I you I'd treat that man better."

Hanging up on Kathy's laughter, she stepped inside to see Dal's outline shadowed against the glass of the front door. He took off across the porch before she could get there.

Suddenly she didn't want him to go away. Despite the lump in her throat, despite the chills that passed over her flesh or the hair on her arms standing at attention, despite it all, she wanted the handsome deputy to walk through that door into her house, maybe even into her life. But it was way too early for that. Wasn't it?

She crossed the room and made it to the edge of the porch just as he ducked to climb into the patrol car.

Be smart. Let him go.

Nope, she couldn't. Instead she shouted. "I'm here. Sorry, I was on the phone out back." Okay, so she wasn't so smart.

Turn, walk back in the house. Slam the door. Walk, hell. Run. Run and keep running. Unable to follow the inclination, she peered in his direction and, like the fool she was, anticipated him standing near her.

For a long moment he squinted at her over the top of the Tahoe, then took off the gray Stetson that was just like Mac's, and tossed it on the seat. In the bright sunlight, his hair gleamed like ebony, and he never took his gaze off her as he crossed the yard. He wore the slate gray official uniform of the Grace County Sheriff's Department, and he was armed.

Though he limped slightly, he still reminded her of a stealthy cat approaching prey as he mounted the steps.

Wrapping her arms tightly around herself, she shivered.

On the porch, he gestured toward the glider. "I brought back your shirt. I washed it."

The folded shirt lay there like a white flag of truce. Not sure what to say, if indeed she could find her voice, she opted for silence.

He eyed her a moment. "Thanks again… for what you did." That easy drawl churned at her insides, stirred a sensual feeling she'd all but forgotten. His demeanor remained as unnerving as ever, and he didn't seem to be aware of it.

Feeling utterly foolish, she nodded again. Why couldn't she think of something to say? It was embarrassing, and not like her at all. Nobody ever caught her tongue-tied.

Until Dallas Starr came along.

He cleared his throat, took a step backward. "Well, I guess I ought to—"

Abruptly, she opened her mouth and let the words out. Not what she wanted to say at all. "Kathy said you found out something about the arrowhead. It'd save me a call if you don't mind bringing me up to date. For the paper."

He tilted his head. "You on the story? Or just fronting for your boss?"

She looked down at her feet. "If it matters, I'm on the story. Parker's too busy. Now, about the arrowhead?"

"Oh, yeah. Sure. I forgot the sheriff asked me to do that since he wouldn't be in his office Monday. He said you'd likely be calling at the last minute like you always do, wanting information that very instant so you could meet your deadline. Asked that I give you a quote you could run with. Whatever that means." His forehead creased, as if he were surprised he could speak in full sentences.

She was a little, herself.

One reluctant glance into his sultry eyes, and she plunged deep inside him. Wasn't that supposed to be the other way around?

Her bare toes curled self-consciously on the rough pine floor. "He's quite a card, our sheriff." There was no controlling the slight quiver in her voice, and she covered it by babbling on. "I was just having a glass of lemonade out back on the deck. Come join me and we'll talk. That is, you can give me that quote."

He darted a quick look toward his cruiser, then his gaze found her bare toes, locked there. "Oh, I don't know. I probably ought to get on my way."

"Busy, are you? Lots of murders and the like to solve?"

Angling his head, he regarded her without replying.

"Besides, there is the quote." Why couldn't she just let him go?

"Yeah, there is that. And no, there're no more murders. Just your bones. I figured it'd be best if I didn't hang around, after the other day. Best for the both of us." His tone rang gruffly, but he made no move to leave, found her toes again.

She felt warm all over, reached out to brush his bare arm. A muscle rippled under her touch, and she imagined being enclosed in his embrace, trapped in his lair.

"Dal, we need to talk. And not just about the case, either. You're here, I'm here. It's a beautiful day. Hey, who knows, maybe, well, maybe something wonderful will happen." That's it, girl, babble on like an idiot, that way you'll run him off.

"Like what?" His expression said he doubted there was anything wonderful left in the world.

"Like maybe we'll become friends so we can stop dancing around one another." She pulled the screen open, tugged at him like one child to another. "I could use a new friend, couldn't you?" Playing games with him could be dangerous, yet her uncontrollable need to do so outweighed the apprehension she felt.

He stepped through the door, took hold of it before it slammed and held it open, like he might bolt and run. Gave her one last chance to back out. "Jessie, are you sure about this?"

She had never been so unsure of anything in her life, but she took a step back, leaving him room to go in first. The moment he did, her life reached a turning point and there was no going back.

8
CHAPTER

Jessie took Dal's hand and led him through her house into the kitchen.

Grandma inviting the big bad wolf inside to view the goodies. And him bringing his own goodies along.

"Come on in. The ice is melting in my lemonade." His hand in hers was strong and warm, the scars from wrestling with the barbed wire barely discernible.

In the small kitchen, she reluctantly let him go. He stood close behind her, his presence dominating the compact space, while she filled a bowl with ice. Shrugging off a lingering hesitation, she handed him the bowl, grabbed another glass and the pitcher of lemonade.

"Get the door would you? My hands are full."

She followed him out, gazed at his fine butt encased in tight jeans. After pouring his drink, she stood beside him at the rail, the only sound the wind in the trees and the bickering of squirrels in a nearby oak. Everything smelled so fresh and clean. Even this man whose tightly muscled arm brushed hers when he lifted the glass to drink.

At last he put it down and reached in his pocket.

No more messing around. Time to get down to business. She spoke at the same time he did.

"Kathy was telling me about…."

"I brought this to…."

Their words tumbled over each other, and she stopped, waited for him to continue.

He held up a clear plastic bag, his eyes regarding her with calmness, reflecting the cool green of the deep woods. On the brink of submission, she reached for the piece of exquisite obsidian and tried not to touch him. He dropped the smooth black object into her hand. It was warm from being against his thigh in his pocket.

"Sheriff says he wants to withhold information about this." He pointed a stern look at her. "You can do that, can't you?"

A huge lump lodged in her throat, but she managed to smile at him. "Yes, I can do that. Can you trust me?"

Abruptly he snatched his gaze away and studied the mountain behind her. "I figure I can. You didn't tell what I did." A lopsided, questioning grin lit his somber face, and her heart melted like the ice in her glass.

Thank God she hadn't spoken to Parker or Mac about him going off like a half-crazed madman. In silence, she studied the exquisite arrowhead, each smooth chip forming a perfect point. Hard to keep her mind on business standing so close to him. Had she gone totally nuts?

Speak, woman. Say something. She cleared her throat. "So Kathy thinks it's probably a piece of jewelry. I do remember back when there were craft fairs everywhere, you saw a lot of these. After they decided it was against the law for people to dig up stuff like this and sell it, some of the craftspeople began to fashion their own for jewelry."

He leaned lightly against her to get a better look. She swallowed hard. "Um, they usually twisted a wire around the shank in such a way they could be hooked to a chain, worn as a necklace. Both men and women wore them. They were wildly popular, but silver arrowheads are more popular nowadays."

His breath feathered against her cheek. She continued with a great deal of effort. "I always wondered if an expert could tell the difference between what the crafters chipped and the real thing."

Shifting a bit more so their thighs touched, he fingered the stone. "Obviously they can. At least the Spaceys did. Wonder if there'd be any way we could find out who might have made this one."

Though she heard him, she couldn't reply. His shoulder, so close she could have laid her head there, his mouth within kissing distance, distracted her.

"No marks or signatures on it. Uh, Jessie?" The question seemed much more than her name, and she glanced up. Caught by the lure of those lips, she stretched to brush them lightly with hers. The immediate shock brought tears to her eyes.

"I didn't want to do th—"

His mouth covered hers, muffled the word.

Too late, oh, *shit,* too late.

She'd stepped right off that edge she walked.

A tingle headed for her toes, slowing to form a tight coil deep in her belly. Now she knew why women swooned.

His lips pulled away and he leaned his forehead against hers for a moment. "Sorry, sorry about that."

"Me too, I mean... no, it's okay. Uh, maybe one of the local craft organizations could help. I could, well, I'll call around if you like."

He straightened so their bodies no longer made contact. His breath came in long swigs before he spoke again, almost sounding normal. "Might be a good idea. Maybe we could get a fix on where our killer might have lived. Go ahead, but it's probably a long shot. And even if you did find the crafter, they probably don't keep records of the names of purchasers. Might not be worth the effort." He looked out across the yard. "Jessie." Not a question this time. Firm, almost harsh.

"Yeah, I know. It's okay. Don't worry about it. So, you'll let me lend a hand?" Tone an octave too high. This was ridiculous.

"Sure, lend a hand."

"Mmm. Okay, I'll see what I can find out. Did Kathy say anything else?" Peeking at him was out of the question, wasn't it? No. She'd just sneak a quick look.

He grinned, rubbed her arm. As if they'd become comfortable lovers. Shit. Not yet, not yet. She concentrated on what he was saying.

"She thinks they have enough bone marrow for a mitochondrial DNA. Too bad the college doesn't have the equipment to do the profile. Now all we need is a female relative. Mitochondrial is passed by the mother, but as I understand it a sister would carry it too. If we had teeth we might get a profile, but the guy has to be in LDLS or SDIS for an ID of him to be possible. Too bad it may be a year or more before we get a DNA profile." He shook his head, then grinned at her. "Sounds like alphabet soup, this new language, doesn't it?"

"LOL," she quipped and they both laughed. How good to joke around with him. Maybe he'd kiss her again, but he didn't make a move, and when he did speak, he was all business again.

"I guess what we have from Kathy is all we're gonna get for a spell."

"Then there's no point going in that direction, is there? I guess someone who's been dead and buried all this time doesn't exactly qualify as an emergency. Looks like we're just going to have to solve this without the help of modern conveniences."

He tilted his head and regarded her with such intensity her heart kicked at her ribs. The moment hung between them while neither spoke. Then he fiddled with his empty glass, and took the time to place it carefully on the small table. Maybe he couldn't think of anything to say either.

Two blue jays squawked and battled their way out of the top of a sycamore nearby, startling them so they turned to watch.

After the birds flew off through the tree tops, he answered her question. "Uh, the arrowhead was not the victim's jewelry. He was naked, so that adds to the probability that he didn't end up there by sheer accident. Our killer was smart enough to take off all the clothes, he wouldn't have left that."

"And here I thought you were communing with his ghost." She smiled and he shook his head.

"You're not going to leave that alone, are you?"

"Nope. You gotta admit, it's too juicy."

"Just don't put it in your paper."

She crossed her heart with an index finger. "I won't, I promise. Now, tell me what else they know about the victim that I can print. I need something."

"Okay, this you can print. It may cause someone to come forward with information. From measurements and condition of the bones, he was probably in his late twenties when he was killed. If they had the skull they could come closer on his age. But as to when he was put in the ground, that's up for grabs. A good guess is more than eight and up to twenty years ago, but Kathy stresses that's not very scientific. She's going by the lack of flesh on the bones and then there was some language I didn't understand."

"That's okay. I'll get that stuff from her in layman's terms. Odd, but I was just talking to a woman whose husband supposedly drowned back in nineteen eighty-nine. That fits in the time frame. She seems a tad nervous about this body turning up. I smell a skunk here somewhere."

His interest perked. "I heard about him at Butch's place. Uh, the Red Bird? I need to talk to this woman."

"Mary Smith. But—"

"Where does she live?"

She gave him Mary's address, and he jotted it in a small notebook he slipped from his shirt pocket.

"Mary wouldn't harm a fly." For a moment she couldn't go on, then made her decision. In this new life she had vowed to be ethical, so ethical she would be. "She—*Mary* was wearing a pair of earrings that looked a lot like this." She held up the arrowhead.

"When was this?" He stared at her, and she squirmed.

"Last week, when I saw her before the city council meeting... Dal?"

His face had gone stone still. "Our killer is a woman. Why didn't you say something earlier?"

A spear of fear lanced through her. "How do you know the killer is a woman? Now you are scaring me." She covered her mouth with one hand. "You can do what they say, can't you?"

Instead of giving her a direct answer, he said, "Two women, maybe only one did the deed. He was abusing both of them."

"Damn, why don't you just go arrest them if you know so much?"

He stared off for a while, then turned to meet her stare. "Funny, but the law won't take my word for it. You can as long as you don't print it. This belonged to a woman. Not necessarily your Mary."

Hair stirred along the back of her neck.

Was it possible he really could commune with the dead? Stranger things happened.

"It's not, uh, I'm not psychic. Well, not exactly."

"Well, what exactly?"

His scowl drove her to change the subject, fast. "What if the person who buried the body didn't kill him?"

He took the bagged arrowhead from her. "Okay, enough. If you were the least bit interested instead of skeptical I'd be glad to discuss it with you."

"What if I'm both interested and skeptical?" He obviously didn't take teasing too well.

He stuffed the evidence bag in his pants pocket, taking his turn changing the subject.

"If we could just find the gun that shot our victim, preferably in the hands of someone who knew the victim… if we knew the victim." He grinned. "Well, there are still a lot of ifs."

"I'd say so, even with your mysterious mind-reading tricks. Do they know how our guy was killed? And can I print it?"

"He was definitely shot. That's off the record for the moment. Kathy and Dave located a crease along the sternum, made by a bullet. From the angle, they determined he was shot in the heart, would have died almost instantly. Of course, he could have been shot numerous times. If the projectile went through the body without hitting any of the bones we have, nothing would now show up. But we do know for sure a bullet that would have been fatal went into the heart. Remained there till he turned to dust. Well, almost."

"We did find a bullet."

"A piece of lead from a thirty-thirty rifle."

"Of course, he could've been shot in the head first."

He grinned widely, and it did fantastic things to his moody features. "You ought to do that more often."

"What?"

"Smile. Smile like you just did. You don't have to be so tough all the time."

A darkness closed over him, wiping away the smile. "Oh, yes. Yes I do."

"Why? What could be so terrible that you can't let down your guard and have a good time?"

"You don't want to hear this." His voice took on a harsh tone, his features a savage blend of emotions.

Now she had stepped over the line she'd sensed earlier. In that moment she hung poised on the brink of danger. This was not the man who had kissed her moments earlier. No doubt about it, she could make a choice here that might put her at the mercy of a crazed man. What was wrong with her that she always wound up in situations like this?

Walk away. Walk away now. Tell him to go. Save yourself.

His eyes, so beautiful, so haunted.

Goddammit, don't *do* this.

Trembling, she brushed the back of his hand, the fingers long and strong enough to strangle her, break her bones. And she leaped off the precipice.

"It's not a sin to be frightened of what you might do, but you can't keep holding it in. Surely you know that." She might have been lecturing herself. If she told him about her own fears, what would he do?

His low resounding reply interrupted her thoughts. "If I don't, it'll kill me."

Another shudder ran through her. "It?"

"This thing inside me. This—"

"What, for goodness' sake? Tell me."

"Why do you care? This isn't something you can fix."

"I care because I'm a fool, I don't have good sense. Ask Mac. I like dangerous men. I like you. I don't know. What difference does it make why?" She grabbed his hand, placed it at her throat so the thumb lay to one side, the fingers to the other.

His eyes flashed, but he didn't pull away. "What the hell are you doing?"

"Squeeze," she said, teeth gritting over the word. She could no longer bear to see the anguish, the confusion written on his face, and closed her eyes, sagging so that he momentarily held her weight with that one hand splayed around her neck.

His grip loosened, he grabbed her shoulders and shook her. "Stop it, stop that. Are you crazy?"

The tears she'd held back slipped down her cheeks. "Yes. No. I don't know." And then she was sobbing, and he pulled her close, her cheek against his chest.

"You said you trusted me. Not a good idea." Her words, muffled by his shirt, were only half of what she wanted to say. She hated herself for making this moment about her terror rather than his. But he didn't seem to mind.

Fingers threaded through her hair, he lowered his lips to nuzzle at her ear. "It's okay. I didn't mean to frighten you. Take it easy, would you? Just take it easy."

The bigger and stronger the man, the less he felt capable of handling a crying woman, so she tried to stop. Huge, hiccupping sobs replaced the torrent of tears. She allowed him to hold her until they subsided, not saying anything more.

Doubling her fists, she pushed against his chest, and he let her go, though he could very well not have. A huge sigh exploded from deep in her lungs and she sniffled, rubbed her eyes, and tried to meet his questioning gaze.

"I'm sorry about that. Look at your shirt, look at the mess I've made of it." A huge wet blotch darkened the front of the crisp fabric.

"I only have one, too." His lips twitched, not really a smile, probably because he was still trying to figure her out. Still studying her closely.

"I'm sorry. You could wear my t-shirt again."

He didn't respond to her attempt to lighten the moment. "There's a laundromat next to the motel."

For a long while they remained in the dappled sunlight of the deck, standing a hair's-breadth apart, staring at each other. One of them had to break the silence so they could move on to whatever was going to happen next.

"Well, what was that all about?" she asked, fingering away the last of her tears.

"You tell me. Are you okay?"

"Uh-hum. Are you?"

"Yes, I think so. But you scared the ever loving hell out of me."

A laugh rolled up from deep inside her clenched belly.

"What's funny?"

"Oh, nothing. I was just thinking how odd it is that we humans hold back what we truly feel until something busts out of us. You and that crazy fling with the barbed-wire fence, and now me with" —she gestured— "with this."

"Some things are just too painful to talk about so they bust right out of us in the strangest ways."

"Okay, so you can't or won't tell me what your problem is, and I can't or won't tell you about mine. So what do we do now?"

"Maybe just cool it and see what happens." He turned his head to stare at her straight on.

"You reckon?"

"Well, you got a better idea?"

She studied him a long time, thinking how, at that precise moment, she'd like to screw his brains out, right here in the bright sunlit afternoon with squirrels and hawks as witnesses. The idea brought on another laugh.

"All I can say is it's a good thing you don't read minds." She squinted up at him. "You don't, do you?"

Green eyes smoky, he backed out of reach. "That's my secret," he murmured, then turned and went into the house.

She followed him through and out onto the porch. Watched him drive off. So much for that. He probably had read her mind and it scared him off.

Not an hour later the phone rang and it was him, his voice all over her like exploring hands. Chill bumps rode down her spine. She hadn't scared him off after all.

"We never finished our discussion. I didn't give you that quote."

He spoke without preamble. "I thought you might like to go dancing tonight. But I need to know the answer to one question first."

Did she dare let this go any farther? It might not be so bad. Oh, yes, it would be terrifying. And intoxicating. Besides, it was already too late. She could feel the pull of him even at this distance.

"Ask," she whispered.

"Are you sure there's nothing between you and Mac?"

"What?"

"Well, you have to admit—"

"Oh, my God. No. Me and Mac?" She couldn't help laughing.

"He treats you so, well, it's unusual, and I—"

"I love Mac and he loves me, but it's not that way at all. He was my grandfather's best friend, for goodness' sake. Dangled me on his knee when I was in diapers." Another giggle escaped and she wondered what Mac would say if she told him Dal's suspicions. He might be flattered. Men were that way, even old men.

"Jessie?"

"Yes?"

"Go dancing with me?"

"Where?"

"What?"

"Where do you want to go?"

"Oh, I don't care. You choose someplace. I don't know the town."

"Uh, yes." She felt stupid.

"See you later, then."

Dizzy with confusion, she hung up the phone with a trembling hand and went to find something to wear.

Charlie's, a western club out on Highway 22, would be perfect. Plenty of noise, and good ole boys and the slow kind of dancing her mother once called making love in public.

From the closet she took a broomstick skirt splashed in wild earth tones, a silk blouse gold as fall leaves, and leather huaraches. She'd go bare legged and bra-less so she could feel him against her nipples, her thighs. A shiver of desire rode roughshod through her and she embraced it like an invisible lover.

He showed up dressed all in black, like the first day she'd met him, except the shirt was western cut with blood-red piping. It hugged his broad chest, was tucked into slightly wrinkled jeans straight out of his suitcase. The snakeskin boots had been polished so the scuffs were invisible. The reptile skin wound round his hat presented a wild fantasy she did her best to ignore.

The cruiser waited out front, and he led her to it, hand snugged around hers. "I'm sorry about the transportation. Hope you don't mind. I flew in from Dallas with only a duffle bag to my name. It's going to take me a while to gather some keepsakes around me."

The statement charmed her totally. "Will Mac mind your taking me out in a deputy's car?" He cupped her elbow in one palm and helped her in.

He had her now, didn't he? Had her bad. And they both knew it.

He ran around to the other side and fitted himself in the bucket seat before he replied to her question. "I talked to him, explained that I'd take care of gas just until I could—"

"Gather some keepsakes around you?" Her grandmother's rocker, her mother's quilts. Yes, she knew how he felt.

"Right. He didn't seem to mind at all. In fact, acted delighted. I'm sorry about what I said earlier about you and Mac."

She shrugged. "It's okay. You didn't tell him, did you?"

He keyed the ignition. "I know how to keep secrets. Where to?"

She gave him directions and they drove along in silence for a while. Remnants of golden sunlight bedded down beyond the horizon and stars glimmered to life in a purpling sky. A sickle moon perched on the dark mountain peaks, following the sun to bed.

"Things are going to change a lot when that highway's finished." He shot her a smile.

Okay, that's good. Let's do talk about something sensible, get these fantasies out of my head.

"I know. It's kind of sad, in a way. Back in these hills there are people who still live the simple life without electricity or running water or telephones, because they choose to do so. Hell, some of them believe we've never walked on the moon or spent time in space. Hard to believe in the twenty-first century, but true. Sometimes I wonder if they aren't better off living in a world where life is so much simpler. I sort of hate to see it end."

His expression turned thoughtful. "Yeah, know what you mean. But most of us have known the awful truth for a long time. The human race is deteriorating, or at least becoming less human. I'm afraid small towns like Cedarton are doomed. It can't remain a no-traffic-light town much longer. It can't retain the laid back life, the safe life, the small town, southern America life. You trust people, you pick up hitchhikers, you don't lock your cars or your houses. That sort of trust will have to end."

"Oh, but I wish it didn't." she said.

"Yeah, so do I. So do I." A long pause unbroken by conversation, then he spoke. "You hungry?"

"Starved."

"Know a good place? I've been chowing down at the trailer with a can of soup or at Butch's for a quick burger."

"There are three places in town to eat. Butch's, Bee Swanger's Restaurant, and the Dairy Freeze out on the edge of town. That's a good place. We can order at the window or eat inside."

"Sounds good to me. I'm glad you're not a tofu and salad freak, or worse, a vegetarian."

She felt so good laughter bubbled out at everything he said. Would he think her goofy? Who cared? "I grew up on pan fried steak, biscuits, bacon and eggs, all that stuff that's supposed to be so bad for you, but somehow has managed to produce some of the hardiest people on the face of the earth. Maybe because you have to be strong to survive such a diet, I don't know."

When she laughed, he joined her. That made her feel even better.

They ate in the cruiser, joking about what Mac would think if they left it smeared with ketchup and littered with french fries.

"Oh, I think it'd serve him right for playing cupid," she said.

"Is that what he's been doing?"

"Don't tell me you hadn't noticed?"

He studied her somberly, then took another bite without answering. "Obviously not. Sorry about earlier. I thought—"

She giggled. "Mac would be flattered." Joking around felt so good. She chewed a bite of burger before continuing the conversation.

"You mentioned a trailer. Have you found a place to live?" Here she was, pretending she didn't already know about the trailer. Wasn't that lying, in a way? Would he know? Maybe she'd have to stop skirting the truth altogether if she was going to be around him much. The thought made her nervous.

His Adam's apple bobbed when he swallowed and he gave her that sidewise glance she was getting to know. The one that made her want to dodge so he couldn't see what was going on inside her head. Then he went on.

"Guess news does get around. It's over near the state park. It's not much, but it suits me. I worked off some of my mad cleaning it up. Could use more furniture though. Most of it looks like a whirling dervish lives there."

"You need to visit the Old Barn. It's close to Fayetteville. They have lots of used furniture and appliances. Almost anything you can imagine and the price is right. There's no delivery, but the owner will haul for a fee. When I found my cabin it was pretty skanky, but I knew I had to live there. It felt so comfortable, so safe. I had a few keepsakes." She glanced at him and he grinned. "Finished up shopping at the Barn. I love it now, except...."

He glanced quickly at her. "What?"

Shrugging, she bit into her hamburger. "Nothing." She still wasn't ready to voice the fear that someone was watching her in that safe place. Dal had already seen her crazy side. Besides, though she didn't want to think it, the sense of someone stalking her had come close on the heels of his arrival. Had he only been checking her out, or had she created the watcher because of how he made her feel? Hard to say. If he could truly read her mind, he already knew her fears, didn't he? Perhaps he was having some fun with her making out like he knew her every thought. Surely that was it.

Later at Charlie's, after they were settled at one of the saucer-sized tables, he rose and held out his hand. Feeling lost and so quivery inside she could scarcely breathe, she laced her fingers through his, slipped into his arms, and molded herself against his hard Leeanness. The top of her head rested in the curve of his shoulder and he curled her into an embrace. She did the same with him and, thigh brushing thigh, they swayed to a slow three-quarter beat before beginning to move around the floor. She went with him, led as if mesmerized by the grace of his movements, the limp not hindering his dexterity one bit.

They danced all the songs, the slow ones and the lively line dances, too, never stopping to sit or drink from the two bottles of beer growing warm on the table.

He took her home at three in the morning and surprised her by kissing her well and thoroughly at her door. And she returned the kiss and the embrace, melting against him in the shadows thrown by the porch roof.

"A perfect end to a perfect evening," he whispered. "Thank you."

Stricken mute by his comment, she rubbed her fingers over his jaw, and in the glow from the yard light, memorized the expression of contentment that softened his sharp features.

She was not ready to slip from his embrace, and so she didn't. Tantalized by the intensity of his desire, making itself known through the tight jeans, she imagined them together, her hands moving up and down that long, lean body, her breasts brushing his smooth chest. Making wild passionate love in the darkness. But it was far too early for that, and there were too many unanswered questions between them. Yet, in spite of the demons that pursued this man, and her own clouded past, she wanted to spend more time with him, get to know him.

Once again, she was on the verge of falling for a man who sent ripples of dark anticipation through her soul.

9
CHAPTER

After spending Sunday afternoon with Kathy and Dave Spacey, Jessie returned to work Monday morning eager to run down more on Mary Smith's first husband and his mysterious disappearance. Until there was a break in the story, it was all she had to go on. She told Wendy she'd be in the morgue if anyone called, and retired to the windowless room to scour back issues of the paper. It didn't take long to find coverage of the night of the twin twisters and floods that ravaged the area in May of 1989.

Time to learn more about Ken's drowning and find out if anyone else had dropped out of sight around here over the years. She had also told Dal she would call the local craft association and find out something about manufactured flint arrowheads.

The editor of the paper prior to Parker had been a young man by the name of Walden Corsair. He had moved on to a larger publication in the eastern part of the state when Parker bought the newspaper from its elderly publisher in late '89, several months after Ken's drowning.

While Corsair hadn't been nearly as talented a photographer as Parker, he had done a credible job as editor, reporter, and photographer in those earlier days when the newspaper was a much smaller publication and layouts were done by hand. A cut and paste operation that computers handled very well today.

In the musty back issues, she found photos of uprooted trees trapped under bridges, fields and roads totally inundated by rushing water. She read first-person accounts of the terrible Saturday night, May 21, when two tornadoes had slammed through the area, one around six-thirty in the evening, the other a couple hours later.

Poultry farmer Randall White was quoted by the reporter:

"We heard her coming before we saw her. I just did get the wife and kids in the cellar when she swooped down and took the roof right off all my chicken houses. Durn near scared us to death. Didn't do them chickens much good either. Missed the house altogether. Those chickens were strewed everywhere. Course we got most of them gathered up. They don't know but to squat where they're at, being raised in houses, you know."

The mayor at the time, Whip Morgan, said, "It was truly God's will for both of those funnel clouds to dodge Cedarton. Never heard of twin twisters in the same day and place. Creeks got up and flooded pretty bad. No wonder. It's rained steady now for several weeks with scarcely a break. And I hear some barn roofs were ripped away out at Dual Wilson's place and over to Sanderson's. Old Dual's tractor ended up in the top of a hundred-year-old oak. Hear they're having a time getting her down out of there. The flooding was the worst of it, I reckon, but thank the good Lord we only had that one fatality. Our condolences go out to Ken's wife and sister. Shame, it is."

The reporter went on to quote Mary on how Ken Norville had left his house to go to the grocery store and never made it back. After the tornadoes passed, his truck was found half submerged in the raging creek waters with no sign of him anywhere.

Jessie made a note to ask Dal before they went to press if he'd learned of anyone else besides Norville who had disappeared who might possibly be the unearthed bones. Or maybe she could get him to make an appeal in the paper for information on anyone gone missing in the past twenty years.

She jotted down the names of a few residents quoted in various articles. They would probably be happy to talk to her about the storms, and might even have pictures she could use for the historical feature piece. If she was lucky, others might have stories passed down through family members of previous floods. Best of all, someone she interviewed might recall a disappearance in the past. It was exciting to be working on a serious news story again.

Leafing forward in the bound issues, she found a report on the missing man. As flood waters receded, the search for Ken Norville's body had expanded toward Norfork Lake fifty miles to the northeast. All tributaries flowed into the lake from the northern slopes of the mountains. And then she ran across the headline—***Body Still Not Found.*** This one reviewed how Mary Norville had reported her husband missing Sunday morning after he allegedly drove off to go to town the previous night to buy beer, leaving Mary and his sister at home.

Maybe Mary was lying about his body being found. But for goodness' sake, why? For some reason, she'd appeared afraid the bones might be her first husband's, and then she'd changed her story. She might not fully understand that someone had to have buried it, but thought it might have somehow washed in under the bluff and been covered by silt. If that were true, why be afraid? The fact that the skeleton had been found with no trace of clothing hadn't been released.

Filled with anticipation, Jessie paged to the following week's issue and stopped at the huge, 64-point headlines that announced the killing of a sheriff's deputy. He had stopped to investigate a van parked on the side of the road leading to the state park and was shot dead for his efforts. Accounts of the tragic event effectively drove the drowning from the limelight. She found no further mention of Norville's disappearance.

Quickly, she leafed back and located the drowning victim's obituary. Memorial services had been held a few days after his truck was found hung on a low water bridge with only the roof showing. There had been no sign of Ken anywhere. She returned to the original story of his disappearance, complete with his picture, and read it carefully once again.

His wife Mary and his sister Jolene, who lived with the Norvilles, were quoted as saying that Ken, known for his foul temper and drinking habits, had downed one beer after another all day Saturday, all the while cursing the weather. Though the women begged and pleaded with him not to go out in the storm, along about sundown, he ran out of beer and left to go get more. He never returned and had never made it to town that anyone knew about.

Though she searched the remaining issues for the entire year of 1989 and into 1990, after Parker took over, no further mention was made of Norville. When all the hubbub of the deputy's murder and subsequent slaying of the lawman's killers finally died down, everyone appeared to have forgotten all about Ken Norville.

Engrossed in reading, she didn't hear Parker until he spoke from the doorway. "There you are. What's up?"

"You were already here in nineteen eighty-nine during the tornadoes?"

"Yes. I came here after Susan and I divorced in eighty-eight. Bought the ranch and then in October of eighty-nine, the newspaper. Why?"

"Do you remember the hoopla when Ken Norville was drowned?"

He cocked his head, scratched at an earlobe. "Vaguely, why?"

"Well, unless Corvair flat ignored it, a body was never found. Mary was lying about that. I wonder why?"

He regarded her quizzically. "So you still think there's a connection between the two?"

"I do. I know I'm jumping to conclusions. A drowned body wouldn't have been buried that deep, even given the amount of silt that washes down when it rains. Besides, there were no clothes. Someone would have had to deliberately decapitate the body, strip it of clothing, and bury it. Ken Norville wasn't… I mean, why would anyone bury the body of a man who had drowned?"

For a moment she studied the newsprint, not sure if she should tell Parker the rest.

"What? You know something else. Come on." His coaxing convinced her.

"When I spoke to Mary the other day she was wearing a pair of black arrowhead earrings that looked exactly like the pendant we found with the body. I'm not sure what it means, but it seems a strange coincidence, that's all. I think she's lying, but I'm not sure about what."

He shrugged. "Well, you know what to do, then. No one buries a body, unless they have something to do with its death."

"What do you suppose happened to the head?"

"Maybe the dogs carried it away."

"Yes, that's possible too."

"Maybe the dailies from that time have more information. By the way, that reminds me, there's been a reporter here from Harrison. Doing interviews, taking pictures. I expect something in today's issue of the News."

"Oh, great."

He grinned at her. "This is our story. Yours. And it sounds like you're already running with it."

Before she could object he held up a palm. "I know, I know, we can't scoop em. They'll be on top of it and have the story out before we can possibly get one on the stands. But, you know the local angles and there's where we'll have the better story as it unfolds. And with what you're uncovering, you know more than our intrepid young deputy does. That is, if you haven't shared with him. It's not about being first, it's about being the most well informed and factual. It's about the people involved. You know that." He touched her arm briefly. "You haven't shared what you have with him, have you?"

Misery crept around her heart. "About the earrings, yes. I had to, Parker. I won't do that anymore. He asked me to keep information about the pendant quiet, but he didn't say anything about Mary and her earrings. Still, would that be ethical of me?"

"You have an interview with her, but you can hardly include that she wore earrings like the pendant if you agreed to keep it quiet."

"Parker, I won't become that shark again, I won't join a feeding frenzy. I can't."

"I know, and it's fine. Get all your ducks in a row and write the story. Do what's right. Despite what many people think, an honest reporter is not an oxymoron. It's not so hard as you think. But you don't have to share your information with Deputy Starr, just as he doesn't have to share with you. Just write your story and make sure you attribute to your sources."

Staring through tears at the photo of Mary and Jolene grieving over their loss on the front page of the 1989 issue of the paper, Jessie nodded.

"Good for you." He squeezed her arm affectionately. "Before you go off half-cocked on this theory of it being Norville's body, check to see if it might have been found weeks, maybe months later and Corvair or I just neglected to run a piece on it. Maybe during the transition, after I bought the paper I missed it. It was pretty crazy around here for a while until I got myself situated in this confound business. Who's to say I didn't miss the release?"

"But then, why would Mary act so strange about it? It was weird, the way she hurried to tell me his body was found, after telling me it wasn't."

"You ought to know by now you never take anybody's word for anything. You have to check it out."

Staring at the news pages, a strange feeling washed over her. Was everything connected? Norville's disappearance, the discovery of the bones, and someone lurking in the woods watching her?

Still, she hadn't mentioned feeling watched to Dal or Mac, now she withheld the information from Parker. He knew about her past, he'd think she was having another breakdown. On the other hand, if someone were truly watching her, who might it be, and for what purpose? Wouldn't it be a good idea to tell someone? Just in case.

There she went again, creating something out of nothing. Miss Drama Queen, not happy to take anything at face value. And well she shouldn't. Journalism 101. That's what makes a good reporter.

The feeling of being watched had started after they found the bones and after she met Dal. That opened up all sorts of possibilities. Suppose Dal had ulterior motives where she was concerned, or for some reason needed to keep an eye on her. Or the killer was still around and didn't like her snooping. Wanted to scare her off. This was the more logical explanation, if she wasn't losing her mind and cooking up the entire thing. Experience told her she was good at that.

Parker was right, though. It was foolish to make assumptions before getting all the facts.

He interrupted her ruminations. "Hey, you okay?"

Coming back from her reveries, she managed a smile. "Yeah, I'm fine. Too much weekending, I think."

"I heard." He peeked at her over his glasses. "Hope you had a good time."

Jutting her chin at him, she said, "I most certainly did, and so did he."

He grinned and nodded. "Good for you. Okay, go ahead and look into this. I'm going down to Butch's and listen to some gossip for a while. Wouldn't want to miss any late-breaking news. Buzz if you need me."

As soon as he left she picked up the phone and punched in a number from memory.

Tinker answered at the sheriff's office.

"Hey, friend. I thought you were still doing duty over at the jail," Jessie said.

"Nah, it's my turn to sit behind the glass and direct visitors and answer the phone. Just like a real deputy. If Mac doesn't loosen up and let me out in the field, I'm going to leave this job and go to work flipping burgers out at the Dairy Freeze."

"I can picture that. Is Deputy Starr around?"

"No, but I can get him to call you. He said he was going out to see if he could interview Caveman Jake. Where shall he call?"

"I'm at the paper, or you can give him my cell number. Did he say how he knew where to find Jake?"

"From someone at Butch's, I think."

"Oh, great. Knowing some of those guys, they may have sent him on a wild goose chase just for a joke. Well, ask him to call me. Tell him it's important."

Tinker didn't answer for a minute, but Jessie sensed something coming. And it did.

"Heard you two went out Saturday night. From all accounts you danced the night away."

"Did Dal tell you?"

"Are you kidding? That man's mouth is rusted shut, for all the talking he does. Lane saw you."

"And couldn't wait to spread it all around, I suppose. And who was our alert Deputy Lane out with? Maybe I can put an announcement in the paper for him."

Tinker laughed. "Did you have a good time?"

"As a matter of fact, I had a very good time, and so did Dal, thank you very much."

"You didn't…?"

"That is none of your business."

"If you don't tell me, I'll think what I want."

"You'll think what you want, anyway. Tell you what, why don't you ask Lane? Call me Friday, let's get a pizza and rent a movie."

"Are you sure you and Dal won't be busy?"

"Say goodbye, friend."

"Goodbye, friend."

Jessie went back to the computer with her notes, and began a feature about the 1989 floods. She called a couple of people and spent some time on the phone getting juicy quotes about the "good old days," asking as well if anyone recalled Ken Norville's drowning or any other disappearances. Those sources, of course, were not trustworthy for facts in a murder investigation, but she had some crazy and good-for-a-laugh suppositions by the time she finished her feature and began an updated news story on the bones out at Kyle Foster's place.

No one could think of anyone who disappeared outside of Ken, except a fella by the name of Larry, who ran away with a waitress. Maybe his wife killed him and buried him, old Jed Loftin suggested with a wicked laugh. Not very likely, but then how likely had it been that Mary Smith was involved?

Jessie called the craft association and they checked their records regarding arrowhead jewelry. Ran into a dead end, other than learning that such jewelry had been available locally back then. Dal could decide what he wanted to do about it. Let him ask Mary where she got her earrings. See what that set off.

After hanging up she glanced at Wendy. "Hasn't Deputy Starr called yet?"

As if in reply to her question, the front door opened and Dal stepped in. Leaning down, he peered in at her.

She waved her fingers. "What's up?"

"Going to see Caveman. Wanna come?"

For a moment she was speechless. "You want me to?"

"Sure. Why?"

"I thought maybe it was Mac's idea."

He smiled. "Nope. Came up with it all by myself. I'm good with the simple stuff. 'Sides, the directions I received were less than clear. What if the black and white cow isn't in the field where I'm supposed to turn?"

Laughing, she grabbed her bag from under the desk. "You're in a good mood today. And I guess I'll come even if you are using me." He probably didn't want to discuss the outcome of the last time she started to show him Caveman Jake's abode.

Besides Wendy's ears were wiggling in anticipation.

He raised an eyebrow, but didn't say anything.

The logging road she pointed out was overgrown but discernible. It led through the woods past the grave site and Dal steered carefully to avoid hidden hazards. Or maybe to show her he wasn't really a maniac. In places, saplings had grown up so they switched at the underside of the vehicle as they passed. Overhead, buds swelled into tiny leaves, and under the trees, dogtooth violets bloomed in beds of old leaves. A slight breeze stirred creamy dogwood petals that floated through the air like huge snowflakes.

The sweet fragrance of spring improved her mood. "Park there. We'll have to walk in."

"Is it far?"

"See those bluffs? There's a cave just under them. We're actually not too far from where we found the bones, but it's easier to get up to Caveman's from here."

"I never would've found this. Don't you think you ought to leave your bag? It looks heavy."

"It is, but I might want to take pictures. Besides, I have emergency supplies in here. What if we get lost in the woods? We might need water or crackers or something."

He stared over the top of the vehicle at her. "Are we apt to do that?"

"No, silly, just kidding."

"I don't know, might be fun."

Flushing with delight, she looped the straps over one shoulder then the other so the pack rested between her shoulders. Together, they moved along a narrow path made by animals, Dal pushing aside low hanging limbs ahead of them. For more than ten minutes they climbed steadily, her leading the way. He bumped into her when she stopped abruptly and turned toward him.

"Whoops, sorry," he whispered, and steadied her with a firm grasp that almost made her forget why they were here.

"Careful, there," she said, keeping her own voice low as well.

"What are we whispering for?" he asked.

Slanting a glance up at him, she grinned and shrugged. A fine sheen of sweat covered his face and formed a damp vee in the back of his shirt.

For a long instant Dal gazed down at her. Being so close to this woman was turning him into a complete idiot, and what's more, he didn't care. Made him almost wish he actually could read all her thoughts, rather than just the occasional fleeting connection. He was pretty good at filling in the blanks. Ought to let her know, but he was having too much fun with it.

A drop of perspiration trickled from her hairline over her temple, and he reached out to capture it with a finger. Bemused by a sudden vision of chasing her through the sun-splashed forest, he failed to hear what she obviously saw. Her eyes widened, bringing him out of the foolish trance.

"Jake, how are you?" she said loudly.

Turning, Dal nearly bumped into a tall, bearded man blocking the path behind him. A long walking stick in one grubby hand, the man wore loose, dirty work pants and shirt. A tattered hat partially tamed his thick bush of salt and pepper hair. The lower half of his face and much of his chest were covered by a dirty white beard. Leathery skin disguised eyes that were mere slits. He didn't reply to her greeting.

The man's appearance so startled him, when he'd imagined them all alone except for birds and bees, that he let out a grunt of surprise.

"You're trespassing," the man said in a gritty voice.

"I apologize. We came to talk to you, if that's okay. My name's Dal Starr, you know Jessie."

"I know who you both are. You're still trespassing. No one asked you up here." He shook the stick, like he might use it if he had to, and Dal stepped in front of Jessie.

"Oh, don't worry, I'm not about to hurt you, but you got no business up here. I don't mess with no one, I appreciate the same consideration."

"I'm a sheriff's deputy, sir, and I need to ask you a few questions. I understand nothing happens in these woods that you don't know about. I thought maybe you could help me out, being as I'm new around here. You know how some folks are about those of us from away."

An amused glint flashed briefly in the squinting eyes. The breeze shifted a bit, blowing a sour odor their way. Since the man hadn't repeated his warning, but continued to stubbornly block any retreat, Dal went on.

"I expect you already know all about the bones Mister Foster's dogs dug up the other day. How long have you lived out here?"

Jake tilted his head and regarded the canopy of trees above his head, then after a moment or two, answered. "Seventy-one. That's when I came here. From away." He stopped long enough to flash a tight grin. "What year is it now? I haven't paid much attention lately. Figure it out for yourself and you'll know."

"It's the year two thousand thirteen, sir," Jessie said quickly.

Dal wished she hadn't, for the news appeared to upset the man.

He twisted in place, almost as if looking for a way to escape, hammering the walking stick on the ground a few times. "That late, huh? Reckon I ought to get busy, then, huh?"

The foul odor emanating off the man might have chased Dal away had he not been so intrigued by what could be hidden in that somewhat confused mind. If he was schizophrenic, he was having one of his better days. And he was definitely more intelligent than Dal had expected.

"I'd appreciate it if you could think back and try to remember if anything unusual ever went on over there in Kyle Foster's pasture. Down by the creek." Dal said.

"Near Jacob's Bluff?" Jessie inserted.

"I believe it was the year of the flood and the twin twisters," Jake said. "Woke me out of a dead sleep. What kind of fool would be out in that kind of weather? A pickup truck, and some idiot had driven it right across the fields yonder." He pointed through the trees down toward the creek. "Water had covered up the road, near filled the lower pasture, and he just drove through the grass, fescue it was and so thick the tires didn't sink in the mud. Headlights swept right over me where I was sleeping."

Dal's interest quickened, and Jessie squeezed his arm. The man could not possibly have dredged this up immediately out of his memory like that. Perhaps he was hallucinating. Or putting him on. That seemed a favorite pastime of people around here.

"What did they do? Did you recognize the truck?"

"'They'? No *they* to it, sir. In the dark, what with the storm, I couldn't see that much. Have no idea what he did. Lots of pickups around, then and now." Jake studied the toes of his shabby boots, lips moving but no sound coming out.

Dal waited a while, then gently nudged the man. "Pickups?"

It didn't work. Jake's head jerked and he glared at Dal. "What are you doing here bothering me? Can't you see I've got work to do? Time's a-passing faster than I suspected. Leave now. Stop invading my privacy. You think I moved out here so I could waste my time jawing? Go on now, leave me be! No wonder I never get anything done." He raised the end of the stick like he was poking at a bothersome dog.

Dal didn't feel threatened for himself, though he tried once again to shove Jessie behind him. She stood her ground, and rather than get rough with her, he gave in.

Feeling sympathy for this man, he said, "I want to thank you for taking time to talk to me. Perhaps I could come see you again later." He took Jessie's hand, inched past the pathetic creature and down the path.

The man hollered after them. "You come up here agin, better come ready to shoot me. I don't know nothing. Nothing."

Out of sight of Caveman Jake, Dal said, "Well, that was interesting. I'm not sure if this was a waste of time or not."

"Dal, the pickup incident could have happened anytime, but Ken Norville drove a pickup and he supposedly drowned and I can't find where his body was ever recovered. I've been going through back issues of the paper. You don't think? I mean, he did say the year of the big flood, and the twin twisters." She gestured wildly as they walked, warming to her subject.

"How many folks around here drive a pickup? The poor man is probably delusional. And who the hell is Ken Norville?"

For a moment she was confused. "Oh, Dal, I'm sorry. I told you about Mary Smith's first husband, but I guess I never mentioned his name. Ken Norville. You know, the old Norville place? We drove by it the other day. Ken and Mary and his sister Jolene lived there until he drowned in nineteen eighty-nine. And you heard Jake. How could he come up with something so on the money if he's just making it up?"

"That explains the two women," he murmured.

She stared at him. "You said it was two women. How did you know that?"

"Don't write this. You're just clutching at straws." He threw down her hand as if it were hot and headed down the path toward the Tahoe, gleaming through the trees.

On the drive back to Cedarton, he tried to think rationally about his tenacious attraction to her. No one could be more surprised than he, for women hadn't interested him since Leeann's death, and then all of a sudden, one showed him a bit of compassion and he ended up acting like a high school kid with raging hormones. And with a reporter, for God's sake. A reporter who now sat at his side, chomping at the bit to ride roughshod over everyone to get what she wanted. Who had kept information from him on an open case. A mere whiff of a story and the thin veneer of humanity split away to reveal what he had suspected all along. A ravenous hunter. He gripped the wheel and tried to concentrate on this Norville information.

"Dal?"

The sound of her musical voice made him flinch and he stared down the road. Don't look at her. Don't.

"You're not going to make a break for the fence again, are you?" The question held an attempt at humor.

"Hell, no." Damn her, couldn't she see the futility of this?

"Well, what then? I'm not sure why you're angry, but then you do tend to go off for no reason."

"It doesn't matter."

"Of course, it matters." She touched him and he tensed. He didn't want her to do that, to touch him, to soften her voice and be nice. It made him remember holding her in his arms while they moved around the dance floor, her nipples hard as beads against his chest, and him thinking maybe he could be normal after all. It made him remember what it was like to kiss her. The world turning upside down and a ravenous joy chewing away at his sorrow and filling all the dark places with light. He wished they could get it all together for each other. Knew they couldn't because of her insidious desire to ferret out a story above all else.

Teeth gritted against his anger, he said, "Tell me more about this Norville who drowned."

And so she told him what she'd learned. "Do you think it's possible he was murdered and buried out there? Who would've done that? I can't picture Mary in the role. She's not really the type, besides she's small and not very strong."

"She could've had help. And there are those damned earrings. Discounting serial killers, most murders are committed by people who know their victim and on the spur of the moment. Motive is usually jealousy, money, or a power thing. Most killers will never kill again and when they go undetected as long as this one has it's almost impossible to uncover any leads. I won't make the mistake of concentrating on this Norville until we know more. There may be others missing, maybe in another county, or state."

"Everyone has a conscience. Mary is already acting strange. She knows something she's not telling. I can feel her out, maybe learn more about her husband's death than she's telling. But this is my story, whether you like it or not. And what I find on my own is too."

"Don't think that surprises me. I ought to get Mac to lock you up."

"Just try it." Her eyes flashed.

She was right about conscience, though. Guilt and the fear of detection often made people behave erratically. "Well, more than twenty years is a long time to keep a secret. In that length of time Mary Smith may have convinced herself it never happened, and if it did she had nothing to do with it. You'd better stay out of it. You're not the cop here, I am, and I don't need your help running down a killer. And I sure don't need you to break the news in the paper that helps our murderer get away."

For a moment, she looked as if he'd slapped her, and her voice shook when she replied. "Then don't come hanging around asking me to go with you. And don't ask me to share what I learn, either. But don't worry, I know better than to mess up your precious case."

"You better hope you do."

Disappointment rode between them like a looming barrier. He'd made her angry, and she was staring out the window. That was fine, he was angry, too.

With much regret, he forced his mind away from her, where it'd never belonged in the first place. The intricacies of this case gnawed at him. Though his job didn't hinge on it, he needed to solve this one, his first assignment. A difficult task considering how many crimes were never solved. But more than that, he needed to get rid of this overpowering need to touch the woman beside him, to kiss her, to love her. To stop the world and haul her off somewhere. Make all the pain go away. He jumped when she spoke.

"Dal, I wish you'd stop being so obstinate. You can trust me."

"Can I?" He pulled to the side of the road and stopped, turned to look at her. The worst thing he could possibly have done.

10
CHAPTER

"I don't want to let us go, not without a fight," Jessie said softly and placed her hand over his on the wheel.

"We seem to do that well enough," Dal grumbled, giving just a little. Not much, but some.

"Yes, but I think, I believe it's only because we're both holding back so hard, trying not to fall."

"That sounds like a goddamned country song title."

She sighed, turned away to stare out the window. How could she expect him to fully trust her? For an instant he wished he truly could read her mind.

Nosing the Tahoe to the curb in front of the newspaper office, he remained immobile, hands fastened around the wheel while she hopped out. He should leave. Fast. But he waited until she crossed in front of the unit and came to his open window. He smelled the sun on her bare shoulders and in her hair.

"Look, Dal, I think we ought to call a truce. There's some stuff in our back issues you should maybe read about Ken Norville's disappearance."

Okay, here's a valid excuse to spend time with her and get some work done too. Not something he dreamed up to satisfy a deep down need to do so. He shut off the engine, sneaked a peek at her lovely face, innocence painted there like someone had brushed it on. Goddamn. Like he could trust her. He hung on to the keys dangling from the ignition. Gotta get the hell out of here. This he did not need.

"I've got some other leads I need to follow up first. No sense going off half-cocked." Good try, but feeble. The minute he'd heard about the two women and Norville's disappearance he'd had a gut feeling that here was the victim and his possible killers. Tying it all together wouldn't be easy, but she was right about catching up on the background. There would be a police report, a file on Ken Norville. Damned if he wanted to admit that newspaper stories were a viable source of information, though.

Irritation crinkled her forehead. "They're tied together. If you weren't so stubborn you'd admit it. Do you really believe in the coincidence of these things happening at the same time in the same place? And besides, Caveman did say a pickup truck drove through the fields to Jacob's Bluff the night of the twin twisters."

"That old man is high on something, and no, I usually don't believe in coincidence. Ah, hell, I suppose it's worth investigating. You do realize that someone else besides Norville may have disappeared. That guy who ran off with a waitress. I'll still have to look into that."

She backed off, started for the office, acting like she didn't care whether he came or not. The key dropped from the ignition into his hand. He opened the door, trailed after her because he couldn't stop himself. Didn't really try.

Streaked hair blowing in a breeze, she glanced over her shoulder. "Of course. Come on in, I won't bite, I promise." Through the trees, dappled sunlight kissed her cheeks.

Damn, he was a fool. Still he scurried to catch up before she slammed the door in his face.

"None of this goes in the newspaper, you understand, none of it. Mac says I can trust you. I hope to hell he's right." He tilted a look down at her. Too late he realized his mistake. He'd stumbled into her space where he could taste her, feel her, smell her. Much more and he'd be touching her. Lost. And he didn't move a muscle.

She gave him that look he was getting used to when he made any remark about her reporting. He shouldn't do that, but he couldn't help it. It was hard to learn to trust a reporter.

She crossed her heart with two fingers of her right hand. Second time she'd done that. "I promise not to print anything you uncover in your investigation until you tell me I can."

He grinned and believed her because he had to. So, he surrendered. Hell of a thing, considering everything.

What was she talking about? Oh, yeah. She'd said she wouldn't print anything in the paper. But her reply was carefully worded. The last time a woman made him a promise his life had gone right down the toilet.

I'll stop the drugs, Dal. I promise. He'd no more than turned his back till Leeann killed herself with that poison. Maybe that's what she'd meant all along. Her permanent way to stop. He'd better listen a little closer to what Jessie had to say.

She glanced back up at him through long lashes, and he let go his train of thought.

He wanted to tell her to stop looking at him like that, to stop looking at him at all. Instead, he only said gruffly, "Don't make me promises. You and I both know there's really no such thing as off the record with reporters."

"There is with *this* reporter."

His lips clamped over any retort he might make. A familiar darkness closed around his heart. It was all he could do to remain standing so close, not run like the coward he was. One minute he wanted to believe her, the next he couldn't. What he'd do was get the most information out of her he could and not turn his back on her for one minute. Figuratively speaking.

She led him between three cluttered desks, deposited her bag on the messiest one, and showed him into the morgue. The place was quiet and musty as its namesake, pitch dark until she flipped the switch that turned on a bank of fluorescent lights. Even then, the room was gloomy, the corners shadowed by stacks of newspapers. A funny smell, like old houses too long shut up. Bound copies of 1989's newspapers lay open on the long table.

"Sit. Read," she said, and stood behind him while he paged through each article, butt perched on a rickety stool.

The light fragrance of his aftershave reminded Jessie of when they'd danced together, her head tucked up into his shoulder. Though she wished things to be like that between them again, she didn't trust herself enough to make it happen. Out there on the trail today looking for Caveman Jake, she'd felt that old reporter's instinct for a story overwhelm all common sense. Dal'd been right to be angry with her, for he saw it too. Would she truly betray him to get this story? A week ago she would've denied such a thing vehemently. But then she had no idea such a temptation would come along. By returning to Cedarton she'd removed herself from that possibility, because nothing much ever happened here. Or at least she'd thought so. Now, it looked like she was going to be tempted after all.

Parker believed in her, and she clung to that. Tried to forget about being first at any cost. Still, whatever she found on her own was fair game. Wasn't it? Parker had said so. But he too was an old newspaperman who might do anything for a story.

She took a deep breath, and touched Dal's shoulder. He was real, warm, and dangerous. Probably the only reason she wanted to get to know him. Nothing new about that. She sure could pick em.

He shifted, shrugged her off, and kept reading. He wanted nothing more to do with her. And who could blame him? He knew her better than she did.

Saddened, but at the same time relieved, she moved away and propped herself on a high stool until he finished reading.

At long last he raised his head, glanced into the dank corners of the windowless morgue. "Helluva thing."

"What is?"

"How fitting the term morgue is for a place where out-of-date, musty newspapers are kept. Yesterday's news, dead and buried." His gaze grew distant and he shuddered as if cold, then went on. "I think we need more information."

He'd said we. "Well, of course we do. But what do you think so far?"

"I can't speculate."

"Nonsense, that's what you were hired for. Share it with me."

"I don't think so."

"I promised."

He shot her a look she couldn't read. Halfway between speculation and doubt. "I need to see copies of the daily newspapers that came out during that time."

"Figured you would. The library has them on microfiche."

He started toward the door.

"Dal?"

He paused, shoulders tight, then with a sigh he paused.

"I'm going there too. Doesn't make sense to take two cars."

Hand out he waited.

On the way to the library she told him about Mary Smith not showing up at the city council meeting after their talk concerning the sale of the Norville land and Ken's body. "I think her no-show is somehow tied to her husband's death and those bones, but I'm not sure how."

"You realize she will be a prime suspect if we find that her husband was murdered, never mind what we learn about the bones."

"Mary didn't kill her husband. She's such a timid little thing. I can't imagine her doing something like that, even though Parker said she might have had good reason. He was a brutal man, a drunk who didn't mind beating her when he was of a mind."

"I think he beat them both. The sister and the wife. All the more reason to suspect she killed him and has gotten away with it all these years. And that," he said gruffly, staring at her a moment, "is not for publication." Damn, why did he keep telling her this stuff? It just came out of him. Easy to see why the sheriff trusted her. She had a way about her.

She raised an eyebrow, glared at him. "On what do you base that theory?"

"I'm a detective." She accepted the words with a tiny grin that lit her lovely features. Damn, there she went again. Giving him all the reason in the world to like her, open up to her.

Apparently oblivious to the effect she was having on him, she went on. "All I know is, Mary didn't kill him, but if she did she had good reason."

"She didn't but if she did? You'd better leave the deducing to me. Think about what you're saying."

"Well, you know what I mean. I don't really think she's capable of such a thing, but I do understand that's how it works with investigations. The most likely suspect is usually guilty, even if it doesn't seem possible. All I'm saying is I hope you're not the kind of investigator who allows the probable to cloud the possible."

That she would criticize his techniques galled him. "It's called target fixation. And yes, I've seen some good cops get caught up by it. But I can do my job. Our speculations are getting way ahead of us is all. We're a long way from identifying our victim, let alone establishing a motive for the killing. Let's take our steps as we come to them. I understand you defending your friend. It's like the way you stood up for that pot grower, though. You need to use more common sense."

Encouraging how he kept saying we this and we that. Still including her, though he really had his doubts.

"Neither of them are friends," she said. "They're just ordinary people I happen to know who are caught up in circumstances beyond their control. And you need to quit seeing evil in everyone."

"Almost everyone has evil shadows in their minds. Be very, very careful who you trust."

A warning tapped at her nerves, but she ignored it. "I don't believe that. There are more good people than bad. Like you, for instance. Are you trying to tell me I can't trust you, Dal?"

"Probably better not," he said, only half joking, and the answer did little to calm her jittery nerves.

She nodded, and they rode along for a while in silence, then she said under her breath, "You haven't been watching me, have you? Since you came?" Immediately she bit her lip. Why had she blurted out such a question? She felt uneasy, disappointed in herself.

He shot her a quick look, mouth grim, eyes dark. "What do you mean, watching you? Why would I do that? Someone's been stalking you?"

"People get stalked in California, in Dallas. Not in Cedarton. But twice I thought I saw a shadowy figure. Someone hanging around the cabin back in the woods where I couldn't really see him. Keeping an eye on me for some reason. I went out there, didn't find anyone, but still, I can't get rid of the feeling. You know, the itch, hair on the back of the neck?" Lowering her gaze, she said softly, "Forget it, I'm probably just imagining it."

"When did this start?"

"I'm not sure exactly." She sighed deeply. "Around the time we found the bones. I thought he was there again Friday night before you came over on Saturday, but not since then. Forget it, I'm being stupid."

"Probably not. We sense much more than we actually realize. Most of us put aside those feelings because we don't believe in such things as second sight or being psychic. Why would you think it was me?"

"I don't know. I'm not sure I did think it was you. Not at first. Then, well, you've been acting so strange and I got to thinking maybe...." Helplessly, she shrugged. She would not tell him about Steve. It was none of his business.

He stomped the brakes hard for the four-way stop. Wouldn't look at her.

"I don't think it's you, Dal. I never said that." Now he was staring at her, eyes dark and menacing. An expression not exactly conducive to proving his innocence. A horn sounded and he pulled back out onto the empty street.

"I hope not, because I wouldn't do such a thing. Have you told anyone? Mac or your boss?"

"No. I decided I was just being foolish. It—well, it happened to me before and I—forget it, Dal. You know what? I don't want to talk about it anymore."

"For Christ's sake, why *not?* What happened to you? Who stalked you?"

"Never mind. I said I can't talk about it. Turn here."

Only Parker knew her background, and if he found out what was going on, he'd surely think she was going off the deep end again. Maybe she had to tell someone, and had blabbed it to Dal because he didn't have sufficient evidence to think she might be crazy. And maybe, just maybe, she wanted to lure him back on her side so he'd stop snarling at her.

Very good. Now she was analyzing herself. But something else went even deeper. If he truly could read her mind, then he'd already have known all this, and all about Steve too, wouldn't he? Bunch of bull crap and he was shining her on, that was all.

Whatever the reason, she wished she hadn't said anything about being watched, considering how he'd reacted. His allowing it might be so only frightened her more.

He followed her directions and pulled into the parking lot of the small library, an old building built of native rocks. Once stopped, he turned toward her, and she could tell he was more frustrated than angry.

"What's going on inside that pretty head of yours?" he asked softly, almost touched her before pulling back.

"Nothing, really. There are things I can't tell you, that's all."

"Oh, I'll just bet there are. So why did you even bring this up?"

Sometimes he sounded as if he were literally spitting words at her, like now.

"I don't know," she said. "And besides, Mister Smartass, if you can read my mind, why then, have at it. I won't have to tell you anything. Besides, it has nothing to do with us."

"Us? There is no us, Jessie. There can't be and I think you know it as well as I. And it doesn't work that way. If I went around being assailed by everyone's thoughts I'd go out of my mind."

Miserably, she nodded. He would have his way, but it broke her heart to give in to it. "Okay, Dal. Never mind. I'll handle it my own way. I shouldn't have said anything." She stared out the window.

The car rocked, the door slammed so hard she jumped. She expected to see him striding off toward the library, but instead he came to her door and motioned for her to unlock it. She did and he reached for her hand, held it as she climbed out, kept it all the way to the entrance, like she was a child he didn't want to stray. But he didn't say one word, not one. His anger was a palpable thing, stiffening his gait, squaring his shoulders, knotting his muscles and silencing his tongue. He hovered over her like a hulking monster. Once more she was vaguely frightened of him.

At the door, she tugged her hand free. "Don't yank me around like I'm your prisoner. I'm surprised you haven't cuffed me."

For an instant he gazed into her eyes, then lifting both hands in the air, gave her an I-give-up look and headed toward the information desk, leaving her standing there feeling even more foolish than she had before. Like the argument might be her fault.

And she had forgotten to mention that Parker wanted her to interview him for a story on his being hired by the sheriff's department. She could imagine his reaction to such a request, and decided to let it wait a while.

At the end of the non-fiction stacks she found him sitting at a microfiche viewer loading a reel of tape into it. There were only a few people in the small library. The hum and click of the viewer in the eerie silence only added to her sour mood. For a while she peered over his shoulder, but then she dragged up a chair and sat beside him. In order to see what he saw, she had to move in close, lean over so they touched. He shifted a bit to give her a better view, but didn't break the contact between them.

Without taking his stare from the screen, he said in a low voice, "I didn't mean to mistreat you. I guess I don't know how to act civilized in the real world. I'm still living with a narc's mentality. I need to clean up my act."

It wasn't exactly an apology, but she accepted it for what she thought it was. An invitation to be friends. Perhaps nothing more, but it was a start.

He stopped looking at the screen, slid his gaze around to her. "Sometimes I think I'm still under, and I act like that man I became." His voice cracked and he moved the film.

"Wait. I think there was something." She pointed at the flashing images.

Sure enough, the obscure article was buried on a back page of the *Harrison News*. In the changeover, Parker had missed the release.

It told how the search for Ken's body had been abandoned. There followed a short résumé of Norville's drowning and speculation that the body had been washed into the lake by the raging flood waters. After combing the river banks and sending divers down into the deep mountain lake with no results, the search had been abandoned.

"So Ken's body was never found," Jessie mused. And Mary had lied to her, to boot.

"Looks that way. I want to go to the courthouse and dig out the file, see what's there."

"Yuck."

"Why?"

"Hasn't anybody told you?"

"I guess they haven't, but that's not unusual. It's not the old 'records have been burned' story, I hope."

"No, but almost as bad. A few years ago they started converting all the county records into computer files. It's been a mess. I think they've worked their way back about five years in some of the departments, in others it's worse. Everything else is in the basement in boxes."

"Well, we'll just have them put one of the clerks on it."

Jessie snorted. "There's only one clerk, so you can dream on. You want it, you find it yourself."

"You're kidding."

She shrugged. "Nope. What's the matter, you got other crimes lined up waiting to be solved?"

His chuckle put them back on easier footing. "Thank God, no, I don't."

"Watch out what you wish for. You might be out of a job."

"That would be fine with me. I could go into investigating insurance fraud or searching for strayed pets, getting cats out of trees for sweet little old ladies, stuff like that."

She liked him better when he abandoned the smoldering rage. Maybe these brief glimpses into a less intense personality were who he truly was, deep beneath that stony, protective façade.

After getting a copy of the story from the printer, he rewound the film, removed the tape, and stacked it with the other beside the viewing machine like the librarian had instructed.

On the way back to the newspaper office he brought up once again the story Caveman Jake had told them. "I can't help but think there might be a vein of truth there somewhere. But he's covering up something. Knows way more than he told us."

"You can't put any credence in what he says."

"It wasn't exactly what he said."

"Oh, that other thing again?"

"That, and why would he make up such a thing?"

"It's not so much that he makes things up. He really believes they happened. But you've got to realize that, even if it did happen, in all probability it wasn't at the same time as our body was buried. He has no sense of time." Jessie shifted and captured a quick glimpse of his profile.

"I thought you believed him. Have you changed your mind?"

"Not really, I like to argue the other side. Sometimes it helps the thought process."

"Well, sadly, you're probably right about him being confused. I probably need another go at him. What a damned waste."

Sadly, he'd said I. Now that he knew where Jake lived, he'd be carrying on the investigation without her. Well, she could do her own investigating and without him. "I feel sorry for him."

"A lot of people endure horrible things. They don't all end up like that. I don't mean to sound merciless. Sometimes we all walk a hair's breadth from that life, I suppose."

From what little he'd told her, he probably had lived as a homeless man on the streets of Dallas in order to apprehend some drug pusher or killer. It wasn't the same as living that way because you had no choice, but perhaps he'd experienced that too. From what Mac said, he'd had a tough life. She hastened to change the subject.

"Parker wants me to interview you, write a warm fuzzy piece about the a-number-one investigator the sheriff's department has hired. You know, standard stuff. Where you come from, where you're going. Who, what, where, when, why, and how."

He jerked the steering wheel, slammed on the brakes, and parked against the curb.

Oh, damn. Without thinking about it, she'd lit on the one thing she should've let ride. Before she could defend herself, he pitched a fit.

"What did you call this piece of garbage? A warm fuzzy? I wondered how long it would be before you got around to this crap. Snooping into my past. Prying until you dug up some dirt. I don't need it. I won't have my name splashed all over your newspaper, and I certainly won't have you digging around in my past. It's none of your damned business. Nobody else's either. And if you throw that 'public's right to know' at me, I swear I'll...." Whatever it was didn't come out.

Well, that certainly wasn't a good choice of subjects. Though she'd expected him to say no, his vehement reaction stunned her, and it took a moment to respond. When she did it was with anger.

"You'll do what, have another battle with a barbed-wire fence? You sure do go off easy, Dallas Starr. It makes me wonder just what you have to hide."

"Oh, I'm sure it does. How many times have I heard that? Anyone who won't sit still for your nosing into their private life must have something to hide. Did it ever occur to you that some people don't want their private lives paraded around for everyone to read about? Well, I suppose you'll do what you damned well please. That seems to be what you so-called journalists consider your right, but I'll have no part in it."

She took a deep breath and wasn't surprised to see her hands trembling. Once again he had frightened her, and it took all her willpower to remain in the cruiser with him. All things considered, she wasn't so much afraid of what he might do to her, as what he might do to himself. This was not getting any easier, but nothing worthwhile did. At least, that's what she needed to think.

"Okay, no story. But you're judging me entirely wrong, Dal. You can't make me into one of those unfeeling reporters you've dealt with simply by saying it's so. The generalization doesn't hold up, and maybe I'll prove it to you one day. I ran away from that kind of journalism when I came here, and I'll never go back to it, no matter the consequences. Why do you think I'm working for this little backwoods newspaper? I've got the credentials to work for any daily in the state."

A knot in her throat prevented her continuing, and she stared out the window into the glare of sunlight, at perfectly normal people walking along the street, their lives as secret as hers.

He didn't reply to her question, and she tentatively laid a hand on his arm. The muscles tensed under her touch, but at least he didn't shake her off.

"I'm sorry if I tread in forbidden waters, Dal. I'll tell Parker you don't want a story. Funny, now that I think about it, he wanted the same from me and I refused. I don't remember being quite so violently vocal about it, though."

His glower showed he thought she was only trying to placate him. "Well, maybe you're just nicer than I am." He steered back out into the street.

Not nicer, really, just unwilling to call attention to her existence. She had plenty to hide, but didn't pursue that avenue of thought. She'd simply told Parker she preferred no announcement of her addition to the staff, and said it was for the same reason she would be writing under the name of Jessie West, rather than JJ Stone. He had ended in welcoming his new reporter, who had recently returned home where she belonged, and let it go at that.

She rode beside Dal in silence, studying the stubborn set of his jaw, determined to get back on his good side.

"Dal, could I fix you supper Saturday night? Maybe we can talk about this. I don't want you angry at me."

He braked at a stop sign, turned to stare at her. "Why would you want to do that? Why do you care if I'm angry at you?"

"Why? Maybe because I'd like to be friends. Because I don't like people being angry with me."

He sighed, but didn't look at her. "I'm not angry, I just think you and I, well, we don't mesh. And I sure don't need you feeding me, trying to get back on my good side."

"For crying out loud, you are the most exasperating man I've ever met. It was just a friendly gesture, not to be confused with acting like a perfect jackass."

"Well, as we've agreed, nobody's perfect. But that's all the more reason for me to wonder why you want to feed me supper."

"I'd like to spend an evening with you. Supper is extra. Oh, just forget it. I'll wait for you to ask, next time. I'm sorry if I offended you or overstepped my bounds."

"Don't expect me to ask," he said. "I don't need the complications."

"You can bet I won't. One minute you're friendly, the next you're like a great bear with a sticker in his paw. As far as I'm concerned you can go curl up in your cave and gnaw out your own thorn."

He didn't reply, and neither of them spoke when he let her out at the office. This time it was she who slammed the door so hard it rocked the cruiser. He stared straight ahead and pretended not to notice.

11
CHAPTER

Jessie's follow-up story on the bones was published on Wednesday, and the next day a pale and nervous Mary Norville Smith visited her at the newspaper.

"Could we talk somewhere else?" She eyed Wendy and the open door to Parker's office.

With a feeling of anticipation, Jessie led Mary through the morgue and into the small shady back yard where Parker had put a table and four chairs so they could get away from the office for lunch or just take a break and enjoy the fresh air. A honeysuckle vine covered the nearby fence, bees buzzing around the sweet golden blossoms.

Nervously perched on the edge of one of the chairs, Mary fidgeted and refused to meet Jessie's gaze. The woman looked like hell. Like she was coming apart at the seams. Each time Jesse saw her something else had gone awry with her appearance. Like the painting of Dorian Gray, she was falling to pieces. Today her brown hair was lusterless and straggly, and she wore no makeup or earrings, her outfit more frumpy than casual.

"I don't know why I—I came. I…." She broke off and gestured wildly, eyes darting.

Jessie leaned forward and touched her arm. "Calm down. What's wrong with you? You're nervous as a bobcat in traffic, and you're babbling. I've never seen you this way."

"That new sheriff's deputy?" Mary aimed a bloodshot challenge at her.

Puzzled, Jessie could only urge her on with a grunted, "Uh-huh."

"He came to see me yesterday. Asked me all kinds of questions about how Ken died. Do they think those bones are Ken's? I mean, hell, what's that deputy up to? He wouldn't answer any of my questions."

Now there was one heck of a clue to file. Her husband's bones?

Jessie weighed her reply, careful not to reveal much. "I don't think it's anything to worry about. He's just looking at all the old unsolved cases. You know how these big city cops are, think no one else knows how to solve a crime."

Gasping, the nervous woman wrung her hands. "A crime? My God, does he think Ken's death was a crime? I read your articles in the paper yesterday. It sounded lik—you think that the sheriff thinks—since Ken is the only one who has disappeared around here—that he might be…." She covered her face with both hands.

The moment the word crime had come out of her mouth, Jessie wished she could take it back, but it was too late. "No, no. I didn't mean it that way. It's unsolved, that's all. What happened to the body. I'm sure he doesn't suspect a crime."

Fingers twisted together in her lap, Mary took a deep breath. Uncertainty chased the wild look from her eyes. "I told you his body was found."

Crap. Now she'd told her too much. "When did that happen, Mary?"

"I—uh." Tears flowed.

"Mary, we know Ken's body was not recovered."

"Oh, dear me. I'm sorry I lied. I didn't mean to. I was frightened."

"I understand, but why are you so concerned about the bones? This body that was found was buried. It couldn't be Ken's, could it?"

She held her breath, watched Mary's reaction closely. Asking that was a calculated risk. What if the woman confessed to something? Then what kind of trouble would Jessie be in? Mary definitely knew a lot more than she was telling. Surely there were explanations that didn't involve Mary being his killer.

She took the woman's clammy hand in an attempt to soothe her.

Hazel eyes wide, Mary continued, as if unconscious of Jessie's touch. "Harold said that if that deputy bothers me anymore he would call the sheriff and complain. Called it outright harassment. He was pretty mad over you nosing around too, said if you didn't lay off he'd be by the office to speak to your boss as well."

"Lot of good that'll do him. Parker will set Harold straight. No one tells us how to cover news for the paper, nor what we can or can't write. You have to calm down. You're getting upset over nothing, I'm sure, I don't think Dal, uh, the deputy, will bother you again. I'm sure it's just his way of clearing up old stuff. Don't worry about it."

With her other hand, Mary grabbed Jessie's wrist so hard it hurt. A vague whiff of body odor assaulted her, as if Mary had been so distracted she hadn't bathed.

Lips twisting grimly, she shouted, "Ken drowned." With a loud swallow, she glanced around, leaned forward, and said through gritted teeth, "He got drunk and drove into a creek and drowned. If that deputy doesn't believe me he should ask Ken's sister, Jolene. She was there with me when the deputy came and told us they'd found the truck. She was with me all that night while we waited for Ken to come back from town. When he didn't, I knew, I just knew. Long before they came to tell us. Ken was a drunken fool and not afraid of anything when he had some liquor in him." She took a deep breath, struggled at control, then went on, as if once begun she couldn't drop the subject.

"I may have been lucky he died like that, you know? His sister too. He was getting, well, dangerously violent. We were both afraid of him. But that doesn't mean I, we, had anything to do with, with his death."

"Of course it doesn't. Did you tell the deputy that?"

Mary's eyes widened. "No. God, no. He'd think the worst, they always do, don't they? Maybe that's why he's poking around where he doesn't belong. He thinks I killed my own husband?"

"Oh, don't be silly." Now this was an interesting conclusion. Perhaps she'd have to change her mind about defending Mary.

The woman's grip on her wrist loosened, but she still held on, making Jessie uneasy. Suppose she did have something to do with Ken's death. Didn't they say after you'd killed once, the second time was easier? What if Parker found her bludgeoned to death out here? And no explanation. Jesus, she was being plain silly.

In an attempt to smooth over the situation, she gently pried away the fingers and changed the subject. "What about Jolene? Did she ever get in touch? About the land, I mean."

"What? Oh, no. We placed personal ads in all the Kansas papers. The offer for the land is too much money to let slip through our fingers, and the place is doing no one but a bunch of cows any good."

Obviously, of the two subjects, Mary now felt more at ease discussing the land deal. Time to get more information.

"You know, it will sure change life around here if they build a retirement community out there."

"Well, we—Harold and I—can't be responsible for who buys the land, can we? Certainly not what they do with it. I mean, is it our duty to sell only to someone who will leave things like they are? Harold says that's ridiculous and he has no intention of worrying about what gets built there. We all die sometime, and then what control do we have over anything?"

"Why did you come to me, Mary? What do you think I can do?"

"Well, you're friends with that deputy, aren't you? I mean, more than friends, I understand, and you work for the paper, so you can find out things from the police that people like us, like Harold and I, can't. I thought you might…." Mary chewed on a nail, watched Jessie.

More than friends? She'd forgotten how quickly things got around in a small town. "He doesn't have to tell me anything, despite what you may think."

"What about Freedom of Information? Harold says—"

"That doesn't cover criminal cases under investigation."

"Under investigation? What the hell am I going to do?" Quite distraught, she tugged at a lock of her hair and gnawed at her lip.

No matter what she said, this woman was ready to climb the nearest tree. "Calm down, Mary. You have to get hold of yourself. This is doing you or no one else any good. Why don't you go home, make yourself a cup of hot tea, and lie down?"

"Yes, maybe I'll do that. I apologize. I really do, it's just that all this has dredged up some very unhappy memories, and then not being able to find Jolene and settle this land deal has only made matters worse."

And it wasn't helping that Harold was on her case. The poor woman hadn't much luck with her men, but then she wasn't the only one, was she?

Shoulders slumped, Mary trudged out of sight around the building. As much as Jessie hated to think it, Dal might have been right in his suspicions. Yet she couldn't believe Mary was actually capable of committing murder and then covering it up for so many years. Still, maybe she did know something about Ken's death she had never told. If anything, Mary's current husband Harold was a more likely suspect.

Yet she'd rather believe that if anyone did away with Ken, it was that crazy old man living in a cave near where the body was buried. He certainly had the opportunity, and look how quickly he'd shut up after saying he saw the pickup that night. Ken's pickup? Certainly possible. If he had killed Ken, what motive could he have had? An interesting question. And one worth pursuing.

Inside, the office remained quiet, and she sat at her desk for a while doing nothing but thinking. No way to get around it, she had to tell Dal about Mary's visit. Finally she picked up the phone and punched in a number. Tinker answered and promised she would relay a message to Deputy Starr. She thought he was at the courthouse.

"He mumbled something about being up to his butt—and a fine butt it is—in old files. Anyway, he's going through records down in the basement over there. You couldn't drag me into that creepy place. Hey, friend, we still getting pizza and renting a movie tomorrow night?"

"You bet."

"And how are you and our awesome deputy getting along?"

"We're not."

"Uh-oh. I figured that was too good to be true."

"For him or me?" Jessie snapped.

"Whoa, friend. I think I'll just change the subject right quick. What time Friday?"

"Whenever." Jessie tapped her pen on the desk top, mind a million miles from pizza and a movie.

She jumped when Tinker's voice came through the earpiece. "You still there?"

"Uh-huh. You say Dal's at the courthouse? Think he'd still be there?"

"Probably, the way he talked."

"Tell you what, just round-file that message. I'll catch him there. I've got something to talk to him about that can't wait."

"Can't say as I blame you."

"Tinker," Jessie warned.

"I know, I know. Say goodbye. Meet you at my place around six tomorrow. Okay?"

"Fine." Jessie nibbled at her lip, tossed the fat daily planner into her bag, and told Wendy where she was off to, uncomfortably aware that she had no business going anywhere near Dallas Starr.

The basement of the old courthouse was not exactly her idea of a great place to face him again. Dark and quiet and very private. All county offices had been moved into the renovated brick post office building in the center of the square. The hundred-and-twenty-year old rock structure with its clock tower and massive, high-ceilinged rooms, was being utilized as office space by a bail bondsman, a couple of attorneys, and an insurance firm. And storage for all the county's records dating back to the founding of Cedarton in 1849. It was also being restored to its original glory.

The old building clung to a steep incline above Cedar Creek, so that the back entrance led into the main floor. The front entrance higher on the hill led to the second floor.

She parked in the lot out back and went inside. Above her head, two men worked from scaffolding. Hooking the backpack over her shoulder, she treaded carefully on canvas spread over the marble floor. Blue, red, and gold light filtered in through stained-glass windows in the high-domed ceiling. The whine of a saw pierced the dusty air. Ducking beneath a cross hatch of two-by-fours, she took the flight of stairs that led down into the basement. She could barely make out the steps dimly lit at the bottom by a weak rectangle of light. A damp smell of plaster and newly sawed wood hung in the narrow hallway. Moving carefully, she spotted a dangling bulb with a chain and pulled it. Nothing happened.

After descending a few more steps she heard a footfall from above and twisted to peer over her shoulder. A shadowy figure paused at the top of the stairs for an instant, then slipped away. A shiver trailed through her, stirred the hairs on the back of her neck and along her arms. Probably just one of the workmen. Her thudding heart didn't believe that for a minute. She hurried down toward the dim glow of light, the heavy bag thunking against her side. The door stood ajar and she slipped through, waited there a moment to allow the thundering in her temples to ease.

From above came the echoes of conversation and laughter broken by a staccato hammering and the continued whine of a saw. A workman, that's all it'd been. As jumpy as she'd been lately, she'd probably imagined the whole thing. Even so, it took a while for her pulse to slow to normal. When it did, she moved quietly toward the room where all the old records were kept, out of which stretched a patch of light.

Dal was seated at a table surrounded by boxes, head bent forward in concentration. A single bulb burned above him and some daylight seeped in through a dirty narrow window to one side. As she stepped into the room something sticky fingered over her face and caught in her hair.

She let out a startled cry and pawed at the thing, which turned out to be an enormous cobweb that latched itself to both her hands.

He came to his feet, knocking the chair backward. "What in hell?"

"It's just me. I'm sorry. I'm not usually so freaked, but I thought someone was following me, and then that thing floated down around me like a shroud. Did I frighten you?" She picked gossamer webs from her face and fingers.

"Oh, hell no, I always look like I've been goosed by a ghost. What are you doing here, anyway?"

Hmmm. Not any too glad to see her. "Well, don't worry. I'm not here to invite you to supper or anything. I found out something important, and when I called to tell you, Tinker said you were over here. It was so strange, weird really, that I decided I'd better just come on over and tell you. Can't have you thinking I'm hiding evidence."

He waited a moment, then asked, "Well, what is it?"

She shifted the bag, took it from her shoulder, and lowered it to the dusty floor.

He didn't return to his chair, nor offer to empty the other one in which he had stacked several file folders. Instead he stood there glaring at her as if he might scalp her, given the chance. "Well?"

"No need to be so kind, I haven't been sick. Mary Smith paid me a visit, and she was acting spaced out. Wanted me to find out what you were up to concerning Ken's death. She said, several times in fact, that the bones absolutely couldn't be her husband's, then promptly supplied herself and her sister-in-law with an alibi for the night he died. Claims very defensively that they were together the entire time."

He lifted an eyebrow. "Oh? That's interesting. What did you tell her?"

"None of your secrets, I assure you. I reminded her of something to bait her, but it was already in the paper. I just said that the body we found was buried and couldn't possibly be her husband's."

He shrugged. "And that's all? You didn't mention anything else?"

"No, of course not."

"Well, what'd she say or do?"

"She admitted to lying about his body being found, then she got off on the land deal and the disappearance of Ken's sister, Jolene. I think she knows something, maybe even who killed her husband. It might be Harold."

"Well, now, there's a leap if I ever heard one. Hell, we don't even know if the body is that of her husband."

His reaction angered her. "You're the one who called her a 'prime suspect.' You even went to see her. That's what sent her running to me. You're the one who's accusing her of murder, not me. So climb down off your high horse. I just said she might know something. As far as I'm concerned we, uh, you ought to look at other possible suspects."

"Thanks for the advice. As for the way I'm running this investigation, I don't owe you an explanation, dammit. I'm the cop, you're the reporter."

"How could I forget it? You remind me every other word out of your mouth. By the way, that's investigative reporter. In the annals of crime and law breakers, some of us often come up with stuff you guys miss. Anyhow, what's your problem with me? What are you afraid of?"

If only he'd tell her so she'd know if it was the same thing she was afraid of. That they'd do something incredibly stupid, like fall in love.

His sharp gaze made her conscious of being alone with him in the dark, eerie basement. Amid the mossy smell of old files and gathered dust, she caught a whiff of his aftershave, felt his body warmth drift over her. He moved closer, picked a strand of cobweb from her hair. Pulse throbbing, she remained very still, staring at the top button of his shirt. His fingers trailed down across her temple in a gentle, brief caress. All she wanted, all she feared, was him taking her in his arms. Then all would be lost.

But he didn't. Instead he tantalized her further.

His fingertips drew warm lines down her cheek, past the ridge of her jaw to her throat, moved under her chin, and tilted it upward. He leaned forward as if to kiss her, and she swept her gaze over the full lips and somber eyes that drifted closed, long dark lashes curling on his cheeks. He groaned softly down in his throat, awoke the passion asleep within her.

Fire glinted in his eyes. If he hadn't caught her she would have dissolved into the dust. He gripped her arms. Hard. She thought for a moment he would shake her like a misbehaving child. Instead, he pulled her against his chest, captured her mouth with his, hungrily devoured her lips in a raw act of possession. Excruciating in its desperation, his sweetly silken tongue explored her mouth, and she twined her own around it. Loosening the vicious grip on her arms, he grabbed fistfuls of her hair, the wild, demanding kiss sucking away her breath.

Caught up in a maddening desire, she closed her eyes and clung to him.

His harsh embrace, the flames of his brutish passion, drove her mad with desire. Her breasts ached, her loins throbbed, and she submitted totally to the demands of his searching mouth, the furtive exploration along her backside, across her belly, upward to cup her breasts. Fear fed her lust until it became a rampaging beast that he freed with his hands, his mouth, his demands. All her past memories faded into the darkened corners of the room, and she gave herself completely to him.

Groaning, he tasted deeply of the inner softness of her mouth. His muscles hardened against hers, the urgency of his desire probed, searched, found.

He lifted her onto the edge of the desk, scattering files to the floor. Frantic hands ripped off her shirt and bra, then tore at the zipper of her jeans. She worked loose his silver belt buckle, yanked his uniform shirt from the waistband of his pants and ran her palms over the rippling muscles, so warm, so alive. Mouth abandoning hers, he nibbled over her chin, down, down, into the crevice between her bared breasts.

He searched out one nipple, then the other, traced each with a tongue hot, moist, desperate. Licking and biting and sucking at every inch of her flesh, his fingers trailed down her belly and between her legs, exploring until she moaned with ecstasy. Cried out and let go the bonds that kept her anchored to reason. Soared beyond reality to a place filled with a thousand stars, a million dreams.

"Give me your hand," he ordered, voice hoarse with passion.

Pulling her back from the edge only a bit. She did, and he placed her fingers around his erection.

"Hold on, Jess. Just—hold on," he whispered. "Don't let go."

His heart beat in the palm of her hand, the skin hot, smooth as satin, burning, rigid, ready.

Slowly, he lifted her. "Okay, move your hand."

She did and, as her legs coiled around him, he slipped deep inside her, drove into her core, and set off an explosive euphoria.

For a long, exquisite moment he did not move, but held her locked to him while he throbbed inside her, became one with her electrified rhythms.

"Is this what you wanted?" he whispered in her ear.

"Oh, yes. Yes."

"Is it all you wanted?"

"I—no. *Yes!* I don't know. What do you want?"

He began to move as if they were dancing until he pressed her against the wall. Through gritted teeth, he matched each thrust with a word. "Fool. That. I. Am. I want this."

The pounding increased, tossing her into a wild whirling storm of fury. Of rage. Of uncontrollable dark cravings. And then he came with that same fury, filling her, clutching at her, nose and mouth buried against her neck to muffle the deep-throated growl that tore from his throat.

Her body's passion raced to catch up, sent her panting into exhaustion until all she could do was hang on. Shed tears of anguish, of pure joy, of terror, as he lowered her to the desk, cupped her face in both hands, and tenderly kissed her eyes, her cheeks, her mouth.

This time kissing him was like sinking slowly into warm water, and being massaged with aromatic oils while night breezes caressed her bare skin. She longed for a bed, clean sheets to lie upon. Longed to hold on to him, breathing in his essence, caressing the ridges, planes, mounds of his beautiful body. Longed to lie with him throughout the dark velvet night.

When he disconnected from her, moved out of reach, she wanted to cry for him to come back, to stay with her. No words would come out.

He turned his back to fix his clothing, tossed her a white handkerchief. "Here, clean yourself up."

The tone of his voice left her feeling abandoned, somehow ashamed of her own feelings. She took his hanky and used it, then buttoned her shirt and zippered her jeans. Her raw insides throbbed with an exquisite gratification new to her.

Never in her life had she had such sex. So untamed and urgent, so loving and tender. So terrifying. She began to tremble and couldn't stop.

"I have to go. I can't—"

"Not what you wanted after all?" he asked, staring at her, standing out of reach. The swaying bulb cast eerie shadows across his unreadable features.

"Oh, yes. I mean yes, it was exactly what I wanted."

"Oh? You'd better go, now that we've both had exactly what we wanted."

The crisp and unemotional words battered at her senses. He was mocking her and she didn't know why.

She gazed at him, feeling him still inside her. His frenzied mouth at her breasts, her nipples rigid with the memory. Aching for more. "You're angry with me."

"I'm angry. Not with you."

For a long moment she regarded him, confused and a bit angry herself. Then she wadded the handkerchief into her pack and picked it up off the dirty floor. "I wish I understood."

"Yeah, me, too. Go on, get out. Let me get back to work."

Jessie drove straight home without stopping at the office. It was late and besides, she needed to run as fast and as far as she could from what had happened between her and Dal.

After she took a long shower that did little to wash away the smell and feel of him, she padded naked into the bedroom. Lying on the bed pillow was a piece of tablet paper. The kind they once used in grade school with the wide lines on it. There were letters, words, scrawled on it, but she couldn't read them. Her eyes went wildly out of focus, blurred by a kind of horror she'd known before.

Frozen in place, she stood there a moment, hands cupped over her mouth, pitiful sounds erupting from deep within her.

Hold on tight.

Don't scream.

Don't let go.

Don't let the terror loose again.

Naked. She wasn't dressed. The shades open. She scrambled to the floor, put the bed between her and the window. Hunkered there, heart thumping so fast and hard she couldn't breathe.

Someone had been in her house, in her bedroom, on her bed. Touching—touching her sheets. Vile body sitting where she slept.

Dear God, it was starting all over again.

She had no idea how long she remained in the evening shadows of her bedroom before she summoned enough courage to read the words on the paper.

I KNOW WHAT YOU DID
LEAVE OR I'LL TELL

She bit her lip and choked on a scream that ran from her mouth in dribbles. She dare not close her eyes, for then she would see Steve's face, twisted with hate, telling her she'd better run far, far away or he would find her and pay her back for what she'd done. She would never forget it, nor her betrayal. Never. How could she forget that her foolishness and desire for a story had caused the end of her own career and destroyed the man she loved? Caused him to hate her with a caustic savagery.

Had he somehow found her? Prowled in her things? Put this here? But to what purpose after all this time? Think. Think about this. No, not him. Not his way. He'd have been sitting there on the bed when she came home, her Steve. But if not, then who? The possibilities were even more terrifying.

Dallas Starr had the time and opportunity.

Hands over her mouth, she let that sink in.

His hands on her, like searing brands that wouldn't cool. Bile surged in her throat and she whirled, stumbled into the bathroom, and knelt gagging over the porcelain bowl.

After a long, miserable bout that left her stomach sore, she brushed her teeth and took another shower. For a very long time she let the hot water wash over her face and into her mouth, but she still felt soiled. In her robe, she checked the doors and windows one more time, then curled into a ball on the couch. Much later, monsters of her dreams chased her awake, drenched in night sweats.

The terror had returned, and there was no place to run.

12
CHAPTER

Startled awake, Jessie crawled from a frightening dream, mouth open in a silent scream, unable to move.

Panic rose up the back of her throat.

Where was she? Her apartment in California? Waiting for Steve to come knocking?

No, not there, but a room, dimly lit by the rising sun.

Hugging herself, trembling, she managed to sit up. Shadows of furniture in the golden glow. A dull throbbing at her temples blinding her so she couldn't identify her surroundings. On closer inspection the familiar recliner, end tables, Aunt Bessie's ugly lamp shaped like a starved elephant. Grandma's rocker padded by one of her crocheted afghans.

Ah, she was in her own home. And she lay on the couch in her robe because? Because he'd been in her bedroom, left a terrifying message on her pillow. But who was he?

Fingers massaging her temples, she stumbled into the bathroom and gulped down three aspirin with icy water. Dared not glance in the mirror, but rather raced back to the living room, dug around in folds of the afghan and finally found the phone, punched in the paper's number. When Wendy answered, she asked for Parker.

When he came on, she croaked, "I'm sick, I can't come in today."

"Sick? What's wrong? Can I do anything?"

"No, I just, I need to take the day off."

"Well, sure, fine. Don't worry, but in the time you've worked here you've never been sick. What is it? Have you seen a doctor?"

"No. What is this? I guess I have a right to a sick day, don't I?" Ashamed of flying off the handle, she disconnected before he could reply.

Damned inconsiderate, snapping at her boss and friend that way. Maybe she should kick the cat, if she had one. She should get one, just in case she needed something to kick later.

The closed bedroom door all but shouted at her to enter, face her torment. She wasn't about to. Not yet at any rate. Not when she had the furniture to dust, the floor to clean, and hey, maybe she ought to wash the windows. In all but the bedroom, that is. Not wise to clean anything he might have touched with his filthy hands. Fingerprints? But that would mean telling everyone what happened. He wore gloves. They always did.

First she'd dress, but her clothes were in there, too. There were those in the bathroom she'd stripped off when she came home, what she'd worn when she and Dal—nope, don't go there, either. He was all over them and she didn't want to think about him either. So, she'd clean in her robe. Nothing wrong with that.

Some time later, she propped the dust mop in the corner. Time to face the demon before she wore out the floors.

Feeling like a coward, she twisted the knob and slipped through the opening, still refusing to look at the bed. She straightened her jewelry box so that it aligned perfectly with the back corner of the chest. Maybe the note had been a hallucination. That was something to hope for, but then she'd have to go have her head examined in one of those tube things that drove people to claustrophobia. Or drove claustrophobics wild.

So, okay, look at the bed. Get it over with. Just a quick peek.

Yep, she was sane. The piece of paper still lay on the pillow, proving she wasn't crazy.

Okay, this was good. Right?

Anger replaced the helpless terror that kept her knees knocking, and she went to the bed, wadded the thing into a tight ball, and tossed it in the waste basket. Still not satisfied, she stripped the bed. He could have lain on it, satisfied whatever psychotic fantasies he indulged in.

When the sheets were agitating in the washing machine with plenty of bleach and detergent, she pulled on a pair of shorts and a sloppy shirt, carried the pillows out on the deck, and tossed them into a pool of sunlight. While she huddled there, arms crossed tightly across her breasts, daring the bastard—whoever and wherever he was—to take a good look, the telephone rang. If she didn't answer, the caller would drive out to see what was wrong, so she went inside and picked it up.

It was Mary. "Parker said you're sick. I'm sorry to bother you, but I desperately need to talk to you."

"I'm feeling better, thanks so much for asking." There she went, kicking the cat again.

"Oh—yes, of course. I didn't mean—I'm sorry. How are you feeling?"

"I'm okay." She sighed and chastised herself. If anything, the woman sounded more upset than she herself. "I'm sorry, Mary. Come on out. I don't have anything catching. In fact, I'm not really sick, it's just one of those days."

"Well, if you're sure. I mean, this is really important or I wouldn't bother you. I'm scared to death and I don't know who to talk to. There is no one but you."

Ah, maybe this would be a break in the story. She cleared her throat and tried not to sound too eager. "It's all right. I'll be waiting with a pot of coffee."

"Thank you. Thank you so much. I won't be but a few minutes."

She had scarcely put on the pot and remade the bed when she heard a car pull up and the door slam. Mary must have run all the way to the house because a loud knocking rattled the screen before Jessie could get there to let her in.

The woman's plunge into coming totally undone had bottomed out. Her hair spiked in all directions, she wore old sweats stained with coffee or tea, and muddy sneakers, and acted skittish as a new colt. Black shadows circled her bloodshot eyes, and she couldn't seem to keep from gnawing on her fingernails. In her free hand, she clutched a wadded piece of paper that she thrust out.

One look and Jessie's heart dropped into her shoes. Tablet paper with lines and the same letters she'd seen earlier.

"Read this. My goodness, I can't believe it. How can this be happening?"

Jessie smoothed the paper and read the crookedly printed words aloud.

DON'T WORRY, I WON'T LET ANYONE HURT YOU.
I SAW WHAT YOU DID, BUT I NEVER TOLD.

"Sweet Jesus," Jessie breathed, and swallowed hard to keep from retching. Same printing, nearly the same message. But this one didn't seem threatening. Sounded almost as if the anonymous writer was reassuring Mary.

"Who do you think wrote it?" Mary babbled. "What does he mean?"

Mary was about to crawl the wall, and Jessie right behind her. To keep that from happening, Jessie squawked a few reassuring words from a throat so tight she could scarcely speak.

"Some sort of joke. 'I saw what you did'? Mary, somebody's putting you on. Someone who's been watching too much television. Kids do this kind of thing when they're bored."

Oh, how she wished that were true. Maybe she ought to drag out her note, show it to Mary. They could compare them. But she was afraid that would really send the woman off the deep end. She was inches from the edge already, with Jessie right on her heels. They could link hands and jump into the abyss together.

Mary grabbed her by the arm. "It's not a joke. That's not all. I—I can't even think straight."

"Come on, let's get some coffee, and go out on the deck. In the light of day, the worst nightmare can usually be put in its proper perspective." Well, at least she sounded convincing.

The distraught woman followed, accepted a mug of the steaming brew, and trotted dutifully outside like an obedient child.

Tossing nervous glances in all directions, she asked, "Can anyone see us?"

Jessie gestured at the hillside and thick woods with a carelessness she didn't feel. Be damned if she'd let this craziness drive her back into old habits. Hiding out for days in the safety of a dark bedroom. Afraid to go out even to buy food for fear he would be waiting.

"Nobody out there. Maybe a bear or deer. Who would be watching anyway?" Be great if she knew the answer to that herself. Quickly, she scanned the area, saw nothing, no one. Even if someone was out there, he couldn't hear....

Could he?

"Mary, where'd you get this note? When?"

"I can't say."

"You can't say? Then why did you come out here, to let me watch you fly apart? Sit now, before you fall over the railing, and let's talk."

"No, I mean I don't know where it came from. The note. I found it on the table in the kitchen when I came home from the store this morning. What does it—" She broke off, eyes wide. "Oh, God, what shall I do?"

Damned if she knew. Despite her own panic, she had to help Mary. "Take it easy. Just calm down."

"Maybe it's Jolene's husband. It's the only explanation I can think of." Mary stared at her, daring her to think otherwise.

Jessie sipped at her coffee, but it tasted like acid. "Why would he write a thing like this?"

"Because she told him. He knows, and maybe they think they can blackmail us into giving them all the money for the place."

"Mary, that doesn't make any sense at all. Knows what? What could she have told him? What are you afraid this guy saw? Have you talked to her? And why would they do a thing like that? This is Ken's sister's husband you're talking about."

"Nothing, he couldn't have seen anything. It's just, he was in my house. I mean, what else could it be but the money? They're trying to scare Harold and me. And no, we haven't heard from them, I just know."

"For God's sake, why?"

"That's what's so strange. I don't know. We've been trying to locate them, you know that, so we can sell the place and share the profits equally. After all, it belonged to Ken and his sister, inherited from their parents, so now it belongs to Harold and me and Jolene and whoever she married."

"What makes you think they're here in town? Did you see them or did they call or something? You're surely not going by this stupid note. I saw what you did," Jessie scoffed. "That's so juvenile."

"Because someone has been watching me, going in my house, and moving things around. You know how I am with my things. And now I find them all over the place. Not where I put them, not where I left them at all. And this note on my table. You know we don't lock our houses. Anybody can come in. Why are we so foolish?" Her voice rose to a hysterical pitch.

Jessie put down her cup and curled fingers around Mary's arm. "Get hold of yourself. I think we need to tell the sheriff about this—or the deputy who's investigating the bones. You know?"

"No, he'll find out. He'll *know*—" She broke down and began to sob.

He'll know she *what*? Holy—suppose *she* had killed Ken?

Woodenly, Jessie patted the heaving shoulder, unable to speak. Suddenly she felt disconnected, her cheeks and tongue numb with shock so she could hardly speak. All she could think of was the note on her bed pillow that all but matched Mary's. This whole thing was connected to the bones and the death of Ken Norville, it had to be. Nothing to do with her past at all.

Nothing else she could think of could explain who would watch them both. Protecting one, threatening the other, for she saw that distinct difference in the notes. He was protecting Mary, while warning Jessie to go away and leave things be. Who could possibly know Mary's dark secrets as well as guess that Jessie might threaten to uncover them? Or know about Jessie's past. Mary's husband Harold, perhaps? For the first time, he became a viable suspect in this puzzle.

"How long has this been going on?" Her voice sounded like someone pounded on her throat.

"How long? Why, I don't know. What difference does it make? This week, last week. Since, well, frankly since you called and asked about the sale of the property." The wide eyes narrowed, focused on Jessie as if she suspected her. "My things are being moved around. Someone has been in my house, and now they're writing threatening notes and I'm scared to death."

"Settle down, Mary. This is doing no good at all. What does Harold say?" Her head whirled until she could scarcely concentrate on her visitor's reply.

"I haven't told him. I haven't had a chance to talk to him. I—I'm afraid to."

Afraid to?

Jessie gazed in amazement at the woman. She wanted desperately to ask her just what she had done that the accusation caused such a frenzy. But she could hardly ask her if she killed her husband, could she? What would she do if the woman said yes, then pulled a gun out from under her baggy sweats and shot her?

Stop such nonsense. Get hold of yourself.

Beyond Mary's shoulder something moved in the edge of the woods. Jessie cried out and twisted away, knocked her mug off the rail. Beside her, Mary let out a squawk and began to whimper. The cup bounced on the wooden deck and rolled round and round with a monotonous racket that she thought would never end. Blood roared in her temples, almost blinding her. She opened her mouth to scream, but found no voice.

"What is it? What's wrong, what did you see?" Mary grabbed her by the arm. "What is it?" Her voice cracked. "He must have followed me here."

Shaking loose from the insistent grip and ignoring Mary's hysterical voice, Jessie stared at a spot between the shaggy trunks of two hickory trees until her eyes ached. No one was there. She shoved a lock of hair out of her eyes with fingers that trembled.

"Calm down. Let's go inside, we've spooked each other, that's all. No one's there. It was just a deer. We're acting like kids being told ghost stories."

"You're frightened of something, too," Mary insisted, dragging at her arm. "I want to know what it is. That cop's been hanging around asking questions about both of us. It's making me real nervous, and now this."

Jessie pulled away, paused in the doorway. A gust of frigid air blew past her. "Both of us? What kind of questions is he asking about me?" She took Mary's elbow and urged her into the kitchen, then closed and latched the sliding door. "And who is he asking?"

"Myrna, at City Hall. He wanted to know when you bought your place. She said he was just awfully curious about you, where you came from, how long you'd worked for the paper. Wanted to know the names of some of your relatives. Cousins, aunts, uncles. Asked if you and I were close friends, all about how long Harold and I had been married, and how long I'd served on City Council. I'm telling you, something strange is going on and he might be part of it. I don't think we ought to tell him about the note."

"Did she tell him?"

"Tell him what?"

"The names of my relatives," Jessie said through gritted teeth.

"I don't know. What's that got to do with anything?"

"Nothing, I guess. You ought to take this note to Harold and see if the two of you can figure out what's going on. If you think someone's been in your house you should call the sheriff and report it."

Mary's head swung back and forth and her eyes widened. "I'm trying to tell you, that sheriff's deputy is part of this. How can I call the sheriff and tell him anything?"

Her grandma would have said a goose walked over her grave. Jessie hugged herself and her teeth chattered. The advice she gave Mary was what she should follow as well, but she wouldn't. Not just yet, at any rate. Not until she could learn more about Dal's interest in her when he was supposed to be investigating a murder that took place long before she returned to Cedarton. His checking on Mary, she understood. And Mac constantly defending Dal and his strange actions. What was that about?

She finally managed to get Mary calmed down enough to send her home with a promise to talk to Harold.

Wishing she had someone she could talk to, she snatched up the phone as soon as the woman left and called the sheriff's private office number. She had to trust someone, and it came down to Mac and Parker.

On the other end of the ringing phone, Captain Anderson picked up and told her Mac was out of town. "Could I help you?"

"No, that's okay. I'll call his cell." But she didn't.

From beyond the open window, a hawk cried out, bringing her back to earth. Considering what Mary had told her about Dal poking around, she just might punch out his lights before they could get around to the good stuff again. Going around asking questions about her. Investigating her? He could well be the one watching her and Mary. But why and to what end? She had to get herself back on track, solve this problem on her own and set her mind at rest.

Hastily, she kicked off the shorts and dressed in jeans and shirt, tugged on sneakers, grabbed her bag and, after securely locking up, headed for the Red Bird. There she ordered an early lunch because she knew she should eat before this caper. She'd need her strength if she were going to commit B & E. And her mind was made up about that. She'd teach Dal to sneak around behind her back asking personal questions. For all she knew he was the one who had left that note.

The six-mile drive along the narrow, scenic road to the trailer park north of town took forever. She wasn't sure how she would manage to get into the trailer he had rented without being seen by the owner of the place, but she would reconnoiter first.

Ina Mae Carter and her husband had bought the Hidden Holler Trailer Park about the same time Jessie had returned to Cedarton. A month or so later, he dropped dead of a heart attack. She was almost ashamed that she would now have to trick the good-natured woman to get a look inside Dal's place, but the end justified the means. At least, in this case. There was much more than a story involved here. She could be in danger from a man hiding behind the badge of a cop.

She found the plump Ina Mae working in the garden between her small home and the trailers she rented out. Careful not to tread on the neat rows of tiny plants emerging from the soil, Jessie waited in the grass at one end. On her knees, Ina poked tomato plants into the moist earth, watered them, and packed soil around the roots. Their tangy fragrance reminded Jessie of when she was a little girl, following her grandfather as he planted row after row of Big Boy tomato plants.

"It's beautiful," Jessie commented by way of a greeting.

Ina Mae blotted her sweating forehead with the back of a white gloved hand. "Oh, hello. Jessie, isn't it? From *The Observer?*"

"Yes, that's me. Your garden is lovely."

"Ought to be, spend plenty of time on my knees out here. But it keeps me from watching the soaps." She laughed, a lusty, friendly sound that made Jessie feel even more guilty for what she was about to do.

"I know this is going to sound strange, but I'm doing a piece on our new deputy, and I understand he's living out here. I—well, I wondered if you'd show me which place is his so I can get some shots of it. It'll mean some publicity for your place, and we can put in a nice plug for the park, too."

"Oh, it's always fun to see your name in the paper, especially when it's about something good. I couldn't let you inside, of course. The deputy's not home and that wouldn't be proper."

Heart thudding in her throat, Jessie tried to keep her voice casual. "Of course not. I'll just take a few shots of the outside, then I'll catch Dal later and get some candid photos of him." Surely this woman wouldn't buy such a weak request.

"Sure. It's the last one in the row there, tucked back where you hardly can see it from the road. He said that's why he liked it, the privacy and all." She rose from her knees, kneaded at her back, and pointed. "See, the fifth one in that line. You can just go on down there and take your pictures. I'm sure the deputy wouldn't mind. He's a very nice man, and you should see how he cleaned up the place. Why everything is spic and span. Unusual for a man living alone, don't you think? I mean, knowing how to clean and everything."

"Oh, yes, I suppose so. Thank you, Ina Mae. You don't know how much I appreciate this. I'm in a hurry and can't wait for him just now, and since I was out this way anyway, I thought, why not kill two birds with one stone." Jessie pinched her lips together to stop the inane chattering. If she tried to explain too much the entire illogical request would fall apart.

The trusting Ina Mae appeared not to notice what a dumb thing Jessie was asking.

She could lose her job or go to jail if she got caught snooping around on private property. But if Dal was not who he claimed to be, she could well be in danger of losing more than her job and her freedom, so there was no contest.

She parked near the last trailer, hopped out, and made sure Ina Mae saw her taking pictures. Then she strolled toward the creek bank. A rocky expanse bordered the stream on the far side. Beyond, tire tracks marked where picnickers and swimmers regularly parked. If she crossed the creek on the main road, then left her car there she could wade the shallow water and approach Dal's trailer from the back side, undetected.

Jessie waved and shouted thanks when she drove past the woman, still bent to her task in the garden. She raised a gloved hand and returned to her work.

Almost a half hour later, Jessie removed her soaked shoes on the back stoop of Dal's trailer, picked the simple lock on the door with trembling fingers, and eased inside. Now she had added breaking and entering to trespassing. Mac would pitch a conniption fit. And Parker? She shuddered to think what he'd say. But only if she got caught, and she had no intention of that.

She left her shoes on the new rug just inside. Her bare feet squeaked on the immaculate, worn linoleum as she crossed the kitchen into the small living area. Large sparkling windows looked out across the water, and Dal had opted for no curtains there. The windows at the front had blue vertical blinds that were closed. Just as Ina had said, the place was immaculate. He hadn't bothered to add many furnishings, as if he wouldn't be staying long and didn't expect visitors.

She shivered, and moved to check the kitchen cabinets. Some men had strange ideas of where to store things. But they were almost empty except for a couple of boxes of crackers, some cans of soup, a pound of coffee and filters. Nested neatly together were a dinner plate, a lunch plate, and a soup bowl. On the counter beside the coffee pot sat a clean coffee mug with a spoon in it. A knife, fork, and soup spoon lay on a napkin. The dish cloth was folded and hung over the faucet, a matching towel looped through the handle of the ancient refrigerator. She didn't look inside. Underfoot, the floor gleamed and there was a light fragrance in the air, perhaps potpourri or one of those plug-in air fresheners. Dal was definitely Mr. Clean.

The kitchen spoke volumes about the man, made her feel sympathy for his solitary existence. He didn't even expect friends over for coffee, or maybe it was that he wouldn't welcome them.

Outside gravel crunched, and she hunched down to peek out the window, heart pitter-pattering in her chest. An older car, Oldsmobile maybe, rolled slowly past and parked at the trailer across the way. Analyzing Dal could wait till another time. She hurried into the living room.

Not much there. Yesterday's daily paper lay on a copy of *Wild West Magazine* on a rickety table next to a new La-Z-Boy recliner. The only new piece of furniture in the place. The man liked to relax. Along the opposite wall was a cheap couch that probably came with the trailer. Where the television should be rested a small stack of CDs, a player, and classical piano on top of a *Best of Hank Williams*. Eclectic taste.

"I'm not impressed, dammit," she muttered under her breath. No pictures on the walls, no personal photos. Sadness washed through her, but she tamped it down. Dangerous to feel sorry for him.

The hall closet yielded nothing out of the ordinary, so she hurried past the tiny bath and into the single bedroom. A neatly made, built-in bed took up half the room. Lying on the floor, a book marked partway through by an envelope from a credit card company. She picked it up. *Dreams to Dust* by Sheldon Russell. *A Story of the Oklahoma Land Rush.*

"Still not impressed," she muttered, but she was. Their tastes were so alike it was scary.

Laying the book back where she'd found it, she turned to a chest built into the opposite wall. Empty drawers, except for one that contained neatly folded undershorts and several pairs of black socks. Finally, she swung open the closet door. Three uniforms hung there, along with a few pairs of jeans, several t-shirts, and the black cowboy shirt he'd worn when they went dancing. On the floor, the Tony Lama snakeskin boots and a pair of work boots. She sighed and rose to check out the high shelf. Lying under the black Stetson with its rattlesnake band was a picture album.

She pushed aside the hat, pulled the album down, sat on the bed, and flipped it open. By the time she had read a few of the newspaper articles encased in plastic, tears poured down her cheeks. No wonder Dal Starr acted as if the demons of hell pursued him. They surely must.

Following several commendations for performance while in uniform, he'd received a Medal of Valor, which he accepted from a wheelchair because he'd been shot. There was a picture of him and a pretty but frail young woman identified as his wife Leeann. They thought he might never walk again, but obviously he had.

He turned up in the news again a few years later. Leeann had been found dead of an overdose in their apartment in Dallas, and he was by then an undercover narcotics officer. By the time the media finished with him as related to her death, he had waded through hell and back. The implication was that he had procured drugs from his connections to keep his young wife supplied.

Jessie knew how that went. Some reporter looking for glory. No wonder he hated those practicing her profession. A motive for pursuing her. Doubt crawled through her. Such occurrences were known to drive people over the edge.

Jessie had no idea what happened to him after Internal Affairs cleared him of any wrongdoing in that death, which occurred about the same time she returned to Cedarton eight months ago. The rest of the pages were blank.

Eyes swimming in tears, she sat staring blindly out the window. Almost forgotten was her reason for coming here in the first place. Dal could well have a hidden agenda where she was concerned, but even the worst of his experiences would not excuse such action against her. She wasn't sure what to do.

Glancing around the sparsely furnished room, she felt sympathy for the life he lived. Not sorry enough to allow herself to be drawn back into his arms though. She did well to keep herself together without taking on someone with his kind of baggage.

It could only explain why he was going around town asking questions about her if he was going to do her bodily harm. She had nothing to do with Ken Norville or the mysterious bones. It wouldn't be easy, but she would simply face him, preferably in a public place, ask him why he was investigating her and try to get him to stop. She understood he was very good at his job, and he might uncover things she didn't want anyone to know. Mac had said he was a natural for getting the feel of a crime scene and following every possible lead, even some that no one else picked up on. That psychic bit hadn't come up, but with Mac, it wouldn't. It kept running through her mind that Mac trusted Dal, and because of her relationship with the sheriff, she trusted him. The entire situation was confusing, to say the least.

If Dal refused to explain poking into her background, she would have to go to the horse's mouth, much as she hated to. Mac would be able to clear things up. Meanwhile, until she had some answers, she intended to stay as far away from the deputy as possible.

A door creaked open and brought her out of her reverie. She scrambled to her feet, but there was no time to escape, because Dal stood in the middle of the living room when she burst into the hall.

Wiping her eyes and sniffing wasn't exactly a defense for housebreaking. Especially not if the house belonged to an armed and dangerous deputy sheriff who had caught her flatfooted. Barefooted. She glanced down, curled her toes as if to hang on to the floor, and waited for him to explode. There was nothing she could say. Evidently, he was stricken dumb as well because he didn't utter a word either, just stared at her, handsome features a scowl of perplexity, jaw muscles throbbing.

Finally he spread his hands. "Working on that exposé, are you?"

God, the tone of voice was deadly. In an attempt to appear calm, though her heart leaped around in her chest like a mad thing, she crossed her wrists and extended them. "I give up, arrest me. Take me to jail." At least she'd be safe there. It would do no good to deny any of his accusations.

"I may do just that. Depends on why you're here."

"You mean there are good reasons, legal reasons, for breaking and entering?" Her voice cracked, but she held on tight to an edge of rationality.

One corner of his mouth twitched, but she couldn't tell if it was from anger or the beginnings of a smile. No doubt it was the former. There was nothing here to laugh about. Another tear escaped and ran slowly down her cheek.

"Why are you crying? You don't seem the type to use that as a weapon."

She sniffed but didn't answer. How could she tell him those tears were remnants left from poking about in his life and learning his tragic secrets?

He moved toward her, and she expected him to whip out the cuffs. Instead, he pulled a tissue from a box on the counter and extended it.

She took it, dried her eyes, and blew her nose lustily. "Thanks."

"Ready?"

Shoulders hunched, she nodded. He was going to take her in, and she might as well make the best of it. Mac would be livid, Parker would be disappointed and Tinker? Well, Tinker would never let her live it down. If she arrived at the jail in one piece. The way Dal glared at her, she might not.

What if he took her off out into the country and they didn't find her body for years?

13
CHAPTER

Instead of handcuffing Jessie, Dal brushed past her into the tiny kitchen. "I'll make coffee."

A huge lump in her throat dissolved. At least he wasn't going to arrest her. Not yet anyway. Since she deserved it, she didn't know whether to be relieved or sorry. What if he had something else in mind? Something he didn't want Mac to know about?

She had to say something—*do* something—so she croaked, "You've only got one cup."

"You counted my dishes?" His look of disbelief spoke volumes.

"I'm sorry, I couldn't help it. But I didn't break in to see how you live."

"I think we both know why you broke in. Reporters will do anything for a story." He shifted a few steps, filled a pot with water, and poured it into the reservoir.

She wanted to deny his accusation, but only a squeak came out, so she gave that up.

While he dipped grounds into a filter she inched closer to the back door and her shoes. If he gave her half a chance she'd grab them and run. Maybe he wouldn't catch her.

Oh, sure. Like he didn't know where she lived.

Settling, she eyed his long legs. Fat chance she'd make it a dozen feet anyway. He was a big man. His very presence in the small trailer dwarfed everything. Despite that limp, he was strong and virile. It was hard to believe they'd once told him he'd never walk again. It must've taken a lot of determination and physical strength to recover from such an injury.

Stop. She was on the verge of feeling compassion. Dangerous.

The aroma of coffee filled the room, mingled with the subtle, pleasant fragrance of air freshener.

"Why don't you sit down?" He gestured toward the faded couch. "It's going to be a long and tough conversation. Where's your car?"

She pointed out the back door. "On the other side of the creek."

"Sneaky. I left mine down by the garden where I had an interesting conversation with Ina Mae." He glanced at the wet sneakers on the rug across the room. "And those are your shoes, I presume."

Lips clamped, she regarded him grimly. Rhetorical question.

He continued to give her the evil eye, but lowered himself into the oversized recliner, making him only a tad less menacing. Though she yearned to stand up, tower over him, her legs would no longer support her. Instead, she perched on the edge of the hideous couch. Without taking her eyes off him, she tucked in her bare feet. He could still change his mind and arrest her. He seemed damned calm for a man who'd found a burglar in his home.

"Did you find what you were looking for?"

"No, I didn't."

"And would you mind telling me what that might be? I have an idea, but I'll let you try to weasel out of this one without any help at all."

The gentle Texas drawl had disappeared somewhere amidst the rigid anger, leaving the voice of a professional interrogator. She was a criminal, he was a cop, and he'd make her talk or else. At least that was a tad safer than her earlier fears.

Offense was her best bet, so she launched an attack. "Mary told me you were asking questions all over town about me. I resented it. I was afraid you weren't who you claim to be. I thought you might be someone looking for me, and so I had to find out."

She didn't mention the photograph album, though he would know soon enough. She hadn't had time to put it away, and it lay on his bed, a silent accusation of her snooping.

"Why the hell would I pretend to be someone I'm not? And why would anyone be looking for you?" His sharp-eyed glance softened, but he didn't look away.

She shrugged off the first question, went right on to the next. "Something that happened to me in California. I was afraid of reprisals, so I uprooted my life and came here to start over. Then I found the note on my pillow and I thought maybe you'd been hired to find me." Regaining some courage, she tilted her head. "Why don't you read my mind, then you wouldn't have to ask?"

His eyes narrowed. "Can the attitude. Let's begin at the beginning. What note? On what pillow?"

"My house. I went home and someone had been there. Left me a note warning me to back off, leave this alone."

A tilt of his head and raised brows told her he didn't believe that. His next words proved her suspicion. "I do hope you saved this mysterious note. Did you break the law out West?"

The question hit her so hard, she had to think it over a minute.

"Uhm, legally, no."

"Who do you think is after you?"

"Just a man."

"What man?"

"A man I hurt?"

"Is that a question? How did you hurt him?"

"Look, I don't think this is relevant."

He snorted through his nose. "I'll decide what's relevant. What did you do to him?"

"It's personal."

He sighed and watched the coffee drip for a moment before speaking. "Okay. Can you tell me this? Are you afraid he's going to hurt you?"

"Not really. Well, maybe. It's only that I...." A tear escaped the corner of one eye and she couldn't go on. How could she tell him she deserved to be punished? That would sound perverted.

"Wait a minute, you can't cry. It's taking unfair advantage."

"Why? You could always shout and yell, or hit me."

He looked as if she'd hit him. "I've never hit a woman in my life. Don't intend to start now, even though you're really pissing me off. But back to the subject." He poured coffee into the single cup and handed it to her. "Want anything in that?"

"No, it's fine." She took a sip and wished she'd asked for something, anything to add to the strong brew.

"Now, about this note." He waited for her reply, and she obliged.

"It was just a note. I thought maybe you came here to—"

"Why would I be looking for you? I didn't even know you existed until the other day when we were digging up those bones. What kind of threat?"

Damn, this was getting tougher by the minute.

How much should she tell him? "Look, all I know is I did things I'm not proud of, and for a long while I expected that I would have to pay. There's always consequences to our actions. It doesn't seem right that he would just walk away. He could have—I mean I guess I wanted him to do something, so I could maybe... Oh, shit."

"You're not making much sense. I don't think you're telling me the truth. I don't believe there was any note, especially not one threatening your life. I don't think anyone is watching you. Why would anyone do that? I think you made it up to give you an excuse to go digging around in my private life. Clever little liar that you are. What are you really after? Information for a story? Digging for dirt, that's what most reporters do. I'll give you this, though, your story is a nice touch. I suppose you destroyed the note."

"I wadded it up and threw it in the trash. It's the truth, I really don't care if you believe me or not. Besides, I'm not most reporters, and there are plenty of us with integrity. And I'm not lying. Not about the note or the other."

"Aw, hell, give me a break. You'd sell your own grandmother for a story that would explode in newspapers and on TV. Integrity. That's bullshit. You can't even use the word in the same sentence with a reporter. Especially not one who's already admitted to being disreputable." He eyed her a moment and she squirmed. "What'd you do? Something not at all ethical, I'm sure. All of you are cut from the same herd. Ethical reporter is an oxymoron."

She leaped to her feet, sloshing coffee out on the clean floor. "No, I'm not like them. I would never do anything like that again. I'd quit first." Biting her lip, she tried to calm down. "You don't know about me, do you?"

He held out his palms, streaked with tiny white scars from his battle with the barbed wire fence. Supplication of a sort. "What about you? What are you talking about?"

It really wasn't fair she knew all about him, and he knew nothing about her. Him and his mind-reading bullshit. Perhaps because of the scrap books, or the sneering hatred he had for all reporters. Or more likely it was the way they'd made love in that dank, musty basement, like hatred and vengeance drove them rather than love or desire. Anyway, she steadied the cup with both hands, collapsed on the couch, and spilled all.

"We were in love, Steve and I. He was a vice cop. Tough, but very sweet to me, like he had to find his tender side in order to keep doing what he did."

Dal's expression softened, like he knew what she meant.

"Anyway, they had a sting going, involving a new drug connection in Los Angeles. They'd worked on it for months. He was undercover, close to the connection. I... he told me about it a week before it was to go down. Pillow talk, passion talk." She stared into the steaming liquid but didn't drink any. "All I could think of was, what a story. How could I wait until it happened and then just be one of the many writing about it?"

Dal took a ragged breath, eyes going dark and dangerous, but he didn't move, didn't say anything. He might have been turned to stone except for the blaze shooting from those eyes.

Tears leaked down her cheeks, but she brushed at them and went on. It was too late to do anything else. "Don't you see? I was young, I wanted a big story. Needed a big story, would kill for a big story. I didn't know anyone would get hurt." She sat down the cup before it slipped from her grasp. "Maybe I didn't care, I don't know. Anyway, I invented sources to quote, and I wrote the story telling all about the setup. It came out the day before the sting was scheduled to take place."

"My God."

"I was greedy for a career. Everything was going so slow. So I was stupid. I wrote everything he'd told me about the drug cartel, right down to names, and I attributed my information to fictitious sources, thinking that would protect him. But it didn't." She glanced at Dal and shivered under the hatred written across his features.

Christ, the look on his face, both fists knotted against his thighs. Like it was all he could do to keep from striking her, but he didn't lift a finger, scarcely stirred.

She met his dark gaze, drew in a long breath, nodded miserably. "I ruined his career and mine."

He stared at her. "You deserved what you got and more. It's a wonder it didn't get him or someone else killed." His eyes batted. "It didn't, did it?"

The question sent a massive shudder through her and she hugged herself, stared at the wall beyond Dal. "No. No. I know I deserved his retaliation. More. How well I know. He, well, then he—he was so *angry.* He hit me, this man I loved—who loved *me*. Hit me. A slap of derision. And I deserved it. I *did!* He told me if he ever laid eyes on me again he'd kill me, and I believed him. Then he gathered his stuff and left. I thought I'd never see him again."

She raised her eyes, glanced toward him, but received not a bit of sympathy. "Thinking about what I'd done, and what I deserved, terrified me. For a long time all I could do was sit in the dark and cry. Sometimes I'd call him and listen to his voice on the other end and say nothing. Other times I'd beg him to call me, yell at me, to scream, do something. But he didn't. At times, I wanted to kill myself."

"Why didn't you?" He turned away, stared out the window as if to continue to look at her was too painful.

Why didn't she stop? She owed this man nothing. It was clear he hated her for what she'd done, yet she plunged on. A sort of cleansing confession, as if he could give her the punishment she'd never received. He looked like he might.

"I didn't have the courage. I loved him. And I was responsible for everything that happened. I finally learned, with a lot of help, that I had to forgive myself, atone in the only way I could by living a better life. He was gone, his phone disconnected. I couldn't find him to apologize, seek his forgiveness.

"Then I started receiving these phone calls. Threats. Someone followed me. He promised if he ever saw me again, if I ever wrote another story, he'd kill me. Then the newspaper got wind of what I'd done. Dug into the story. Found out about the false leads. They fired me. So I did the next best thing. I came back to the only other home I've ever known. And I vowed never to do anything so terrible again."

She finally met his harsh gaze in time to see him flinch as if she'd hit him.

"This is the reporter Mac Richards expects me to trust? Does he know all this?"

"Not all, just some," she whispered. "But he knows I can be trusted. I would never do anything like that again. It all but destroyed me. I thought it was going to. He only knows something terrible happened, and he's watched over me like I was his child for a long while. He's a good friend."

She glanced toward the bedroom where she had left the scrapbook lying open on the bed. "Dal, I'm sorry. So very sorry. The person I am today would never do anything like what they did to you."

Glance following hers, he rose from the chair, pinned her with feral eyes. Oh, Sweet Jesus.

She clamped her hands over her mouth. How stupid, to let him know she'd seen the album. Much better if he'd found out after she left. Give him time to cool down before he could get to her.

"Like who did to me? What are you talking about?" His voice crackled. "What did you do?"

In a few long strides he was in the bedroom, and she stayed right where she was, teeth clenched. There was absolutely no point in running away.

Out of sight he spat an epithet, then burst into the hallway.

Black fury transformed his features into a terrifying mask that fueled her desperation to run. Hard to remember what he'd said about having never hit a woman. This might be the first time.

Never taking her eyes off him, she set the coffee cup down on the rickety table. Chin thrust forward, she met his stare without blinking. Somewhere beneath all that twisted rage was a man deeply hurt, a man searching for forgiveness. How badly she wanted to reach out and calm him. Tell him she understood. But that probably wasn't a good idea at the moment. It would be like trying to gentle an injured wolf.

"Dal, I'm so sorry. Please believe me, I didn't know. I had no intention of prying."

"No intention? You broke into my house. My *home*. We're supposed to be safe in our home, even from the prying eyes of unscrupulous reporters. You opened this...." He shook the album at her, and she dodged, threw up her hands. "You dug into my privacy. Well, tell me, sweet Jessie, *innocent* Jessie, what do you think now? Isn't this a juicy story for your piddly-ass little newspaper? And don't tell me you won't use it. You have a history." He raised the book, and she thought for a moment he might throw it at her, but he slammed it to the floor. It banged like a cannon shot.

She jumped. Because looking up at him made him appear all the more formidable, she leaped to her feet in a defensive stance. While she deserved his wrath, she wasn't about to let him hit her.

Bracing the backs of her knees against the couch, she said in a quavering voice, "I will not write one word of that in our newspaper. Not one word. After what happened out in California, how could you think I would?"

"That's exactly why I know you will."

"No. I apologize for prying into your personal life. I'm terribly sorry for your loss. I only wish you could trust me, I wish I had trusted you. Then none of this would have happened." She swallowed hard, refused to cry any more. "Now, if I'm not under arrest, I'd like to go."

He waved toward the door. "Go on, get the hell out of here. If you hurry you can make your deadline and write one hell of a story. Because that is what you'll do. You're crazy if you think I'll ever trust you again."

Shaking with relief and a sorrow so deep her body ached with it, she grabbed her shoes and scurried out the door. She had purged her soul to him, leaving her insides hollow. He once held her in his arms, and now he hated her. Deep down, she didn't blame him.

She had come so close to falling in love with him.

Still sobbing, she sat on a boulder at the edge of the stream to put on her shoes, and glanced back at his trailer. He was watching her through the huge window. Just standing there looking out like he didn't care if she saw or didn't. She wanted to throw herself on the ground and bawl as if she were a child again. Instead she rose on shaky legs, splashed through the water, slipping and sliding on moss-covered rocks, and headed for her car. It took a very long time to make the short walk because she couldn't see for the tears, could scarcely walk on legs weak and trembling.

Anger seething like a dark and evil thing, Dal stood by the window long after Jessie disappeared into the shadows beneath the trees. What had possessed her to put herself in such a position? You'd think she'd have learned something out there in California. Said she had, but hell, if that was true what was she doing breaking into his home? And that story she made up about thinking he was leaving her notes. Looked like she could've come up with something better than that to excuse what she'd done.

But he'd guessed at her treachery all along, hadn't he?

Time to put his mind back on the case where it belonged, but all he could think of was her poking her nose where it didn't belong. Her and her smooth skin and silken hair. Body warm against his while they danced. Everything a lie. All of it. After this got out, no one around here would trust him. He'd have to move on, get back to the case. Solve it quick and forget about Jessie Ann West and settling down here.

There was a connection between the bones and the disappearance of Ken Norville. Had to be.

But all he could think of was this evocative woman with her mane of wild hair and eyes that glinted golden as a tiger's.

The aroma of coffee pulled him away from such thoughts. He drank from her cup without washing it, lips over the rim where hers had been. A terrible loss engulfed him. He'd wanted her. Goddammit, he'd imagined him and her together. He rinsed the mug and turned it upside down on a paper towel. Then he went to the car.

Keying the radio, he checked in, then headed for the old Norville place. He had a hunch if Ken had been murdered, the act had been committed there. Besides, he had nothing better to do than poke around the old house.

Kathy Spacey had managed to extract enough bone marrow for an mtDNA test, and once that came back, he'd have the results run through the index of missing persons in CODIS. From what she said, though, that could take months. Besides, it was probably fruitless anyway. Law enforcement knew little about preserving evidence for DNA in 1989 when Norville disappeared.

Right now, this minute, there was the empty house, a good way to simmer down and attempt to reach the spirits who dwelled there.

The two-story structure sat back off the road, surrounded by huge trees, as if hiding from view. Clumps of last year's dried grasses slapped at the undersides of the car. He parked in the deep shade cast by the old house and approached through a carpet of blue spring beauties. The lap siding was bleached gray, the windows dark and glassless. Brambles and wild roses grew over a caved-in cellar door. And a lost voice called to him, distant at first, but increasing with each step he took.

One corner post of the porch had collapsed and its roof sagged precariously. He tested the boards cautiously, avoiding rotten spots. The front door lay on the floor inside, and he stepped through the opening into the dust-ridden gloom, emerged in a room about fifteen by fifteen. Shards of broken ceramic figurines lay on the dirty floor. He pictured the dank space with furniture. Brushed fingers over the faded wallpaper and was overpowered by a frantic hopelessness.

Houses embodied echoes of those who had lived in them, spoke to those who would listen. Some called them ghosts, but he knew they were the lingering spirits of lives so vivid the memories remained. All life, he learned from his Cherokee grandfather, left a trail as bright as a shooting star, the particles remaining long after the effervescence faded. He'd read somewhere that we were not humans who would one day become spirits, but rather spirits who had become humans for a short time only to return to that world from which we'd come. It was true because he heard the voices, felt the emotions.

Closing his eyes, he reconstructed the room, placed Mary and Ken there with sister Jolene. She helped with the housework, had been a companion to Mary when Ken was off on a toot, stood up for her when he wanted to give her a good belt. Got herself knocked around as well.

He waited and listened to a clatter of disturbing echoes, wails of feminine suffering. Bellows of an attacker's rage. The bastard had beaten them both, and they never lifted a finger to stop it. Just took it like the gentle, dutiful women they were. The brute could handle both of them, and often did.

Had that extended to the bedroom as well? Were they both victims of his sexual rage?

That personal room and its vivid tragedies would have to wait. He was drawn into the kitchen by a dreadful reek of blood, the smell as pungent as if it had been shed this very day.

Feet crunching over broken glass, he stumbled into a wall of terror that sent him reeling backward. He swayed, opened his arms to embrace the images, to share their pain. The agony of a torturous death.

Dear God. He'd been right. This was the killing room. And these spirits wouldn't rest until he found who had done this.

Damn, he was not an *ada'wehi* with supernatural powers. Never claimed to be. Only the greatest shaman could invoke the human and spiritual world. Grandfather said none of these special men were alive today. Yet, Dal received not only the thoughts of those whose spirits had passed into the next world, but of those who still walked this earth. They brushed over him like gusting winds from the mountains. Begged for release. It was not a thing he took lightly. Still, he wished with all his might he was not so blessed. Wished they would go away and leave him alone.

Grandfather said he must embrace the small powers he had been given to help those in such terrible need. All they wanted was to be set free to move into the next world, yet they clung to this earth.

He staggered under the sense of anguish, of brutality and despair, a rotten stench of gore. Tilting his head back, he allowed the lingering spirits to flow into him. A man and woman locked in combat, something terrible outside, like a lament from hell. The house rocked under his feet, around him the sound of shattering glass, voices shrieking, an unthinkable roar.

He sucked in a deep breath, clenched both fists, held steady. No words. He never heard words, just emotions that lingered like tenacious ghosts. Love turned to hate, despair over loss, terror and rage, deep regret and unending loneliness.

Here, in this place, two completely different sets of out-of-control emotions, a man and a woman. Then another woman. All the while the roaring outside grew and grew until the walls nearly exploded. He covered his ears with both arms to shut out the clamor.

Breathing heavily, he dropped to his knees, grunted with a sharp pain that shot into his back. Eyes closed, he held steadfast against the physical discomfort and spread one palm against the wide pine boards, brushed away dust and debris to take the pulse of the house with sensitive fingertips. Not only had violence exploded in this place, someone had died in this very room, on the spot where he knelt. Terror splashed like blood into every crack and crevice, covering any happiness that may have once dwelt here.

When he could not bear to absorb more, he gathered a protection around himself that shut out the turmoil. Something his grandfather had taught him so he could remain sane. Escape to another place, a peaceful place. Settle his own soul. Deal. Slowly, the darkness crept away, letting in the warm rays of sunlight through the kitchen window. Helping himself to his feet using one wall, he stumbled from the room and its violent tale back into the front room, perhaps a parlor or common room.

No children here. Ever. No joy. Ever. Pain and sorrow, yes. Betrayal too. In the twisted lives there'd been no happiness. He had little trouble seeing Mary Smith locked in such an atmosphere. She had a weak spirit and was easily detached from reality.

At last he took a deep breath, broke away from the darkness and out on the porch where he could breathe without sucking in the cluttered past. He'd had enough for one day. First Jessie and her disruptive, deceitful spirit, then this place. Clean air filled his lungs, and after a moment he went to the cruiser, waited till the tremors left his voice and hooked up the radio.

"I want a crime forensics unit out at the Norville place," he told the dispatcher, "and find Mac, tell him we need a warrant."

"I'll have to call the State Police."

"Then do it. I'll wait."

Ten minutes later her voice came over the radio. "It'll be late tomorrow."

He cursed under his breath.

"They said it's waited all this time, it can wait another day. They're tied up on something else. Said to tell you this ain't Dallas."

He gritted his teeth. Well, this was what he wanted, wasn't it? How could he embrace the peaceful lifestyle, then criticize those who knew better than he how to make a life here?

"No, thank God, this ain't Dallas," he told her. "Thanks. I'm going home, then, unless there's something else. You can reach me there. What about the warrant?"

"Mac said he'd see to it."

When he passed the lane to Jessie's house he tried not to check to see if she was home, but couldn't help himself. Nor could he help the disappointment he felt. A light burned in the front room, but her car wasn't there. Must plan on being out late. It was Friday night.

Exhausted from the encounter at the Norville house, he wanted to sit in a dark bar somewhere, sip at a glass of Johnnie Walker, watch some pretty lady do the two-step with a slightly tipsy cowboy. Laugh when a woman next to him told an off-color joke or made a play for him. Inhale her flowery fragrance, her musky aroma. Maybe go with her when she beckoned.

Not just any lady would do, though. Goddamn it, he wanted Jessie. Her gentle hands as they'd doctored his palms. Her laugh like the sound of sunshine lighting his soul. Her writhing, sweating body pinned by his against a dank wall. Her dangerous soul.

Though it was out of the way he drove to Charlie's Country Bar where he had spent such an enjoyable evening with her before everything fell apart. He'd liked the live music, played way down low and gutsy, not all that hammering and shouting the kids went for today. He wasn't sure what the rules were about him drinking in uniform. Technically he was off duty, but realistically he was never off. Twenty-four-hour call, the sheriff had said.

Well, what the hell? He'd be lucky to have his job when the next issue of *The Observer* came out.

He parked out front so as not to be accused of being sneaky, hooked the radio in place on his belt, and went in. How long would it be before Grace County deputies were equipped with rovers to clip on their shoulder, leaving their hands free to deal with trouble? Jesus Christ, what was wrong with him tonight? The last thing he wanted was for progress to come to this place and ruin it. He wanted it to remain just the way it was. He wanted to be here with it. Sadly, that probably wasn't going to happen.

Inside, he checked out the room. It was early yet. Only a few patrons sat at tables and the bar. A couple of flattop guitars, an electric bass, and a sax were propped beside chairs on the small stage in back of the dance floor, and a hand-lettered sign said the music would begin at eight. He glanced at his watch and ordered Johnnie Walker on the rocks. A half hour. He might wait for the music, he might not.

Leaning on the bar, he took a slow sip of bourbon, savored the fiery smooth taste. An image of Leeann, never far from the surface, emerged from his subconscious. Blinking, he raised the glass to his lips again. Liquor had a way of blurring the pain, but he dared not use it. Too often he had seen what dependency on any drug did to a human being. So he'd keep his rule, one drink, and only occasionally when the pain and sorrow dug way too deep.

Someone laid a hand roughly on his shoulder. "Thought that was you."

He turned to see Harold Smith, a smart-ass expression on his face. Damn, he'd like to punch him one, would have had he not removed his hand. The man introduced himself and Dal let him, even though he well knew who he was.

Dal nodded. "Care to join me?" Hoped he wouldn't.

Smith immediately slid onto the stool next to him and raised a finger toward the bartender. "Jimbo, bring me a bourbon and branch water, and give the deputy here another of what he's drinking."

Dal shook his head at Jimbo, who looked like an ex-rodeo cowboy who'd taken too many falls. His Adam's apple stood out so sharply it threatened to cut his skin. "Thanks. One's my limit nowadays. Wouldn't want folks to get the wrong idea."

"I figured drugs were your vice of choice," Smith said.

Dal swallowed a burst of anger with a long sip, kept his voice level. "Now why would you think that?"

Smith shrugged. "Heard it somewhere."

Dal didn't bother to deny it. His and Leeann's story was probably all over the Internet, and this man the kind to search. The world offered no privacy anymore, and folks were foolish to expect it.

"Did you want to talk about something in particular? If not, I'd rather be alone," he told Harold.

Smith studied him with a hard scowl. "Yes, I did want to speak to you. This may not be the best place. Why don't we go outside?"

"What about your drink?"

"Jimbo'll keep it for me till I get back, won't you, Jimbo? This won't take long. Just want to talk to you about trespassing on my land." He raised his voice so that several patrons glanced at them. They would remember the two men leaving together.

Dal swallowed the last of the bourbon and stood. "Fine by me. We'll talk outside." He dropped a five on the bar and followed Smith through the dimly-lit bar.

Lavender dusk shadowed the streets, and from somewhere far off to the southwest, thunder rumbled across the land. A chunk of bright moon hung in the clear eastern sky, fearlessly waiting for the dark thunderclouds to swallow it up.

Smith moved away from the entrance between two parked pickups, and turned to face Dal. "I want you to leave my wife be. And stay away from my place."

Spoken like Dal and Mary might be having an affair. "I don't think I understand. I'm not doing anything to your wife. And I was just looking around. Understood your place was for sale. Might want to buy it, being new around here."

It was just light enough to see the sneer twist Smith's features before his hand shot out, wadded a fistful of Dal's shirt. The action so startled Dal that for a moment he didn't react at all. Then, in one lightning-fast movement, he clamped the man's wrist, curled a thumb around his, and twisted the hand backward. The move forced Smith to one knee, cheek crammed up against the door of a muddy truck. The man did not go down easy, but he went down and let out a grunt of surprise and fury.

Dal released him immediately and took one quick step backward. "I'm sorry, sir. I guess I misread your gesture. You meant it to be friendly, seeing as how you're too smart to assault an officer of the law. Hope I didn't hurt you. Now, what was it you wanted to tell me about your wife and your property?"

"You bastard," Smith spat. Rubbing his arm, he lurched to his feet. Dirt smeared one side of his face and the knees of his trousers. For a moment, Dal thought he might come at him, but he didn't.

"You quit bothering me and my wife, and you can tell that nosy reporter the same. Got no business asking my wife questions. And you stay away from our place. That's trespassing unless you've got a warrant. I think you'll find out I'm well-connected. I'll have your badge if you don't back off. Now."

Without speaking, Dal studied Smith for a long moment, and the man finally swiveled on one heel and stumbled back inside, rubbing his wrist.

A damp wind carrying the promise of rain followed Dal to the cruiser. Technically, Smith was right. He had trespassed on the Norville property when he took a look around earlier. Funny how fast word got around, but Smith's violent reaction wasn't funny at all.

If the property sale went through, Smith would benefit because he'd married the dead man's widow. And if they could identify the bones as being the skeleton of the only other heir, he and Mary would have it all, unless the missing sister turned up. If they could find her, DNA would tell them if the bones were those of her brother. Eventually. Without other relatives, or teeth for a dental ID, they might never prove who the bones belonged to. If Harold had done the killing, then Dal figured the man had a real problem. One that wouldn't go away very easily. How eager he must be to lay hands on the money from the sale of the property.

Eager enough to see that the head turned up and the body was identified? Eager enough, maybe, to have helped the dogs out a bit in their digging frenzy?

Something was missing in that equation. It had been so long that Ken would already be considered legally dead, so why would Harold have any interest in exposing and identifying the bones? That could only lead to a search for the killer.

At least Dal had a direction in which to go. Search for Jolene, attempt to turn up hard evidence at the Norville place, wait for CODIS to kick out something. Make sure no one else was missing who might be the body. Cover all his bases. Still, there were no easy answers. This case had been cold a hell of a long time, but it wouldn't remain that way if he could help it.

Huge drops of rain splatted on the windshield, dragging him from his thoughts.

Surprised to find he was still parked in the lot beside Charlie's, he keyed the ignition. Time to go home. He'd had enough for one day.

Might as well drive by Jessie's and make sure she was tucked in. Despite his doubts, if she wasn't lying about someone watching her, he didn't want anything to happen to her. Damned if he hadn't wanted to grab her up in his arms when she stood there in the center of his living room, eyes big and wide, tears on her cheeks. How he could go and fall in love with a reporter was beyond him, but truth be told, that's exactly what he'd done. Now he felt like his heart had cracked in two. She'd betrayed him by searching his house. What the hell had that been about? So, he'd go by, check on her without letting her know. He well knew what it was like to lose someone he loved. Try as he might, he couldn't stifle the feelings he had for Jessie.

When next week's paper came out, he fully expected an exposé on the new criminal investigator Sheriff Richards had hired, and he expected the byline to belong to Jessie West. How he would handle that, he had no idea, but he wasn't about to let her run him out of town without a fight. And that went for Harold Smith as well.

14
CHAPTER

Tinker glared at her friend, then handed her a margarita. "Here, drink this. You'll feel lots better."

"I wish." Jessie took the glass and drank deeply. "Damn, that's good."

"Okay. Tell all."

She ran a finger around the salty rim and licked it. "What?"

"What nothing. You've been all swole up like a wet chicken since you got here."

"Well, it's raining, but thanks for the compliment."

"You know what I'm talking about. Come on, Jessie. We've been friends long enough I know when you're upset. Share. You'll feel lots better. Trouble at work?"

"Not exactly. It's just this story I've been working on." She really didn't want to get into this, but knowing Tinker she might as well tell her something.

"It's our sexy new deputy, isn't it?"

How the hell had she guessed that? "I don't know what you mean."

"He's been stomping around like someone stole his horse. Biting everyone's head off for the slightest thing."

Tears poured from her eyes and she couldn't stop them. Barely able to see the table, she reached out to set down the glass.

Tinker steadied her hand, helped her place it without tipping it over. "I knew it. I knew you two had a falling out. Listen, you've got to patch it up. I think you two were meant for each other if you could both get past the stubbornness."

"He's just so—" She broke off, unable to continue for the emotion clogging her throat.

"So like you."

"Baggage."

"Yup, baggage. But hell who don't have baggage? Long as he don't blame you for his troubles."

"He'd like to, though."

"Long as he don't. You like him, don't you?"

She nodded, unable to speak. "Give me that glass."

Tinker did so, waited till she'd drank deeply, then rescued it. "I've never seen you so upset over a man. Why don't you two just make up? No wonder he's going around like a bear with a thorn in his paw. Get with it, Jessie, before you lose this chance."

"He'll never speak to me again. I broke into his house."

"You *what?* Whyever for?"

"I thought—I mean, it seemed like someone was watching me and I was afraid it was him."

"So you broke in his house? Don't make sense, girl."

"I know. Now that I think about it, I know. He didn't believe me about someone watching me."

Tinker watched her for a long moment. "Why do you think someone is watching you?"

She shook her head, took a tissue from the box on the table, and wiped her face. "I'm probably just being stupid." She didn't dare tell Tinker about the note. She'd have a fit, insist she stay in town with her, that whole thing about living in the country would spring up again. She just wasn't up for it.

"Let's watch a movie. You did get one, didn't you?"

Tinker grinned, obviously glad this whole crying jag thing was over. "Yep. George Clooney."

"Just what I need." Jessie waited while Tinker loaded the disk into the DVD player.

She left Tinker's around eleven, driving carefully through torrents of rain that camouflaged the narrow, curving blacktop so it blended into the surrounding darkness. Tonight she had no desire to stay with her friend, yet dreaded going home. What if she found another note? Or worse, suppose whoever left it was waiting for her in the dark?

A knot formed between her shoulder blades and she hunched forward over the wheel. During the past few days payback for her sins had lurked in the background like some unknown monster. Someone had disrupted the uneasy calm she'd worked so hard to attain, replaced it with a fear as familiar as her own image in a mirror. Was she yet to pay more for what she'd done? Maybe she wasn't supposed to be working on this story, and this was a sign.

Oh, get a grip. Grow up. Face life.

None of those silent appeals to her saner self, if indeed there were such a thing, muffled her fears.

At her turnoff, she slowed almost to a stop, squinted through the curtain of rain, and spotted the opening in the trees. Once in the lane, she sucked in a breath. No lights shone from the cabin. No security light. Was the electricity off or had someone put it out?

If she didn't stop this nonsense she'd be a babbling idiot.

Shoulders hunched, she approached the cabin. A brilliant slash of lightning lit the yard and house, cast eerie fingers into the hovering woods beyond. The sweep of her headlights caught a scurrying figure. Looked like a man, bent over and making for the tree line.

Blinded by terror, she slammed on the brakes, slithered to a halt in the mud, and hung on to the wheel, unable to move. It was so dark, the roll of thunder so loud, she could neither hear nor see an intruder, if indeed there had been one. Maybe her imagination working overtime. No, someone had been there. Not Steve but a stranger. The Steve she remembered wouldn't wait out in the rain. He'd jimmy her door and help himself to a drink, be waiting for her on the sofa as if he belonged there.

Hands clutching the steering wheel, she began to tremble. Her teeth clattered and her heart hammered till she could hear it over the slap of the windshield wipers. Her headlights formed a path to the porch. She ought to do something. Drive away or turn off the engine and get out. Something. But she couldn't. It was all she could do to breathe.

Someone banged on the side window, and she screeched, almost wet her pants, tried to summon enough nerve to take a quick look. Couldn't even do that. If she could only make her foot punch the accelerator, but nothing worked.

Turn. Look. That's all she had to do.

Simple, huh?

Sure.

Filled with terror, she swiveled to peer through the glass. A face squinted back, features drenched, ebony hair plastered by the rain. Abject fear swallowed her up in a thick, black river that threatened to drag her under. Someone had unlocked the gates to hell, her own private hell, and shoved her through.

The mouth moved, the words at last penetrating her numbed brain. "Open the door, Jessie."

Dallas. Dallas Starr. Nearly sick with fright, she unlocked the door and pawed at the latch, shaking so hard she could barely function.

He would not hurt her. In spite of everything that had happened between them, or maybe because of it, she knew he would not hurt her.

When she could finally release the lock, he yanked the door open, leaned in, "What's going on? Are you hurt?"

Still she couldn't move from the seat, even with the blast of cool, wet air that hit her full in the face and left her gasping. All she could do was stare at him. What was he doing here? Oh, God, suppose he'd decided to get back at her, after all.

Speechless, she yanked on the door, tried to shut it against him.

But he had a good hold on it. "Stop, Jessie. I won't hurt you. Stop it."

"Did you see him? Who was that?" She pointed toward the trees, dropped her hand. "Not you?"

"Not me." He touched her, cupped her chin and held on, made eye contact. Said her name several times, then, "Come on, turn off the engine, get out."

She swallowed, gagged, shook her head, but could make no sound at all. Couldn't move.

He twisted the key from the ignition, maneuvered her legs around, and pulled her to her feet. He caught her as her knees buckled, slipped an arm under her legs, another around her back, and lifted her effortlessly.

In desperate need of something to hang on to, she locked both arms around his neck. Vaguely, the annoying *bong, bong, bong*, sounded from inside the car. Door open, lights on. Who cared? She was safe in his arms.

"Hey, it's okay. Relax. Let's get you inside." Voice husky, breath warm against her rain-soaked cheek.

"No. No. Nonononono." She cried against the flesh of his neck, tried to warn him about the man. Out there. Somewhere.

Watching.

The garble that came from her mouth meant nothing. She gave up making sense, gritted her teeth, and held on.

He carried her through the soggy darkness and up onto the porch. There he produced a key ring and opened the door without putting her down.

"Where? Couch? Bed? Floor?"

Bleary-eyed, she looked around, felt for an instant as if she were in an unknown place. Yet she was safe, safe with this man. Anger in his tone, but surely not aimed at her.

From outside beams of light cast a meager glow in the room, leaving shadowy humps where furniture sat, dark corners where someone could hide. All she wanted was for him to hold her, keep her safe. For the first time since coming here, she couldn't face being alone.

"Jessie?" An impatient whisper in her ear.

She licked her lips, tried out a reply that emerged shaky. "Floor. Put me down. I'm fine now."

He obeyed, but kept a grip on her upper arms. Reluctantly, she let go his neck, gazed up into his glowering features.

"Can you tell me about it? What happened? Why were you so terrified? I was driving by, saw your car sitting there with the lights on. Got worried. What happened?"

"I thought I saw someone. Out there. I can't—I don't… Oh, please." She shivered and he touched her cheek, pushed back a lock of hair.

The power came back on and the light she'd left turned on flickered, lit the room. Outside, the security light cast a comforting glow into the night.

"If anyone was out there, they are long gone. Get out of those wet clothes, I'll wait. You okay now?"

Warily, she backed out of his reach, nodded like some crazy marionette. He had rescued her, but where had he really come from? Now that she had time and the sense to think, she hadn't heard him drive up. Maybe that had been him she'd seen skulking around in the yard. Oh, God. And now he was in her house. He'd opened her door with keys. All the things she'd thought of him gathered like a great ball in her chest. She scurried into the bedroom, slammed the door, and stood against it, dripping onto the floor.

This was utter nonsense, and she had to stop. She was beginning to act like a madwoman. If he'd meant her harm, he could have done it when they were alone at his place. When he was so furious with her. Thinking of how safe she'd felt in his arms, she snapped on the light and peeled off her wet clothes.

Damn, she couldn't stop shaking.

He tapped on the door, and she jumped. "Jessie? Where are the towels?"

She told him, then grabbed a robe and scurried past him and down the hall to the tiny bathroom. Adjusting the water so it steamed, she stepped in and stood immobile under the shower until her teeth stopped chattering. Until she brought her wild imagination under control. This man was not here to hurt her, he wanted to help. She had to believe that, not pass judgment on him for what had happened in her past.

At last, she returned to the living room, wrapped warmly in an oversized terry robe, wet hair shrouded in a towel. Silhouetted against the kitchen window, he stared into the rainy night. Caught by the power of his image and a fluttering in her belly that had nothing to do with the earlier encounter, all she could say was his name.

He had removed his soaked uniform shirt. The wet t-shirt hugged his broad chest. The trousers clung to his legs. The belt, with all its equipment and his gun, hung over the back of a chair, and he had dried his hair so it was rumpled. A blue towel was draped around his neck. In silence, he turned to gaze across the dimly lit room, then moved to meet her. Gentle hands cradled her face, big thumbs wiped the tears from her cheeks, warm lips kissed her with tender desire. On the forehead, each eyelid, the tip of her nose, one cheek then the other, finally moved to her mouth with such fierce devotion she melted into his arms. Could only hold on and match his sensuous exploration with her own. The towel unwound and slipped away, releasing her hair in a veil around them. If she let go, her trembling legs would dump her to the floor.

After a long while, he leaned back to study her, eyes smoky with passion. His fingers brushed errant damp locks from her cheeks.

"I've tried to stay away from you. Mad as you make me, stupid as I know it is, I can't. I was on my way to let you know how I feel when I saw your car sitting out there."

Tears pooled. One escaped and ran down her cheek. Shivers quaked through her. "I'm so afraid of this, I don't know what to do. God help us both. We may destroy each other."

He gazed at her. "Don't you think I know that? And right now I wish I could walk out that door and never look back, but I can't. I can't stay away from you. When I'm with you I can't even think of the reasons I shouldn't be. I don't know if this is good or bad, but I can't throw it away.

I need to be with you. I hate what you did, what you do, yet I just can't turn away from you. And I can't let you get hurt or be frightened. Does that make sense at all?"

After he uttered the declaration, he took a step away so they no longer touched. Waited for her to say something.

"What's happening, what it's doing to me, is making me so angry." She swayed but held her head high. "I don't want anyone to protect me. I can take care of myself. Or at least I should be able to. That's what I keep thinking, and then there are questions I need answered."

"Fine. Ask them, now, before we—"

"Where did you get a key to my front door?"

He glanced toward the table at the ring of keys. "They came out of your car, silly. Just a minute ago."

"I'm sorry, I need to stop being so suspicious."

"We both do. But can we?"

"I hope so, because I feel connected to you. I feel like you and I have to be together. To make things work in our lives."

He nodded with relief. "Connected, that's how I feel. It's like something in you speaks to me. To my spirit. Sometimes we all need someone. You need me. Jessie, I need you too. Don't you see it's okay for us to need each other? We'll work it out, I promise."

"Never promise, Dal. I'm so sorry, what I did to you. I really didn't come there for that, and then there it was and I needed to know what had happened to you to make you so, so bitter."

He remained out of reach, and she shuffled forward, rested a hand on his shoulder. His muscles quivered under her touch. "It makes no sense, yet it does. You're cold. You need to get out of those wet things."

"Do you think that's a good idea?"

Running both hands down his chest, she nodded and slipped her fingers under the tail of his t-shirt. "It's a very good idea."

Even with her hands caressing him, Dal did his best to deny this attraction. Did everything he could to walk away from this very dangerous affair. They could so easily grow to hate each other. But he couldn't go back to existing behind the wall of loneliness he'd constructed with such great care. She offered him love in spite of who he was and what he'd done. Could he offer her less? She had paid dearly in ways he should understand. Desire for her was a pain he could no longer bear, and so he took her in his arms, held her close, inhaled her essence, and accepted whatever was to be.

She stirred, took his hand, led him toward her bedroom.

He followed, paused at the door. "Are you sure?"

Her eyes sparkled. "How can you even ask?"

Now that she had committed herself, Jessie moved with deliberate concentration. Heart thumping, she slowly folded the quilt and placed it on top of the cedar chest. Glanced shyly at Dal, who watched as if seeing her for the first time. When she started to turn back the sheet, he covered her hands with his, guided them to his waist.

"Touch me," he whispered. "Make me believe this is real."

For a moment she hesitated, then slowly lifted her hands to undo his pants and pull down the zipper. She remembered doing this before, a long time ago, it seemed now, but that was because so much had happened so quickly. They had never made love, only had sex. Shyly, she glanced up to read his expression.

A slight grin lifted the corners of his mouth, and he spread the front of her robe open, cupped her breasts with both palms. The touch electrified her, desire thrummed low in her belly. The zipper hung and she yanked it free, tugged his jockey shorts down. Trailed her fingers through coils of hair and over satiny flesh, pleased by his arousal.

He moaned, guided her hand to grasp him. Warm, soft, and silken skin belied the rigidity, the pulsating heat, the compelling hunger. She'd been here before, they'd been here before. This time the urgency was not driven by savage lust but by a serene desire to explore and enjoy every moment.

She guided him backward onto the bed where he worked loose the constrictive clothing. Her fingers trailed over the ring hanging round his neck. Without hesitating he slipped the chain over his head and let it fall to the floor.

Languidly she crawled on top of him, stretched to fit her curves to his. When he touched her she captured his hands, pushed them above his head, and tasted of his mouth.

To prolong the ultimate satisfaction of their needs, she crawled all over him. To make him ache for her, to entice her own desires until they reached the breaking point. Fires ignited at the tips of her breasts and between her legs, yet she continued the teasing game. Pulling back each time he tried to enter her.

Though he could easily have overpowered her, he only played at trying to free himself. Letting her lead the way was new to him, but he liked it. Even though he was ready to explode.

Finally, when he thought he could hold out no longer, she straddled him and lowered her mouth to bite playfully at his nipples. His throbbing sex tantalized her inner thighs and still she teased, reaching for the ultimate peak.

Suddenly, he lunged and tossed her on her back, loomed over her with a feral growl.

"My turn, now." He took her breast in his mouth while keeping her arms pinned above her head. He caressed her with nothing but his mouth, leaving no inch of flesh untouched, right down to the tips of her toes.

"Oh, please, now," she begged, writhing with a wild, heated passion.

"Now?" he asked, a glint in eyes.

"Yes, now."

He turned her over and lifted her hips. Nested close and entered her slowly, oh, so slowly. By this time she was begging for release, shoved upward against him in a move that must have caught him off guard, because he shouted with surprise. Or perhaps delight? And shoved back.

Rolling this way and that, drenched in sweat, panting and crying out, they did not, could not stop. His need was insatiable, hers unquenchable, until both lay limp and exhausted, limbs entwined, her head on his chest, his fingers threaded through her damp, wildly tousled hair.

The sound of harsh breathing, the aroma of sex, crowded the room, masked the rain slashing at the windows and pounding on the roof.

"Are you—"

"Don't ask," she ordered. "Can you move?"

"No."

"Then don't."

"I won't."

"Me either."

She drifted off, vaguely aware that something had been left unsaid. She dreamed he told her he loved her and was complete.

Soft night breathing fanned over Dal, filling him with a painful need to hold her forever, never let her go. All he wanted was to keep this newfound feeling of total contentment. But this time would pass, this time of bliss. And then what? Sometimes love simply was not enough. But damned if he knew what was.

Oh, God, he didn't want to think about facing that world out there, where she did things he couldn't fathom. Shutting out the dreary thoughts, he held her, closed his eyes, and drifted off.

She awoke with the warmth of sunlight bathing her face. Sat up lazily. She was alone. Before she could wonder where Dal had gone, the front door slammed.

His voice echoed down the hall, "Rise and shine, sleepyhead. Guess what we did?"

"Oh, I know what we did." She stretched sore muscles. Satisfaction drenched her like warm water and she peered at the waiting world through slitted eyes. Time would be changed forever. It had to be.

He stood in the doorway dressed in a wrinkled white t-shirt and uniform pants and eyed her with a joyful grin, amusement lighting his emerald eyes. "We left our lights on and both batteries are dead. Looks like we're stuck here for a while. Mac is going to love this."

So good to see him happy. "Well, isn't that just too bad? This is Saturday, why worry about your job? Come back to bed."

"Good idea, but I'm on call. I'll have to get the unit running." As if in direct reply to his statement, the radio in the other room belched static and his name. He made a face, and went to answer.

Crawling from the bed, she worked a t-shirt over her head and followed, walking gingerly to appease her aching loins. What a wonderful ache it was, though. Leaning against him while he talked, she caressed his smooth, coppery skin.

He folded one hand over hers, squeezed, spoke into the radio, "I need a ride. Someone will have to stop by. I'm at Jessie's place. I need a jump. My battery is dead."

A familiar feminine voice touched with humor. *"Excuse me, Deputy Starr, you're where?"*

Her friend Tinker. Jessie laughed and covered her mouth. Joy filled her. She'd forgotten how good it felt to love someone. To wonder if anyone noticed. To keep the secret close to her heart until the proper time to spring it on best friends. Still, Tinker would surely guess.

Dal took his finger off the button and whispered, "Be careful what you say. We're on an open channel here. Scanners can pick this up."

Once more he keyed the radio. "Dispatch, would you send a cruiser out here? My battery's dead and I need a jump. Out."

He laid the radio down, and both of them chuckled when Tinker said, *"Ten-four, Deputy."*

Jessie laughed with delight. "Well, we'll never live this down. She won't give us a minute's peace."

"I don't care." He swooped her off her feet and carried her out onto the deck, kicking and screaming. Stood her near the rail where they remained, hand in hand.

She didn't want to think of the man she'd seen last night, but Dal finally brought it up, as if reading her mind. He did that a lot.

"We'll find him, you know."

"Will you?"

"Oh, yes. And until we do, I'll see you're protected."

If someone really wanted to get to her, they would, no matter the protection. He knew it as well as she, was simply trying to soothe her. So she said nothing.

The deputy who drove out to provide assistance for Dal's cruiser was young and fairly new on the job. He introduced himself as Wally Preston, and carried with him a message from the sheriff.

"Mac says he's got a final report from the Spaceys on those bones Miss Jessie found? He thought if you weren't too busy with anything else, you might want to come by his office. He said you could bring Miss Jessie along if you so desired. Said it would save him having to tell her all about it later." The deputy's blue eyes flashed, and he bent to clamp on the jumper cables.

He looked like the red-headed kid on the old *Happy Days* reruns, what was his name? He was old and bald now. She imagined Wally bald and giggled. "Could you ask Mister Wally to stop calling me Miss Jessie?"

Dal grinned. "You ask him."

"I heard," the young man said from beneath the hood. "What should I call you, er, her?"

"Just plain Jessie will do. Wally."

Dal led her back toward the house.

"Sometimes Mac thinks he's my father, you know."

"Mac's not a bad choice for a father—and you make him a damn fine daughter."

"I mean, let's not tell him about my scare last night. I don't want to worry him."

He hugged her so close for so long she thought she'd stop breathing. His heart thumped hard against her.

At the sheriff's office, they found Mac leaned back in his chair, booted feet propped on the desk. Mischief glinted in his blue eyes.

"I warn you, Mac," Jessie said, shaking a finger. "One word and I'll publish that picture I took of you at the Halloween carnival. You know the one I mean."

"You told me you destroyed that."

"Well, I lied."

He held up both hands. "You two are looking radiant. Had a nice night, I reckon."

"Mac," she warned, "No need to be so cocky."

"Sorry, I couldn't help myself." He handed Dal a file. "An official report from Dave and Kathy. May get an ME's report in a month or two, DNA from the lab sometime next year. This isn't exactly a priority case, and the lab is backed up."

"Yeah, so I've heard." Dal flipped the folder open, read in silence. "Yep, just what Kathy told us, only she's just used bigger words for the file. Our bones were the victim of foul play. A ridge angled along the gladiolus of the sternum was caused by a bullet, and at that angle it would have been fatal, going directly into his heart."

He slapped the file against his thigh, glanced at her. "I wonder if they are connected after all. Ken Norville disappeared, this victim was murdered, during or around the same time frame. Considering the lack of disappearances or crimes around here we have to treat it as possibly one and the same. All we gotta do is tie up all the loose ends."

"Mary Norville Smith definitely knows something she's not telling," Jessie added. "She's our key to the whole thing."

"Now, about that search warrant for the old Norville place." Dal pointed a direct gaze at the sheriff.

Mac nodded with satisfaction. "Let's get some of the kids from the college to do a search for the skull too. Can't hurt, and they just might find it. Those kids like to get out and do that sort of stuff. Be better than spending their last few weeks in school locked up in a classroom." He glanced at Dal. "Give the Spaceys a call. They can take charge of that. Use my phone."

Dal picked up the instrument, then glanced at Jessie, who supplied the number. It only took a few short sentences to arrange the search, and he hung up.

"Doc says they can probably get it started today. Should one of us be out there?"

"Probably," Mac said. "I'll go. I need some time out of this office."

"Good," Dal said. "I want to try to run down this Jolene Norville. We'll need her DNA for comparison. Doubt Ken is in CODIS, but we'll run the results anyway. Can't presume it's him. I haven't been able to find any other outstanding missing persons that could be our guy."

Jessie told them about the note Mary had found and her being so frightened. "Someone also has been in her house, just like someone has been in mine."

"When was this?" Mac pinned her with a glare. "You didn't tell me someone had been in your house."

"I told Dal when I—" She broke off, glanced at Dal.

He shrugged. "The note. I'm sorry I didn't believe you. Thought you were just saying that to get on my good side."

"Oh, you have one?" she quipped.

"I'm trying." He caught her stare, held it somberly to let her know she wasn't making things any easier.

"What about these notes?" Mac asked, bringing them back to the case at hand.

"They were almost alike, except mine was threatening and Mary's was meant to console her."

"Where are they?" Dal glanced her way.

"I think I wadded mine up and threw it away." Jessie glanced from one man to the other. "Not too smart, huh? It's still in the wastebasket. I saw Mary's, but she took it with her. She wanted to show it to Harold."

"Damn," Dal muttered almost in sequence with Mac's harsher expletive. "I really like Harold for this."

"Well, see if you can get the notes," Mac said.

"I'll do that."

"Now, what's this other stuff you're hiding from me?" Mac said. "Sounds like there's things going on here I need to be apprized of. What's up between you two?"

"It's personal, Mac," Jessie finally said with a furtive glance at Dal. "It's early on, yet. We're working it out." Father figure or no, he didn't need to know everything, especially not her love life.

Dal glanced over the report, changed the subject as if too nervous to discuss the matter. "Even if our bones aren't Norville's, something suspicious went on at that old house, I'm convinced of it. Have you heard from the State Police? I called for a forensics team yesterday to go over the place and dispatch said this evening."

The sheriff nodded. "Sergeant Pepper called first thing this morning to verify that. Said they'd be out late this evening, if our investigator could meet them there. Fluorescing requires it be dark, you know." He paused, eyed his new deputy. "Harold Smith is fit to be tied over this. Called me at home last night, said I was to call you off. You should have waited for a warrant."

"It's the scene of a crime, Mac."

"It's the alleged scene of a more than eighteen-year-old alleged crime. You can't just go stomping around on private property, not even out here in the boonies. What if you'd found evidence?"

Dal eyed him with skepticism. "After all these years? Nothing I could carry away, at any rate. We'll get some with the warrant and luminol though, I'm convinced of it. Did you get it?"

"It's done, but the warrant is strictly for the forensics team to check for signs a crime was committed there. Blood spatter, other bodily fluids. Bullets in the walls. You know the drill. We don't look for marijuana or coke or weapons. He'll be strict about that." Mac glanced at Jessie.

She made a face. "Like he's liable to keep stuff like that in that old place open to the elements and prowlers."

Mac nodded. "Okay, fine. Technically the disappearance of Ken Norville has never been a closed case, according to the file you found at the courthouse, and our search will be to continue that investigation. Now, if you wouldn't mind letting me in on it, what's the point in forensics going out to the Norville place?"

Dal frowned, tapped the sheaf of papers from Kathy Spacey. "Something evil happened out there. Just call it one of my darker hunches." Secretive mask well in place, he glanced at Jessie, then went on. "The file was in the basement in the courthouse. Shouldn't have been down there if this case was still open. I also checked for any other missing persons during that time frame while I was in those files."

Mac scowled at the presumed criticism. "Find anything?"

Dal held up a hand. "Nope, and I didn't mean to be a wise-ass. At the time Ken disappeared, Mary and Jolene told identical stories, like they'd rehearsed them. That's fishy in itself, but it seems no one was too worried about it then. Clearly, the old bastard needed killing, and I guess everyone was relieved that he'd gone and drowned. Too relieved to check into it further, I'm sorry to say. But I've been out to that place. Something happened in that house. Something bloody, and I don't think it was a hog butchering."

"You can tell that after all this time?" Jessie's voice was skeptical.

He relayed with silence that he wasn't about to discuss it with her, at least not at the moment.

Mac twisted in her direction. "Young lady, this is an ongoing investigation. I'll see you get a press release Monday in time for next week's issue, but none of this sees print, you hear?"

Relieved at the change in subject, she acquiesced. "Do me one favor, though, Mac. Don't send the dailies a release until we're on the streets. That story they ran yesterday was pretty bland, but this forensics thing will likely stir them up."

Dal studied her somberly. "Scoop them at all costs?"

The judgmental tone of his voice nagged at her, but she came right back at him. "Yes, scoop them if we can. No, not at all costs. It's hard enough being a weekly, but when a big story comes along, we're at an extreme disadvantage. I want my story out there before theirs. It's my job.

"Parker gets upset when we're scooped on something in the county, even though in theory he agrees that the true concept of a community weekly newspaper is not to scoop anyone. This is big enough to really get his dander up, and it's right at our front door. He won't let up on it. You can count on that. And he'll want me doing my best."

A frown creased his forehead. He didn't quite believe her. Feared she was hot on a story and would let nothing stop her. But it wasn't true. What intrigued her about this case was the mystery of fitting all the intricate puzzle pieces together, and she itched to interview Mary again.

"Why don't you turn it over to another reporter, then?" Dal asked.

"The same reason you don't get one of the other deputies to handle the investigation," she said, the words coming out sharper than she intended. "Besides, we're a small newspaper. When it comes to reporters, I'm it except for Parker. You're better off with me, trust me. He covers the police beat like a blue tick hound on the scent of a coon. He'd have you up a tree, bare-ass naked, in a minute. Count on it. I found the bones, I'll finish it." Happily, this was the first time she'd felt sure of herself. She would finish the story, and she would do it ethically.

Before Dal could come back at her, Mac dropped his feet to the floor with a loud thud. "You two take this somewhere else. I'd like to have some time off to eat before we begin that search. It'll likely run till dark unless we find something right away. Now, let's get moving. And I don't want her left alone, you hear?" He jerked his head toward Jessie.

"I've got to get on the computer, see if I can find Jolene." Dal unfolded his long body from the chair.

Jessie rose eagerly. "I'd like to help, if it's okay."

"Fine, but only because I'm under orders not to leave you alone. What we find is off the record till I say different."

"All right." Satisfied, she followed him out, wiggling her fingers at Mac before the door closed.

15
CHAPTER

Dal sat at an empty desk in the office, indicated another for Jessie. "Make yourself useful. Google Jolene, see what you can come up with. I'll start with DMV records. You did say she moved to Kansas."

"It's what Mary told me."

Without glancing at her, he went to work. After two hours he leaned back, rubbing at his eyes. "No driver's license, car registration, insurance, property taxes, electric, or phone bills. Nothing anywhere. It's like she dropped off the face of the earth."

"Same here," Jessie said, manipulating her fingers. "Jolene Norville is not exactly a common name. None of the searches turned her up. Looks like she's hiding from something."

"And doing a damned good job of it, too. Wonder what that might be? Did Mary mention anyone at all, even a first name? Maybe the guy she married?"

"Nope, all she said was she got married, but she didn't know the man's name or exactly where they were living. Nothing."

"Still, searches under her maiden name ought to have revealed *something.*"

"She must have changed her name other than getting married."

"If she did it legally, I'd have found it. Dammit, people like her shouldn't know how to disappear into thin air."

"You don't suppose she… well, this sounds crazy, but what if she died and is buried somewhere else. We could search death certificates."

He stared at the toes of his boots, head shaking slowly. "I'm just not getting that, but I suppose it's possible."

"Maybe your psychic connection is broken."

Even though she grinned, he regarded her seriously for a moment, as if considering the possibility. Then he too smiled, rose, and rubbed the back of his neck. "Well, whatever it is, I'm tired of this." He glanced at his watch. "We've worked right through lunch. Let's grab a bite to eat, then go on out to the Norville place. The State boys will be there by seven or so, I hope."

"Guess that means I'm going with you."

"That or I lock you up in a cell."

"Don't you dare. What a story that would make. New deputy charged with false arrest."

"Okay, okay. I heard what Mac said about taking care of you, and everyone's busy, so I guess you're with me. Come on, let's go."

She grabbed her backpack, followed him to the car, and climbed in when he held the door open.

They ate burgers at Butch's and, since it was early, walked around town, her educating him on the residents and some history. When the sun went down, they climbed in his Tahoe and headed out to the Norville place.

Because he seemed lost in thought on the drive to the Norville place, she kept her mouth shut.

The forensics team hadn't arrived, and he parked in the yard. For a moment he sat very still, hands gripping the steering wheel.

He was deep in thought, no doubt talking to his spirits. Not wanting to disturb whatever was going on in his head, she checked out the place. This was the first time she'd been this close to the old house. It beckoned to be explored. In the yard, a lone dogwood shed the last of its creamy petals into the still, warm air. They floated to the ground as gracefully as butterflies. Yellow forsythia formed a riot of color in a wild tangle along one end of the dilapidated structure.

What a great place for a murder. Was he right and someone had been killed here?

"You're kidding, of course," he murmured. "I mean about it being a great place for a murder."

His reply to her silent thoughts sent shivers through her. "Okay, I forgot you read minds. I'll have to be more careful. Besides, I was thinking in the abstract."

He shook his head, acted as if it were perfectly normal for him to carry on conversations with someone's thoughts.

"Come on, tell me how you did that."

"What?"

How could he look so innocent? She sighed, stared at the house in the lowering shadows. This was truly creepy. She'd made love with a man who could eavesdrop on her every thought at will. Not good.

"Okay, if you don't want to talk about it, fine. But just don't be so serious. What happened here was a long time ago. I'm sure it was terrible, but it's in the past. This is today. The house looks like it could be haunted."

She stopped suddenly, grabbed his hand. "That's it, isn't it? There are ghosts here. Come on, let's go in before the State boys get here, and you can use your powers to conjure them up. Oh, that's right, not ghosts. Spirits. You can introduce me." She squeezed his fingers. Why couldn't he lighten up a bit? Have some fun.

He was having none of it, but didn't pull away. "I don't conjure up spirits. And haunted is a misnomer. If I were a true *ada'wehi* I'd know what happened here, who it happened to, and the killer's name. Lone Bear Stands tells me I'm gifted. He was a true shaman."

Dal refused to watch her while he tried to explain what he did. Instead he gazed at the windows. The place was haunted, all right, but not in the way she thought. No white robed figures peering out at them. No chains rattling nor ghostly moans. And she was being damned quiet. He must've spooked her.

He gave her a quick glance, but she wasn't spooked at all. She was excited, her features dancing, a grin turning up her lips.

"Hey, you're right," he said. "Such a beautiful evening should be enjoyed, especially in the company of a gorgeous woman." That said, he was fixing to get her pissed at him. Big time.

"I'd like to borrow your camera. I want to look around and take some pictures before the state boys get here."

Her hand left his and she honored him with a scowl. "Hey, I can take my own pictures. Doesn't the department furnish you with a camera?" She tilted her head, looked at him suspiciously. "You're not letting me in there, are you?"

Should he admit she was right? She might bonk him one with that pack she lugged around. Knock him silly.

Instead he dodged the issue. "I don't have my stuff yet. You know that. And there isn't a camera at the department either. I think they put the cart before the horse hiring me before they equipped my department."

Clenching his jaw, he reached out for her camera.

She was having none of that, grabbed up her pack and shoved open her door. "Tell you what, Buddy, you show me the subject, I'll take the pictures. This camera belongs to the paper and Parker'd have a hemorrhage if I, or you, broke it. I'm going in there, too. You just don't want me to watch you commune with your spirits."

He bailed out of the car and hurried to catch up with her, favoring that damned right leg. The doctors had told him he'd never get any more out of it, but he kept pushing anyway.

"Dammit, Jessie. I'm not going to break it, for Christ sake. Is it made of glass? Just give me directions on how to use it. Get back here. You'll contaminate the scene of the crime."

She hauled up at the foot of the rickety steps and tossed him a glower. "After more than a decade, I hardly think that would be possible. I'll bet the coons have pooped all over it, and forget what the squirrels and rabbits have accomplished, to say nothing of the pack rats."

Sneaking a look at her expression, he read the stubborn determination there. No damn way was he going to keep her from going in that house short of hog-tying her, and he wasn't sure he could accomplish that without hurting her. That he would not do.

"Okay, okay. At least be careful. It's dark in there." He took out his flashlight, illuminated the floor. "Those boards are old and rotten. Don't fall through."

"I think I can manage."

Looking contrite, she held out her hand and he took it. From inside, the roiling spirits licked at him like smoke off a smoldering fire. What would she think when he reacted to the horror of the past within those walls? He had trouble controlling how he dealt with them when he was alone. She was absolutely right. He didn't want her to witness what could happen. It might not be pretty.

At the doorway, he hauled up short, assailed by cries of pain and despair. Sucking in a deep breath, he beat them back. "Jessie, if you insist on writing this story, I'm not so sure you should even be with me during the investigation. It's not, well, it's unorthodox, to say the least."

Her pretty mouth tightened and those cat eyes flashed a warning. She was steaming all right.

"I don't care what you think. You brought big city ideas with you carried here from the filthy streets and alleys you're running away from."

She paused, set down her pack, and dug around in it until she found her own flashlight. Shook it at him and turned it on. "You're not dealing with pot heads and scumbags here. I've been there, too, you know. And for your information, I'm not about to wait here like a good little girl while you conduct your investigation. Not unless you handcuff me."

"Well, believe me, I'm considering it. You don't know what's about to happen in there, but if you're dead set on going in, come on. Just don't say I didn't warn you. And don't touch me."

She studied his face a moment, trying to figure out if there was real danger. "You're just trying to keep me out. Trying to scare me."

"Damn right I am."

She jerked her hand from his, stepped around the fallen door, and put her foot down on a rotten board. Through her leg went, clear to the thigh, a nail ripping a gash along her calf. When her foot hit solid ground the other leg bent, one knee cracking onto the floor.

He caught at her, missed, and she fell forward, flinging the backpack aside to catch herself with both hands.

Her flashlight rolled away with a clatter.

"Jessie, you okay?" He bent to help her, touched the floor with one hand and all hell broke loose.

Tendrils of terror shoved her and the present out of his mind. The musty smells of yesterday blended with dim echoes of violence that had all but soaked into the aged hardwood floor where his hand rested. The terror that lived in this place reached out and squeezed his soul. The screams of women in fear for their lives mixed with a brutality gone wild. A gunshot thundered, a searing pain clutched at his chest. He hugged himself, fell to the floor, agony pinning him there. He couldn't speak or move.

Blood, blood. Everywhere blood.

And outside the storm raged, literally shaking the walls.

"Dal, are you all right?"

She grabbed his arm, jerked him from the past, and he peered at her. Superimposed over her face were twisted features spattered in blood, mouths open in endless screams. One after another, the gory images shook him to the core. He must have blanched, for Jessie clung to his arm and scrambled to pull her leg loose.

The nail that had caught her going down dug into her flesh. "Ow, dammit." She yanked at the jagged board, but couldn't pull it away. "For God's sake, would you stop rolling around on the floor and get me out of here. I fell in the hole, you didn't."

He crawled to her, sweat pouring off his face and darkening the fabric of his shirt.

"I told you not to touch me, didn't I? I told you to stay in the goddamned car, didn't I?" He ripped the rotted wood away until she could ease her leg free.

"Well, I would have if I'd known you were going to have such a fit. What in the world happened?" She inspected the jagged tear along her calf, pawed around in her bag, and came out with a pack of Kleenex to dab away the blood.

"I warned you and you wouldn't listen. This is a killing scene, and the spirits of those involved are still here."

"Oh, yeah, sure. And one of them shoved me through the floor."

The noise she made sounded like a raspberry, but he ignored it and held the flashlight where she could see to mop at the cut. "That looks bad, probably needs stitches."

She pushed his hand away. "It's just a cut." Again she searched her bag. "I've got some antiseptic pads in here somewhere. I'll clean it up and it'll be fine."

"That's a rusty nail, no telling what it had on it. You had your shots?"

"What? For hydrophobia?"

Despite the situation, he couldn't help but chuckle, an act that placed the terror at bay. "No, for tetanus." The day she'd asked him that very question flashed back on him, as did her gentleness and compassion toward his pain. Anger drained away.

"I think so, yes, I'm sure I have."

"Uh huh. Well, the bleeding has stopped, but it'd be a good idea for you to check with your doctor."

Having located an antiseptic pad, she ripped it open and cleaned the cut thoroughly. "There, all better, and I will."

"Oh, shit," Dal muttered, twisting away from a new attack fingering through his brain. A gasping, sucking noise, an obscenity of muttered threats. "I think we'd best get out of here till the lab boys come."

"What's the matter? Evil spirits after you again?" She tossed everything back into her bag and stood, retrieving the flashlight before reaching down to give him a hand.

"Thanks." He held on to her longer than he intended, considering her flippant remark. But the silken feel of her skin, the fresh smell of her hair, the expression in her eyes that belied what she'd said, distracted him. At least the screams had faded.

"What about the pictures?"

"We'll take em while they're working in here." Hopefully, with company, the spirits would settle down.

Outside, the roaring of car engines announced the arrival of the state forensics team, and the choice was made for them. Three young men stampeded across the porch and inside, sounding like a herd of buffalo. Each one was loaded down with equipment. Dal left Jessie and went to talk to them.

Sergeant Pepper, a lean redhead with a dusting of copper freckles over his nose and cheeks, looked more like somebody's teenage son than a forensic specialist. It was difficult to take him seriously. Dal wondered at the way men oft times fit their names.

He introduced himself and filled Pepper in tersely. "Check for blood. It may be concentrated in the kitchen, spatter on the cabinets and walls too. This place has been partially open to the elements for a lot of years, but we may get lucky with the luminol. The weapon may have been a thirty-thirty."

Pepper nodded, squatted to open a large bag, and jerked his head in Jessie's direction. "Your partner?"

"Hardly. Miss West is a member of the press, so be careful what you say." Though he tried to sound unconcerned, he knew he hadn't succeeded, and Jessie stared a hole through him.

The trooper raised an eyebrow. "You both need to put on gloves, if you're remaining on the scene."

The older officer handed them both a pair of latex gloves, which they pulled on.

Dal turned away. "I'm going upstairs."

"Do you want the camera?" she asked sweetly.

"When I get back."

Miffed at his curt dismissal, Jessie watched him climb the stairs, favoring his right leg. His mood shifted from light to dark so quickly she had trouble sorting out her feelings toward him. If she hadn't been in love with him last night, it was as close as she'd ever come. His demeanor today was disconcerting. But love was like that. Wasn't it?

She hung around the scene to watch the forensics team. While one mixed several chemicals together in a spray bottle, another took photos of all aspects of the room, and yet another slipped a pair of colored goggles over his eyes and slowly shined a light on various surfaces in the kitchen.

She stood on the periphery until Pepper approached. "Ma'am, you'll probably want to leave now. This stuff isn't toxic, but it sure is unpleasant."

"Do you think I could stay? This is intriguing, and I've never been at a crime scene at this stage before. Maybe I could get a couple of photos of you guys at work?"

Pepper glanced at one of the men, who had already donned a respirator and glasses. "Get the lady a respirator, Dan. It won't hurt if she watches. Take your pictures now, ma'am, before the boys get started luminescing."

She snapped the photos as the men finished preparing the chemicals, then slipped on the mask and goggles Dan handed her. Dal would probably have a conniption when he came downstairs, but let him. This was exciting. Darkness fell like a cloak over the work space. Flashlight beams sliced the room into eerie triangles and rectangles, turning the scene ghostly.

"We're shooting baseline control photos for comparison before spraying the luminol," Pepper told her. "It reacts not only to blood but to bleach and various minerals, so sometimes it's an educated guess. There's a new product that is more specific to blood, but we don't have it yet."

After photographing and marking sections of the wood for removal, the technicians went to work spraying the area Dal had indicated. Vague patches where they sprayed the pine board floor glowed like blue ghosts under the UV light. The men looked like aliens on an exotic planet. The whoosh-whoosh sound of the respirators added to the spooky ambiance.

"Good God almighty. Looks like a slaughterhouse," Pepper said, voice distorted by the paraphernalia he wore.

Good quote. She'd remember it. Horrified by the pattern the light revealed splashed over the front of the wood cabinets and all over the floor, she retreated to the doorway. Sweat poured from under the mask. Was that blood? Further, was it Ken's? Swallowing bile, she cleared her throat.

"I didn't know it would show up like this after so many years. Do you think it's blood?"

Pepper nodded. "Probably. We can tell at the lab. Sometimes the older the blood stains are the better they come out when we treat the area." Carefully, he scraped samples from the aged and cracked doors, collecting each in a separate bag that he marked and sealed.

Hanging the camera over her shoulder, she took out her pad and scribbled notes. Hard to see in the gloom and with the goggles on, but she did her best. The sound of a saw buzzing added to the noise. One of the men was removing a section of the flooring near the door.

Shuddering, she moved back into the parlor, avoiding stepping where the splashes of blood had glowed earlier, as if they were fresh. The men had removed their masks, so she did too. A vague scent remained in the air, but it was a relief to be unfettered by the bulky equipment. Easy to understand why television shows about forensics ignored masks and protective clothing. Everyone looked damned weird in such get-ups. Sure couldn't look sexy on camera.

Dal clumped back downstairs and stood in the doorway, one gloved hand braced on either side, eyes closed. She quickly snapped a shot of him. Thank God he didn't notice, or he'd probably have tossed her and the camera out the front door.

Did he really hear the dead speak? Surely not. What a crock that was. But the way he acted, he thought he did, that was for sure. Did that make him crazy? Or better at what he did?

At the moment he appeared to be in some sort of trance. It was a peculiar way of dealing with a crime scene, and one she'd only seen in movies. Maybe there was something to it after all. He'd referred to shamans with supernatural powers known as *ada'wehi* in Cherokee, yet claimed he was not so endowed. Sure seemed to be effected by something weird.

Away from the distraction, she flipped on her tape recorder, stowed in the outside pocket of her bag, and questioned a balding trooper who was dusting surfaces with a black powdery substance. "Can you still get fingerprints after this long a time?"

"Oh, some surfaces hold prints better than others, but no telling how many people've been in here, you know kids and all, since then. We'll try, but I doubt they'll be much use. Now if you could get us the murder weapon and it'd been well wrapped and dry all these years, maybe." He shrugged, and went on with his minute inspection of the wall.

"What're you looking for?"

"Bullet holes, preferably with a chunk of lead intact."

"Oh."

"Normally, at a scene, we arrive soon after the crime occurs. We bag hair and fabric and tracked-in mud, all kinds of possible evidence. An older scene like this, it's a lot different, though, as you saw, blood that's been around longer tends to show up better under luminol. Probably find more in the cracks between the boards. That's why we're taking more than one section. But any hair we find probably came from a possum or a coon, maybe a curious deer." He grinned up at her charmingly. "Or maybe you. All that loose long hair. I trust we can eliminate any of your hairs from our crime scene." He laughed. "Not much here really. It's mostly the blood and a possible bullet hole. Through and through."

"Then this is a waste of time?"

"Not at all. We'll take out sections of the floor and wall where the luminescence showed up, others where there wasn't any for comparison, take em back to the lab, and maybe learn something. It's not always just blood of the victim, you know. If we get lucky and find more than one type, well, who knows? And today with DNA, we have a better chance if there's enough uncontaminated blood to do a work-up. These days we can even extract STRDNA from sweat or cigarette butts or blood diluted by other sources. Course, DNA's no good without a suspect unless again, we're lucky and CODIS has our perp or he gets hauled in."

"What's STRDNA?"

"Short tandem repeat. But as for your remains, mtDNA may help in identification. Old remains lack nucleated cells. So hair shafts, bones, and teeth unamenable to STR or RFLP will yield mtDNA samples."

The young man was cooperative, and she smiled sweetly at him. With all that technical stuff, she was pleased she had turned on the recorder. What a story this was developing into. What was best, she could use these interviews without Dal's permission.

"What's RFLP?" she asked, but the subject of her thoughts came out of his trance and glared at the trooper, who shrugged as if innocent, but shut up.

Miffed, Jessie watched for a while longer and snapped a few more shots, just to show him he hadn't run her off, then went outside to poke around. She could get on the Internet and find the answer to her question about DNA that he'd cut off. Even, she suspected, learn more about DNA profiling.

Dal seemed to have lost interest in taking his own photos, probably because the forensics team was taking so many. It looked as if someone was actually murdered here a long time ago. Strange how he knew that. But no way would she believe a ghost had clued him in. That was utter nonsense.

Except, there was a moment there, caught up in the dark room surrounded by swords of light and strange-looking apparatus, when she could easily have believed in spirits of the dead.

Nonsense. Her story was the thing, and it would go beyond the killing, to the real people involved and what life had done to them. This had been a murder of some passion. A murder that had affected the lives of those involved for many years. It was beginning to look as if Mary Smith most probably was involved.

She would begin writing the first piece, using quotes from these investigators and Mary as well. Put it in the pending file where she could work on it in her spare time until this case was solved. The daily down in Harrison would probably want to print it, and that might get her noticed. It would go out on the wires where other newspapers could pick it up.

A worry worm crawled into her mind, burrowed around there and settled in. She dare not think that way. Dreams of fame and fortune. That was the old JJ Stone, the blonde girl wonder who'd shot her wad and gone down in flames. She had killed all her chances with one big flash. Yet she was still standing on her two feet and working at what she loved.

Dal came up behind her. "You ready?"

Startled, she turned, and was once again swept away by his moody good looks. "Are they finished?"

"No, but we are. I'll take you home."

Guiding their way with the flashlight, he lifted a length of yellow and black crime scene tape stretched around the old house. She ducked under and he followed, then led her through the weeds toward the cruiser. Without another word, he opened the passenger door for her and handed her inside. His mere touch sent a shiver through her.

When they arrived back at her cabin, him silent all the way, Wally was leaned against the cruiser parked under an old oak tree. "Sheriff asked me to keep an eye on the place," he explained.

While Dal talked to him, she went on to the house. Fishing around in her bag, she realized that she'd left her keys inside. Dal had taken them from the ignition the previous night, and considering what had happened later, it wasn't any wonder she'd forgotten to put them in her bag. It didn't matter, though.

Glancing toward the two men who were deep in conversation, she ran around the corner and up on the deck. The space under the planter where she kept a spare key was empty. Only vaguely alarmed because she had a bad habit of misplacing things, she glanced at the sliding glass door. It stood open. For an instant she thought of calling Dal, instead rose and slipped inside. She could take care of this herself.

The house embraced her with a deathly silence. Everything looked okay, but felt strange. The maple dining room table and four chairs, Dal's morning coffee cup rinsed and turned upside down on a paper towel, hers sitting in the sink. The living room slightly askew from their abrupt leave-taking earlier.

Still, the shiver climbing her spine urged her to get the two men. Not go any further. The intruder could still be here. But she never listened to that still small voice. Why start now? She crept past the bathroom, where damp towels hung over the edge of the tub, and into the bedroom. Stopped, clenched both fists over a scream that nearly choked her.

The bastard. Damn him.

The room was littered with fluffy down, gutted from the ripped comforter and shredded pillows on the bed. Feathers floated in the air like delicate moths in rays of sunlight, drifted over the cedar chest and dresser. One drawer hung open and a handful of her panties lay about on the shiny wood floor like dying flowers.

Stricken mute, she stood in the center of the devastation, fists clenched at her sides, battling the demons that gnawed at her. Then she turned and fled, out the door and through the yard, gasping and pointing back toward the house, unable to utter an intelligible sound.

Dal met her, caught and shoved her toward Wally. "Hold on to her, and *stay here.*"

Drawing his weapon, he crossed the yard and crept up onto the porch, stood aside and reached to open the front door before he realized it was still locked. What the hell was going on? He sneaked around the cabin and eased onto the back deck. The door stood half open.

He had no more than hugged his way around the sill, weapon aimed, when Jessie ran into him, Wally Preston hot on her heels.

"Dammit, *get down.*" Voice husky, he blocked her way. "I told you to stay outside."

"I couldn't stop her," Wally said.

"I'm familiar with that experience."

Jessie swiveled to gaze at the two of them. "What? Why?"

"Might still be in here." He trapped her behind him.

Wally cleared his weapon, pointed it at the floor, and dug in on the opposite wall.

"No one's here, I looked." There was her smirk again.

"Hush and wait. For once do what I ask."

She stiffened against him, but he didn't have the time or the inclination to placate hurt feelings. Nodding at Wally, he slinked around the room and into the hallway. Covering each other, they checked out the closets, the bathroom, and then darted through the open bedroom door to stir up clouds of white fluff.

"Holy cow." Wally stared. "I swear, no one came near this place."

Dal gestured toward the closet door and jerked his head.

Wally took the message and, standing to one side, yanked it open. Down lifted from the floor and floated out to meet them, clung to their pant legs and settled in their hair. The closet was empty.

"It's clear." Dal moved into the hallway.

Jutting her chin at him, she dared speak. "Do you feel better now? I told you no one was here, but you have to go get bossy on me." Anger melted into dismay, and she raised both fists. "Damn him to hell. Who's doing this? Why can't he leave me alone?"

One look into the depths of her tear-pooled eyes and Dal gathered her close. "It'll be okay. We'll find this sick bastard. He's not going to hurt you."

"But I'm liable to hurt him." She gagged and covered her mouth.

"Hush, now. Wally, get her some water, would you please?"

The young deputy moved to obey, tracking fluff through the hallway toward the kitchen. A few wads trailed after him.

"I will not go through this again. I can't."

He patted at her back. "It'll be okay."

She stiffened against him. All he could do was hold her and soothe her, offer her the glass of water Wally brought from the kitchen. Get her settled down enough to get some sense out of her.

Wally hovered, looking contrite, so Dal sent him home.

She drank the water and watched him over the rim. Distraught, almost comical with his downy hair. Some clung to one ear, another wad stuck to his chin.

She finally pulled herself together, and because she enjoyed being in Dal's arms way more than she should, moved out of his embrace.

"Thank you, I'm sorry I acted like such a fool. I guess all this is getting to me. Him making it personal and all."

"You think this might be that Steve fellow?" Dal asked.

"It's not Steve. I promise you that. Believe me, he wouldn't do it this way."

"Never mind," he said, rubbing her arms gently. "It was a thought, but if you say no, then it's no. We'll find out who it is, but until we do I don't want you out here alone."

"I don't need a keeper. I can take care of myself."

He glanced at the bedroom, then back at her. "I'm sure you can. But you shouldn't have to. I'll spend the night and tomorrow's Sunday. We can do something together. But I have to be back on the job Monday."

"I said I don't need a keeper. This has to have something to do with the bones, but what?" She waited, scarcely breathing, watching him.

"Could you go stay with your friend Tinker or maybe the Spaceys?" he asked. "Just till we catch this maniac."

She strode angrily outside, stood at the deck rail staring off into the woods, wishing she'd see someone she could point to and say, "There he is, go get him." But all was serene. A beautiful, peaceful spring night, a partial moon coming up like an enormous egg over the mountains. A soft breeze kissed her cheeks.

He came up behind her, enclosed her shoulder in a hug. Unable to hide her desire for his touch, she leaned into his warm strength. "He will not drive me out of my home."

He kissed her temple. "We'll get him, Jessie. I promise."

"You can't promise something like that. We both know it." She shivered, and he pulled her closer.

"Tinker and I have a standing invitation to Dave and Kathy's every Sunday. Come with us, we'll figure something out. I can't let this man disrupt my life. And I won't leave this place. This is my home. I belong here. I have no other place to go. Damn him. Damn him to hell."

After a long silence, he took her shoulders and turned her to face him. "I promise you, we'll get this man… this person. I won't let him hurt you."

She touched his cheek. She wanted so badly to get closer to him, to know him better. "Someday, you need to tell me about Dallas. And about Leeann."

His expression darkened, shut her out. "You already know all there is to tell." Moonlight shadowed his face, gleamed in his eyes. "We'll see," he finally whispered.

Stubborn. That's what he was. She'd opened up to him, but he wasn't about to reciprocate.

He lowered his mouth to hers for a tender kiss that rapidly grew intense. Still, there was no time for what they both apparently had in mind, and so they pulled apart.

"Later." He traced her jaw line with a finger.

With his help she managed to clean up some of the mess left by the intruder. When she picked up the chain and ring he'd taken off the night before, he took it without a word and dropped it into his pocket.

"I can't sleep in here tonight." She led him out and closed the door.

They made love on the couch, and she fell asleep in his arms. He lay awake for a long time before he could get the occurrences at the old house out of his mind.

16
CHAPTER

Though Dal was withdrawn into his own world, Jessie enjoyed their visit with the Spaceys and Tinker. After a picnic dinner that included Dave's special barbecue of mixed beef and deer steaks, they sat in the shade. Everyone attempted to talk about anything but what had been termed the Old Bones case. The sun balanced on the mountains to the west and Tinker crawled from the lounge chair.

"I need to get. Us working girls have chores to do."

Dal glanced up at her silhouette. "I have to work Monday late, and since our Jessie here refuses to stay somewhere else, could you come out to her place after work and spend the night with her?"

Before Tinker could reply, Jessie said, "She doesn't have to do—"

Dal lifted a hand. "It's that or you don't come home after work. I'll send someone out to check your house around five. You'll be home by then."

It wasn't a question. Jessie gave in with a long sigh.

"Yes, I'll be able to do that." Tinker smiled so sweetly at Jessie that she laughed.

"Okay, guys. Now that you've sufficiently planned my life for me, I think I'd better go home, if that's all right with everyone."

Back at the cabin, she waited in the car while Dal went around to the other side and opened the passenger door, then let him take her hand. In spite of her earlier annoyance, she enjoyed the old-fashioned chivalry.

"I do appreciate this special care. It's kind of nice to have my own private deputy, even though I'm sure there are other things you need to be doing."

"Part of my job, ma'am," he said when he slipped the key from her fingers and unlocked the front door. "Stay here a minute."

He soon returned, took her hand, and led her inside. "Okay. Nobody here, no signs anyone has been either. Got any coffee? I could sure use some. Tell me where it is, I'll make it."

"I'll make the coffee. You relax."

He nodded and moved to stand at the glass door, gazing through the evening haze while she took out a filter and opened the blue canister on the counter. He was about as relaxed as a leopard stretched on a limb overlooking a tethered goat. She smiled at the comparison.

Aching for him to touch her, sweep her away from this mundane task and into the bedroom, she scooped coffee into the filter. By the time the pot began to gurgle and burp, filling the air with its rich aroma, they were in each other's arms. A long enjoyable time later they showered and went to the kitchen to drink coffee.

"Well, that was nice," he said, grinning over the rim of his cup.

"Didn't see it coming, did ya? Some psychic you are."

"I'm not psychic," he grunted.

"I was just teasing."

"Not entirely, you weren't."

"Well, then, explain it to me. I want to know about your ghosts." She reached across the small table and grasped his hand, their fingers twining around each other. Making love with him had been at the same time gentle and urgent, leaving her sweetly satisfied. But he appeared moody, as if he regretted the act. Hard to know how to take him sometimes.

He continued to gaze into the distance. Probably didn't even notice the way apricot light streaked through the dusky sky. "There are no such things as ghosts. If we see them as they were, that's only from our imagination. They are well and truly buried, their bodies gone back to Mother Earth. It's more a spiritual thing. Handed down by my Cherokee grandfather, a true *ada'wehi* who could sense the presence of spirits. He had no choice in the matter and I don't either. It's not something we take lightly. Only the greatest shaman truly has supernatural powers. I am not like that."

He sounded so serious that she tried to make amends. "I didn't mean to treat it lightly. Tell me more."

When he raised an eyebrow, she said, "Yes, please. Tell me. I want to know all about the you that talks to spirits. Every single detail."

For a moment, she thought he would refuse, but then he blew out a breath. "That's a tall order, but I'll try. It's more a connection to the inner spirit of those around us. Some who have passed on but linger. We believe that every living thing has its own—the closest I can come to the translation is aura—that lingers after it leaves this earth. Some of what we are is left behind like the trail of a falling star. It's warm and soothing if the spirit departed in peace. We call that spirit *asgi`na*. But at the scene of violence, it seethes with a white hot malevolence. Begs to be avenged. That spirit is *anasgi`na*. My grandfather taught that we are all spirits waiting to move on from this place to the next and because of that we can sense those who have moved on, be they at peace or vengeful. Everyone could do it if they would only believe and open up to the possibility."

He glanced at her as if he'd revealed too much of his secret self.

Enveloped in a rush of affection, she lifted his hand and kissed it. "It sounds wonderful. I wish, well, I wish I knew it were true."

"You mean, like you know the sun will come up tomorrow or that star out yonder will always shine?" He gestured toward the evening star, bright in the eastern sky.

"No. More the way I know that you are standing here beside me, that I can touch you. That I…." Why couldn't she tell him she loved him? Not yet. Too much fear lurking in the shadows of her heart.

He raised an eyebrow, waited for her to finish. She did, but not what she'd intended to say. "The way I know I'm safe when you're with me. Even though I can take care of myself."

The flinty green eyes sparkled and he laughed. "Even if I am slightly nuts?"

"I don't think you're nuts at all. Not even slightly."

His laughter joined hers.

The French doors framed umber shadows that slithered through the forest leaving behind perfect hiding places. Tendrils of darkness crept out of the woods and crossed the clearing, fingering at the cozy kitchen like curious ghosts. She hadn't turned on the lights, so his features were in shadow. Feeling an urge to study his expression, memorize each curve, line, and dimple for a time when he might no longer be there, she rose, moved toward a wall switch. She didn't tell him, but if she did indeed believe in prescience, she would have been frightened out of her mind by the nebulous feelings of lurking danger that overpowered her at that moment.

Glancing out across the deck, Dal took her arm. "Leave the lights off for now."

"Do you see something? Out there?" she asked, pulse skipping.

"Not really. No."

Despite his reassurance, she sensed he was keeping something from her. A shiver walked up her spine.

He slipped an arm around her waist. "I don't want you frightened anymore. I hate bullies who do this."

"Sometimes we deserve to be punished for what we do."

"That's not true. We make mistakes. That doesn't give anyone the right to do this."

She wanted to change the focus away from herself. "What if, I mean, suppose Ken was beating Mary, trying to kill her? Then, doesn't she have the right to... well, if she did kill him, I mean."

"I don't know. I honest to God don't know. Only she does."

A smoky passion darkened his eyes. His breath tickled her cheek. Still, she resisted the urge to forget it all and go into his arms.

He covered her mouth with his in a gentle kiss that drew her into its core and spoke to her ravaged heart.

What tomorrow might bring, she dared not think about. A volatile, sexual relationship without commitment was just what neither of them needed. Not with each other, at any rate.

A while later he asked, "Want to go to bed?"

She shuddered. "I'll sleep here, on the couch. You take the bed. Get some sleep. You have to work tomorrow."

For a long while after he pulled a knitted afghan over her, he stood at the sliding glass door in the kitchen staring out into the darkness.

The waxing moon came up huge and golden, throwing a blanket of light over the valley. Fingering Leeann's gold ring stuffed in his pocket, he dealt with a few scattered thoughts of his dead wife. For some reason her memory didn't hurt as much as it once had. He thought of her now the way he had always wanted to and never could. As a laughing, happy, young woman, not yet wasted by drugs or life's disappointments. The visions soothed him so he was able to put the memories away. Able to forgive Leeann for her weakness. If he ever forgave himself, he'd be surprised.

Thinking of Jessie soothed his soul. He couldn't stay away from her. Would she betray him as she had another man she loved? He saw that as a distinct possibility. Maybe he should put an end to it now, before things went too far. Even the thought told him it was already too late. For, God help him—and her too—he loved her. And he might do her as much harm as she feared doing him.

To stop torturing himself, he let his mind drift to the bones and Norville's supposed drowning, the money involved in the possible sale of the family's land, and who might still be around to profit from it. Certainly not a motive for the original killing more than eighteen years earlier.

If, as he believed, Mary and Jolene did do away with an abusive husband and brother, how did that explain this man stalking both Mary and Jessie? And be damned if he'd let that go on any longer. Mary Smith knew more than she was telling. She had a lot of questions to answer, and it better be soon.

Dal poured himself another cup of coffee and went to sit in a chair and watch Jessie sleep, a lock of hair caressing her cheek. He wanted things to work out between them more than he had wanted anything in a long, long time. But it was a tough world, and we didn't always get what we wanted. Or if we did, it wasn't always best. He hoped she would realize her own dreams, even if that meant she would go back into investigative journalism. He might have to love her enough to let her go rather than hurt her and himself.

She'd been hurt enough. And by God, so had he.

Beyond those memories, he must have slept, for he awoke with a crick in his neck and a backache. He could walk that out. It wasn't unusual, not since the shooting. On the couch, she opened her eyes, blinked dreamily at him before reality set in.

He rose, stretched, and went to her, smiled in a rush of warmth. "Are you hungry?"

She shook her head, sat up. "Time is it?"

Tousled hair tumbled around her face, and he pushed it away to give her a kiss on the cheek. "Time to rise and shine. You up to going to work? I can drop you off or follow you in. Either way." His tone brooked no disagreement, and she nodded.

He went on. "I want to touch base with Mac, see if we can't figure out what's going on here. He may have some ideas."

"I'll freshen up and get changed."

"Yeah, me too, right after you."

She went into the bathroom, flipping him a determined grin. Tough lady. She would come through this, with or without him, even though right now she didn't think so.

Staring in the mirror at her haggard features, Jessie stuck out her tongue like a child, took up her toothbrush, then bent to splash water on her face. The telephone rang as she raked a brush quickly through her hair. The sound of his voice came from the other room as he answered.

In jeans and shirt, she padded back into the living room where Dal was buckling on his heavily-laden belt and weapon, a puzzled look clouding his features.

Her heart thrummed in her throat and it was a moment before she could speak. "What is it? What's happened?"

"I just got a call from Mac. It seems Mary Smith's husband tried to kill her, and she's hysterical. Says she'll only talk to you. They're waiting, but not very patiently. We'd better get a move on."

"I knew it. And I'll bet that's who's been skulking around. I never did like Harold." A weird sensation crawled along the back of her neck. That awful man in her house. She'd have to fumigate.

"I've been thinking, maybe it was him, maybe not."

"Who else? I'd better call Parker, fill him in."

Dal offered no more, and they rode in silence to the Smith place.

Several patrol cars, including the sheriff's, sat at odd angles near a large, two-story white house with a southern verandah on the front. Blue and red lights flashed against an overhang of maple trees. A small crowd had gathered, but was being kept out of the yard. Among them, Jessie spotted Parker with his camera. Ready to back her up if she ran into trouble.

She patted her bag that contained her camera and tape recorder. He nodded and wiggled his fingers in a wave.

A deep down itch to get going on the story quickened her pulse.

Dal jumped out and hurried around to where she waited, pack slung over one shoulder. "Let's get in there before Mary changes her mind."

Mac met them on the porch. "Glad you're here. Come on, both of you."

He led them across the porch and through the front door. Overstuffed furniture lay scattered about, brocaded drapes had been ripped off the windows, the thick carpet was littered with broken lamps and bits and pieces of china and porcelain. The terrified woman huddled in the corner of the couch hugging herself and sobbing.

"What happened here?" Dal asked.

"All I can get out of her is her husband tried to kill her. He evidently was frightened away. By what, we don't know, but I've got men on foot trying to track him. Others out in cars. The city and state boys are helping out, but we don't have much to go on. Is he on foot or in a vehicle? She won't say, but I've got an APB out on his truck. It's nowhere around here." Mac shifted his attention to Jessie. "What we need is for you to get something coherent out of her. Says she'll only talk to you."

Mary sat on the heavy couch, the only piece of furniture that remained upright in the room. Jessie went to her, lowered herself gingerly, and put her arms around the sobbing woman.

Shouts arose from the yard. "Freeze, police. Freeze, dammit,"

"What in tarnation is going on out there?" Mac cleared his weapon and headed for the door, but before he could check it out, Harold Smith stormed into the room and bellowed, "What the hell's going on?"

Mary took one look at her frenzied husband, screamed and tried to crawl over Jessie, who sat frozen in place on the couch. At the same time, two deputies squeezed through the doorway, guns drawn. In the small quarters, fighting Mary, Jessie stared at the weapons and hoped none of the deputies panicked.

Mac shouted. "Put those away before you shoot someone."

Wally Preston stopped dead in his tracks, holstered his .38, and grabbed at Smith. The other deputy, a part-timer she'd seen around but didn't know, tried to yank Smith back without putting away his weapon. It pointed in all directions and Jessie resisted dodging in favor of praying. Mac waded through the melee toward the young deputy, and Smith jerked from their clutches, lunged toward his wife who remained entwined around Jessie. Mary clawed at the back of the couch and wailed.

Confusion reigned. Jessie couldn't tell who did what next, but Mac came away with the armed deputy's pistol, and she heaved a sigh of relief, even though Mary continued to use her as a ladder.

Smith, seeing an advantage, lunged forward, reached out for his wife, and socked Jessie in the temple. She reeled and everything around her went black. She could hear what was going on, as if from a long tunnel. Dal somehow crawled through the flailing arms and legs and scooted in beside her.

"You okay? Honey, say something."

"That hurt like hell." When her vision returned, she squinted to see Sheriff Mac Richards with his gun drawn and pointed at Harold. Definitely a hallucination.

This was probably the first time in his long career in Grace County he'd drawn down on someone, and he was so pissed that when he spoke the room got real quiet. Even Mary's sobbing subsided.

"I'd sure hate to shoot you, Harold. But by God, I will. Now behave."

Hauling up short, Smith stared into the steady barrel of the semi-automatic, and appeared to wilt. He might not have feared the young deputies, but the iron-jawed sheriff was another story. As if cold-conked, he sank to the floor near where his wife huddled against Jessie. Head in both hands he began to rock to and fro, emitting a pitiful sound.

Jessie touched her head gingerly. Dal rubbed her arm, glared at Harold like he was sorry the sheriff already had the drop on him. As for herself, it was hard to feel sorry for the old coot with pain shooting through her temple.

Holstering his weapon, Mac said, "Okay. Everyone just settle down. Get this man out of here. Now. Cuff him and put him in a unit. Take him in and charge him with assault of a law officer. And next week, by God, we'll have some more training. Be damned if any of you'll shoot an innocent citizen on my watch."

The two deputies cowered, even as they escorted Harold outside.

"I'll be out in a minute to talk to him." Mac turned to Jessie. "You okay?"

She nodded and her head whirled some more. Mary continued to hiccup, hand over her mouth, but at least she'd quit climbing.

"Then do something with her." He waved a hand toward Mary. "Settle her down. Get her story before anything else happens. Everyone else, go, except you, Dal. You stay. It's your case."

As if by magic, the room emptied. Taking his cue, Dal rose from where he knelt beside Jessie, righted a chair, shoved it into a shadowy corner of the room out of Mary's line of vision, and perched on the edge.

Mary's heavy breathing filled the silence.

Jessie put an arm around her. "He's gone. You're safe. You've wanted to tell me something for a while now. Whenever you're ready, I am." She reached into the pack that had survived the excitement and switched on the recorder, then handed Mary a bottle of water.

The shaking woman drank deeply and took a few breaths before she sat upright and wiped her face. "It wasn't him, I didn't mean him. Not Harold. Don't put him in jail, please."

"Then who, Mary? For God's sake, who?" Harold had looked ready to kill his wife, and she'd reacted as if he intended to. So what was the woman talking about?

The poor woman swallowed so loudly her throat crackled. "Ken. We killed him," she whispered. "Jolene and I. Or at least I thought we did. But now he's back and he wants revenge."

From the corner, Dal drew a loud breath. The words struck Jessie mute.

This sophisticated woman couldn't be a killer. And even if she was, what could she mean? That Ken had returned from the dead?

Shocked into silence, she and Dal stared at each other. Outside, the excited deputies exchanged words, car doors slammed. Powerful engines revved, filling the void of silence in the house. Blue and red strobes flashed through the window, splashing deathly shadows through the gloom in the parlor, then they were gone.

And Dal, who claimed he wasn't psychic, damn him, was busy proving it. He appeared as puzzled as she, staring at Mary like she might have just hatched out of an egg or something.

Shouldn't Mary have a lawyer before she confessed anything? Dal hadn't Mirandized her, so anything she said wouldn't count later, would it? He read her mind then, and nodded imperceptibly. At least, it seemed so.

Her voice croaked when she finally asked, "What happened, Mary?"

"Ken was a drunken bully. Oh, God, I don't know why we stayed with him. Both of us. Stupid and weak-willed. I don't understand. We buried him out there, and now he's come back to punish us—punish *me* for what happened."

Fear crawled up Jessie's spine. "You can't truly mean to say it was your dead husband who tried to kill you here? And not Harold?"

Mary nodded until her neck popped. "He came back from the grave. He wants me." Her voice rose to a wail.

Dal hunched forward, nodded his head once more, and listened with an intensity that darkened his eyes. Moving her worried look back toward Mary, she hugged the woman, patted at her shoulder.

"No, honey. No, that can't be true. Calm down. Tell us what happened. You're safe here. Harold is under arrest. You can tell us what he did."

"Harold, he didn't do anything but scare me half to death." Mary straightened, composed herself by taking several deep breaths and tucking a stray lock of hair behind one ear. Then she began to speak, fingers twisting together in her lap. Her story came to life in the quiet room, and Jessie could almost see it play out.

"It was a Saturday, May twenty-first, nineteen eighty-nine. It had rained for a month or more, the creeks and rivers were overflowing, but Friday it cleared off and got hot. Saturday the heat was worse than if it were July. We should've known something was going to happen. It was like living under a steamy wool blanket. Sucking for every breath." She brushed her hair back, as if wiping remembered perspiration from her forehead.

Jessie patted her hand, waited. This time she didn't even glance at Dal. He appeared off somewhere with his spirits anyway.

"Then the storm hit. By four o'clock, the clouds were black as night with that yellow glow, and we knew it was coming. The tornado. We never could've guessed there'd be two of them. Or what would happen." She shuddered so hard the couch vibrated.

"And Ken, the worse the storm became, the madder he got. It'd thunder and he'd bellow. Then he saw there was no more beer and he really got furious. The approaching storm roared, he roared louder. I'll swear I don't know what made the old house shake worse, him or God's wrath. He ranted and raved, threw things until the floor was covered with broken dishes."

"Where was Jolene?" Jessie asked when Mary paused and wrung her trembling hands together.

Dal cleared his throat and she glanced at him, could read nothing in his expression. Beyond his shoulder and outside the window she saw Mac filtered through the fading glow of the setting sun. Puffing on a cigar. Waiting patiently. All the deputies were gone. She turned her attention back to the woman's bizarre story.

"Jolene was hiding upstairs, where she always went when he got like that. Outside, it sounded like a freight train coming. A tree fell and the house shook. Jolene came running down screaming that we had to go to the cellar or we'd all die. Finally, she was more afraid of the storm than her maniac brother."

This time Mary's pause grew longer while she struggled with the memories. Jessie spread a hand over the woman's fists, gripped in her lap. "It's okay, Mary. Take it easy." Under the toe of her shoe a shard of painted china with an exquisite rose caught her attention. One of Mary's prized possessions. She sensed movement and glanced up, but saw no one. Dal switched his attention for a moment, as if he too had seen or heard someone. They had, for at that moment Mac moved into the shadowy doorway, still as a ghost. No longer able to wait outside.

Lost in the past and unaware of her surroundings or the sheriff's presence, Mary continued, catching their interest once more. "Ken, he grabbed her around the throat with one hand. His own sister, and he's trying to choke her. For a minute I couldn't do anything. The storm screamed outside like some sort of banshee let loose. A window exploded and glass flew everywhere. I felt the floor shake. I prayed for that horrid monster to swoop down and carry us off, prevent this horrible thing that was about to happen." Her teeth ground, her jaw tightened. "I could see it coming, sure as the Devil himself." Her tumbling words halted and the silence was deadly.

In the destroyed room where they listened to the terrible tale, the only light came from a lamp in the far corner that had escaped the earlier melee. Its glow didn't reach the shadowy recesses where fear and evil lurked.

Before continuing, Mary wet her lips.

"Still holding on to her, he smacked me with the other hand, knocked me up against the wall. Oh, God, I can still see the look on his face, cut from the flying glass, dripping blood, a fearful wildness in his eyes. In my dreams I still hear the crunch of his boots when he crossed the floor." Unheeded tears poured down her cheeks, but she couldn't be stopped now. The story was hers to tell all the way to the end.

Jessie could hardly catch her breath, caught up in the scene as if she were there. Two terrified women being threatened not only by a madman, but by nature gone berserk.

"And when I finally stumbled to my feet, I saw he had Jolene backed up onto the counter, holding her by the throat, her feet off the floor. Kicking. Going bang, bang, bang, against the cabinets. He was killing her. Killing her. Oh, God. Oh, God forgive me. I… I went in the other room and grabbed his rifle out of the rack. He kept it loaded. Always. And I went back in there. I told him to let her go. I screamed it at him, and he turned to face me, but his hand held on to her. He was killing her and I'd be next." Eyes huge and glazed, she stared Jessie full in the face. "So. I. Shot. Him."

A ghastly grimace masked her features. "Odd, you know. I didn't even hear the gun go off, the storm was so loud. I didn't even hear it go off."

Silence stretched between them. No one spoke. Jessie's stomach churned and she fought an urge to run outside, glanced once again at Dal for reassurance. He gave it with a nod.

She jerked when Mary spoke again in a voice that rose an octave. "He didn't let go of her right away and I thought I'd missed, but then he bellowed like a bull in heat, his knees buckled and he fell, Jolene on top of him. I just stood there, I couldn't move. The house shook and lightning flashed and I thought I saw some kind of monster staring at me from across the room. But it was only my reflection in the mirror over the wash pan. I became a monster that night."

"You're no monster, Mary. Why didn't you call the police? It was clearly self-defense."

Unable or unwilling to stop until the tale was told, Mary's voice droned on. "Liked to never've got his body loaded in the pickup. Drove out across the pasture and up toward Jacob's Bluff where I knew we could dig. Under there the ground was soft, not too rocky. After we—after we got him—covered up, we drove the pickup in the creek and went home. That was that, or at least I thought it was till today when I saw him."

Again she shuddered and hugged herself, gazed at Jessie with eyes big and wet.

"I swear we thought he was dead. We buried him, out there where you found the bones. I thought you'd found him, till tonight. God, I don't understand. How could he be alive? How could he? He's come back to kill me for what I did, and I guess I deserve it."

"Nonsense, Mary. You deserve nothing of the kind. Besides, the dead don't rise up from the grave."

Startled at her own words, she stared, first at Mac then at Dal.

Grim-lipped, Dal moved over to kneel beside Mary. It was time he asked some questions that would finalize this investigation and allow him to put the remaining pieces together.

"Mary, you remember me? Dal Starr? Can you answer some questions?"

Woodenly, she nodded. "I'll try." She studied her nails, not looking up.

"Why did you remove his clothes?"

Her features spasmed. "His clothes? We didn't. I mean, I don't remember taking off his clothes."

Unable to bring himself to ask this poor woman the next question, Dal shot a look at Mac. How did you talk about decapitating a man to his wife? Surely she had nothing to do with that. What the hell was going on here?

He touched her arm, and shuddered, rocked from head to toe by what he sensed. The sheer terror of that night shot from her through him as if he'd touched a live wire.

Everything came clear. He saw the two women taking turns digging the hole. Breath gasping in and out of their lungs. Covered in mud, clothes hanging heavy with rain, they struggled to drag the limp body from the back of the pickup and into the hole. On their knees, both women sucked at the wet air for a long while before they could bring themselves to shovel the mud into the watery grave.

And the pendant. The black arrowhead. It slithered from around Mary's neck to rest amid puddles of muddy water covering the body.

The vision passed like a flash of lightning and he was listening to a man, yelling, screaming, breaking things. "You won't tell them, you can't. You stupid bitch. You want to ruin it all. Keep quiet, you hear? You hear?"

The man's face came clear, the man who had only recently been dragged from this room. Harold had threatened his own wife and poor Mary, in her condition, transferred that threat back all those years to her first husband. In her frantic mind, Harold became Ken.

"Tell us what happened to Jolene, Mary," Dal said softly.

"I don't know, she ran off, that's all. She didn't even leave a note." She cleared her throat, fingered a doily on the arm of the couch. "We couldn't look at each other after that horrible night. We were always so close, and after that we couldn't… I mean, how do you talk about something like that? And how do you not talk about it? We could neither one live in the house, so I moved to a little place here in town and Jolene, well, she left.

Went to Wichita, I think, and got a job there. She wrote once, then I never heard from her again, but someone we knew told us she'd married. I guess that's true."

She stared at Jessie with tears running down her cheeks. "I hope she got a good man."

Jessie continued to hold her hand, felt the woman tremble. "You said you thought she and her husband had come back. Why did you think that?"

"I don't know. I thought I saw her in a car that went by earlier, but maybe I was wrong."

"Why did you say Ken tried to kill you?"

"Who else would it be?" Mary shook her head, said in a sing-song voice, as if all the strength had gone out of her. "You know, we were no more than back to the house when the second storm hit."

Puzzled, Jessie studied Mary for an instant before she realized she had gone back to that night so long ago.

"I thought it was the wrath of God come to strike us dead for what we'd done. We huddled in the storm cellar till morning, both expecting to be hit by lightning at any minute, punished for what we done. But we weren't. Don't you see, we weren't?" She held out a hand to prove she was alive.

Jessie glanced at Mac. "I think Mary needs to stay with someone till this is over, don't you?"

"Just a few more questions. Then we'll take her wherever she wants to go." He turned back to Mary. "Did you tell your husband about what you did? Does Harold know?"

"He found the note." Mary buried her face in both hands and sobbed.

Jessie tightened her arm around her hunched shoulders. The poor woman had had enough, but Jessie understood the need for her to answer this one most important question.

"Honey," she said, glancing at Dal. "Does Harold know about what happened to Ken?"

Wide eyed, Mary replied. "Yes, I told him the afternoon after you and I met at Butch's and spoke about the body. I thought he was going to hit me, but he just stormed out of the house. Said he'd fix things."

Jessie exchanged a quick look with Dal, but neither spoke.

17
CHAPTER

Mary's voice broke the silence like a wispy breeze. "If I go to jail, he's afraid we won't get the property."

With a sigh, Jessie met Dal's fixed stare, patted Mary's shoulder. "Honey, is there someone, a friend, you can stay with?"

"Yes, my cousin Susan."

"I'll put some things in a bag for you and someone will take you."

Rising, Jessie caught a glimpse of Parker, leaned against a tree. Even though he'd assigned her to the story, he couldn't stay away. Ever silent, Mac continued to hover in the doorway. No doubt keeping an eye on the proceedings.

It was over, and what a story this would be. She had it all. Every word from the lips of the only one who could tell it after all these years. No one could ever get it as right as she could. And it was hers to write.

Dal grasped Mary's arm, gently steered her toward Mac.

"I doubt she'll even be charged, but if she is a good lawyer will get her off," Mac said.

Dal nodded. "This confession will go no farther than this room. Not until this is all over." Gaze aimed directly at Jessie, he went on, "I didn't Mirandize her, it's no good in court anyway. And even if it was, not one word will find its way into print, until the PA decides on charges."

The warning stirred a dormant anger in Jessie, and she hated that he'd felt it necessary to say it. At the same time, he was right not to trust her. It pissed her off that he could know her so well.

"I've got the story, and it's mine. But it won't be published as long as it might incriminate her."

Mac gazed at Dal. "The thing now is to catch whoever this is running around out there threatening Jessie and Mary. Be it Harold Smith or someone else."

"Well, we know one thing for sure," Jessie said under her breath.

Both men stared at her.

"It's definitely not Ken Norville."

Dal nodded. "It's whoever dug up that body and took away the clothes and head to keep it from being identified. That well could be Harold Smith trying to protect his wife. He may be too self-centered to care about her, but if he thought she might not get the money from the sale of the property, and therefore he wouldn't get a share, well that's different."

Mac nodded in agreement.

Jessie fetched Mary some clothes, stuffed them in a bag she found in the closet and, as she carried them to her, she spotted Parker waiting patiently just outside the open door on the porch. The sheriff's radio chattered and he stepped out of Parker's hearing to answer.

Dal watched the sheriff for a moment, then told Parker there would be a press release soon, and that Jessie had the rest of the story but had been told not to release it yet.

Parker fumbled around in his camera bag a moment, came up with a folded newspaper. "I thought this might be important."

She craned her neck to get a look at the paper. Dal must've decided it would do no good to keep it from her, since it was Parker's discovery, so he didn't move away.

"What is it?" Dal opened the paper. *"Wichita Eagle Beacon?* Where'd this come from?"

"A room in the motel. The owner said a couple checked in there day before yesterday. I found it in their room."

"You went into their room?"

As if it were nothing unusual, Parker nodded. "It was open for the cleaning lady. Besides, I'm not bound by your regs. They registered as Mister and Missus Bob Brown. Almost as original as John Smith, isn't it?"

He glanced at Jessie with a victorious grin, turned and left, without waiting for a reply from Dal.

Across the room Mac clicked off his radio. "Dallas, they've picked up a man driving Harold Smith's truck. He says his name is Bob Brown."

"Our mysterious Jolene and hubby." Dal slipped his hand down Jessie's arm, twined his finger with hers. "Come on, I'm going to take you home. Mac, can you take Mary to her friend's place?"

"I'm not going home," Jessie said. "Not yet. I need to go to the office. I have work to do. Parker will drop me off when we finish."

"You're going to write the story now?"

"I said I was. It's my job."

"It better not come out in this week's paper."

She jerked away as if he'd slapped her. "Tell you what, Dal. You go catch the bad guys, and I'll do what I do. And if we're going to be friends, you'd better learn to trust me."

Without sparing him another look, she swept her bag off the floor and went out to join Parker. This time she would do everything right. No cheating, no lying. Just write the story and be fair to everyone. Wait to release it, like she'd promised. And if Dal couldn't trust her, then he'd better back off before things got more complicated.

In spite of her silent resolution, she felt a rush of regret. Getting to know him better was definitely on her agenda and she hated to give up, but this was her life and she wasn't about to let someone else run it. Especially not the man she loved. That admission surprised her, but there it was.

Weary, her head reeling from the blow she'd taken and all that had happened in the past twenty-four hours, she caught up with Parker.

"Could you give me a lift to the office? I want to get started on this while it's fresh in my mind."

"Glad you decided to do the story?"

"You were right. I have to prove I can be a good journalist without all that other hoopla. It's a good story. Why, didn't you think I would?"

"I never doubted it for a minute. You're a fine writer, better than most, but you had to get your head out of your—"

"Okay, okay. I get the picture. You don't have to get graphic."

Chuckling, he climbed in his beat-up old Scout and waited while she swept aside plastic coffee cups and candy wrappers from the passenger seat. The sky lit up, followed by a clap of thunder that shook the ground. Large drops of rain spattered the canvas rooftop.

Back at the office, she shook droplets from her hair, sat down at her computer, and went to work. While the tape turned, Mary Smith's voice filled the silent room and the story flowed from the tips of Jessie's fingers through the keys and onto the screen with an effortless ease.

Nineteen years ago, with storms battering her home, Mary Smith struggled through a life and death battle with an abusive husband.

Today, Mary told this reporter a hair-raising tale of years of terror and the final blows struck on that night so long ago.

Jessie leaned back and closed her eyes, listened to the tape for several minutes, imagining the next sentence, then her fingers moved over the keys.

Words spun out as if she had never been away from serious reporting all this time. She would continue to love the historical writing, but this was what she lived for. Satisfaction settled in as she related the abusive home Mary and Jolene had existed in, their fear and degradation, and at last, that fatal moment when, pushed to the very edge Mary had reacted in the only way left to her. And paid dearly for it during the years that followed.

It was a long story and there was a gap that would be closed once they caught whoever had dug up Ken's body and learned the motive. There was also Jolene and her story, which she hoped to get first hand. She leaned back and stretched the kinks out of her muscles, noticed with some surprise that it was getting dark outside. She'd worked through lunch and a usual afternoon break and long past normal quitting time. Hadn't even heard Wendy leave.

"Ready to go?" Parker asked from the doorway of his office.

She jumped. "Oh, you scared me. Guess I was still in there." Cocking her head toward the computer, she pushed her chair away. Tomorrow she would hone the words and phrases until each touched the readers' hearts. It was much more than a news story, it was a feature to be proud of. Better than anything she'd ever written. It shouldn't take long for the PA to declare no charges would be filed, and Parker would run her story, even if they hadn't yet caught whoever had messed with the body and written those notes.

If Dal or the sheriff had caught up with the guilty party, they would have surely called. So, that meant the man who threatened her peace of mind was still on the loose. Could be at her place now doing no telling what.

Tinker would be there soon, might even beat her out to the cabin, late as it was. Despite her fear of dark places, her friend wouldn't let her down. She felt a twinge of guilt, but let it go. We all had to face our fears sometime. She'd certainly learned that over the past few weeks.

Parker was silent during the drive to the cabin, and she was lost in her own thoughts. The rain momentarily let up, but against the horizon another storm rumbled. She was relieved to see lights on at the cabin when he steered into the lane.

"Looks like Tinker's here. Thanks for bringing me home."

"Don't see her car."

"Oh, she probably parked it around back. It's closer to the door that way."

"I'll just wait till you get inside."

"That's not necessary. Go on home, you look tired."

"I'll wait."

She wasn't about to ask him to come inside with her, make sure Tinker was indeed there. He looked exhausted. And besides, the lights were on.

"Bye. See you tomorrow." She closed the Scout's door firmly.

By the glow from the porch light, she inserted her key into the lock. When the door swung open she sensed a hidden menace. How terribly sad that this, her safe haven, now represented fear. Squaring her shoulders and swallowing the apprehension, she stepped inside, closed the door, and turned off the porch light. For a moment, she watched the taillights of the Scout recede into the rain like eerie red eyes.

"Tinker? Tink? Where are you?" She put down her backpack and moved toward the kitchen.

Cautiously, heart in her throat, she padded into the back of the house. No car. An alarm went off in her head.

Where was Tinker? What was going on? Who had turned on the lights? Don't panic. No time to panic.

She ran to the front windows, but Parker was gone. Frantically, she dug in the pack, pulled out her cell phone. Heart in her throat, she carried it with her and searched the silent house for signs of a visitor, peering into every closet, under the bed, and behind the shower curtain. As far as she could tell, no one had been here, and she relaxed a bit.

Still, what had happened to Tinker? She should've been here before dark. Better give her a ring. She might have had to go home for something first. They hadn't spoken today. It was possible her ditzy friend had forgotten she'd promised to spend the night to satisfy Dal's request.

Only a bit worried, she punched in the speed dial. On the other end, the phone kept on ringing.

"I'm sure she's all right," she told herself aloud. "Why isn't the stupid answering machine picking up?"

Don't panic. Don't let this thing get hold of you. No one has made any threats against Tinker. She could've decided to stop off somewhere, been delayed at work, chickened out, any number of things.

But she would've called. No matter what, she would've called, unless.... Jessie called the sheriff's office, got the night dispatcher.

"Has Tinker left yet?"

Silence for a moment, then, "Yes. Who is this?"

"Sorry, this is Jessie West. She was supposed to come to my place, and hasn't shown up. I'm worried about her."

"Maybe she went home instead."

"I called her cell. No answer, straight to voicemail. I'm wondering if you would mind sending someone by her apartment to check? What with all that's been going on?"

"I think Wally's in that area. I'll give him a heads up. Okay?"

"Yes, thanks."

She started a pot of coffee. Before it was even half full, the phone rang and she punched the talk button.

"Jessie, this is Wallace Preston. We've got Tinker. She had a flat on her way out to your place, and I guess she must've panicked. Found her hiding in her car, all the doors locked and the lights burning. Every one of em, even the dome. Liked to never got her to open up. Can't get much out of her, but she's okay. We're gonna take her home and put her to bed with a sedative. She says tell you she's sorry, she's sure you'll understand." Wally paused. "You may, but blamed if I will. She out-shoots me on the firing range and she ain't afraid of nothing. 'Cept the dark. Oh, Mac told me to head out your way shortly. Lock the doors and wait."

"Yes, I'll do that. I'll be fine."

The pretense that everything was okay deserted her when she disconnected. Shaky on her feet, she leaned against the counter and closed her eyes. The coffee smelled good and strong. A cup of that would either steady her nerves or put her on a caffeine high. Either was preferable to this. She took down a mug, reached for the pot, and spotted the corner of a slip of paper sticking from under the blue sugar canister.

The same lined tablet paper!

Heart pounding, she slipped it free with fingers that trembled so she could hardly make out the scrawled, now-familiar printing. Once she did, panic crawled into her throat. It took a while before she could read the words.

IF YOU WANT TO KNOW WHAT REALLY HAPPENED THE NIGHT OF THE TWISTERS COME TO THE CAVE ALONE TONIGHT

It wasn't signed, but she knew who wrote it. Felt as if his scrawny hand clutched her heart. The reference to the cave could only mean that this came from Caveman Jake. That meant he'd written all the others, been in her house. The dirty old man. She'd felt sorry for him, but now terror roiled in her stomach, and he became the boogey man. Still, she would do as he said because this would be the rest of her story. Hers alone, without Dal's interference, and before Wally Preston arrived to stop her. Damned if she was afraid of one scruffy old man.

Yeah, she should keep telling herself that—even as she got ready to walk into his trap.

Rushing into her bedroom, she dug around through a drawer, came up with a black t-shirt and socks, and dragged a pair of dark jeans from the closet.

Quick now. Get the shirt off, pull on the tee. Wally could show up any minute. Put a stop to her leaving. Ruin everything. Dancing on one foot, she stuck a leg into the jeans, reversed, and jabbed the other in. The long, slightly damp hair she clipped tightly into a twist. Sitting on the bed, she slipped on socks and walking shoes. Might as well take the backpack. No sense going without a flashlight, tape recorder, and camera, water too. God knew what would come in handy out there in the wilderness.. Everything was in there short of a defibrillator, and she might need that before the night was over.

As she fitted the pack on her back, fear rose in her like a wicked wind. But she would not stop, not when she was so close to figuring this thing out. They knew who the bones belonged to and how they got buried, but she was about to face the man who'd been skulking around scaring the pants off both her and Mary. Find out who had dug up the body, decapitated it, stripped it naked, and then re-buried it. Mostly, she would find out why. It might not be Harold Smith at all, but someone else. Looked like it might be Caveman Jake. Or maybe he only knew who did or they'd worked together. So many possibilities.

Drawing in a tremulous sigh, she eased open the French doors at the back of the house and slipped out into the rain-washed evening. Thunder continued to rumble to the southwest. Another storm on its way. Time to hurry. At any moment, headlights of Preston's unit might sweep down the lane.

Velvety darkness lay over the bottomland, engulfed the cabin and surrounding forest. If she took the car to Foster's place, she might meet up with Wally. Better to walk. So she raced across the yard toward the woods. A damp breeze cooled her sweaty brow. The sweet fragrance of honeysuckle mixed with a vague stench of her own fear.

Once in the trees, she turned on the flashlight and headed toward Kyle Foster's farm, where she could cut through to the old logging road and reach the cave. The night was as black as the inside of that cave. Fighting low hanging branches that whipped water all over her, she stumbled over rocks and exposed roots that the flashlight missed.

Hurry, hurry. This was taking too long.

Even now, Wally could have notified Dal that she was gone. Nothing she could do about that but keep moving.

Windows glowed at the Foster house. The dogs that had started this whole thing by digging up the bones raised a ruckus. She kept moving, crept along a path blazed by deer and small animals.

A screen door slammed and she froze in her tracks, cut off the flashlight.

But Kyle was only yelling at the dogs. "Shut up, you worthless, bone-digging curs."

No wonder he was pissed. After some of the college students found his marijuana while looking for the lost head, the deputies had showed up to uproot his plants. He'd have to start all over, maybe move his next planting to another spot deeper in the woods. Meanwhile, he was out on bond.

For a while after the door closed, she crouched in darkness before moving on, cupping the light in one hand. The dogs continued to bark, the noise fading when she started up the incline toward Jacob's Bluff and the grave. The steady drumming of her heart sent blood roaring through her veins. For a moment she paused, caught her breath, and dealt with the hammering in her chest, brought on not so much by the exertion of the climb as by a deep-seated terror of what might await at its end.

Once she had felt only pity for Caveman Jake, but no more. He was in this up to his filthy neck, and there was much more here to fear than a schizophrenic old man. Perhaps everything she'd run from by leaving California would come to pass out here in the dark. Sometimes you couldn't outrun retribution for your own sins.

"I see you." A spooky voice undulated out of the darkness around her, eerie as a haint.

Gripping the flashlight with hands that trembled, Jessie aimed the beam toward the soulful noise floating out of the darkness. She called out, "Is that you, Jake? I came, just like you asked. Where are you?"

With Jolene and Lester Bennett—AKA Mr. and Mrs. Bob Brown—

safely locked in a holding cell next to Harold, who didn't even glance up at their arrival, Dal headed for his desk, but paused at the dispatcher's window.

"Hey, Troy. Heard from Mac since I got back?"

"Yeah. He went home. Said you were handling things fine and he was tired. Reckon this thing is about settled?"

"I expect it's coming close."

"You hear about Tinker?" Troy asked.

"No. What happened? She's not hurt, is she?"

Troy laughed. "Reckon it ain't funny, really. But they found her locked in her own car out on Cedar Creek Road, on the brink of hysteria. Seems she had a flat and was scared to get out in the dark and fix it. Couldn't even use her own cell phone she was shaking so hard. Gal tough as her, too. Who'd a thought it?"

"Wait a minute. When was this? Who found her?"

"Jessie called in she hadn't shown out there. Deputy Preston found her. Tinker, I mean. They liked to not got her to open the door and let them in."

Dal didn't wait to hear more, instead hit the door at a run and jumped in the Tahoe. Jessie was alone at the cabin. He didn't feel a bit better about Harold and Lester being in custody, either. Lester swore he didn't know anything about leaving anyone notes. Said him and Jolene came down to take care of the Norville property matters with the Smiths. Had no explanation, though, why they were registered at the ratty motel as Bob Brown and wife. There might be a bit more to the story, but Dal wasn't caring much right now. Figured they were running from some nefarious deeds in Kansas. As for Smith, he denied everything and Dal believed him.

So all he could think of was Jessie out there alone and someone dangerous after her.

He ran the siren and lights all the way, and to hell with the cows. They could just stampede, for all he cared.

Lights blazed in the house. A sheriff's unit sat next to Jessie's Jeep out front. He hammered on the locked front door, shouted, then ran to the back. If anything happened to her, he wasn't sure what he'd do.

Around back, he found Wallace Preston trying to jimmy the locked French door, and joined him calling her name over and over.

"Can't raise her," Wallace said.

Dal held up a hand, took some deep breaths. "Stop. She keeps a key under the flower pot."

He dug it out and took several stabs at the lock before he shouldered the door open, banging it so hard against the wall the glass shivered. Weapon drawn, he pointed to one side of the room and Wally nodded, moved in, gun in both hands. Dal checked out the kitchen, while Wally made a hurried round of the bedroom. They met back in the middle of the quiet kitchen again.

This time he slowed down to take a closer look around.

A pot of coffee sat in the Mr. Coffee machine. The light glowed.

On the countertop lay a sheet of tablet paper that looked damned familiar. Struggling to control the urge to break something, he held still only long enough to read the words.

"The cave. She's gone to the cave. You go call the sheriff to get some backup. I'm headed on up there before that crazy son of a bitch hurts her."

Wally raced outside to his car.

"Dammit, Jessie. What have you done? Dammit." If he'd ever wanted to punch a hole in the wall, this was the time.

For a frantic instant he couldn't move, thinking of her off out there in the dark, on her way to meet this madman. Alone. Just like her, too, to go off on one of her wild quests to prove herself. Why hadn't she called? Asked for help?

He knew the answer to that before the question was even out. She was stubborn, independent, out to prove she was strong and quite able to take care of herself. And she wanted a close to her damned story. To hell with everything else.

Balling the note up in his fist, he raced out to the Tahoe, hollered at Wally.

"I'll drive as far as I can, might beat her there."

Wally waved an arm to show he'd heard.

Why in hell she'd left on foot, Dal had no idea, didn't take the time to mull it over. The woman he loved was in danger and the thought she might be hurt dug into his gut, nearly making him sick.

He couldn't let anything happen to her. Be damned if he'd lose the only woman who meant anything to him, even if she was stubborn and mule-headed.

During the wild ride toward the logging road, he told himself Caveman Jake wasn't a killer, but it did little good. He should've taken the old man in the first time he laid eyes on him. Come up with something, anything, to charge him with. Then none of this would've happened.

"Stupid. Stupid, stupid," he muttered, hammering at the wheel, then twisted it to make a sliding turn onto the faint ruts leading into the woods. The road ended and he cut the headlights, pawed the door open and stomped through drenched weeds.

Rain pattered on the trees as he made his way toward the cave. It was quiet, way too quiet. Where was she?

"I see you." A sing-song rhythm like that of some childish song floated through the misty woods.

Dal stopped dead in his tracks. Turned slowly, trying to figure out where the words came from. Then he moved carefully in the right direction. Thank God it had rained so he made little noise creeping over wet leaves that littered the ground. He paused as the voices grew nearer. Jessie's then what must be Caveman Jake's.

"Can we talk? I need to ask you some questions. I think you can be a big help," she said.

"Come on up then." At this point he sounded almost sane.

Silence, then some scrambling and grunting sounds, then him again.

"Just a few more steps."

"And then you'll tell me what you know?"

"Maybe will, maybe won't."

"You promised."

"Oh, a promise is a promise. Bad boys break promises." Still singing in that goofy way.

Was he totally loony? By then, Dal could've reached out and touched them, but he waited, frozen in place.

"Where did you go?" the man shouted, frantic.

"I'm here, I'm here," she muttered, then screeched, "Let me go. Turn me loose now, damn it."

Dal burst through the bushes just in time to hear a solid thud, then nothing but her harsh breathing. He grabbed her and she went berserk, screaming and kicking, but he held on tight.

18

CHAPTER

Whoever it was grabbed her from out of nowhere.

She reached backward, knees trembling, and felt clothing, muscles bunched in knots, an arm, a hand, strong fingers holding her.

"Calm down." The whispered command pierced her roar of mindless fear. A familiar voice in her ear. "I ought to handcuff you to a tree. What is wrong with you, coming out here alone? Putting your life in jeopardy? I was right not to trust you. Dammit, woman. Where is that lunatic?"

"I don't know. I hit him. Hard." Despite his scolding words, relief surged through her. "You scared me half to death."

"Oh, really? And being up here in the dark with an insane nutjob didn't? How could you be so fucking reckless? Besides, who told me to go do my job and catch the bad guys and leave you to do yours? Is this what you call your job?"

"I—I guess not. But I—I wanted to finish the story."

"No excuse."

They'd been hissing at each other in exaggerated whispers, until he put his arms around her, said in a voice husky with emotion, "Jesus H. Christ, girl, I was afraid something had happened to you."

Sensing his relief, she relaxed against his chest. "I'm sorry. I just had to find out who was doing this. How did you find me? Why did you follow me? I only wanted to—"

He put a finger over her lips. "When I found that note and you gone, I knew how much I cared for you. How badly I wanted you in my life. No matter what our problems may be. I give a damn if you get hurt or killed. And I can't let you go running off half-cocked after some crazy story. Not if it puts your life in danger. We'll talk about it later. That's so you'll understand why I followed you here. Now, if I turn you loose, you aren't gonna hit me with that, are you?" He pointed at the bag she still gripped.

She sank limply against him. "Dal, oh, my God. Of course not. I'm glad you're here, but how'd you— Where'd you—?"

"Hush. I'll ask the questions. And my first one is, how could you come up here like this, alone, for a damned story?"

"It's not just a story. It's my life. Please, let's not argue about it now. He left a note. He said, well, I thought he knew who dug up the bones. How did you find me?"

"When I found out Tinker had some kind of fit and didn't get out to your place, I thought I'd just drop by, you know, see if you'd been murdered in your bed or something. I thought I might find you cowering in a corner because our friend had left another calling card. I should've known you'd go running into danger without a single thought."

"Oh, I gave it plenty of thought, believe me. But, yes, you should've known, if you'd been paying attention to me, that I'm not going to, as you put it, 'cower in a corner.' Not ever again. You'd better get used to it, if you really care for me."

His breath whooshed in and out under her ear. "Okay, I do know that about you, but dammit, you could've called me. Let me do my job." Again the words mocked her.

Unable to explain her actions further, she rested in the protection of his arms. "I don't really have an excuse that you'll like. But I know one thing."

"What?" he demanded harshly, his breath tickling the back of her neck.

"I'm sure glad you came." She twisted in his embrace, brushed her lips over the taut line of his jaw. "And I do know you have the right to care. I really do. And we'll have to talk about this later. Right now, I'm worried. He's awful quiet. Do you think I killed him?"

"Nope, but he probably wishes you had. He's breathing like a busted bellows. It appears he's really mixed up bad in this."

"I thought so, or I wouldn't have come out here. Remember he described the truck, and then Mary told us almost exactly what he said he saw, and it's obvious he wrote all those notes and tore up my bedroom. He was messing with us, but I'm still not sure why. I didn't get a thing out of the dirty old coot before you showed up."

His chuckle against her cheek temporarily distracted her and she nuzzled him again. "Sure is a pretty night out here, isn't it?"

He tightened his hold, wrapping his arms so tightly around her she could scarcely breathe. "Indeed it is."

"Dal, he's not going anywhere."

He read her mind again, and his mouth found hers, muffled what she'd been about to say. The kiss, indulged in as it were, in the middle of the dark woods with adrenaline still pumping, enhanced her desire far beyond the point of her recent terror. It was an unusual and quite alarming sensation, to want to make love with danger barely held at bay. But she'd heard that about humans. Hadn't been sure she believed it until now. She wanted to get naked and roll around with him in the dark woods while the rush still roared through her.

Moaning, she locked her arms around his neck. "I need to screw your brains out." She deepened the kiss, tasting his shock and rising passion.

Under her attack Dal staggered backward against a tree. If they didn't pick the damndest times to go all hot and bothered about each other. He struggled to shift his weapon so it didn't poke her, though he was definitely poking her with something equally as hard. He'd never met a woman quite like her. Though this wasn't the time or place, his passion rose to meet hers, and he didn't give a damn where they were. It crossed his mind that Mac could arrive at any minute with the cavalry, or that crazy old man she'd clobbered could come up off the ground and God only knew what he might do.

A dark presence took over, hovered in the dark. Beckoned for his attention. Before he could get a hold on it, her tongue probed deeper in his mouth, her breasts pressed against him, and she made that little sound in her throat like a wild cat purring and came at him some more.

He pushed away the lingering spirit and cupped her buttocks in both palms, shifting her closer amid the awkward equipment on his belt. He'd taken Human Psych 101 and knew all too well what extreme danger could do to people. It set the juices flowing, and no matter how rational your mind might be, you couldn't overcome it. Hard as he tried, he only wanted to have her or go crazy. Here and now, even with all his senses screaming at him.

A groan that didn't come from her distracted him, but only a tiny bit. How could he concentrate on anything with her hands and mouth doing the things they were doing to him? Under his shirt, in his hair, his mouth, his eyes, ears. She wasn't missing an inch of his flesh on the way to the main event, and his body had only one thing on its mind.

The groan became a hideous cry, alerting his brain and cooling his body's passion. He un-peeled her, shoved her aside as Caveman came out of the night and hit him waist high, taking him down. Hard. Air whooshed out of him. Jessie's screams undulated through the night.

Arms locked around the matchstick bundle of the old man, Dal rolled over and over, sucking at air, kicking up leaves, and tumbling painfully about in the rocks.

The old geezer was strong, and must've been able to see in the dark. He punched at Dal's face, gouged his eyes, ripped at his hair, took a bite out of his arm. It was the sort of fight Dal expected with a pumped-up junkie in the streets of Dallas, not here in the backwoods of Arkansas.

The surprising attack had caught him unawares, considering what he and Jessie were up to. But the height of sexual attraction was akin to the violence of battle and he was charged to the max. One thing he knew was how to subdue such violence. Summoning a renewed burst of strength, he twisted out of the old man's clutches, wrapped an arm around his throat, and horsed him to the ground where he ground one knee into his back.

The poor old fellow let out a dreadful groan.

Keeping him in a choke hold for very long would kill him.

Good enough!

The need to do just that shocked him to the soles of his feet.

He'll kill you if you don't do him first. A message from his old self he'd done his damndest to leave behind in Dallas.

Caveman kicked and flailed around like a wounded animal, his cries fading as the air to his lungs was shut off. The urge to crush the wild man's larynx remained. Crush it and be done with this. Squeeze, squeeze, squeeze until the old man's feet and hands stopped twitching.

Enough!

Gasping and staggering backward, Dal released the poor old codger.

Breathless, he hunched over, hands planted on his knees while he dragged in great drafts of air. Whatever unknown monster in his soul had urged him to twist the old bastard's head off fled when he thought of Jessie.

"Jessie. Where are you? You okay?" He could see nothing in the blackness, and shut up to listen for her reply.

Thankfully, her voice echoed back at him. "Here, I'm here."

He took the big flashlight off his hip and shined it around until the beam caught her, scrambling to her feet a short distance down the incline.

Eyes bright and wide, she scrabbled to his side. "What happened? Oh, my goodness, is he dead?"

"No, but near enough. I thought you said he was harmless," he joked in an effort to drive away the boogeymen for both himself and her.

"I guess I was wrong about that. He acted like a maniac or some kind of crazed animal. What'd you do to him?"

"Tried to keep him from killing me. The son of a bitch bit me. Hope to hell he doesn't have some damned disease. Who'd have thought it? Why do you reckon he wanted you up here?"

A sudden attack of the shivers immobilized her. "He said he wanted to tell the truth about what happened." She stammered out the words through clacking teeth.

When she tried to go on her voice shook so badly he couldn't make sense of the words. Allowing them to dribble away, she staggered into his arms, buried her nose in his shoulder.

He could taste the fears that had crowded into the darker spaces of her life. She'd come home to leave it all behind, but they had clung to her like a burr that attaches itself and won't let go. Her struggle to defeat the past was a valiant effort. He wanted to help her, but wondered if she'd let him.

For now, he could hold her. "Here now, don't fall apart on me. You're doing just fine."

She fisted up wads of his shirt and took a ragged breath, drawing his strength inside herself. Fortified, she stiffened in his arms.

"That's better. You're going to be okay. Backup should arrive any minute. Wally to the rescue." The attempt at joking fell flat and he leaned her against a tree.

"Hang on. I'm going to try to get Jake here ready to travel, and I don't want you tumbling off down the hill. This fellow's ready to talk to me now, aren't you, pal?" Dal played the beam over the old man on the ground.

Jake wheezed in, whistled out. "Okay, okay. But she didn't have to hit me. I wasn't going to hurt her." He let out a gasp between every few words, moved about as if to rise.

The old fool didn't act like he remembered attacking Dal, or much else except what he considered Jessie's betrayal.

"Jake, what happened the night of the twin twisters?"

"When?"

"You told Jessie you knew what happened that night."

He managed to drag himself into a sitting position and fingered some leaves from his beard. "He was a sumbitch. On quiet nights when the owls hooted, I'd hear them women screaming sometimes, plumb up here."

"Yes—and?"

"I wanted to help em, but I was afraid. Men ain't supposed to hit women." He swung a rail thin arm toward Jessie. "And I wasn't gonna hurt her, either. She didn't need to hit me."

Dal struggled to get him back on track. "She's sorry. Aren't you, honey?"

She hollered yes, as if Jake were deaf.

Dal went on. "And so you saw what happened down there?"

Caveman stared away from the light as if he'd spotted something in the thick trees, didn't answer Dal's question for a minute.

Then, "Yeah, and after, well, they—they come a huntin for him. Lots of men on horses, and I was afraid they'd dig him up and figger out who he was. Put them women in jail when they didn't do nothing but protect themselves. So I—"

Jessie whispered to Dal. "He's talking about the manhunt, when that state trooper was shot. That wasn't long after Ken disappeared. They combed the hills for a week before they found the killers hiding in an old house over in Madison County."

"So what did you do, Jake, when the men came on horses?"

"If there ain't any teeth, it's harder to figger out who a body is."

"And so...?" He had taken the corpse's head. He might be smart, but he evidently knew nothing about DNA in bones. Been living in a damn cave too long.

Dal waited, held tight to Jessie, who shook so hard she could hardly stand.

"Oh, shit," she breathed. "He cut off his head."

The old man echoed the words, as if he hadn't heard her. "I cut off his head. With a axe. Waited till they was gone and cut off his blamed head and hid it where no one could ever find it. Took off his clothes too and chopped off his fingers, in case they found him and could still get prints." Seemingly exhausted after the revelation, Caveman fell back and said no more.

"Dal, do you think he's telling the truth?"

"Yes, I do. It's here, somewhere close."

"It?" she asked in a tremulous voice.

"Ken Norville's head." Dal shivered himself, but he wasn't lying to her, or trying to scare her. The sense of the brutal man's evil presence had settled deep within him, had prodded at him earlier when she'd been in his arms, and understandably he'd ignored it. And then later, when he fought Caveman, but he'd thought it was only his own paranoia making itself known. Even in death, Norville remained a destructive force.

Jessie took another ragged breath. "I don't want to be here anymore."

"No, neither do I."

"Reckon can I get up now?" Caveman whined. "She hit me so hard I wet myself. I'm sorry I messed up her place, but I thought she was gonna find out and put them women in jail. I just wanted to scare her off."

Jessie could not sort out the jumble of words. He was talking about her. But why had he gone to Mary's?

Dal hoisted the gaunt man to his feet, asked softly, "Jake, where is the head?"

"Could I go home now? I won't bother her no more, nor the other one either. I wanted to tell her it was okay, I wouldn't let them git her, nor the other one neither, for killing that worthless man of hers, but I got scared. I was just looking around. Didn't mean no harm. I want to go home."

In the glow from his flashlight, she watched Dal's features cloud over as if he might hit the old man, but he obviously thought better of it.

At his side, Jessie tugged on his arm. "Jake, if you really want to help both of them, you'll tell us where you put the man's... uh... his head. And his clothes. Mary needs to know so she can have some peace."

Jake cocked his head, studied her with beady eyes. "You didn't have to hit me. All you had to do was ask. I'll help her. Alls I ever wanted to do was help Mary."

"It's in his cave—where he lives," Dal whispered. "It's what I've been feeling all along, I thought it was coming from the grave, or Jake, here. But it's Ken's spirit. The evil, abusive monster that he was. We'll find Ken

Norville's head in this old man's 'home' and then this thing will be over."
He studied Jake. "Come along, pal. You're going to have visitors."

Taking Jessie's hand, he shined the powerful beam along the trail.
"Let's go, get this over with so I can take you home."

From far away a hoot owl called, another answered directly above
them. Jessie's skin crawled, but not from the nocturnal birds. A trickle
of sweat ran down her back as she followed the old man up the steep
incline, Dal bringing up the rear with the light. Going to retrieve a
head. See if you can put that in a story. At the dark mouth of his cave,
Jake halted as if reconsidering.

Jessie did not want to be in on this discovery. The thought of finding
a skull hidden amongst the old man's things nauseated her. She had no
idea what she'd do if they actually did find it.

"Dammit, Jake. Do I have to take the place apart?" Dal asked.

Caveman appeared to come to his senses and dived into the gaping
black hole, disappearing from sight.

Taking a step forward, Dal shone the light after him, but Jessie hung
back. She did not want to look at the dead man's skull. And she sure didn't
want to go in the cave.

Before Dal could enter, the tall, gangly form emerged, face a rictus of
monstrous glee. In one hand he held a skull, ivory bones gleaming in the
slash of Dal's light, upper teeth grinning grotesquely.

"Oh, my God," Jessie breathed. Her stomach clutched and she bent
forward, gagging. Nothing there to come up.

"Bring it here, Jake," Dal said.

"No," Caveman screamed and, using both hands, threw the thing
toward the dark trees as if it were a basketball.

For a long moment no one said a thing, then the grisly missile crashed into the distant upturned branches, and Caveman began to laugh. The sound sent tremors up Jessie's spine.

"Son of a bitch," Dal muttered, and put his arm around her waist.

"What do we do now?"

"It's sort of moot, what with Mary's statement, but I'd like to recover that thing, bring this to a close. We can get those students from the university out to look for it. They seem to enjoy tramping around through the woods. Can't say as I blame them if it gets them away from their studies and out in the air for a while. Damn, did you see that throw? He ought to play basketball."

Sensing the release of emotions he'd held in check, Jessie stretched up to kiss him on the corner of his mouth.

"It's okay. We're okay." She kissed him again. "I think I'd kind of like to get out of here."

He wrapped his arms even tighter around her. "When I found you gone, I thought you were dead. Don't ever scare me like that again."

She avoided making him that promise. "We're both alive. Now, can we get out of here?"

Grunting, he shifted and hooked the radio off his belt. "Mac ought to be close. Don't suppose the old codger got lost, do you?"

She laid her head against his shoulder while he fussed with the radio and received only static in reply. "Damn thing still isn't working. No signal. We'll have to go on down to the cruiser. Wally ought to have backup down there by now."

"Let me have that," she said, and took the flashlight he'd retrieved, shining its beam ahead as he helped her slip and slide down the hill.

"What about Jake? Are you going to arrest him?" she asked when they stood safely in the clearing again.

"He'll have to go in for questioning, but he's not going anywhere. So far, I don't want to arrest anyone, not even Mary. Doubt the PA will press charges. This is one hell of a murder case. Tragic, really. We'll have to sort things out once we find that skull and get an official identification of our body back from the lab. We've got Jolene and we can compare the DNA to hers. When and if the profile comes back. Then we'll go on from there. Even without all that, I'm satisfied and I'm sure Mac will be too."

Jake was nowhere in sight, having retreated to his cave. Dal guided her down the path to the cruiser. In the distance two sheriff's units, lights flashing, made their way along the logging road.

"Need someone to go pick up Caveman Jake and take him into custody. He's a material witness," Dal greeted Mac when he climbed from the first unit. "I'm taking Jessie home."

"Y'all okay?" came back the familiar voice.

"A bit of damage, but we're fine, or at least we will be."

Will we? Jessie wondered, studying Dal's strong profile in the glow from the dash. She had to finish Mary's story, but didn't want to put their relationship in jeopardy. At the same time, what sort of life could they have if they couldn't both do what they loved?

Mac's reply interrupted her thoughts. "Harold and Lester aren't talking. Not yet anyway. And Mary decided not to press charges against her husband. Said she was mistaken."

"You up to going in, or you want me to drop you off at home?" Dal took her trembling fingers in his.

"What? And miss the rest of the story?"

He darted her a glance and she smiled. "Don't worry, I'm okay with this."

"Just thought you might want to clean up."

"That'll keep. I want to see this through."

"You are one tough little cookie."

"Cookie? You're kidding."

He shrugged. "Sorry, I was being kind."

She grabbed his hand and chuckled, let him put her in the Tahoe.

It had become clear that she cared a lot for this man, but at the same time she would not allow him to make decisions for her. Their relationship would suffer and die if that happened.

He moved around the cruiser, climbed in, and keyed the ignition.

She waited till he steered onto the road to town before speaking.

"You know, Dal, I've put in a lot of time on this, taken some bruises and bumps. It's been mine all along. I promise you, what I did in California will never happen again. I won't lie or cheat or steal or commit any other illegal or immoral deeds for a story. But I love this job. I didn't know how much when I ran away from that other life, but I know it now. No matter what I do with my life, no matter what you do, we have to stand on our beliefs, be true to ourselves. I don't want to hurt you, but I'll not hurt myself either." She stared him in the eye. "And I'll never let a man do to me what Steve did, no matter the reason."

It was a long speech and he didn't interrupt. The only sound inside the Tahoe was of tires on pavement and the occasional static on his radio. When she didn't go on, he cleared his throat, as if having a difficult time speaking.

A hand clutched her heart, and she squeezed her eyes shut in a silent prayer. She didn't want to lose him, but she would stand her ground.

"I know you're right, even though I don't like it. I know something else too. I'm not Steve, I'm not like him. My life's been filled with violence, granted. But I'm rid of that now. I came here for peace. I care a lot about you, and that's enough—for now."

"We'll make it work, you'll see. You know, all in all, we did pretty good together on this case. Maybe—"

"Whoa, there. Let's hope we don't have any more cases like this. And you can go back to your historical pieces."

She laughed and he did too.

Guilt over Leeann's death loosened and slipped away. It had sustained him long enough, and if he chose to be vulnerable, at least it was for the right reason. Taking one hand off the steering wheel, he placed it over hers.

Velda Brotherton writes from her home perched on the side of a mountain against the Ozark National Forest. Branded as *Sexy, Dark and Gritty*, her work embraces the lives of gutsy women and heroes who are strong enough to deserve them. After a stint writing for a New York publisher, she has settled comfortably in with small publishers to produce novels in several genres. She enjoys reading mysteries, but it never occurred to her she could write them until Dal Starr and Jessie West emerged from her background in the newspaper business, and the *Twist of Poe* mysteries were born.

Facebook: Author Velda Brotherton
Twitter: @veldabrotherton
http://www.veldabrotherton.com

www.ingramcontent.com/pod-product-compliance
Lightning Source LLC
Chambersburg PA
CBHW020840060726
PP18531500001B/12